# Love for Real

*A Big Brah cozy mystery*

## by Ishwar Chandra Sen

**Publisher: Sen Fiction, Hawaii**
**(www.senfiction.com)**

Sen Fiction, Hawaii

ISBN-13: 9781957022048

Learn more about the author at:
https://www.senfiction.com

Editor: Mele Sen
Cover artist: Rita Sen
Editorial and Publishing Assistant: Rita Sen

Published in the United States of America

*For my island family:*
*mahalo for all the aloha.*

# Contents

# Chapter 1 Tahitian gardenias

On our island of natural beauty and aloha, fake love perished and pure love blossomed. Settled cozily in my chair at the kitchen table, I was busy reading a novel of my favorite mystery series. Big Brah was outside, patiently tending to the many details of our sprawling garden, as the beginning of spring demanded. Kali was there with him.

Big Brah and Kali were enjoying the gardening because they were together. Kali had caringly brushed Poli`ahu and Wiliwili in the morning, and in love's afterglow, the cats snoozed in their chairs on either side of me. The breeze had the sweet scent of gardenias and soothed my skin with its gentle touch. To check on Big Brah and Kali, I looked out of the large kitchen window.

The sun was out in a mostly blue sky. A couple of clouds shaped like sea turtles floated by together. Songbirds sang love songs. Amorous doves cavorted. Butterflies chased each other.

I smiled. Naturally toned and tanned, Big Brah and Kali were dressed alike in wide-brimmed hats, t-shirts, shorts and gardening boots. Their voices carried in through the open window. With a hint of joyous laughter, her voice was higher and musical. His voice was deeper, melodious and full of wisdom.

Kali wanted more Tahitian gardenias. Big Brah approved of her choice. He would make her wish come true. Big Brah wanted cucumbers. Kali would make a trellis for Big Brah's cucumbers. For making the trellis, the bamboo in the yard was the best. Big Brah and Kali had been talking and tending to the garden all morning long.

Pure love.

It was a serene day, a Saturday, the first day of Kali's month-long spring vacation. She wasn't just Big Brah's soulmate, she worked for the county as a medical examiner, the only one on the island. For her break, a substitute from a neighbor island carried on her work.

After working with the departed year-round, spring provided Kali a much-needed reminder of new life. Of course her favorite thing about the break: she worked for the Waialeale Detective Agency.

Big Brah ran the agency, the spiritual master. I was his assistant, the apprentice of the spiritual master. I was also his one and only younger brother. My attention was drawn back inside to the TV screen on the kitchen wall.

I had the TV on mute. But I had followed the breaking news all morning. I could not resist a real-life mystery. The "Honeymooner," a luxury boat had been found on the dangerous northside rocks. Empty. Authorities had launched a search for the occupants.

The broadcast cut to the video of the marooned luxury boat. On the rocks, the red and white boat was tilted at an unlikely angle. The waves rolled in big here and crashed onto the black rocks. The ocean sprayed water on the large boat. *Aue.*

Talk about a bad place to ride your boat. Big Brah had left his phone on the kitchen table. It was the agency phone. Big Brah carried it most of the time. While he gardened that morning, I had instructions to answer all calls. The phone jingled.

I reached for the phone. The phone screen showed "Duke Mahio." I recognized the caller instantly. Duke Mahio was the owner of one of the island's two big shopping malls.

Duke Mahio owned Mahio Plaza. His rival, Jim Bordeta owned the Bordeta Shopping Center. Rumor had it, they weren't just business rivals.

Mahio and Bordeta didn't get along.

In the local business section, the Island Times featured both businessmen often. Small island.

I answered the phone and introduced myself.

Mahio was a big man on our small island. He did not sound big. In a small, troubled voice, he said, "I-I have something to show Big Brah, is he available?"

# Chapter 2 Island-crafted heirloom jewelry

It was the first day of Kali's vacation. Big Brah would be super reluctant to interrupt his time with Kali. Understandable. As long as we worked together as a family, I didn't mind the excitement of an investigation. Kali was always onboard for detective work with Big Brah.

I said, "Big Brah's in the garden, can I take a message?"

"This can't wait, I need Big Brah's help!" Duke Mahio said.

So he needed our help urgently. If anyone needed our urgent help, Big Brah would choose to assist for sure. "I'll have him call you back," I said.

"Mahalo, Umi, but please, hurry." Mahio finished the call.

Within minutes, Big Brah, Kali and I gathered inside the office. I pulled the blackout curtains. The spring day flooded in through the windows. The teak-paneled walls were decorated with framed photocopies of our private investigator certificates.

Big Brah's neat desk had a swing-arm lamp. Without turning on the lamp, Big Brah set the phone down on the desk. I sat behind my desk cluttered with my stuffs: books, sketchpads, notepads, paintbrushes, pencils, pens, markers and a heap of rolled canvases. In the visitor's chair, Kali sat across from Big Brah.

My desk was at an angle to Big Brah's. I observed both Big Brah and Kali. Big Brah initiated the callback on the agency phone.

Duke Mahio's voice sounded over the phone's speaker. "Big Brah, I need your help!"

Big Brah spoke at his reassuring best. "I'm listening, Mr. Mahio. I have Kali, my colleague, and Umi, my assistant here with me in the office. How can I help?"

Duke Mahio sounded thankful. "I need you to come and see. Some invaluable heirlooms, been in the family for generations, have been stolen from the safe."

The Mahio family jewelry was legend on the island. Still. Stolen family heirlooms did not sound too serious.

Big Brah said, "Are you sure it's stolen and not just misplaced?"

Duke Mahio's voice got stronger. "I've been looking all morning, I'm sure they're stolen."

Not so sure, Big Brah, Kali and I looked at each other.

Duke Mahio said, "There are clues, I just can't make any sense of them."

He had clues. Big Brah was best at making sense of clues. We would have to do something.

Duke Mahio insisted. "You must come," he said.

Big Brah was reassuring. "We will see you shortly, Mr. Mahio," he said.

On the short drive over in the big, black truck, the beauty of the spring day shot up several notches. The Mahio mansion had a hill all to itself with picturesque views of the ocean. The asphalt road up the hill morphed into a parking lot. The mansion was a neat building painted ocean blue.

Big Brah parked the big truck. A concrete pathway took us to the front of the ocean blue home. A flight of concrete steps led to the wide, pillared lanai. Duke Mahio waited for us in front of the massive front door, pacing in anguish.

I knew Duke Mahio from the photographs in the Island Times. His thinning hair was colored a youthful black. His business-like glasses didn't hide his warm, soft eyes. Duke Mahio was dressed casually in shirt, cargo shorts and sandals. Yes, definitely dad. He had a son who was a young man.

Tattoos in triangles, bands and solid black adorned his neck, arms and legs. Very traditional. His son would have a tough time, if he swerved away from tradition. But right now, Duke Mahio was in great pain.

His face contorted, he regarded us. "Mahalo

for coming so soon," he said.

Big Brah said, "I can see you are bothered by the theft, what can we do to help?"

"Maybe you're the only one who can help. The jewelry is just part of it. What I couldn't explain on the phone is that my son, Kaipo, he's missing. I'm worried."

His son was missing. No wonder he was so distraught.

Big Brah said, "Have you filed a missing person report with the police?"

"I-I can't," he said.

Big Brah, Kali and I looked at each other, puzzled. We wanted to help.

Duke Mahio said, "It's difficult to explain, but I can show you. I have clear footage from the security camera of the theft."

Clear footage. Not much of a mystery then. I didn't know how wrong I was about the mystery.

"Please, come in." Duke Mahio swung the large front door open and ushered us into the foyer.

The large foyer had a shiny, hardwood floor. Duke Mahio gestured toward a doorway to our right. "The safe's in a special room, let me show you."

We followed him into a darkened room. Ceiling lights turned on as we entered. The room was secure. It had no windows. There was a metal safe on the far wall. The safe had a keypad and a handle.

In front of the safe, the floor had a thick, oval rug. The rug had a red and yellow sunrise pattern on it. A signboard up on the wall to our left warned of a surveillance camera video recording everything. I looked up at the sinister lens of a security camera. Duke Mahio strode over to the safe and punched in a security code on the keypad.

He turned the handle and opened the safe. Jewelry boxes littered the top shelves, as if someone had tossed them into the safe haphazardly. Some of the boxes were open showing their glossy insides empty of jewelry. Others were closed, likely empty.

Duke Mahio said, "The jewelry, it's all gone."

The bottom shelves stored documents. The documents looked organized and untouched.

Duke Mahio said, "The important documents, estate and business, they're all there, thank the Goddess!"

Big Brah said, "When did this happen?"

"During the day, while I'm at work, the front door is usually open, the housekeeper, cook and cleaning staff enter and leave, no problem. The theft occurred then," Duke Mahio said.

Big Brah nodded, sympathetic. He looked up at the security camera. "Did the camera record the evidence?" he said.

Mysteriously, Duke Mahio shook his head. "You'll see, come."

Big Brah, Kali and I followed Duke Mahio out

of the secure room, through the foyer to an old-style living room. The room was big, with a high ceiling and beautiful bamboo and rattan furniture. Light and air poured in through the living room's many windows.

A big screen TV was mounted on the wall. The breaking news about the "Honeymooner" found on the rocks played silently on it. The ongoing report was about the massive land and ocean search launched for the boat's missing occupants.

"Sit, sit," Duke Mahio instructed us.

Big Brah and Kali chose a loveseat. I sank into a sturdy armchair. Duke Mahio went about drawing the curtains.

The room darkened. Duke Mahio returned to us. "For privacy," he said, picking up a remote from the coffee table.

He pointed the remote at the screen still playing the news. The screen turned blank. "This is the footage of the theft taking place, or it looks like that to me, but please, I need another opinion. There's no audio, please look carefully," he said.

He had all our attentions on the screen. A video played. The sunrise patterned rug in front of the safe came into view. The view was from the top. The camera was angled so you could see the large wall safe, the rug and the empty floor all the way to the doorway. The camera recorded everything. There was no one. Then someone walked into the room.

A woman. Tall, scrawny, black hair. She was talking to someone behind her. A man came into view. He had curly, black hair and dark glasses. A bead bracelet with a yellow gold plate gleamed on his wrist.

The man and the woman seemed to be in deep conversation. When they got to the safe, she used a code to open the door. The woman reached into the safe.

The man and the woman continued to talk. She took out a couple of yellowed documents and looked at them closely. She carefully folded the papers and put the documents in her bag. The man helped her close the safe. They left. The camera showed an empty room.

Before Big Brah, Kali or I could ask any questions, Duke Mahio raised a hand. "Wait, there's more footage. Watch what happens 23 minutes later."

The footage started again, showing the empty room. Someone strode into the room. The same curly-haired man with dark glasses, but he was alone. He carried a black duffel bag and he now wore latex gloves. He unlocked the safe and swung the door open. He looked back, as if he had heard a sound.

Then he turned back to the safe. Audaciously, he reached into the safe. Swiftly he emptied out more than a dozen jewelry boxes, one after the other, into the duffel bag. I watched his gloved hands, horrified.

Necklaces, bracelets, leis, rings, a tiara, many precious shells and then an open box of multi-stranded leis of pearls and shells interspersed with shiny diamonds. There were lots of precious stones and diamonds. It was a treasure of gems, diamonds, gold and invaluable island-crafted heirloom jewelry.

It was amazing how casually the thief gathered all this into the duffel bag, locked the safe and left. The footage ended.

"Do you recognize the individual taking the jewelry?" Big Brah asked.

Duke Mahio said, "Yes, of course, I do recognize the individual. It's Kaipo, my son."

Kaipo. His son. My brain did a somersault. *Say what?*

# Chapter 3 Deep enmity

"I know you don't know Kaipo, let me show you," Duke Mahio said.

He restarted the footage and paused where we could clearly see the man grabbing a Ni`ihau shell lei. He had on latex gloves, but the bead bracelet with a yellow gold plate was visible on his forearm. The yellow gold plate had a name stylized in cursive on it.

Kaipo.

Duke Mahio looked extremely remorseful. "Look, it is Kaipo. But it makes no sense!"

I agreed, silently. It made no sense.

Duke Mahio shook his head. "It's all my fault, we don't talk much."

Lack of communication. A common problem in families sometimes.

Duke Mahio said, "My wife, Luana used to take care of Kaipo, but ever since my poor Luana passed away...."

A much deeper problem. My heart softened.

Big Brah said, "I'm sorry."

Duke Mahio nodded, acknowledging Big Brah's sympathy. "Kaipo does his own things, I know I can trust him, so I let him. I tell him he has to be his own person, be independent, figure things out for himself. I always have."

Big Brah believed a loving parent had to be a lifelong guide. A loving parent did not just cut the child off at a certain age in an act of tough love. But Big Brah was highly accepting of other parenting styles. He didn't say anything, merely keeping his face impassive.

Duke Mahio said, "But why would Kaipo take his own jewelry? He's my only child, so all this belongs to him anyway."

Big Brah said, "Where is Kaipo?"

Duke Mahio looked sad. His shoulders sagged. "I don't know. He's studying to be a marine biologist. His mother loved the ocean and he has inherited the love from her. Last evening, he told me he was going out on a field trip.

"He left at around 6 p.m. Told me he'd be back in the morning. I tried calling him today and discovered he left his phone in his room. If Kaipo left the phone by mistake or he planned it, I don't know...." His voice faltered.

Duke Mahio really did not know his son. He shook off his regret and got back to the footage. "You saw the woman in the recording?"

Big Brah, Kali and I exchanged looks. We had seen the woman with Kaipo. Big Brah nodded.

Duke Mahio said, "That's Helen Hokui, my property manager. Other than me, she and Kaipo are the only ones who know the security code of the safe. She had a good reason to access the safe. She was straightening out the deeds of a couple of old, disputed properties. I'd asked her to do so.

"I was at work. Helen called me to report afterward. She told me she'd found Kaipo near the safe, he was surprised to see her, but she found it normal. They talked, you saw the footage, he walked her to the front door and she left. I tried calling her, just in case she knew where Kaipo was, but she's not answering.

"Don't blame her, it's the weekend, she works hard enough during the week to deserve the rest. I looked for Kaipo everywhere, here at home, places he may go to, I even called relatives, but I can't find him."

Big Brah said, "The field trip, did Kaipo tell you anything about it?"

Duke Mahio shook his head. "Regret it, but no. I count such matters as his college work, something he should be able to do on his own. I think any reasonable parent would. Come to think of it, he did mention he'd be renting a boat for the field trip at the eastside harbor.

"I asked him why he didn't take one of ours, and he said there'd be others, you know, his college mates, so they'd rather rent and share the costs. Sounded like responsible behavior, I forgot about it."

One of our cousins ran the rent-a-boat business at the eastside harbor for locals and tourists. Big Brah nodded, satisfied he understood the situation. The search for the truth had started. We were headed to the harbor next.

But Big Brah was still not ready to commit to take on the case. "Mr. Mahio, let me make inquiries, then get back to you," he said, cautiously.

Big Brah drove and the big truck rolled toward the eastside harbor. My stomach cautioned me a refill was required. Besides, driving around the island made you extra hungry and thirsty. I didn't know when, but Kali had magically packed musubis and coconut water.

Kali made an awesome Big Sister.

Kali handed the musubis out from the passenger seat. We ate hungrily. Sitting alert in the backseat, I savored the aromatic rice, the wholesome meat and the delicate seaweed of the musubis. Afterward I washed all of it down with the sweet-salty coconut water.

When Big Brah, Kali and I exited the big truck, the sun was warm on our backs. We were in the parking lot of rent-a-boat, harborside. The front office was a wood shack painted white. Behind the shack was a bigger structure painted sky blue: the boathouse, situated in an inlet. Ocean water lapped around the boathouse.

To the right of the office and boathouse was the green-painted front office and hangar of another rental business, "Fly like a Bird." Outside the hangar, a tethered seaplane bobbed on the ocean water.

As we climbed the few steps to the front door of rent-a-boat's office, the door swung open. Our cousin, Keni emerged, a frown on his usually smiling face.

Keni was a short man with a ponytail. He had a wife and a daughter and he doted on both of them. He wore a red rent-a-boat t-shirt and navy-blue shorts. At the sight of us, his frown melted away.

Keni smiled. "Oh, it's you, Big Brah. What a relief. How did you know? I was about to call you. I need your help."

Big Brah chuckled deep. We had many cousins. All our cousins loved to help out. If Keni was part of your team, you could count on him to volunteer for the toughest tasks always with a smile. Not that Big Brah would ever let Keni do such tasks. Big Brah reserved the toughest tasks for himself.

But Big Brah liked Keni. Big Brah patted Keni's tattooed arm affectionately on the way inside. "What's the trouble, Keni? Tell me."

No matter Keni had troubles, but he did not forget to hug me and Kali with a smile. Pure aloha. Keni then followed us into the compact office.

The office had a low ceiling. The walls were plastered with posters, prices and pictures of the boats. A window overlooked the parking lot. Beyond the parking lot, the palms swayed near the ramp private boats used to get onto the water and the dock. Through the other window, you could see the boathouse and the boats bobbing gently on the water.

The door to the boathouse was next to the window. The sales desk had a tablet on it presumably for reservations. On the far side of the sales desk was a chair for Keni. There were chairs for customers.

Keni had us sit down in the customer chairs and went around the desk and seated himself. A small screen on the wall played the breaking news about the "Honeymooner." The search was still on for the boat's missing occupants.

Keni pointed his index finger toward the small screen. He frowned. "That's my boat!" he said.

I would have connected the boat with Kaipo, but Big Brah beat me to it. "Who did you rent it to?" he said.

Keni picked up the tablet, did something, then held it up, so Big Brah, Kali and I could see the screen. "I rented the 'Honeymooner' out to Kaipo Mahio, see," Keni said.

I took a good look at the proffered screen. The boat had been rented out on Friday, April 9 at 7 p.m. The reason for renting? Field trip.

My heart sank. Then, Kaipo was truly missing. Sad for Duke Mahio. He was already regretting his hands-off parenting. Now, he would have to deal with this. And I wasn't prepared for the shocking truth about Kaipo's character we were about to learn.

Big Brah said, "Have you informed the police?"

Keni said, "Didn't have to. I got a visit. Not a squad car either. A homicide detective visited me. A lieutenant. Loni."

Loni graduated from the island high school the same year as Big Brah and Kali did. The similarity ended there. Loni ran the island's tiny homicide department.

"Why Loni? What's homicide got to do with this?" I said, puzzled.

"That's what I'd like to know, that's gonna tell me how much trouble I'm in," Keni said.

"What did Loni say?" Big Brah asked.

Keni glanced furtively out of the window. The parking lot was empty but for our trucks. He lowered his voice. "Loni didn't say much. He asked the questions, I answered. But I didn't tell Loni something important. I'm worrying if I should have, but he didn't ask, and he had told me to just answer his questions a few times already, so I couldn't decide whether I should volunteer the information or wait to be asked about it."

Curious, I asked, "What is it you didn't tell Loni?"

"I was going to tell Big Brah," Keni said.

"Yeah, tell him, he'll know what to do," I said.

Keni looked over at Big Brah and Kali. "Kaipo

was doing something bad. This wasn't the first time he rented a boat from me, he's done so many times before. Every time, the same excuse: field trip. But he was never going on a field trip."

"Weren't there others from his marine biology class with him?" Big Brah said.

Keni shook his head. "Never. He was always alone."

"Alone?"

Keni took a deep breath, then let it out slowly. "One time, I got curious. A couple months ago. Kaipo would drive past the parking lot, park his truck under the palms near the dock. I suspected someone was with him, someone who didn't want to be seen.

"Then Kaipo would walk back here to rent the boat. Every time, he got the boat out the boathouse, then took the boat up the inlet and turned left, so he could dock the boat. I suspected the someone he had left in the truck, joined him then. So."

We waited. All three of us were caught up in Keni's story.

Keni pointed at the door to the boathouse. "As soon as Kaipo went out that door to get the boat, I ran out the way you came in. Hiding behind palms, so I wouldn't be seen, I raced up near his vehicle. Kaipo docked the boat, as usual. Neither of them saw me. But I saw her. She left the vehicle and joined Kaipo on the boat."

Keni looked at each of us, willing us to ask

him who she was. But all three of us knew better. Asking a question would only take away from his story. We stayed silent.

Keni nodded, satisfied. He had expected nothing but the best from us. "I don't have to tell you about the Duke Mahio and Jim Bordeta enmity, do I?" he said.

Silently, we shook our heads.

Keni said, "You know they fought over the same woman, right? Kaipo's mom, Luana. And she chose Duke Mahio. When she died in a boat accident a few years ago, Jim Bordeta is supposed to have blamed Duke Mahio for her demise. Deep enmity."

We nodded, again.

Keni lowered his voice further. "Mind you, Kaipo may have had another reason to be secretive. The business next door, 'Fly like a bird,' its owner, Ross Alba, he's a friend, talks to me often. Says he started college with Kaipo, marine biology, but Ross Alba, he dropped out.

"Doesn't ever tell me why. But he does talk a lot about his hatred for Kaipo. He's told me he'd kill Kaipo, if he could. Funny, he was out flying early this morning, and he's the one who sighted the 'Honeymooner,' on the rocks."

Big Brah nodded. "Interesting," he said.

I agreed, wordlessly. Here, Kaipo was missing. And we had at least one person, Ross Alba, who wanted Kaipo to go missing permanently.

Ross Alba was the person who had reported

the empty boat. How had he even known to find it?

Interesting, for sure.

But what was going to be even more interesting was the identity of the woman with Kaipo.

Keni said, "The woman was none other than Jim Bordeta's daughter, Nohea Bordeta."

Nohea Bordeta. *Say what?*

Keni said, "I was sure of it. I was shocked, how could Kaipo Mahio and Nohea Bordeta be together? They know their family history. No way was either of their fathers ever going to accept them together.

"I blamed Kaipo, after all he was the one renting the boats from me. Terribly irresponsible. I made inquiries. I found out Kaipo and Nohea studied marine biology together. But I hesitated to say anything to him, after all, it's the island, and hey, when it comes to love, pure love...pure love conquers everything, right?" He looked searchingly at Big Brah and Kali for affirmation.

Big Brah nodded, approvingly. Kali took Big Brah's big hand in hers and smiled. Theirs was pure love. Watching them, I forgot we had seen Kaipo steal his family jewelry on surveillance video a short while ago.

Big Brah said, "Kaipo and Nohea studied marine biology together. Kaipo rented your boats for field trips. Perhaps they couldn't tell their fathers even that? They needn't have been in love or anything."

Keni nodded, slowly. "You may be right, I really don't know. All I know is they were hiding being together."

Big Brah said, "On these trips, where did they go?"

Keni said, "I asked Kaipo, and he was all vague about it, told me they go out on the open ocean, far from the island. But trouble was, I could tell from the fuel I pumped into the boat, they really didn't go too far.

"Still, they could be on a field trip to study the ocean somewhere close, so I let it go. It isn't something I bother myself with. Once a boat is rented, it's really the renter's responsibility."

Big Brah said, "What happened last evening?"

Keni shrugged. "Kaipo came in, the same as usual. He had parked near the dock. I presumed Nohea Bordeta was there with him. Loni had the truck towed to the PD. Anyways, Kaipo was unusually excited, told me it was a special occasion, wanted to rent the 'Honeymooner.'

"Much higher rent, the inside of this boat was a beauty. Included a luxury bedroom suite with a walk-in closet. Perfect for couples. The boat is all ruined now. I still thought it was irresponsible, even risky behavior on Kaipo's part, given they could never really come out being together, but I didn't stop him. I regret that."

Keni looked ruefully toward the small screen

TV that continued to play the breaking news about the search for the occupants of the "Honeymooner." "Both of them may have gotten into harm's way, they're missing," he said.

Kali nodded, concerned. Big Brah glanced her way, then bowed his head. He was thinking.

Finally, Keni said, "Sorry, I unloaded my troubles on you. What are you here for really?"

Big Brah raised his head. "We're looking for Kaipo, he didn't return home this morning, Duke Mahio called us," he said.

"Duke Mahio! He gonna cause trouble, Big Brah!" Keni said.

Big Brah said, "No, brah, with Kaipo gone, Duke Mahio is in trouble."

Keni fell silent.

Big Brah said, "Right now, I need time to think about everything we've found out about the 'Honeymooner.'"

Helpfully, Keni said, "That's everything I know. I'm always here to answer anything."

"I'll tell you all about it, later," Big Brah said.

Keni relaxed. "Makes me feel better, you looking for Kaipo, Big Brah. I know you'll find him," he said, with a smile.

Outside, the afternoon sun was as warm as Keni's smile. Big Brah suggested a stroll around the harbor. He had mentioned he had to think. Also, this was the place Kaipo was last seen. Big Brah would like to commune with the place.

The harbor birds were quiet. They would get

noisy with their end-of-day feeding excitement soon. From rent-a-boat's parking lot, Big Brah, Kali and I strolled down Harbor Road toward the dock. We passed tall coconut trees and a few parked cars. There were not many people around. We strolled along the dock's lapping water. It was cool waterside. Big Brah and Kali held hands. From time to time, I skipped pebbles on the ocean water. The nifty strum of an *ukulele* gradually filled my ears.

Playing the ukulele, his skin darkened by the tropical sun, a man in dreads sat in a backpack chair under a coconut tree. He deftly manipulated the strings of the ukulele, his long fingers a joy to watch. Music Man, as he was known on the island.

As long as anyone knew, Music Man had always sat here at the harbor and played music. He lived in a shack near the harbor. The island rumor mill, the island wireless had it that a girl broke Music Man's heart. Since then, he played music to fill his broken heart. We stopped by to watch.

Music Man looked up at us and grinned. He strummed harder. His fingers blurred. Calm, poised and all grown-up as they were, Big Brah and Kali couldn't resist the temptation.

They broke out into a *hula* dance to the fast music. Inspired by the music, I threw a pebble that broke all my previous bounce records of the day. The big, black truck was still parked in rent-a-boat's parking lot. We returned laughing.

Inside the truck, we settled into our seats. Big Brah grew solemn. "I was trying to think of a way forward without seeing Jim Bordeta."

Kali said, "Seeing Jim Bordeta is sure to complicate matters."

Sitting in the backseat, I shrugged. "I don't see why we should bother. Kaipo is a thief who stole his family jewelry before eloping with a girl his father, our prospective client, doesn't approve of," I said.

Big Brah peered at me on the rearview mirror. "Which is why meeting with Jim Bordeta may complicate matters, Umi."

Kali said, "Even if Kaipo is bad, Nohea Bordeta may be innocent."

Darn. Kali had a point. "The innocent must be protected, right?" I said.

"Right," Kali said.

Big Brah nodded, approvingly.

I spoke with renewed enthusiasm. "Then, let's go. Bordeta House," I said.

The mission was clear. Find out where Nohea Bordeta fitted into this mess. The Bordeta House was located on the hill next to the one the Mahio Mansion was built on. The sun dazzled and the sky was blue. Big Brah drove the big, black truck up the winding road.

The hill was a little more inland. The views of the ocean were nonetheless spectacular. The home was a modern-day glass, wood and concrete mansion. Friendly curtains fluttered on its big windows. Fragrant flowers bloomed in the front garden. The steps leading up to the lanai were painted red. Surely, Big Brah would deduce a feminine touch in the curtains, choice of flowers and the color of the steps. So did I.

But I knew better than to disturb Big Brah with trivia, just as he pressed the button of the ornate doorbell on the wall. The front door swung open and a girl emerged. She had thick, black hair, big eyes and shapely chin. In tank-top, shorts and slippers, she was attired like a typical island girl.

A disappointed look came over the girl's face. "Oh! I thought it was Nohea. She's my older sister. She's missing since the morning."

Kali said, "We'd like to have a word with your parents, are they available?"

The girl's eyes widened. "Wait a minute! I know you, from the news, you're Kali, aren't you?"

Kali smiled and then nodded briefly.

Nohea's sister appraised Big Brah. "This must be your forever boyfriend, Big Brah," she said.

Big Brah bowed, pleased.

The girl turned her attention on me. "Umi!"

I bowed also.

She giggled and clapped her hands. "Wow. You're an awesome trio. My friends and I talk about how you solved the Hale Kiai mystery. We were all glued to the news, the entire week. I'm a big fan! Oh! My name's Iekika."

Iekika turned hopeful. "Say, I've never seen you here before, have you come with news about Nohea?" she said.

Kali said, "Yes, it is about Nohea."

From behind Iekika, an older woman called sharply. "Who're you talking to, Iekika?"

Uh-oh. The older woman was a strict hen, scolding her straying chick. Our youthful fan had grownup censors. Discreetly, Big Brah, Kali and I exchanged glances. *Careful, now.*

# Chapter 4 Ripe like the July mango

Iekika turned her head back toward the voice. "Stop treating me like a kid, Mom. I'm sixteen!" she yelled out.

I flinched. Big Brah and Kali smiled at me. Some sixteen-year-olds could act like babies. Agreeing, I smiled back at them.

Iekika turned to us and confidentially lowered her voice. "You couldn't have come at a better time. Mom's real worried about Nohea. I'm sure she'd like to talk to you about her, come in!"

Kali followed Iekika into the home. Big Brah and I followed Kali. The walls of the large, well-lit foyer were decorated with cute knick-knacks. Wicker art. Paper flowers. A child's art. We entered a large living room.

The large living room had its many windows open letting in the afternoon light. The full-curtains had been pulled open. The colorful half-curtains fluttered in the breeze. A trendy conversation set, leather and chrome armchairs, loveseat, sofa and coffee table adorned the carpeted floor. Farther in, the carpet turned pristine white and more luxurious, as did the furniture. There the armchairs, loveseat, coffee table and sofa were full-sized and plusher. Nearer us, on a fancy glass entertainment center, a muted TV screen played the breaking news about the "Honeymooner."

The spokesperson for the PD was about to make an extraordinarily important announcement. My curiosity was ripe like the July mango. A woman in a flowery housedress walked toward us.

Her wavy, long and plentiful hair was done in an elaborate bamboo sticks hairdo. She looked a lot like Iekika, only plumper.

Iekika's mom. Her face was all scrunched up, stressed. Her eyebrows were straight-lined, and her forehead was creased with worry lines. Older daughter, Nohea, missing. Younger daughter, Iekika sassing her. Plenty reason to be worried and stressed.

She saw us. Her round face brightened. In wonder, her eyebrows arched. She gasped. Like Iekika, she must have recognized us from the news. "Kali! Big Brah! Umi! I'm Jean Bordeta, what brings you here?" she said.

Kali stepped forward. "It's about Nohea," she said.

"Nohea? Do you know where she is?" Jean Bordeta said, looking distraught.

"No, but we're looking for her." Kali gave the

distraught mom a quick hug.

Jean Bordeta said, "Is she in trouble, my Nohea?"

Kali said, "We don't know, but we're making inquiries on behalf of Duke Mahio, his son's missing too."

*Clean dive right into the complicated part,* I thought.

Jean Bordeta looked horrified. She put an arm around Iekika, protectively. Iekika too shrunk to her mom's side, her eyes wide.

Jean Bordeta said, "You mustn't say that name, my husband, he'll be furious."

Iekika nodded vehemently, agreeing with her mom. She looked fearfully behind her in the direction of the door. A man strode into the living room.

He approached us. His hair was brushed back and stiffened by hair gel. Something different about his eyes. One a lighter shade of brown than the other. Straight-line mouth. I had no problems recognizing him from his pictures in the business section of the Island Times. Jim Bordeta. He halted by his wife and daughter.

Jim Bordeta addressed us. "I couldn't help hearing what you just said, our daughter, Nohea, she's missing, but it can't have anything to do with Mahio's son, impossible," he said.

Jean Bordeta looked relieved her husband had stated the facts succinctly. But something was going on with Iekika. She was looking up at her dad and shaking her head. I glanced at Big Brah to see what he was making of it.

A faraway look came on Big Brah's face. He gazed past Jim Bordeta, as if he had seen a vision. Coming to an understanding, Big Brah nodded. Then, he returned to the present.

His eyes regained their focus. "Impossible," he murmured.

Jim Bordeta took it that Big Brah was in sympathetic agreement. His demeanor changed to that of reconciling. "Look, I know about all the good work you do. Big Brah, Kali, Umi." He paused to nod at each of us, as he said our names. "But, really, I have notified the PD. At my request, the police are already investigating the disappearance of my daughter."

Jim Bordeta seemed to care for his daughter. "If it's true you're acting on behalf of the man I hate, I say we have nothing more to talk about, not this time!" he said.

Jim Bordeta did not care for Duke Mahio. The enmity was for real.

Big Brah, Kali and I were about to turn away, disappointed. Iekika yelled out, "Wait!"

Both her parents frowned. Iekika broke away from them and raced to the fancy entertainment center with the TV on it, picked up the remote and turned on the sound.

I understood why. The police had started making the announcement of extraordinary importance about the "Honeymooner." Trouble was the person making the announcement wasn't the usual boring police uncle.

Instead, it was detective Loni, of homicide.

For homicide cases, Loni prided himself on handling all aspects of the case. He would have sent the regular spokesperson home.

Loni looked into the camera, his thick, black mustache bristling importantly. "A body has been found by the boat, a young woman's body. Due to the ongoing investigation, I can't disclose the identity of the woman."

Loni paused. A TV reporter asked him how long it would take for him to release the identity of the woman.

"No questions at this time, I'm focusing on the murder investigation," Loni said, importantly.

The TV screen dissolved into a commercial. Iekika's big eyes had filled up with tears. Her mom looked terrified. Even Jim Bordeta had gone silent, frowning fiercely.

The terrible thought must have crossed their minds that the young woman's body could be that of Nohea Bordeta. Big Brah, Kali and I looked at each other.

Cousin Keni had told us Kaipo Mahio had rented the "Honeymooner." Kaipo usually took Nohea Bordeta on the boat with him. And now, the police had found the body of a young woman by the boat. I shivered. It had to be Nohea Bordeta.

Dead.

I looked at Nohea's mom, dad and sister. I felt their pain. *No, please, no,* I prayed to the Island Goddess.

Big Brah stepped forward and placed a supportive hand on Jim Bordeta's arm. "Why don't I make inquiries with Loni about the body, get back to you. I'm sure you'd like to know what's going on."

Jim Bordeta said nothing. But both Iekika and her mom nodded fervently. Back inside the big, black truck, Big Brah called Loni, while Kali and I listened on.

Loni knew Big Brah didn't call him lightly. Despite being in the middle of an investigation, he answered immediately. That's how much even Loni respected Big Brah. Big Brah asked Loni about the young woman's body.

His voice brisk over the connection, Loni said, "Why don't you come down to the rocks, Big Brah? I'm here, be happy to show you what we got, talk it over." He disconnected.

Big Brah glanced at Kali, pleased. Kali smiled back at him. Loni and Big Brah clashed often during an investigation. But Big Brah helped Loni, always, and sometimes, Loni helped too. The coastal highway took us high above the rocks. A sandy track from the highway spiraled downward.

Big Brah drove the big, black truck down the sandy road, until the ground leveled somewhat and the track ended. An unmarked green sedan was parked here. I recognized Loni's car.

Big Brah parked the big, black truck next to Loni's sedan. It took us several minutes to trek down to the rocks. Loni was there, waiting.

He greeted us somberly. "The others, mostly forensics, they all left about when you called, I waited." He pulled at the ends of his thick, black mustache. "Just curious, what's your interest in this, Big Brah?" he asked, shrewdly.

"I'm looking for Kaipo on behalf of his father Duke Mahio," Big Brah said.

Loni raised his eyebrows theatrically. "Then, why is it Duke Mahio hasn't declared his son missing to the PD?" he said.

Before Big Brah could respond, Loni said, "I'll tell you why Mr. Mahio hasn't come to the police...it's because he knows his son, Kaipo, is guilty of murder!"

The only other person on the boat with Kaipo had been Nohea. If Loni thought Kaipo was guilty of murder, then Kaipo could only have killed Nohea. The afternoon sun had subsided. It was cool on the rocks.

I shivered.

I looked away at the big, white boat stranded on the rocks. The boat was tilted at a weird angle. Its name, "Honeymooner," glittered on the side facing up. Blue, foamy ocean water now swirled around it.

Loni pointed to the boat. "It's simple, really.

The boat crashed last night. Early this morning, the boat was spotted by the owner of 'Fly like a Bird,' a man by the name of Ross T. Alba. Following my instructions, forensics has more work to do on the inside. Sorry, can't take you in there."

Loni looked smug. "But if you want to see the boat, I can show it to you, tomorrow. The body of the young woman was found on the leeward side of the boat, in calm waters, dead by head trauma."

Loni glanced over at Kali. "Your substitute, the medical examiner from the other island, he's pretty sure the cause of death was the head trauma.

"He also fixes the time of death between midnight and 4 a.m. I waited to release the information, so I could investigate first. Kaipo Mahio rented that boat from the rent-a-boat at the harbor.

"The rent-a-boat owner, I interrogated him, he's sure of it. How Kaipo got the young woman on the boat is still a mystery, but the more I investigate him, the more resourceful he seems to be. So, somehow he did. My theory is they had an argument, neglected the boat.

"The boat crashes, but they survive. Now, the boat's gone. The argument gets worse, turns into a fight. In a rage moment, Kaipo picks up a rock and kills her. He then treks up the sandy road, hitches a ride on the coastal highway, and now, he's gone into hiding.

"Kaipo thinks he can get away with it, but I'm going to find him. I'm sure of it!" Loni looked from Big Brah to Kali then me, checking to see if any of us doubted he would find Kaipo.

Big Brah shook his head, slowly. "Kaipo may have rented the boat, but you found the body in the water, right?"

"Right." Loni nodded.

Big Brah spoke slowly. "So why did you conclude Kaipo killed her?" he asked.

Loni smirked. "I expected you to ask that question, Big Brah," he said.

Grandly, Loni whipped out a zipper bag from his pant pocket. He held up the transparent plastic bag, so we could all see what was inside.

A bead bracelet with a yellow gold plate.

All three of us had seen it in the surveillance video of the Mahio safe robbery. The yellow gold plate had "Kaipo" stylized in cursive on it.

Proudly, Loni said, "I found the bracelet myself. It was buried under the water, on the rocks next to the body. The bracelet must have come loose in the struggle. Undeniably, Kaipo's."

"What about a motive, why would Kaipo do such a thing?" I asked.

Loni displayed white teeth under his black mustache. "You're an able assistant, Umi. Good question. I thought of that, too." He held up two fingers. "Two nights ago, Kaipo had an argument with the young woman at 'The Tavern.'"

Wait just a minute. Loni had suddenly stopped making sense. The Tavern was the place islanders gathered to have fun. Kaipo and Nohea had been careful not to be seen even at the rent-a-boat. Would they argue openly at the Tavern? But Loni didn't give me a chance to say anything.

Loni continued. "I have a reliable witness. A family owns the Tavern, one of the sisters, Mohua." He turned to look at Kali. "She's your friend, right?"

Kali nodded. "Mohua's my friend. She's reliable, totally. What did she say?"

Loni said, "Kaipo and the young woman had a fight. She says she heard Kaipo threaten the murdered woman, his exact words were, 'I'll kill you.'"

Astounded, the three of us gazed at Loni. Both Big Brah and Kali must also have picked up on the strangeness of Kaipo and Nohea arguing at the Tavern. Big Brah and Kali exchanged looks.

Big Brah said, "Can you tell us the identity of the young woman?"

Loni grew grim importantly. It wasn't often he got to tell Big Brah things. "You know why I haven't released the identity of the young woman? It's because my chief suspect is Kaipo Mahio. The Mahio family is involved. Obviously that makes it a big case for the PD. The chief's asked me to keep him in the loop.

"Now, you say you're looking for Kaipo? So am I. Tell you what, Big Brah? I'll strike you a deal.

Work with me to find Kaipo, and I'll tell you the identity of the woman."

Big Brah always worked with Loni. Even the chief appreciated Big Brah's help. No problem there.

Big Brah nodded. "All right," he said, pleasantly.

Loni said, "The victim was Duke Mahio's property manager: Helen Hokui."

The woman with Kaipo in Duke Mahio's surveillance video. *Wow.* The victim wasn't Nohea Bordeta. The Bordeta family would be relieved. But, why would Kaipo Mahio kill Helen Hokui, the property manager?

Total mystery.

Besides, our rent-a-boat cousin Keni had been sure the woman on the boat with Kaipo was Nohea. How and when had the switcheroo to Helen Hokui happened? The sun was setting and the western sky blood red. We made it back to the big, black truck parked at the end of the sandy road. Loni had walked with us. He departed in his unmarked green sedan with a friendly wave. We had left the Bordetas worried.

Big Brah called Jim Bordeta. Told him the young woman wasn't Nohea Bordeta. Jim Bordeta didn't say much. When Big Brah asked if we could visit Bordeta House and talk story about Nohea's disappearance with him, his wife and his daughter, Jim Bordeta quietly agreed. Then he disconnected the call.

Big Brah gazed out at the ocean stretched out in front of us. "Search and rescue crew are still looking for Kaipo out there. Loni thinks Kaipo is hiding, on island. If so, finding Kaipo should be easy.

"What Loni isn't following up on at all, because he didn't bother to find out about it, Nohea may have been there with Kaipo when the murder happened. It's important we find out the circumstances of Nohea's disappearance," he said.

Made sense. Distances were generally short on the island. The coastal highway circled most of the island. You had to use the highway to go almost anywhere. Big Brah drove the big truck toward Bordeta House, as the evening darkened.

The lights were on at our destination. Big Brah, Kali and I followed a pathway through the garden. The fragrance of evening blooms was thick in the air. The lanai lights cast an eerie glow over the red-painted steps. The large front door opened, just as it had during the day.

Iekika emerged. Big eyes wide. Thick, black hair a mess in curls. She wore a tank-top and shorts. "I heard your car come up the hill, then your footsteps up the lanai." Then, sotto voice, she added, "Dad told me you want to talk story about Nohea."

Jean Bordeta's voice came from behind Iekika. "Iekika, bring our guests inside."

Iekika popped her head inside. "Of course,

Mom!" She turned to us, bright-eyed. "Come in!"

We followed her in. The large living room was lit up by lamps. Jim and Jean Bordeta were already seated on the trendy chrome and leather conversation set. The TV on the glass entertainment center was turned off. Big Brah and Kali chose the loveseat. Iekika hopped onto the sofa with her parents, and I got an armchair.

I settled into the armchair. This was turning out to be a long day. I was completely unprepared for the revelation we were about to have about the case.

# Chapter 5 Pure love telepathy

Self-consciously, Jim Bordeta ran a hand over the top of his head. Brushed back and stiffened by hair gel, his hair was in place. One eye browner than the other, his mismatched eyes appraised us coolly. His mouth stayed a straight line.

Jim Bordeta gestured with his hands. "In times like this, we don't know where Nohea is, the mind is overcome with fears. So mahalo for calling and clearing that up. I left a message with Sergeant Rice, assigned to investigate Nohea's disappearance. I asked him the same question, but he hasn't called back," he said.

Big Brah saw the good side of people. He nodded. "I know Sergeant Rice. You couldn't find a better person. I'm sure he'll call you back, he must be busy," he said.

Sitting next to her husband, Jean Bordeta clasped and unclasped her hands. The bamboo sticks had come out of her hairdo. Her hair fell straight and plentiful onto the shoulders and front of her housedress. "Did you find anything about our Nohea?" she said, tearfully.

"I'm afraid not, ma'am," Big Brah said.

"Oh!" Jean Bordeta clasped and unclasped her hands.

"I'm here to find out from you the circumstances of her disappearance," Big Brah said.

Jim Bordeta rescued his wife. "Jean and I, we weren't home. Last evening, it was a Friday, we were at a party, a friend's house. Iekika and Nohea were home alone, weren't you Iekika?" he said, turning to look at Iekika.

Iekika looked distressed. Her face was all scrunched up. "Not really home alone, Dad. I told you, Heki was with us," she said.

"Of course I remember you told me," he scolded her, "that boy is always here!"

Jim Bordeta turned his attention back to us. "As I was saying, my wife and I, we'd left the three of them at home. Heki is a friend of Nohea's, more like a young admirer. Heki hangs out here all the time. He's a pest, but he's like family, we don't mind. Nohea was supposed to leave at 7 p.m. to join other members of her marine biology class on a field trip."

"A field trip," Big Brah said, softly.

Kali and I exchanged glances. For some unknown reason Iekika looked even more distressed. Her face was so scrunched up, her big eyes were now just slits.

Innocently, Jim Bordeta said, "Yes, Nohea's

gone on field trips before. She told us she'd be back in the morning. Jean and I, we didn't see any cause for concern.

"Nohea's a college junior, she's been doing this for a while. We hugged her, we left, around five. The rest we got from Iekika. Everything was normal.

"At seven, Nohea left, Jean and I got back at ten. By then, Iekika was in bed, we didn't disturb her. This morning, when Nohea didn't come back, we tried calling her. Surprisingly, her phone was in her room."

I remembered Duke Mahio tell us how Kaipo had also left his phone in his room. I would too, if I wanted to run away untraced. *They have got to have planned it together*, I thought.

But, why?

Iekika was about to shed light on why.

Big Brah said, "So Heki, Nohea's young admirer, he must have left with Nohea, right?"

Jean Bordeta wiped a tear and then frowned at Iekika. "I thought you said Heki left with Nohea. Didn't he?" she said.

Iekika cleared her face and shook her head. "No, Mom, Nohea, um, didn't. I mean, she and Heki, they didn't leave together."

"But Heki follows Nohea here, why wouldn't he leave with her?" Jean Bordeta said.

Iekika jumped up, curling her fingers into fists. "Mom! You know nothing!" she said.

Jean Bordeta was exasperated. "What is it

that your father and I don't know?" she said.

"Tell us, it may be important." Kali urged her.

Iekika took a deep breath, looking at Kali, Big Brah and me intensely. Then she gazed down at her parents. "Mom, Dad, what I'm going to say is true. You may find this hard to believe, but Nohea is in love."

"What? Nohea is in love? With whom? Heki?" Jean Bordeta said.

"Not Heki. Leave Heki out of this, he's innocent!" Iekika said.

"Then, who?" Jean Bordeta said.

"At seven, the doorbell rang, and Heki opened the front door. You know why? Because Nohea told him to. She also told me who was going to pick her up. The man she loves. Kaipo Mahio."

Both parents gaped up at their daughter. I sat up straight. The cat was out of the bag.

Big Brah said, softly, "How do you know she loves him?"

Iekika said, "Nohea has been seeing Kaipo, for months now. I know what they do, together. Nohea's told me. Nohea's learning to surf, they go surfing together!"

Jean Bordeta gasped.

Iekika turned to look at Big Brah. "Nohea's been scared of sharks, all her life. Suddenly she loses the fear of sharks, she goes surfing. With Kaipo. Why do you think? She's in love with Kaipo!"

Love made you fearless.

"Where do they go surfing?" her mother asked, her voice quivering.

"They rent a boat, then go to Forbidden Beach."

Jim Bordeta jumped up. "Forbidden Beach? The waters are too dangerous. I forbid it," he said.

Iekika rolled her eyes, dramatically. "You forbid it? Nohea doesn't care, she's gone."

Her shapely chin up in the air, Iekika stormed out of the room. Jean Bordeta recovered first.

She grasped her husband's hand. "I'm sure this isn't true, my dear. Nohea wouldn't!" she cried out.

Jim Bordeta bowed his head, sat down and said nothing. Big Brah got up. Kali and I followed. Much as we wanted to help them, we knew we couldn't.

This was up to the Bordetas. All we could do was give them time together as a family to reconcile with the fact Nohea was in love with Kaipo.

Hard, with Nohea missing. For us, Nohea had left with Kaipo. Both were still missing. Were both of them responsible for the murder, then?

Time would tell. Outside, a near full moon lit up the night sky. We made our way back through the fragrant garden.

Big Brah and Kali held hands. I could tell both of them had been moved by Iekika's confession about Nohea's love. Somehow, I felt better about Kaipo knowing Nohea loved him.

On the island, when a girl chose a boy, and the love was pure, almost always, the love made a man of him and a woman of her. But in this case, Kaipo had stolen and possibly killed.

Didn't sound like pure love. Fake love, then? Time would tell. I sniffed the fresh night air. On the next hill, the lights of the Mahio Mansion glowed. Big Brah never jumped to conclusions, especially when it involved others.

We had learned about Nohea from Keni. And now, Iekika had confirmed it. My guess? Big Brah was now ready to tell Duke Mahio about Nohea.

Duke Mahio wasn't going to be pleased either. But Big Brah had told Duke Mahio he would report back. And what Big Brah said, Big Brah did. Duke Mahio was almost sure to ask Big Brah to find the killer assuming the killer wasn't Kaipo. Would Big Brah agree to do so? We reached the big, black truck.

I didn't bother Big Brah with questions on the short drive over. He was quiet, thinking things over, and so was Kali. From time to time, they looked at each other and smiled.

A pure love smile.

The shared smile meant they were thinking of the same thing: whether to take on solving the murder mystery. We ascended the concrete steps leading up to the pillared lanai of the Mahio Mansion. The soft lanai lights were on.

The massive front door opened. A young woman in a simple, black dress stood framed by the doorway. The bright foyer light streamed out from behind her. At the sight of us, she bent her torso and bowed her head. She had pink hair cropped at the shoulders. She gestured with her hands for us to enter. In the foyer, she greeted us with a bright smile.

She had a mole on her chin. "I'm Lily. Uncle Duke has been waiting to hear from you, for news about Kaipo. You're Kali, Big Brah and Umi, aren't you?" she said.

We nodded. She looked oddly familiar.

Kali said, "We have news, not all good."

Lily's smile faded. She lowered her voice. "Sorry to hear. I live in the quarters behind the house with my mother. She's the housekeeper, everyone calls her Aunty Maria.

"My mother and I, we couldn't leave Uncle alone on an evening like this, so I'm here. Come sit, I'll go get Uncle."

We followed Lily into the spacious, old-style living room with its high ceiling and beautiful bamboo, rattan furniture. A cooling breeze blew in through the big windows. Big Brah and Kali chose a loveseat, again, and I snagged an armchair. Lily left the room. The state-of-the-art big screen TV mounted on the wall had breaking news about the "Honeymooner" playing on it. The update?

The search and rescue crew had worked throughout the night, still looking for the boat's occupants. A reporter had traced the boat to rent-a-boat. An interview with Cousin Keni started to play. Rent-a-boat was open extra-long hours on Saturday night, Keni explained, so he was available. Yes, he knew who had rented the boat.

Man by the name of Kaipo Mahio. Yes, Duke Mahio's son. No, he didn't think Kaipo had murdered the young woman whose identity the police were withholding due to an ongoing investigation. But the police could better answer that question. Lily following close behind him, Duke Mahio entered the living room.

Since we last saw him only a few hours ago, Duke Mahio had aged. His clean-shaven face had the shadow of a white beard. He had developed a permanent stoop. Incongruously black now, his thinning hair looked even more depleted. He gestured for us to stay seated and settled down on the couch. Lily sat next to him.

Duke Mahio adjusted his business-like glasses in a tired way. He looked toward the TV. A commercial now played on it. "I was watching the news in my bedroom. So it appears Kaipo did rent that boat, but the rest of what they're saying is bogus. No way did Kaipo murder the young woman, whoever she may be. My boy isn't a killer. Far from it. He doesn't fish, he doesn't hunt, he's a peace-loving boy...." His voice faded away, and he lowered his head.

Lily glanced his way, sympathetic. She took his hand to comfort him.

"You tell them, Lily," he said to her, and to us, "Lily's his childhood friend, they're good together, she knows him better than most. Lily and Kaipo, they went to school together, and now college."

College. That's it. That's why she looked familiar. Most of my courses were online. I didn't go in often. But on one of the few times I did go in, I remembered seeing her. The island college had plenty fashionistas, but pink hair still stood out.

Lily looked at us and rubbed the mole on her chin absent-mindedly. "It's true, I've known Kaipo a long time. He's been a friend, sweet, romantic, I can't imagine him killing anyone."

Did that mean Lily had a romantic interest in Kaipo? Duke Mahio wanted it.

Duke Mahio looked up and nodded. "I've always wanted Lily and Kaipo to hook up," he said, with a sudden smile.

Something had gotten Duke Mahio to smile in the circumstances. Lily looked pleased. She patted his hand. "You know, Noah's my boyfriend. He better not hear what you said. Noah will be mad. Earlier this week, maybe it was Monday, no Tuesday night, we'd met at the Tavern, and I was telling Noah, how good Kaipo will be in love, he won't hold back, and Noah got so jealous," she said.

Duke Mahio shook his head, sadly. "I know, I know, it's always Noah, Noah with you...."

Lily let go his hand.

"Ah, I'm joking." Duke Mahio gently patted Lily's head to bless her silently. He turned to Big Brah, "So what did you find out?" he said.

I glanced at Big Brah. Learning about Kaipo and Nohea being together wasn't going to be easy for Duke Mahio. The raging Mahio and Bordeta enmity. *Here's the tough part*, I thought. Big Brah would have to find a way to soften the blow.

Big Brah said, "I have good news and bad news."

"Tell me the good news first. I could use some this very minute," Duke Mahio said.

Big Brah said, "There may have been another woman involved. Someone who could have been with Kaipo at the time of the murder. Someone who could be his alibi."

Interested, Duke Mahio sat up. "An alibi for Kaipo. Who's she?" he asked.

Big Brah had softened the blow.

Big Brah bowed then raised his head to look squarely at Duke Mahio. "Nohea Bordeta," he said.

"Not one from *that* Bordeta family." Duke Mahio cried out.

Big Brah nodded, empathizing. "Nohea Bordeta is the daughter of your business rival Jim Bordeta."

Duke Mahio was up on his feet, agitated. "Impossible," he said.

Big Brah and Kali exchanged glances.

Impossible. Jim Bordeta had reacted the same way.

Patiently, Big Brah explained. "We just talked to the Bordetas. They confirmed Kaipo picked up Nohea from her home at 7 p.m. last evening. My cousin Keni of rent-a-boat also confirmed Kaipo had rented boats from him previously, all to go out with Nohea."

"Why? What did they do?" Duke Mahio said.

"They surfed," Big Brah said.

Duke Mahio said, "Surf?" He fell silent, thinking.

Big Brah waited, always patient.

Duke Mahio adjusted his business-like glasses. "I suppose surfing's possible. I told you Kaipo gets his love for the ocean from his mother. He loves to surf, I'm proud to say, he's good at it. But why would he need a boat to surf?"

Big Brah said, "They didn't want anyone to see them, they went to Forbidden Beach."

"Forbidden Beach? But that's private property, part of Alika's Whale Reserve, and it's dangerous!"

Big Brah nodded. "They definitely wanted no one else to know they were seeing each other."

"I see." Then, silence. Duke Mahio knew only too well why Kaipo and Nohea wanted to keep their seeing each other a secret.

At last, Duke Mahio cleared his throat. "Was that the good and bad news then?" he asked.

"There's one more thing," Big Brah said.

"What is it?" Duke Mahio said.

"About the victim," Big Brah said.

"Who is she?" Duke Mahio asked.

Big Brah said, "Helen Hokui."

"The goddess help us! Why would Kaipo kill poor Helen? She's my employee, a good employee," Duke Mahio said.

Big Brah said, "Two nights ago, Kaipo and Helen Hokui had a fight, at the Tavern. Kaipo threatened to kill her in front of witnesses."

Duke Mahio said, "I know nothing about this. Look, Big Brah, something's terribly wrong with this. Please, you must help. You must find the real killer. My Kaipo couldn't have done it!"

Big Brah and Kali exchanged looks. They had thought about this moment. Time to decide whether to take on the case or not.

Big Brah said, "Mr. Mahio, did you observe any change in Kaipo lately?"

Duke Mahio nodded. "Yes, yes, a very big change."

A very big change. Interesting.

Duke Mahio said, "For the better. He was taking on more responsibility in the business. He did his college work. He's always been academically brilliant.

"I'd say the biggest change in him in recent months, he was happy. Five years ago, his mother passed away. Kaipo's always been sensitive, he missed his mother.

"Can't blame Kaipo, I miss Luana too. She was

everything to both of us. But lately he's been happy, you know, like he used to be, before all this happened."

Happy. Very interesting.

Big Brah glanced over at Kali. Kali nodded, briefly.

Big Brah said, "All right, Mr. Mahio. I'll find the real killer."

The real killer. Outside, in the cool night air, I took a deep breath. This was going to be a tough case. Usually, when he took on a case, Big Brah liked to visit our family heiau or temple dedicated to the Island Goddess.

Today, Big Brah had his goddess, meaning Kali, with him, so he wouldn't be in a hurry to go to the heiau. But Big Brah said we all needed food to produce good work. Big Brah and Kali held hands all the way back to the big, black truck.

Inside the truck, Big Brah said, "I'm hungry. Besides, I want to know more about Kaipo's fight with Helen Hokui. Let's go to the Tavern, get some grinds and see Mohua."

Big Brah found us a space in the crowded parking lot of the Tavern and parked the truck. It was close to midnight, a Saturday night. Islanders partied. Under the familiar neon sign, we strolled in through the sliding door.

Inside, it was darker. Island reggae blasted from the dance floor. The aroma of food enveloped everybody with familiar comfort. People was happy! Big Brah, Kali and I strolled past the gleaming screens displaying the specials of the night. The *loco moco* with bacon burgers caught my attention. Yes, I was ready to eat big. We ambled past the busy bar.

Next to the bar, the dancefloor was crowded. The real excitement was on the dancefloor. Fun. We turned right. The sprawling, well-lit restaurant with tables and chairs interspersed with potted palm trees came into view.

Some of the tables were occupied others empty. From a counter near us, a petite woman stepped out to greet us. She had big eyes, long, dark hair down to her hips and a sweet smile. Kali's friend, Mohua.

Kali said, "Mohua! We need to see you."

Mohua fluttered her big eyelashes, importantly. "It's about the woman who died in the boat accident today, isn't it?"

Kali smiled fondly at her friend. "Mohua, you're so clever, how did you know?"

Mohua tilted her head modestly. "In the last news report, the TV reporter, looked sleepy, but she said the Waialeale Detective Agency was investigating on behalf of Kaipo Mahio's family, and that's you," she said, smiling sweetly at each of us in turn.

Kali smiled back. Big Brah nodded. I bowed.

Mohua hurried back to behind the counter and returned with three menus. "You must be hungry," she said hospitably, "come on."

She took us to the table by the window at

the back. The window had a view of the clear sky, the silvery moon and the mountains bathed in moonlight. A lush palm next to the table provided privacy.

Mohua knew the table was our favorite. And Mohua was just being polite. We didn't really need the menus. We had the menu memorized.

Big Brah ordered the Prime Rib topped with sautéed mushrooms and onions. Creamy mashed potatoes, steamed broccoli and spicy horse radish on the side. Kali ordered the rich goat curry and flavorful fried rice. I ordered the loco moco with juicy bacon burgers, of course.

All three dinner entrees came with a fresh, colorful salad and a drink. Along with our salads, Mohua got us a pitcher of mango-flavored iced tea. Soon she returned with our dinner plates and a complimentary platter of hot tempuras fried golden-brown. It was a party. The food was yummy and our appetites big.

The loco moco plate had a blend of brown and white rice. The rice was topped with a couple of big bacon-burgers and sunny side up eggs. A bowl of rich, brown gravy was served on the side. Mohua was sweet.

Mohua was Kali's friend, after all. She let us eat first and fill our empty stomachs with the delectable food. Satisfied, we sipped the cold tea. It was pure aloha.

Then Mohua joined us. She sat down in the empty chair next to me. "Why did you want to see me?" she said.

Kali sat across from Mohua. "Tell us about the fight Kaipo Mahio had with Helen Hokui," she said.

Mohua poured iced tea from the pitcher into a spare glass and sipped the cool drink. "It happened on Thursday evening. The woman, Helen Hokui, she came in first. Around eight o' clock. I knew her.

"Tall, slim, black hair. She and her brother moved in from another island, year and a half ago. At the time, she told me she worked for Mahio Plaza. Her brother was busy looking for suitable employment.

"Since then, both of them ate at the Tavern often, sometimes together, other times alone. Brother's name is Randall Hokui, Randy. On Thursday, Ms. Hokui was alone. When I approached her, she told me she wanted a table for two.

"Naturally, I asked her if her brother was going to join her. Ms. Hokui, she shook her head, told me, the someone who was going to join her wasn't her brother. She's in here often, a regular, I knew her well.

"I teased her. A date, then? She looked nervous, she laughed. She didn't say yes, or no. I let it go. People come to the Tavern to relax, I don't bother them with questions. But she told me the man she was expecting was Kaipo Mahio, did I know him?

"Of course I knew Kaipo Mahio, he spends a lot of time in here with the other young men, so I told her yes, I knew Kaipo. I'd be happy to bring him over to her, soon as he arrived.

"Ms. Hokui smiled gratefully and asked for a table at the back, I figured they wanted privacy. When Kaipo showed up, all tall, dark and handsome, I brought him to her right away.

"The tables were crowded, the waitresses busy, I brought them their dinner myself. At first, they were happy, like any two people spending the evening together. But, by the time I brought them dessert, Kaipo was frowning, Helen unsmiling.

"I figured they were having a rough moment, who doesn't? I went away behind my counter. Next, I heard a commotion from the tables. I ran to see what it was. There, at the back, Kaipo had Helen pinned on the wall.

"I was shocked. I had never imagined Kaipo to be violent. He's always so dreamy, so easy-going. If he's on the dance floor, all the girls seek him out, and he's kind to them. He makes them feel good. Kaipo makes everyone feel good. Never messes with anyone. But there he was, his hands around her neck. I can't explain. From the other tables, people were screaming.

"A couple men ran to hold Kaipo back. I think everyone heard him. I know I did, and I was standing far away. Kaipo kept repeating 'I'll kill you,' until the men pulled him back. He didn't fight them. By the time I got to him, his anger still hadn't subsided, but I think he was aware of the scene he was creating.

"In a huff, Kaipo left. I asked Ms. Hokui if she was hurt, and she shook her head. I took that as a no, told her, if it made her evening any better, the food and drinks were on the house.

"She smiled and shortly afterward, after a trip to the restroom, she left. Now, I've already told Lieutenant Loni all this. I don't know whether this helps you or not."

Mohua paused to sip her drink. Engrossed by her story, I had forgotten my drink. I reached for it now. Mango, I like.

Kali said, "Mohua, you've been a big help."

Big Brah nodded, approvingly. "Invaluable," he said.

Big Brah and Kali were satisfied. My stomach was also satisfied. Mohua's invaluable testimony swirled in my head as Big Brah, Kali and I exited the Tavern.

The Tavern's parking lot was lit up by moonlight. We boarded the big, black truck. In minutes, we were on our way home via the coastal highway. Big Brah drove.

Kali rode in the passenger seat and I had the backseat to myself. We were all silent, no doubt pondering the next step. The truck took the turnoff for our home, entered the driveway and swished past the light above the reader board displaying "Waialeale Detective Agency."

The truck turned the corner.

In front of us, like in a dream, our darkened two-story home was a beckoning big boat surrounded by an ocean of moonlight. But Big Brah wasn't finished.

With the big truck parked in the garage, Big Brah glanced at Kali. "How about a stroll to the heiau?" he said.

Kali looked at me questioningly. I happily agreed. For a stroll to the heiau it was a gorgeous moonlit night. Big Brah, Kali and I strolled down the garden path to the beach. I didn't bother turning on the flashlight I had picked up from the garage. The clamor of the ocean got closer. The cool breeze was in my face. The water silver and the froth of the waves bone white, the ocean looked surreal. Soon we were walking on the soft sand of the beach, the clamoring waves close by. The heiau was built on the sand.

The heiau had an oval boundary built of black lava rocks placed next to each other. We stopped outside of the boundary. Giving the much-loved heiau a divine glow, the moon shone down on the familiar collection of whimsical shapes and figures made out of the same black lava rocks.

Dedicated to the Island Goddess, the heiau was a memorial to our family lost in an ocean tragedy. Big Brah and I were kids, fighting grief. We had put the heiau together painstakingly one rock at a time. There was a time I couldn't look at the familiar collection without tearing up.

Tonight, it still hurt, but I didn't tear up. Instead, the murder played on my mind. I knew how hard it was to lose a loved one. What had Kaipo and Nohea got to do with the murder? Where were they? Along with Big Brah and Kali, I closed my eyes.

I prayed to the goddess. "Let nothing bad have happened to Kaipo and Nohea…let nothing bad have happened to Kaipo and Nohea…let nothing bad have happened to Kaipo and Nohea…." I said, over and over again.

I opened my eyes. Big Brah and Kali were holding hands, all solemn, patiently waiting for me to finish. I was always the last to be done praying. We did a warm group hug and then headed home.

Both Big Brah and Kali were silent, as we made our way back across the sand. Big Brah didn't take on a case very easily. He always helped with advice and support. He took on a case only if he was sure he could help. I remembered him looking at Kali and Kali's brief nod back at him, right before he told Duke Mahio, he would find the real killer.

I had been with Big Brah and Kali the entire time. I had heard everything they had told each other. Never once had they exchanged words about whether to take on the case or not. Not a word. But Kali had known. Big Brah agreed with her. I wanted to know their secret. I did know how they had pulled it off. Pure love telepathy.

Anyways, I had to verify why they had been sure.

I said, "How is it both of you were sure you wanted to work on this case?"

Big Brah chuckled. "I knew you'd ask, Umi."

He knew I'd ask?

Kali giggled, nodding.

She knew I'd ask too. But how? As we walked on the sand, the moon high in the heavens, the cool breeze whispered the answer to me. Pure family love telepathy. Obviously! I was warmed.

Kali said, "Iekika was very sure Nohea was in love with Kaipo. With Kaipo, Nohea's gotten over a fear, a fear she has had since childhood: sharks!"

Big Brah said, "I believe she's in love. Then, Kaipo's father, Duke Mahio told us Kaipo had been happy recently, like he used to be, before his mother passed away. I believe it's because he fell in love, with Nohea."

Wise, very wise. I nodded, understanding.

Encouraging, Big Brah patted my back. "Umi, this time, we're working to protect love!"

To protect love. A worthy cause. Still, I had my doubts. There was the surveillance video of Kaipo stealing from the safe. His bracelet by the body at the murder site. What about the scene at the Tavern? Mohua had vividly described Kaipo attacking Helen Hokui unprovoked. We had reached the garden path to the house. We walked up the sloping path in silence. The sound of the waves was behind us.

I said, "Iekika could be mistaken. Duke Mahio could be wrong. How can you be sure Nohea and Kaipo, theirs is pure, not fake love?"

We walked some more in thoughtful silence. We were almost at the house.

Big Brah said, "I'm sure Kaipo and Nohea, their love is for real."

Kali nodded, vigorously. "I know it. Their love is pure," she said.

Big Brah and Kali were island doves, always lovey-dovey. This was their secret: they instinctively believed Kaipo and Nohea's love was pure. Still my doubts backed by the mountain of evidence started an intense staring match with my trust in their instincts. It wasn't like Big Brah or Kali to make assertions without proper evidence.

Big Brah patted my back, again. "Time will tell."

Kali said, "The truth will be revealed."

Big Brah said, "We must search for the truth! We're detectives."

I was getting it. "We'll expose fake love," I said.

Kali smiled. "To protect pure love it's essential to expose fake love!"

"Let's find the love killer," Big Brah said.

The intense staring match between my doubt and trust ended. My trust in the lovey-doveys won. *Here we go again, this time for love*, I thought. I nodded with enthusiasm. It was close to 3 a.m.

by the bedside radio alarm clock when I finally flopped onto the bed tired. It had been a long day, but I didn't need the alarm clock to wake me up.

Big Brah woke me up, early morning.

I cracked an eye open and gazed up at his caring face. "Let me guess, we have to go somewhere," I said.

# Chapter 6 Don't hide love

Big Brah said, "Right on, Umi."

"Where?" I asked.

Big Brah said, "Nohea and Kaipo used to rent a boat and go to Forbidden Beach. On Friday night they rented a boat."

Friday night had been the night of the full moon. Or *hoku* as our ancestors called the full moon. "Perfect night for surfing," I said.

Big Brah said, "Yes, they'd have headed to the Forbidden Beach, like always. At the beach, or somewhere between the eastside dock and the beach, something changed. So, to investigate, we take the big boat, travel the way they did, all the way to Forbidden Beach."

I opened my eyes and gaped up at him, wide awake. Forbidden Beach? The beach was part of the Alika Whale Reserve. It was forbidden to enter the reserve. It was *kapu* or sacred law. The Alika family enforced the kapu. Around the island, the Alika family was well-known and liked.

The Alika children dominated surfing events. They were fun to be around. The matriarch of the family, Kala Alika practiced an ancient art of our ancestors: hand-tapped tattoos. Discerning celebrities often dropped in on her to get inked. The entire family made us proud to be islanders.

The present-day patriarch of the family, Makoa Alika had always been serious about the kapu. He had to be serious. He belonged to a line of high priests, kahunas, who worshipped at the sacred heiau or temple there.

In ancient times, the heiau had been a refuge to those who needed it most. The whale reserve was a recent addition, but every islander respected the kapu.

I worried. "There's a story about Makoa Alika every year. About how relentless he's in enforcing the kapu."

Big Brah said, "I agree. We may meet Makoa Alika today. I want to ask him if he saw Kaipo and Nohea."

Kaipo and Nohea had better not have gotten on Makoa Alika's wrong side. I mimed my fiercest *haka* face.

Big Brah smiled. "Did you know, despite his scary image, Makoa Alika is also a songwriter. A poet, he composes meles," he said.

*Meles?* I loved the song-poems. I loved music. I loved poetry. I loved sketching. I loved painting and I loved meeting artists. It was going to be an interesting day.

I leaped out of bed. I had a brainwave. Kaipo and Nohea had surfed on Forbidden Beach. "Are we bringing our surfboards?" I said.

Big Brah laughed like he did when he was proud of me. "Surfboards. For sure, Umi," he said.

Downstairs, in the kitchen, the lights were on. Kali greeted me with an affectionate smile. "Good morning, Li'l Brah," she said.

I gave her my bright grin. I was awake now, excited. Big Brah and Kali had made fresh musubis and chocolate chip cookies.

We packed the musubis and cookies along with plenty coconut water into a cooler for consumption later. For breakfast, Big Brah and Kali had made a savory rice mashup with soft-boiled eggs, butter-fried salmon and potatoes. The potatoes were Big Brah's addition.

Yummy. Did Big Brah and Kali get any sleep at all? I had another brainwave. No sleep was required when you worked to protect aloha. I rode the aloha wave. On the brief stroll to the boathouse, the sun wasn't up.

It was light outside and the air was cool and bracing. I hugged my surfboard. Big Brah and Kali carried their surfboards underarm. Excited by the birth of a new day birds called. At the boathouse, we took a moment to contemplate the big boat.

Peacefully flying Old Glory, the big boat had a sizable, shiny and V-shaped hull. The wide deck had many seats. There was a stylish navigation cabin on top and private cabins below. The big boat was perfect for venturing out to wider waters and partying.

Big Brah and Kali used the big boat to meditate. The boat had its name, "Meditator," painted on its side. I had chosen the name. Big Brah and Kali had let me choose. We got the cooler onboard, and we were off.

The big boat moved powerfully forward toward open water. A thrill surged through me. Big Brah and Kali were in the navigation cabin, while I enjoyed the ride on the large deck. In order to avoid the dangerous rocks, Big Brah took the boat away from the shore. The horizon reddened. The sky changed color.

The boat cut back in an arc toward the island and the bay with Forbidden Beach came into view. The water turned clearer, the waves just right for surfing. A hill covered by lush wild grass fringed the golden sand of the beach.

Pure nature.

Beautiful setting. For Kaipo and Nohea, the perfect place for romance, no doubt. The sand bar was not far from the beach. We anchored the boat easily there. There was not a soul in sight.

From the deck, Big Brah pointed to a solar-paneled rooftop glinting under the trees on the left of the beach. "I believe that's the boathouse the Alika family uses. It's their only way to enter and exit their property," he said.

"There must be a way to contact the main residence from the boathouse. Let's head for the boathouse, they must have visitors like us sometimes," Kali said.

"Here's where we surf!" Big Brah said.

I was first in the water with my surfboard. I knew we were on serious duty. But I couldn't resist a joyous whoop. *Cheehoo.*

Big Brah and Kali jumped into the water alongside me, and to my surprise, they cheehoo-ed louder. We laughed at each other.

Soon I was up and riding my surfboard. The soft touch of the ocean spray was in my face. The wind kissed my bare shoulders. Kali and Big Brah were close behind me. A movement on the shore caught my attention.

An imposing figure, a man in the garb of our ancestors stood on top of the hill. He had on a feathered helmet, a *mahiole,* and a feathered cape, an *ahuula.* A *kapa malo* hung from his hips.

The rising sun illuminated the red feathers of his mahiole and ahuula. In the ways of our ancestors, the red feathers were a sign of his esteemed rank as the highest. He was a kahuna, a spiritual master.

In the same red rays of the early sun, an evil-looking spear glinted in his hands. I knew better than to point. That would have alerted the man watching us.

I called out instead, hoping the sounds of the ocean around us would drown my voice. "Big Brah! Kali! Look, on top of the hill!"

I heard Kali say, "I see him."

Then, Big Brah said, "Let's get on the sand. I

want to meet him."

My curiosity was at high tide. The beach got closer and closer. I raced out of the water, surfboard tucked under my arm. Big Brah and Kali followed me out of the water more leisurely. The man on top of the hill had disappeared. I hadn't seen him leave.

One moment, he was up there. I had felt his eyes on us. Next moment, gone. Big Brah, Kali and I regrouped on the sand to catch our breath.

I heaved a breath, looking toward the wild trees. "Don't know where he went," I said.

Big Brah was standing closest to the trees. Suddenly, the swish of something dangerous, something that flew fast, hard and deadly. It had to be the spear in the man's hand. The weapon landed inches from Big Brah's feet.

"Careful, Koa!" Kali said.

My heart skipped a beat. But Big Brah didn't even flinch. Instead, he stood his ground, gazing intently in the direction of the trees. The spear had been flung from behind one of the wild trees. Helmet, cape and malo in place, the same man emerged from behind the weathered trunk of a wild tree.

The man had a long beard. He was older. He walked slowly up to us. His piercing eyes on us, he picked up his spear. It was his weapon. Big Brah didn't move.

The frown lines between Spearman's eyebrows deepened. He struck a menacing pose.

Big Brah spoke, soothingly. "We're guests on your property—"

"Leave!" Spearman said.

Big Brah was livid. "How could you be so unwelcoming to guests?" he said.

The man raised his voice. "I was welcoming enough. If I was being truly unwelcoming, the spear wouldn't have landed at your feet, it would have pierced your heart."

I shuddered at the image of the sharp, hard spearpoint piercing a human heart.

"Leave, it's kapu!" The man repeated.

Big Brah spoke even-voiced. "Brah, aren't you forgetting another sacred law?" he asked.

The man's voice dropped to a menacing growl. "You gonna teach a kahuna sacred law."

His sarcasm was as sharp as his spearpoint.

Big Brah was unperturbed. "Brah, this is also the kapu of our ancestors: a guest has to be welcomed first!"

The man relented. "Okay, okay, welcome."

Big Brah introduced us. "My name is Koa Waialeale, these are my associates, Kali and Umi."

"I'm Makoa Alika. Now, leave!"

Big Brah, Kali and I stood our ground, unmoved.

Makoa Alika was annoyed. "Why're you here?" he asked.

Fear of the spear forgotten, I was compelled to speak up. "We work for the Waialeale

Detective Agency," I said.

Makoa Alika threw out his chest and laughed a surprisingly high-pitched laugh. His bare chest was intricately tattooed in the method of our ancestors. Kakau. His wife's art, no doubt.

Makoa Alika had on a whale tooth necklace, another sign of his high rank. "Detectives! What're you investigating, the tides?" he said.

Big Brah just ignored Makoa Alika's made-up, eccentric humor. "We're investigating the murder. The body of a young woman was found by an empty boat stranded on the dangerous rocks nearby."

"It was nearby, so you're here, is that it?" Makoa Alika said, irritably.

"Not really, we have a good reason to be here," Big Brah said.

"A good reason, let's hear it," Makoa Alika said.

Taking his time, Big Brah took a deep breath. "Two people. A man and a woman used to rent a boat and surf here, quite regularly. Have you seen the couple?"

"A couple?" Makoa Alika repeated, quickly. Too quickly. He knew something about a couple.

"Tell me their names," he said.

Big Brah told him the names, slowly. "Kaipo Mahio. Nohea Bordeta."

Almost immediately, Makoa Alika said, "Those two, yes I know them. I caught them breaking the kapu several times these past few months."

Darn. He sounded honest.

"They bother you?" Big Brah asked.

Makoa Alika dug the spearpoint deep into the sand. The spear stood, upturned. Makoa Alika had given up the idea of scaring us with the weapon.

He heaved a sigh. "You know what? Since you ask, at first, they did bother me. They came here often." He gazed past us at the open bay.

In the distance, anchored on the sand bar, the big boat bobbed blessed by the rising sun.

Makoa Alika returned his attention back to us. "They weren't fully grown up. He was just a boy, she just a girl. He surfed. She didn't. She was learning from him.

"It bothered me, they were so far away from their homes, no family around. All this I could tell looking at them from afar. One day, I decided to confront them.

"I caught them right here, on the beach. It was a clear afternoon, I remember. They were surprised to see me. They'd already visited a few times, never seen anyone, must have assumed the place was empty.

"I informed them about the kapu. Heck, everyone even calls it the 'Forbidden Beach.' They had to have known.

"They told me, they did know of the kapu, but they'd rather face the kapu, than face the consequences of being seen together."

Makoa Alika took off his helmet, revealing long hair. He stared down into the helmet for a long while. None of us said anything. We were all intrigued by his story reliving the afternoon, when he had talked to Kaipo and Nohea, while the couple were healthy and happy together.

At last, Makoa Alika looked up at us. His face darkened. "What kind of parents allow their children, a good, responsible boy, and a good, loving girl, to hide their love in this manner?

"When you find love, you're supposed to climb the highest tree, climb the highest mountain, ride the highest wave, shouting your love. Don't hide love.

"I was aghast. Two kids couldn't declare their love on our island of aloha and natural beauty? At first, I was mad at them. Told them not to come here. Then I saw their sad faces.

"I melted. I told them they could come here, as often as they wanted. They wouldn't bother me. That's all I know. After that, I saw them often, from a distance.

"I waved to them, sometimes. They knew me, by then. Knew I was around. They used to wave back, always happy together. Sweet couple." Makoa Alika looked away toward the big boat.

Big Brah said, softly, "The boat, found on the rocks, was theirs."

Makoa Alika turned his gaze back on Big Brah. "I have no idea how the boat got there."

"So they didn't come here to surf on Friday

night?" I asked.

Makoa Alika turned his piercing eyes on me. He gazed at me for a long moment, as if looking into my soul. His gaze struck me breathless.

"Surf? Not that I know of," Makoa Alika said, slowly.

I nodded, silenced. My throat was dry. Suddenly, I had no more questions or witty remarks to make. Kali had been silent this entire time. She was great at relieving tension.

She planted her surfboard on the sand and leaned on it. "I have heard the story of Pilialoha. How this whale reserve came about," she said.

The permanent frown lines between Makoa Alika's eyebrows relaxed a little.

"Is it true?" Kali asked.

Makoa Alika fixed his piercing eyes on Kali. "It's true. Pilialoha, our whale. She was a baby then.

"I saw her thrashing trapped by an abandoned net. Luckily I had a dagger with me that morning.

"I swam out to save her. The entire day, she thrashed. I tried to free her. The evening, the night, they passed. Finally, the following morning, I was almost dead with exhaustion after the long struggle.

"Pilialoha swam free. Ever since, she always returns every year, to have her babies, right here. I swim out to meet her. To me, she's like a daughter," he said.

Makoa Alika looked out at the bay. "Pilialoha left, only a few days ago, otherwise you'd see her. She's gone North, her yearly journey. Pilialoha will be back, same time as every year."

Wow. What a story. The sun was out, warming the sand at our feet. I gazed at Makoa Alika. In the soft light of a new day, despite the wonderful story Kali had gotten out of him, the kahuna looked mysterious. Somehow, I got the feeling, he wasn't exactly leveling with us.

What was he hiding?

"You look like a nice family," Makoa Alika said.

Big Brah, Kali and I were proud of our family. We simultaneously melted at the compliment. We were pleased. Modest, all of us stayed silent.

"Stay as long as you want," he said.

I was totally impressed. Such generosity from the kapu upholder.

Makoa Alika fixed his piercing eyes on Big Brah. "But don't forget, you have a bigger task."

What was that again? I glanced at Big Brah. Big Brah didn't say anything. He made an inquiring face.

Makoa Alika said, "The body found by the boat. You're investigating the death of the young woman. Isn't it urgent you find the killer?"

So much for his generosity. He was back to reminding us of our task. *Okay, we get it, you don't want us here, one way or the other*, I thought. Big Brah merely nodded, agreeing.

No surprise. Big Brah stayed calm no matter the provocation. Back on the big boat, Big Brah, Kali and I dried ourselves on the deck. The morning sun helped. I had mixed feelings about Makoa Alika.

I toweled my hair vigorously. "One thing we can all agree on about Makoa Alika, he didn't like Kaipo and Nohea having to hide their love."

Big Brah finished toweling his back and tossed the towel into the bin for the used towels. "Right, and he blamed the parents for it," he said.

Towel wrapped firmly around her torso, Kali stepped out of the pool of ocean water she had created on the deck. "Makoa Alika blamed the parents, he got that right, and he got Pilialoha right, don't know about anything else," she said, moving toward the steps to the cabins below the deck.

Big Brah and I glanced at each other. How well Kali summed things up.

Big Brah smiled fondly in her direction. "So, how're you enjoying hands-on detective work?" he called out.

Kali paused. She turned back to look at him, her smile radiant. "I'm lovin' it."

She blew us kisses before disappearing down the steps to the cabins.

Soon she was back in a fresh sarong dress. "The victim has a brother. We should go see the brother, don't you think?" she asked.

Big Brah was impressed. "I was thinking the exact same thing," he said.

Kali smiled bigger. She exchanged a look with me, as we always did, whenever either of us impressed Big Brah. Yes, she was enjoying hands-on detective work.

Big Brah glanced my way. "Kali's right. Let's go see the brother," he said.

But first we sat on the deck and enjoyed the musubis, chocolate chip cookies and coconut water from the cooler. I was hungry.

The coconut water cooled my parched throat. The food tasted sublime. Afterward, with all three of us cozy in the navigation cabin, Big Brah expertly navigated the big boat around the northeast corner of the island.

The "Honeymooner" came into view. The boat was still stranded. Waves crashed against the dangerous rocks. White spray leaped skyward. A crew had arrived to tow the damaged boat away. Surely the boat required extensive repairs. Cousin Keni had a lot of work ahead. Still looking for a missing occupant, a couple of helicopters caught the sun's rays. Back on the eastside, Big Brah, Kali and I exchanged the big boat for the big truck.

I used my phone to find out where Randy Hokui lived. He lived with his sister, the victim. They had shared a home. The home was on the coastal highway, eastside. Nothing was too far away on the island.

Soon Big Brah drove the big truck through a crowded neighborhood. Many streets, one after the other, forked away from the highway on both sides. Lots of homes, mainly rentals.

Tourist rentals were showy and closer to the coast. Locals overdid or underdid the keeping up. Local homes were easy to spot. The victim's home was kept up in the same modest way long-term rentals were maintained on the island.

The small home on a tiny lot had a privacy hedge and a gate. Big Brah parked the big, black truck streetside near the gate. A short driveway connected the gate to the two-vehicle car port. There was a lanky man on the short driveway. He was rinsing down a white truck with a garden hose. He had to be Randy Hokui.

Randy Hokui was a thin man, his casual tank-top and shorts loose on him. Something was the matter with his legs. He limped sideways. Limping, he continued to rinse the white truck.

In the light of the clear morning, everything seemed so regular. Who would have thought such a big tragedy could unfold here? Big Brah, Kali and I entered through the gate.

The man turned the hose off and flung the nozzle onto a dry flower bed. He had an untrimmed beard that partially hid his face. "Aloha, I'm Randy Hokui. What can I do for you fine people?" he said, pleasantly.

Big Brah introduced us. His voice softened with sympathy. "We're investigating the murder of Helen Hokui. I understand she was your sister," he said.

A lost look came over Randy Hokui. His eyes filled with tears and his voice trembled. "I-I'm lost without Helen, she-she's the only family I had," he said.

Big Brah said, "I'm really sorry." Sincerely, both Kali and I murmured our condolences.

Randy Hokui nodded slowly accepting our words. "Helen and I, we lost our parents, they died together in an accident. Ever since, we-we've been family for each other, and now, this," he said.

Familiar. Big Brah and I had also lost our parents in an ocean tragedy. Too familiar. I got *chicken skin*, you know, goose bumps. Randy Hokui blinked his tears away. He limped toward the house. A walking stick was propped up against the front wall.

Randy Hokui gripped the stick, slipped the wrist strap on and turned to face us, miserable. He sighed heavily. "I suppose, you'll want to know everything. I'll tell you best I can. Come in."

The living room was messy and smelly. The couch and loveseat looked used, the furniture dusty and the rug under the coffee table dirty. The floor was littered with beer cans and pizza boxes. There was a wet spill. A beer can had overturned. A slice of pizza languished next to the spill. The only window had a blind.

The angled slats of the blind let in the

morning sunlight. Dust motes danced in the sunlight. A corner table had a small TV and a lumpy armchair nearby. Using the walking stick, Randy Hokui limped his way to the armchair and seated himself. He propped the walking stick against the chair.

He gestured for us to sit down. "I'm really sorry for the mess, my sister was the neat sibling. With her gone, I don't know what to do. The problem isn't just my leg, I can handle the limp, but I have a problem bending as well."

Seated in the lumpy armchair in the unclean living room, the lost expression on his face, Randy Hokui looked so pathetic that we all felt pity for him. We did not want to judge him in this terrible time. Pretending everything was normal, Big Brah and Kali valiantly chose the loveseat to sit on. I sat on the couch.

When we were all seated, Randy Hokui said, "I have already told Lieutenant Loni everything. Whatever I know. He called me in the morning, yesterday. Around this time. Asked if I could drive down to the rocks, where the boat was. When he called, he didn't tell me about the boat, but—"

Randy Hokui pointed toward the small TV on the corner table, tiredly. "I had the TV on. The boat was in the news. I am so stupid, I still didn't connect. In my defense, the police hadn't announced finding the body.

"Apparently Loni wanted to talk to me, first.

He had me identify the body. I identified my sister...." His mouth moved, but no words came out.

# Chapter 7 Regret is such a thing

Randy Hokui's eyes filled with tears, again. We stayed silent, allowing him time to recover. His grief was profound.

Eventually, he pulled himself together with an effort. "I'm sorry. I don't mean to break down so often. But all this is so recent."

Big Brah soothed him, his voice filled with sympathy. "Please, take your time. We're in no hurry, we understand," he said.

After a while, Randy Hokui, his voice small, said, "Funny thing is, she called me, she called me, twice. I slept through her calls."

Big Brah said, "You mean, on Friday night, your sister called you?"

"Yes, twice. I was on the couch, drinking beer, watching TV. Being useless. I don't even know, when I passed out. But my phone showed a record of the missed calls. They came in right after 1 a.m., minutes apart. I was passed out right here, on the couch. Here, I'll show you."

Randy Hokui fished out a phone from a pocket of his shorts and fiddled with it. He held up his phone so we could see its screen. Sure enough, the missed calls log displayed the two calls at 1:23 a.m. and 1:25 a.m.

Sadly, he put the phone back inside the pocket. "If I hadn't been so negligent, if only I had taken the calls, my sister, she'd be alive! You see, she must have called me, when she felt she was in danger. She didn't leave any voicemail, the danger must have been imminent.

"My sister and I, we have always had this bond, since we were so high, she always called me, if she was in trouble. And she must have been in trouble, she was murdered."

I remembered Loni saying the substitute medical examiner thought the murder occurred between midnight and 4 a.m. Those calls were well within that time period. Yes, Helen Hokui could have been fighting for her life, when she made those calls, as her brother was suggesting.

"I couldn't save her." Randy Hokui leaned back in the armchair, weary. "I let her down," he said.

*Regret is such a thing,* I thought.

Randy Hokui said, "Now, I've told you my sad story, what's yours? How're you involved in all this?"

Big Brah cleared his throat. "We're investigating the murder on behalf of Mr. Duke Mahio," he said.

At the mention of Duke Mahio, Randy Hokui's demeanor transformed. His eyes widened.

He sat up. His shaking hand reached out and

gripped the walking stick. "Wait just a minute, I have told you the truth. But you never told me you're investigating on behalf of Duke Mahio. I don't even know if I should be talking to you. I don't know if you understand this or not, but his son, Kaipo Mahio, deliberately trapped my sister and killed her!"

Kali flinched and I gritted my teeth.

Big Brah remained his usual calm self. "That's a terrible accusation, do you have any evidence?" he said.

"Evidence? Of course I have evidence. First thing I told Loni was how violently Kaipo had attacked poor Helen at the Tavern, just the night before. How Kaipo, in front of everyone, everyone, threatened to kill her. And he did, the very next night."

Big Brah said, "Your sister must have told you what the fight was about."

Randy Hokui relaxed his grip on the walking stick and withdrew his hand. "Of course, she was my friend, my confidante. We hid nothing from each other. I told you, we were family, ohana. Helen told me what the fight was about."

Was the fight over love?

Randy Hokui said, "You know, Helen was working as Duke Mahio's property manager for the last year and a half. Now, Duke Mahio? He's a good man, but a little too simple, if you ask me. Or, maybe it's because he misses his late wife.

"Either way, Duke Mahio has a soft spot for

his son, Kaipo. He's fine in everything else, but when it comes to that brat of his, Duke Mahio is blind.

"Blind, I tell you. Kaipo Mahio has harassed my sister from the very beginning. She needed the job, we were poor. With my disability, I haven't been able to find a proper job, so she kept quiet. At first, it was just small requests. Like Kaipo made a large purchase, impulse buy. He'd ask Helen to hide the expense from his dad.

"Then, things got worse. Finally on Thursday night, at the Tavern, Kaipo asked my sister to rob the Mahio safe with him!"

Rob the Mahio safe? This was definitely not a love situation.

Randy Hokui said, "You see, my sister was quiet, a good worker. Duke Mahio trusted her.

"Duke Mahio had even given my sister the code to unlock the safe. My sister was a loyal worker, she never shared the code with me, her only family. The day Duke Mahio gave her the code, she told me it was a privilege she cherished.

"Problem was Duke Mahio had already given the code to his beloved son. Kaipo knew Helen also knew the code. So he hatched a plan. Steal all the family jewelry. His father had enough money, wouldn't miss it.

"Kaipo was prepared to share the profits from selling the jewelry in the black market with my sister. She was innocent, she didn't even know, if you could sell stolen jewelry in the black market.

"Kaipo assured her he knew how to get it done. Out of loyalty for Duke Mahio, as well her need for the job, my sister bravely reasoned with Kaipo, the monster, to stop him.

"But Kaipo was persistent. He kept asking her to steal. At last, my sister, poor thing, she was forced to say no. And, Kaipo? He flew into such a rage!

"That's when he attacked her. If it hadn't been for all the people around at the Tavern, he'd probably have killed her there and then. After all, if Kaipo was going to rob the safe, he wouldn't want her to live to tell.

"He threatened her, so she wouldn't say anything, and killed her the following night, as soon as he could. You know the rest." Weary again, Randy Hokui leaned back in the armchair, resting his cadaverous body.

His story sounded so plausible. His story really fitted all the facts we already knew. Things looked bad for Kaipo.

Big Brah said, "Even if this were to be true, Kaipo didn't really need your sister to rob the safe. He already had the code, so why would he ask her?"

Trust Big Brah to figure out the flaw in the story. Fast. Kali and I exchanged proud looks, as we did, when Big Brah shone. But Randy Hokui had all the answers.

For the first time that morning, he smirked. "Loni asked me the same question, and I'll tell you, what I told him. You know, sitting here, in this house, while Helen goes out to work, Kaipo Mahio's just a person in her workplace.

"But I got to know Kaipo. Through her. I can almost read his mind. Kaipo asked my sister to join him, you know why? So he could blame her for the theft later. Kaipo knew, his father would never believe he was a thief, it would be easy to frame my poor, innocent sister for the theft!"

Big Brah said, "That may be true, but if your sister knew Kaipo really wanted to kill her, she wouldn't get on the boat with him."

Randy Hokui heaved a sigh. "She called me, earlier in the night. Around nine. I hadn't drunk as much beer, at the time, I was up. She told me she was on a boat with Kaipo. I was concerned.

"She told me not to be concerned. If anything, Helen could be naïve sometimes. That's why she needed me, so I could tell her, if I saw dangers in her path. I never got to talk to her about it in any great detail, but she told me how Kaipo pressured her into going."

I remembered the surveillance video. Helen Hokui had indeed been talking to Kaipo, just as Randy Hokui was saying. Both Big Brah and Kali knew about the surveillance video, but neither Loni nor Randy Hokui did.

Randy Hokui continued. "Kaipo convinced her, she said, with you know, sorry, I lost it last night, won't happen again, I really didn't mean it...Helen was soft-hearted.

"She fell for Kaipo's words, followed him into the boat like an innocent child went after the piper, and me? It was a Friday evening, I was drunk, what can I say?

"Bad judgment. I let her talk me into thinking everything was all right between Kaipo and her. I even slept, wasn't there for her, when she needed me the most...."

I got chicken skin all over my arms, again. Darn, things looked bad for Kaipo.

By the time we got out of the depressing home, the sun had climbed higher. Big Brah started the big, black truck. He looked around at the two of us. It was always hard to see a grieving family member.

Both Kali and I had on our solemn faces. His face was solemn too but with Big Brah that didn't mean anything. Sometimes he joked solemn-faced. Kali had gotten us to Randy Hokui and it had been a total disaster for our side.

Big Brah rested his gaze on Kali. "What do we do next, Kali?" he said, sweetly.

"We do, what we must, as detectives on a quest to find the truth," she said.

Big Brah was impressed. "Wise, very wise," he said.

Wise and triumphant, Kali looked at me in the backseat. "In order to determine the truth, we need to examine the 'Honeymooner,'" she said.

I chimed in glad to be getting in on the action.

"That's right, Loni told us, forensics gonna be done. He'll be able to show us the boat today, let's take him up on his promise," I said.

Big Brah nodded, approvingly. "We're all becoming better detectives," he said, "now, let's go see Loni."

Loni's office at the PD was in the same two-story, gray county building as Kali's office. As we walked from the parking lot to the gray building, Kali looked longingly in the direction of her office located to our right. Big Brah glanced her way quizzically.

Kali took his arm and smiled up at him reassuringly. "No, Koa, I don't miss my office at all. I was only thinking about the autopsy. My substitute has forty years of experience, he's thorough, I have faith in his work," Kali said.

Big Brah and I had faith in Kali's judgment. We walked the rest of the distance to Loni's office in contemplative silence. The chief's office was in the center of the building and Loni's office was at the left end. Over the years, with Big Brah's help, the PD's homicide department had grown in reputation. Loni, the departmental head had a steady job.

Loni had a corner office. A big window brought in all the light anyone could need. The window had a view of a few quaint rooftops of the island's picturesque downtown and beyond the rooftops pure nature: rolling plains and mountains. Loni had an ample desk.

He had framed photographs of his pretty wife and two daughters of school-going age on the desk. Behind the desk, Loni lounged in his executive chair. As Big Brah, Kali and I entered the office, another man, huge, rose from one of the chairs in front of Loni's desk.

The man was built like a lineman. He had no hair on his head and face. Just eyebrows. We knew him well. He had played varsity football in our high school. I had watched him sweat it out with the other big players on the football field. He helped win Island College a championship. He loved the island. He didn't want to leave the island. He chose to fight vice. He was head of the PD's vice department.

He had on a friendly grin on his face. "Rice from vice," he said, introducing himself, as he always did, adding, "you homies know me!"

Big Brah and I shook hands with him. Kali gave him a hug. There had been times when we had worked together on a case.

Big Brah said, "It's good to see you again, Rice. Hope we're not interrupting."

Rice shook his head. "No, you're not interrupting. In fact, you've come at an opportune moment. Loni here, and I, we were discussing the 'Honeymooner' case. Loni told me you're investigating on behalf of Duke Mahio, is that still true?"

Big Brah nodded.

Loni gestured at the empty chairs across from

his desk. "Well, sit down then, all of you, so we can talk about it," he said, cordially.

We sat down, Rice included.

Loni addressed Big Brah. "Rice was just telling me about an interesting development in the case," he said.

"What is it?" Big Brah asked.

Rice was sitting next to Big Brah. He swiveled in his chair to look at Big Brah. "I'm working with the Bordetas in the search for their daughter Nohea. I understand you were present when the Bordetas discovered Nohea had left with Kaipo on Friday evening, is that true?"

Big Brah nodded. "Yes, it's true," he said.

Loni leaned forward, his eyes narrowed. His mustache bristled. "Then, Big Brah, why is it you didn't come forward with that information?" he said.

Big Brah was surprised. "Jim Bordeta mentioned you, Rice. You were investigating the disappearance of Nohea Bordeta. I naturally assumed you'd report it to Loni."

Rice looked relieved. "That I did," he said.

But Loni wasn't done yet. "Rice, you're being too simple, homicide requires smarts. I believe, you Big Brah didn't come forward with the information, because you're working on behalf of Duke Mahio." Loni looked at Big Brah accusingly. "Correct me if I'm wrong, but it's in your client's interests, the fact be hidden your client's son, Kaipo had left with Nohea," he said.

Big Brah said, "Why? I told Duke Mahio, if Kaipo had Nohea with him, it was good news. Nohea will provide an alibi for his son."

Loni was on fire. "She won't be an alibi, Big Brah, she'll be a witness to his crime, a witness!" he said.

Big Brah looked aghast. Somehow, Kali showed no feelings. I didn't know what to make of it, yet. Rice ran a finger under the collar of his shirt, uncomfortable with Loni's tone with Big Brah. He had more respect for Big Brah's skills.

Big Brah said, "What are you suggesting, then?"

Loni kept up the uncomfortable tone. "I'm not suggesting, Big Brah, I'm telling you. Kaipo murdered Helen Hokui, and Nohea Bordeta almost certainly witnessed the crime."

Big Brah frowned. He never frowned, unless he was beyond the pale exasperated. "So, what?" he said.

Loni leaned back in his chair and laughed an unamused laugh. "You'll just continue to act dumb. Okay, Big Brah, I'm getting no help from you. I'll tell you what this is all about.

"I was just trying to convince Rice here about it, when you walked in. Kaipo is a dangerous murderer. He has captured Nohea, the only witness to the murder. Naturally, that puts Nohea in great danger," he said.

Kaipo was a dangerous murderer and a witness kidnapper. Nohea was in great danger. I looked at Big Brah right before panicking.

Big Brah made a puzzled face. "Great danger, how?"

Loni took a deep breath and made a placid face. "You're making me spell out every little detail, Big Brah, but Patience is my middle name. So, I'll say it. Nohea is in great danger, because Kaipo is unlikely to let the only witness of his crime survive."

Big Brah cracked a smile. I had no idea what he found funny in what Loni was saying. Kali still looked relaxed. "Loni, brah, what are you insinuating?" Big Brah said.

"I'm not insinuating, I'm telling you, Big Brah. Kaipo has kidnapped Nohea for now. But in the near future, he may murder her," Loni said.

Another murder by Kaipo!

Big Brah laughed out loud. "That's ridiculous! Kaipo and Nohea are in love. Kaipo won't harm her!" he said.

Loni clutched his head, theatrically. "Love? Love, Big Brah. Now, we're going to bring love into a serious investigation?" he said.

Big Brah chuckled. "Why, not?" he said.

Loni spread his hands. "I don't know how you conduct your investigations, Big Brah. But the police, we work for the people. We can't be so frivolous," he said, firmly.

Big Brah looked at Rice. "Am I being frivolous, Rice?"

Rice looked at Big Brah and then at Kali and

me. He had an apology written all over his clean-shaven face. "I know you're not being frivolous, Big Brah, but Loni here has a point. If Nohea is a witness, it does put her in danger. Even if, as you say, they're in love, well, even lovers can hurt each other, can't they?"

Firmly, Kali shook her head.

Big Brah said, "Well, good lovers don't hurt each other. Bad lovers may, but then, theirs is fake love, and it doesn't count."

Eager to make peace Rice shot a glance Loni's way and then turned his gaze back on us. "There, you said it yourself, Big Brah. You didn't know Nohea and Kaipo before this, did you?"

"No," Big Brah said.

"There you go, I thought so, you didn't. So, there's no way for you to verify what Nohea and Kaipo have isn't fake love, right?" Rice said.

Kali spoke up for the first time. "Actually it's easy to verify Kaipo and Nohea's love isn't fake."

"How?" Rice said.

"From the testimony of others," she said.

Rice frowned. "Testimony of others? That's hearsay. Anything else?"

"There are signs," Kali said.

"Signs? Really now, Kali, this is a dangerous matter. Nohea Bordeta's life may be in danger, we can't be relying on signs," Rice said.

Both Big Brah and Kali sat silenced. Loni and Rice exchanged looks, as if to ask each other who would break the news to us.

As usual, Loni took it on himself. "The police must act! First, I'm advising Rice to inform the Bordeta family about the danger Nohea is in, because of Kaipo."

That was sure to aggravate the hatred Jim Bordeta had for Duke Mahio. After all, it was Duke Mahio's son we were talking about.

Loni tugged at the ends of his thick mustache, importantly. "As you know, the ocean search and rescue operation is continuing, we won't stop that."

I thanked the goddess. Another way to find Kaipo and Nohea was still on.

Loni said, "In addition, I'm going to the chief right this minute, to ask he approve the biggest island-wide hunt we've ever launched, for Kaipo Mahio.

"In order to protect Nohea Bordeta, we'll let it be known, we're looking for both of them, as persons of interest in the murder investigation. That way, Kaipo doesn't feel threatened, he spares Nohea Bordeta."

Big Brah had regained his calm self. He sighed. "I hope the police find them, fast. No one's better at it than you. As soon as they are found, we will all know the truth."

Loni said, "We can agree on that, Big Brah. By the way, I forgot to ask, what brought you here?"

Big Brah rose. Kali and I got up as well.

Big Brah said. "Oh, nothing. We just wanted to look inside the boat, talk about the evidence you no doubt have… and such."

Loni nodded. "Rice, I have to see the chief. Why don't you show Big Brah the boat?" he said, suddenly generous.

Rice looked relieved the meeting was over. He got up. "Be my pleasure," he said.

Rice looked glad to get out of Loni's office. The boat had been moved to the yard behind the gray county building by the rescue crew. Big Brah, Kali and I exited by the building's back entrance, Rice leading us.

The sun was above us, our shadows small. The PD's yard had a few towed vehicles and the "Honeymooner." The boat's name was painted with glitter on it to put you in the mood for love.

In the stark police yard, the shiny glitter did not fit. But it made me wonder. Love, sublime. What had happened in there? We were about to find out. The boat was a luxury cruiser.

The rescue crew had propped the boat up on a brick and concrete support. The sleek, sporty exterior was painted in red and white bands. The exquisite red was the color of love. Pure white was the color of peace. Rice heaved himself up the boarding ladder over the twin engines.

Big Brah, Kali and I followed. The rear platform was clear. We crossed over the platform to climb into the cockpit.

Transparent plastic sheets protected much of the cockpit. Teak floor. Stainless steel appliances. The grill. Built-in cooler for drinks. Luxury seats.

Pilot chair. Digital throttle. Joystick. Wheel. Plastic sheets draped them all.

Rice explained. "The plastic sheets, forensics been searching for fingerprints and DNA in all those places and more," he said.

Rice pointed at two large cup holders above the digital throttle. "Those cup holders didn't have any drinks, but Helen Hokui's phone was found in the holder on the left. The phone's one of the two ways we're placing her on the boat, for now.

"Her brother identified the phone, instantly. Forensics is also bound to get fingerprint and DNA matches, in a few days. Loni thinks the victim was piloting, certainly she had to have been inside this cockpit. Her phone was here, and doubtless, Kaipo and Nohea were here with her." Rice paused to study our faces. "So far so good, sleuths?" he said, jovially.

Big Brah nodded and Rice took us down to the deluxe suite. Daylight streamed in through the portholes, illuminating the confines.

We were in a living area with low, cozy seating. The walls were decorated with prints of romantic paintings by island artists. Beyond the living area, there was a fully functional galley with storage drawers and refrigerator.

Rice said, "The galley was squeaky clean. No, really, it didn't look like it had been used at all." He walked us into the bathroom.

The bathroom had his and her towels on a

rack. All unused. Next, a large bedroom. Big bed. Its silk sheets and luxury pillows looked fit for a fairy tale prince and princess. Untouched.

Rice halted by the big bed. "I understand your cousin, Keni owns the boat," he said.

"Yes," Big Brah said.

Rice broke into a smile, gesturing at the bed. "All this is customized. Keni must be a romantic," he said.

Rice had no idea how big a romantic Keni really was. Big Brah smiled, agreeing. Rice stopped outside a door with a knob.

His face turned solemn. "This is a walk-in closet, we found more evidence in here," he said.

Rice turned the knob and swung the door open. Big Brah, Kali and I crowded behind Rice to peer into the closet. The empty closet had a shelf on the left wall. Below the shelf, there was a wooden rod with clothes hangers.

The clothes hangers were wooden with metal hooks. A hanger had fallen on the teak floor. Otherwise, the floor was clear but for a couple of painted white circles.

Rice spoke in a hushed tone. "Those white circles. In those places, we found discarded wrappers. The green kind, of a popular cereal bar. We also found the victim's bag here. Loni had the wrappers and the bag moved to be presented as evidence. The bag had a few more of the same cereal bars. Her brother confirmed she loved those bars, she snacked on them all the time.

"Loni figures, this is where Kaipo kept the victim locked. The victim, scared, but hungry, passed the time by snacking on her favorite cereal bars. If you find this hard to believe, then look on the reverse side of the door, the side the victim was on."

One by one, Big Brah, Kali and I looked at the other side of the door. The evidence was near the bottom. A dent in the door. The damage didn't extend to our side of the door. But cracks extended from the dent, up, down, sides, all around.

Rice let the door go, and it swung slowly back into place with a click. "This was the perfect place for Kaipo to hold the victim prisoner, before he killed her. Can you sleuths tell what caused the damage to the door?" he said.

Without waiting for us to answer his question, Rice jovially volunteered the answer. "The victim didn't like being locked up. She was wearing shoes. She kicked at the door, damaged it," he said.

Big Brah agreed. "The damage does look like it could have been caused by a kick or kicks," he said.

"Yes, and forensics found shoe fabric trapped at the edges of that dent. They think the fabric came out of the victim's shoes. It's really very clear what must have gone on here," Rice said.

Was it really very clear? We got back to the cockpit, blinking in the bright light of the afternoon.

"That's all I had, folks," Rice said, with finality.

Rice left to follow up with Loni and the Chief on the status of the big search for Kaipo and Nohea. The show over, Big Brah, Kali and I trudged back to the big, black truck, wordlessly. The facts were against Kaipo.

All we had was the knowledge that Kaipo and Nohea were in love and together by the testimony of a sixteen-year-old, Iekika, and that of a completely unreliable witness, Makoa Alika. Meanwhile, with help from Rice, Loni had branded Kaipo a murderer, a kidnapper and a possible double murderer.

I was perplexed. If there was a flaw in the way the police viewed the situation, I couldn't see one. So what was Big Brah going to do about it? All three of us stayed silent all the way home.

# Chapter 8 Love made you know things

First thing Big Brah did when we got home was head to the kitchen. Kali joined him. They cooked. I cleaned up the kitchen table. I fed the cats salmon. Then, Big Brah, Kali and I sat down to eat at the table.

The cats climbed onto their chairs, licking their whiskers. They were done eating, for now. Salmon was always a favorite. Big Brah and Kali had cooked up a quick lunch.

A delectable milkfish curry. The fish stir-fried just right was then soaked in a simmering concoction of ginger, basil and coconut milk. A yummy fried rice with cabbage in it. For dessert, sweet banana bread.

Once we had polished off dessert, Big Brah spoke. "Well, Loni and Rice are doing their jobs, so should we," he said.

Kali and I looked at each other. Sure, we should do our job, but how?

Big Brah said, "Two questions bother me. One, why didn't anyone but Iekika mention

Nohea?"

I shrugged. "Maybe because Kaipo and Nohea guarded the secrecy of their love really well. No one else knew about it," I said.

Big Brah said, "We'll see if that's the case. The second question is even more pressing and requires an immediate answer: how did Helen Hokui get on the 'Honeymooner?'"

When a question was pressing and required an immediate answer, Big Brah did what he was best at.

Big Brah meditated.

That afternoon, Kali and I played the snakes and ladders board game on the living room rug. The cats were stretched out next to us. Behind Kali, Big Brah lay on his back and stared up at the high, open-beamed ceiling.

After a while he closed his eyes. To the uninitiated he was sleeping. Kali and I knew better. To get the answer Big Brah had gone deep. For sure he would have the answer. Kali and I had to wait patiently. Our anticipation ran as deep as his meditation. We focused on getting our pieces past the snakes to the end. At last, Big Brah opened his eyes.

He was on his feet, suddenly alert. "The only way Helen Hokui could have got on the 'Honeymooner' is if she was at the dock with Nohea and Kaipo. In that case, there's one person who must have witnessed them boarding the boat. Music Man!" he said.

Kali and I gaped at each other. Big Brah was right. Playing music all day long, Music Man sat on his backpack chair under a coconut tree right close to the dock. He saw everything.

Music Man would know who had boarded the "Honeymooner" with Kaipo. Why hadn't we thought of that? Because we had Big Brah, of course! I folded the board up.

The game had many more hours of pleasure left in it. Kali put the pieces and the board away in the bin for board games. Soon we started for the eastside harbor in the big, black truck.

The late afternoon sun was fast losing its warmth, by the time the truck slowed to a crawl outside the office of "Fly like a Bird." From the truck's window, I could see the seaplane was still there.

The tourist business was slow on Mondays. Next, rent-a-boat. The "Honeymooner" had lived inside rent-a-boat's sky-blue boathouse.

The truck moved forward slowly, getting closer to the dock. My eyes stayed on the strip of water the "Honeymooner" would have had to take in order to get to the boarding dock.

The strip of water from the boathouse joined the wider harbor. Kaipo was alone inside the boat. To get Nohea, Kaipo would have had to turn the boat left. That would bring the boat alongside the harbor. In all this, where was Helen Hokui?

Big Brah parked the truck at the end of the

harbor road. The coconut trees were nearby. Like last time, a few other vehicles were parked. I got out of the truck. The strip of water joining the dock was still visible. Now, to find Music Man.

As we walked briskly to the coconut tree under which we had found Music Man the previous time, no music greeted us. The coconut tree stood alone. No Music Man. Darn. But Big Brah was not the one to give up fast.

He took out the agency phone he carried from the pocket of his cargo shorts. "Let's call Keni. He'll know where Music Man lives," he said.

Following Keni's directions, Big Brah, Kali and I trekked into the wilderness. Music Man's shack was not too far from the harbor. The shack was painted the same green as the tall grass, the bamboo and the foliage of trees around the home. Music Man sat outside his shack.

Music Man's dreads looked freshly done. His skin was darker than I remembered. The strum of his ukulele greeted us. He saw us. He decided something was up. The music stopped.

Music Man set the ukulele down on the grass by the folding chair he sat on. Big Brah and Kali approached him, me behind them. Music Man rose slowly from his chair, a frown on his face.

Big Brah said, "Sorry to bother you, brah, but I need your help."

The frown on Music Man's face melted away, replaced by a smile. "How can I help?" he said, with aloha.

"Mind if we sit down and talk story?" Big Brah said.

On the island, no one was more welcome than someone who wanted to hang out with you and talk story. Music Man grinned. "You wait," he said.

Music Man disappeared into his shack. Hospitably, he returned with folding chairs for Big Brah, Kali and me. We took the chairs from him and unfolded them. He gestured for us to sit and disappeared into his shack again.

This time, Music Man returned with a carafe, mugs and a canister full of rice crackers. He unscrewed the lid and passed the canister around. We all took the rice crackers.

Music Man poured the steaming drink from the carafe into the mugs. "It's only ginger water and honey, warmed. But if you sing a lot, your throat, it hurts. This drink, it soothes the throat. I make it for the long night. But you're here, we share!" he said, grinning.

Big Brah, Kali and I raised our mugs in appreciation of his incredible sharing. Pure aloha.

Music Man also raised his mug. "You look for me at the harbor?" he said.

Big Brah said, "Yes."

"I try be there, but I have to come back here, for a break, sometimes. Today was one such time, sorry," Music Man said.

It was early evening. The sun was close to

setting. The birds chirped and a cool breeze stirred.

Big Brah leaned back in his chair, at ease. "We're big fans of your music. Nothing more we'd love but to sit here and listen to you play and sing," he said.

Music Man picked up the ukulele he had set down on the grass. Searching for the right song to sing, he strummed the ukulele reflectively. He found the song.

The strum of the ukulele strengthened. He sang a familiar romantic mele about a prince and a princess, in Hawaiian. Big Brah and Kali held hands and listened, swaying together with the beat. I sipped the warm, soothing drink. Tapping on the grass, my feet danced on their own. Finally Music Man stopped. We clapped.

Music Man bowed his head modestly. He set the ukulele down on the grass again. "Okay, we can have more music later, but first tell me, how can I help you?" he said.

"You sit at the harbor, you must see all the boats come and go," Big Brah said.

"Yes, yes, I do, I do, but it's not how it used to be. Years ago, the eastside harbor used to have boats, big boats, small boats, all sizes, docked, but now, no more.

"All the boats, they're docked in the new harbor. This harbor now used only by the seaplane rental, the boat rental and the ramp is used by a few private boat owners. Who do you want to know about?" Music Man said.

Big Brah spoke even-voiced. "Kaipo Mahio."

Music Man threw his head back and laughed. "I no watch TV, but even I know that boy is in trouble. I hear things from people, you know?" he said.

Big Brah nodded. "Did you see him on Friday night?" he said.

"Of course I see him on Friday night, and many more times before."

"Did he interact with you in any way?" Big Brah asked.

"Every time. He comes to me, wants me to play the same reggae tune, says he and his girl like the song. I tell him, I'll sing for him and his girl. Maybe he'll have the luck with his girl. The luck I didn't have with my girl." Music Man shook his head, sadly.

Big Brah was silent for a moment in memory of Music Man's long-lost love. Then, softly he said, "Did you ever see Kaipo's girl?"

"Every time! She sits in the truck, watches for him to dock the boat. Then she boards the boat. I play their song, and they leave. That's the routine."

"Was there any break from routine on Friday night?" Big Brah asked.

"If you mean, did I see the murdered woman get on the boat with Kaipo and Nohea? Yes, I did!"

Big Brah, Kali and I gaped at Music Man.

Big Brah said, "Are you sure it was Helen

Hokui?"

"Sure, yes. I hear the dead woman was tall and thin. She had dark hair. I see such a woman. She got there, after the couple. She had her own vehicle. You'll find it parked where she left it, near the end of the harbor road. A red sedan," Music Man said.

"A red sedan. Then what happened?" Big Brah asked.

"Then Kaipo, he walk away to rent boat, his routine. He return on boat, tether the boat to the dock, come see me, the same. I notice, this boat, it was bigger, better. While he talk to me, his usual girl, from their truck, Nohea runs into the boat. Again, same, usual.

"I realize now, maybe Kaipo asks me to sing, so his girl can run inside. They good at hiding. I play the song. The boat is ready to leave. But, something happen, never happen before.

"Both of them run out of boat and go to their truck. In the meantime, the red sedan woman come out of her car, she runs into the boat. I say to myself, this must be plan.

"I am still singing, maybe they think I not look. Sometimes I don't. But this time, I look. I see the red sedan woman dash into the boat. Clear, no mistake.

"Then, I see Kaipo and his first girl come back from their truck. They carry bottles, drinks. I think they forget drinks, but I say no. Kaipo has been deceiving, many months, with one girl.

This weekend, he's taking two girls with him.

"Maybe why he got the bigger boat. I shake my head. I thought his love was real, but two girls? No, his love was fake. And all this to hide from being seen. I no like. But what can I do?

"I only play music, while the boat leaves. Now, brah, you want to know all this, what you in for?"

Big Brah sighed. Kaipo, Nohea and the victim had all left together. It wasn't what he had wanted to hear. "I'm investigating the murder on behalf of the boy's father," he said.

Music Man's eyes widened. "I hear of you too! You the famous detective. Waialeale, right?"

"Right," Big Brah said.

"Then, you'll want to know one more thing," Music Man said.

"What is it, brah?" Big Brah said.

Music Man took a deep breath. "The three of them, man and two woman, they left together in this big boat, then things happen. Another man, he also follow them. He watch them, he sit in his truck, boat in tow.

"Kaipo leaves. This man use ramp to get his boat onto water, he follow Kaipo and his girls. I'm sure of it. Then.

"The seaplane brah. He races the seaplane, flies low, then high. I'm sure of it, he also follow Kaipo," he said.

Big Brah was intrigued. "Two men. In a boat and a seaplane. They followed the 'Honeymooner.' You're sure of it?"

"Yes."

"Do you know when they got back?" Big Brah asked.

"Well, I no stay the night, I be home. When I get to harbor, Saturday morning, the man with boat, his truck was gone. I think he get back from ocean, drive away in the night. And the seaplane brah, I hear him, when he come back. He the one who find the boat on the rocks, so he up early."

"Interesting. Can you tell us more about the man with the boat, who was he?" Big Brah asked.

"His boat, not very big, but fancy. He alone, young. It could be...."

Big Brah leaned forward, interested. "It could be what?" he said.

"It could be, boat name have his name."

"Do you remember the name?" Big Brah asked.

"Noah's Ark."

Big Brah sank back in his chair. Kali and I exchanged glances. Noah. Lily's boyfriend.

Could this be the same Noah?

Music Man had made the mystery even more mysterious. We stayed a while longer. We sipped the ginger-honey drink, ate the rice crackers and talked about love, romance and everything else under the sun.

At last, Big Brah rose, regret written all over him. "Brah, we've got to get back home, work on this case. Otherwise nothing I'd love more than to continue talk story with you all night," he said.

"Come back anytime. Look for the red sedan at the end of the harbor road," Music Man said, helpfully.

The red sedan was parked exactly where Music Man had told us it would be. Big Brah had a decision to make. If he called Loni and reported the red sedan, and the red sedan turned out to be Helen Hokui's, the evidence against Kaipo would pile higher.

On the other hand, Big Brah couldn't not report the vehicle, knowing it was evidence. In the end, Big Brah did, as he always did. The right thing.

Big Brah called Loni, reported the red sedan and read out the license plate. Within minutes, Loni confirmed the red sedan belonged to Helen Hokui. He would have the vehicle towed to the PD's yard. We were helping the police in their case against our client's son. It had grown dark.

The harbor lights had turned on. Looking out at the dark ocean, Big Brah, Kali and I stood near the coconut trees by the big, black truck. When Kali had proposed we meet the victim's brother, we had met with disaster. This time, Big Brah had even meditated and then proposed we see Music Man. Bigger disaster. Irony.

I smiled to myself. A cool breeze blew in from the ocean, rustling the fronds of the coconut trees. Kali had a spare jacket in the truck. Big Brah brought Kali the jacket. She donned the jacket.

She slipped her hands into the pockets of the

jacket for more warmth. "I was cold," she said, smiling up at him sweetly.

Big Brah lived for Kali's sweet smiles. Is why he had gotten Kali her jacket. He just gazed fondly at her.

"How did you know, Koa?" Kali asked.

Big Brah said, "I know these things."

Love made you know things. I was warmed by their aloha.

Kali said, "I know you know what we do next, Koa."

Big Brah rocked on his heels, smiling. "Well, Music Man did confirm Helen Hokui was on the 'Honeymooner' with Kaipo and Nohea. Loni got it right, I agree.

"But, at the same time, Music Man told us two other people chased after Kaipo and his two girls. A man with a boat named Noah's Ark. And Fly like a bird's Ross T. Alba."

I said, "It's funny, but it's the second time the name Ross T. Alba has popped up. I remember cousin Keni saying, Alba wanted to kill Kaipo. I remember thinking, how had Alba known to find the 'Honeymooner' in the morning?"

Kali wrapped her arms around Big Brah and snuggled close to him. She had found a better way to stay warm. "Yes, I remember thinking that too, and now in the light of what we just learned from Music Man, Alba followed the 'Honeymooner' out into the ocean. Definitely suspicious," she said.

Big Brah hugged Kali affectionately, glad to be keeping her warm. Pure warm love.

I said, "Then, can we all agree, the thing to do next is to march down the road, go see Alba?"

Arms linked, Big Brah, Kali and I marched down the deserted harbor road. The first thing I noted, the lights were on inside the "Fly like a Bird" office. Good. Alba was in. Rent-a-boat's office came up first. A big new rental car was parked in the lot outside. Tourists. The open window revealed cousin Keni with a brightly attired tourist family.

Keni helped the customer by explaining the virtues of each of his boats. With a smile. But this evening, Keni had an apologetic air about him. After all the "Honeymooner" accident had caused his innocent business bad publicity. But that didn't stop him from speaking animatedly making small hand gestures. Cousin Keni was not a quitter. Next, Alba's office.

There was a "Welcome" sign on the door of Alba's office. Still, Big Brah used his knuckles to gently knock on the door, all polite.

A man's nasally voice replied. "Oh, please come in!" The man sounded eager for business.

We entered a room with a low ceiling. The low ceiling had light fixtures, illuminating the room. On the wall behind the desk there was a copy of a pilot's license enlarged and framed for prominent display.

A large window overlooked the water. In the

wash of the exterior light, the moored seaplane bobbed on the water. Behind a clean, organized desk, a man rose from an armless, swivel chair.

The man was of regular build. He had an athletic air about him. Regular jeans, t-shirt. A green "Fly like a Bird" baseball cap covered his hair. His ears fanned out, his small eyes were too close together and he had a big nose. Made him look like an island bat.

His face fell, when he saw us, and he sank back into his chair. "Aw, shucks, you must be the detectives. Keni told me about you, I knew you'd come," he said, his voice turning even more nasally.

Big Brah said, pleasantly, "Alba, brah, this won't take too long, and I'll appreciate your help."

Alba looked up at Big Brah. "I know who you are, your reputation, Big Brah, and I have respect. But I'm just so done with Kaipo Mahio," he said.

Big Brah drew himself up to his full height. "What do you mean, you're done with Kaipo?" he said.

Alba threw up his hands. "I just can't get rid of him from my life," he said.

"Can't get rid of him, what is that?" Big Brah asked.

Alba sighed. "Sorry, I'm talking in riddles, aren't I? Please, please sit down, all of you. I apologize for my bad mood. Allow me to explain."

Alba had a couple of chairs in front of the desk and a few folding chairs stacked up against the wall. Big Brah gestured for Kali and me to sit down. He unfolded a chair, turned it around and then sat on it hugging its back.

Big Brah fixed his gaze on Alba. "All right, I'm listening. Explain," he said.

Unsure of the impression he was making on Kali and me, Alba shot us an uncomfortable glance. Neither of us let on anything.

Alba returned to Big Brah. "Look, I started college with Kaipo Mahio, we did the core science classes, together. For the laboratory work, we were even in the same group. He made a terrible lab partner.

"Kaipo had no time or inclination for the work, I had to work twice as hard for the both of us. But, he managed to snag good grades, I don't know how. I hate Kaipo," he said.

Wow. Alba hated Kaipo. He wanted to get rid of Kaipo. A few more minutes and Big Brah would have Alba confessing all. I listened expectantly.

Big Brah said, gently, "If Kaipo didn't do the work, what did he do?"

"Oh, Kaipo was busy with extra-curricular activities, he was always busy organizing events around the campus. Debate club. Drama club. Trivia club.

"Kaipo was involved with everything, everything other than his real college work. I just don't know how he got his grades, it made me hate college," Alba said.

"You dropped out of college, was it because of Kaipo?" Big Brah said.

For the first time, Alba relented. "No, I don't blame him for the choice I made. Kaipo was going to study marine biology. I wasn't interested. We'd have parted ways in any case," he said.

"Then, what made you say you couldn't get rid of him?" Big Brah said.

Alba threw up his hands. "When I quit college to start this business, I thought I'd got rid of him. Imagine my chagrin, last several months he's made it a habit to come to the business next door, to rent a boat."

Big Brah chuckled. "Renting a boat next door can be aggravating, but brah, aren't you forgetting to tell us something important," he said.

Alba was up on his feet, agitated. The swivel chair he had been sitting on rolled backward, hit the wall and stopped suddenly. "Who told you that? Keni? I knew it, he wouldn't be able to resist telling his relatives, you!" he said.

Big Brah was completely calm. "Keni didn't tell me anything. I'm a detective, you called me a detective, give me props. Your story of hating Kaipo isn't adding up. No one can truly hate someone for being a bad lab partner or renting a boat next door. I figure there's something important you are hiding from us," he said.

Alba fumbled for the chair behind him. His eyes never left Big Brah. "Okay, it's useless. I won't hide it. Even if I do, with all this murder mess, it's bound to come out."

Alba found the chair and sat down. "I'll tell you myself. It's true, in college, I had the biggest, hugest crush on Nohea Bordeta."

# Chapter 9 Love is blind

Kali and I exchanged knowing looks. Of course we were proud of Big Brah for figuring out Alba's crush.

Big Brah closed his eyes. Sometimes he liked to just listen. "A crush, yes, a crush can cause a lot more trouble," he murmured.

Alba blew out a breath. He spoke in a bitter tone. "There, I have said it, and I'll say it again. I had a huge crush on Nohea Bordeta in college," he said.

Big Brah still had his eyes closed. "Then what happened?" he asked.

Alba gulped. His tone lost its bitterness. "But she, she loved him," he said.

Silence. Big Brah still had his eyes closed. Alba had a faraway look in his eyes. Kali and I exchanged glances.

Big Brah blinked his eyes open. "And he loved her," he said.

"No!"

"No?"

"Never. Kaipo's incapable of loving anyone, but himself. Just think. Even by loving her, he was putting her in danger. They could never be together, together. The whole island knows the story of the enmity between their fathers. From their college days too. Kaipo didn't care, he cared only for himself. But, but, she-she's a sweet girl, she loved him.

"I couldn't bear to see the disaster, as a couple, they were heading for. I didn't like college anyway, I quit. Not being around for the disaster, a bonus. Then, he started coming here, renting boats, taking her out on the ocean. Dammit. Did he have to do that? I have a conscience. I couldn't let him play with her. I kept watch over them. It was easy."

Alba looked out of the sole window at the white seaplane with its wings spread out on the water. He smiled, proudly. "I call her my albatross, you know, like the bird. Wherever Kaipo took Nohea in a boat, I flew over them."

"Did they know you were doing this?" Big Brah said.

Alba shrugged. "What does it matter? Even if they knew, what could they do about it? They couldn't stop me. To be honest, in college, Nohea barely knew I existed, and Kaipo, but for the lab work, we were strangers. So I don't think they cared, plus, I fly trips all the time. They wouldn't suspect me," he said.

A silence, again. This time, Big Brah had his eyes open. "Friday night, what happened?" he said.

Alba said, "Usually, they go to Forbidden Beach. Again see, Kaipo is close to legend in surfing. Go to any event. It's either him or one of the Alika kids who wins."

Local boy knew the surfing scene.

Alba said, "Nohea's his opposite. Conservative parents, overprotective, don't even allow their daughters to go surfing. Shame, since surfing's island heritage. But what does that mean? In surfing, Kaipo has a huge, unfair advantage over Nohea. It's the kind of advantage, he prefers. So, he takes her surfing. He's a show off."

Alba let out a nervous laugh. "Friday night was no different. Sure, when I saw the boat he rented, I got troubled. It was better than any boat he had ever rented, cost more.

"I immediately thought Kaipo had something special planned. But I swear, all he did was head over to Forbidden Beach, same as usual. It was a full moon night, the waves big, perfect night to surf.

"How long could I wait to see them start surfing, especially from the air? Nohea was safe with him, at least Kaipo was the best in the water. I turned back.

"Here, I waited for them to come back. Keni has a secure arrangement, renters return the boat anytime. I waited late, but the Honeymooner didn't return. Don't know when, I fell asleep.

"When I woke up, it was morning. I ran

to the bird. I set course for Forbidden Beach. I didn't even need to get there. I found the 'Honeymooner' much before. On the rocks. I called 9-1-1. I told you, Kaipo Mahio is trouble."

"You're sure, they went to Forbidden Beach?" Big Brah said.

"I'm sure," Alba said.

Big Brah, Kali and I gazed at Alba speculatively. Was his testimony biased?

"See, Kaipo can't stay out of trouble," Alba said.

Kaipo sure loved trouble like fish loved water. Outside, the evening had cooled down a lot. Kaipo and Nohea had gone to Forbidden Beach. Of course, Makoa Alika had already denied seeing them that night.

Makoa Alika would be no help. But at least we had a witness who was sure of it. Progress, in ounces, not pounds, but progress, nevertheless. Back home, Big Brah and Kali got busy making dinner.

I sat at my place at the round table in the kitchen, doing homework for an online class. Poli`ahu and Wiliwili snoozed on either side of me. The agency phone was on the table, in my care.

The phone's jingle now got me out of the homework. Poli`ahu sat up. Wiliwili cracked open an eye. Big Brah and Kali turned away from the range to look my way. I raised my hand to reassure them all. I was on it. I never forgot a face. Or a voice.

I recognized Jim Bordeta's voice. "Is this Big Brah?" he said.

"I'm Umi, his assistant."

"I'd like to see Big Brah, it's urgent," he said.

I mimed Jim Bordeta's request to Big Brah. Big Brah mimed me back an answer: tell him to come here and I'll meet him in the office. I told Jim Bordeta and he agreed.

While Big Brah and Kali wrapped up a few things in the kitchen, I went to get the office ready. The lights turned on, as I entered the office. I pulled the blackout curtains aside, opened the windows and let in the fresh air. When we had a visitor in the office, and Kali was present, Big Brah shared his desk with her.

For Kali, I rolled a chair from the conference table to his tidy desk with its swing-arm lamp. In no time at all, a vehicle approached the house then stopped outside. I ran to open the door.

I ushered Jim Bordeta into the office. I seated him in the visitor's chair across from Big Brah's desk. I sat down behind my cluttered desk. I glanced at him curiously.

Jim Bordeta wasn't letting his daughter's disappearance get in the way of his grooming. His hair was gelled carefully in place, as before. He had shaved recently. He had on a smooth silk shirt and trousers creased in the right places. His leather sandals were practically new. His mismatched eyes scanned the walls in a cold, hard stare.

The office walls were decorated with keepsakes of our many pursuits: cooking, art, fire dance, surfing, boating, aviation, martial arts and entomology. My award-winning poem: "Pure aloha." Numerous awards: best security professional, top private investigator, meritorious service and lifetime achievement. Framed photocopies of our private investigator certificates.

A corner of Jim Bordeta's straight-line mouth turned upward. Finally, his gaze rested on my sketches of the family: Big Brah, Kali, Poli`ahu, Wiliwili and me. The sketches must have reminded him of his own family. Jim Bordeta's clean-shaven face filled up with anguish.

The expression of anguish was gone as fast as it had appeared. Jim Bordeta was putting on a tough face. He was suffering, inside. Big Brah and Kali must have heard the sounds of his arrival. Still clad in their home wear, tank-tops, shorts and rubber slippers, they entered the office through the inside door. Jim Bordeta fixed his cold, hard stare on them.

Big Brah spoke politely, as he made his way to his desk. "I'm sorry to keep you waiting, Mr. Bordeta. Kali and I had to wrap up a few things, we were cooking dinner." He slipped into his chair behind the desk smoothly.

Kali sat down next to Big Brah. From behind my desk, I had a good view of the three of them.

Big Brah planted his elbows on the top of the desk, interlaced his fingers and studied Jim Bordeta. "So. What did you want to see me for?" he said, pleasantly.

Jim Bordeta continued to stare hard at Big Brah. He still didn't say anything.

Big Brah smiled, benignly. "Are you going to say something, brah?" he murmured.

Voice choking with feeling, Jim Bordeta finally spoke. "Have you found that boy?" he said.

"Kaipo? No, I'm still looking for him," Big Brah said.

"Sergeant Rice informed me Kaipo Mahio has kidnapped my daughter," he said.

"I don't know why Sergeant Rice would do so. I mean, I know why he told you. I was in the meeting when the decision to inform you was taken. But I assure you, he was just taking a precaution," Big Brah said.

"A precaution. In case something happens?" Jim Bordeta said.

"Yes," Big Brah said.

"Something like, he kills her!" Jim Bordeta shouted.

Big Brah soothed. "No, no, why would he kill your daughter?"

Jim Bordeta spoke in his normal voice. "Rice explained that to me. She witnessed the murder."

Big Brah leaned back in his chair, his interlaced fingers now over his chest. "Yes, but I have reason to believe Kaipo still wouldn't hurt your daughter."

"What reason?"

"Love," Big Brah murmured.

"Love? My daughter, she couldn't possibly love Kaipo, she knows how much I hate Duke Mahio! Nohea, if anything, she's sensible, why would she do something so stupid?" he said.

Big Brah heaved a sigh. "The answer to that question, brah, you'll have to figure it out yourself."

I could have told Jim Bordeta the answer: love is blind. Big Brah, Kali and I knew it. But Jim Bordeta had a different answer. We were about to find out.

Jim Bordeta leaned forward. Animated, he tapped the top of Big Brah's desk. "I know the answer. This is all a trick."

"A trick?"

"Yes, a trick, but before I get into my suspicions, I want to tell you why I came to you, Big Brah," he said.

Big Brah nodded, encouraging. "Yes, please, tell me."

"I know your reputation for honesty, but you're also Duke Mahio's man," he said.

Big Brah demurred. "I wouldn't characterize it quite like that--"

Jim Bordeta raised a hand to stop Big Brah. "I don't trust Duke Mahio. We have fought for years, and I have grown to respect his cunning, but I don't trust him at all! But I know about your honesty, your commitment to justice, you go for the truth!

"I appeal to the side of you that is fair. I love my daughter. I don't want her harmed in any way. If Kaipo has her, I'll do anything, anything to free her. You must help me, even if you work for my enemy!"

An intense expression on his face, Big Brah sat up. He planted his elbows on the desk, interlaced his fingers and rested his chin on them. "What is it you suspect?" he said.

Jim Bordeta said, "Something's not adding up in all of this. Duke Mahio isn't going to the police to find his son, why? I'll tell you why. Because he's the perp!

"I believe Duke used his son to trap my daughter Nohea. She isn't in love, or anything. It's all a charade played by father and son! My daughter, sweet child, she's just a victim. That's what I believe not just suspect."

Big Brah, Kali and I listened intently.

Jim Bordeta's voice took on a pleading tone. "Please, Big Brah, find Kaipo, free my daughter. In this investigation, remember, Duke Mahio should be your chief suspect. He has the motive to harm my daughter, our enmity. That's all I had to say."

I shivered. He had told us a lot. After he left, Big Brah, Kali and I gathered back in the kitchen. Bad enough Kaipo was accused of kidnapping and murder.

Now, Duke Mahio was to be the chief suspect. In silence, Big Brah and Kali returned to the mutton stew they were preparing. The aroma of food comforted. I got back to the homework. Poli`ahu raised her head and then sank back to sleep. Wiliwili pricked his ears and then relaxed realizing everything was normal.

But it didn't stay normal for long. Once again in my custody, the agency phone on the table jingled. The entire family, Big Brah, Kali, Poli`ahu and Wiliwili looked my way.

I recognized the voice immediately. "Hello, this is Duke Mahio." The client himself.

"This is Umi, Big Brah is busy, can I take a message?" I said.

"Umi! I haven't heard from Big Brah all day, I'm beginning to get worried. What's going on?"

I said, "A lot's been going on. It'll be hard to explain over the phone."

"I can come over," he said.

I mimed his intention to Big Brah. It wouldn't hurt to talk with the client.

"Okay," Big Brah mouthed.

Soon, Big Brah, Kali and I were back in our places in the office. The blackout curtains had been pulled aside. The windows were open. Fresh spring air poured in. Sensitive to movement, the office lights illuminated the room. Dressed in a crumpled black shirt, khakis and sandals, Duke Mahio sat in the visitor's chair.

Duke Mahio had allowed the white beard to

grow. His thinning hair was all messed up. He still had the stoop he had developed recently. He sat bent in the chair.

He adjusted the business-like glasses on his nose and gazed at Big Brah. "Any news of Kaipo?" he asked.

"I'm afraid, no," Big Brah said.

"The police are searching for them as persons of interest. It was in the evening news," Duke Mahio said.

"It's in everyone's interest Kaipo be found," Big Brah said.

"Yes, my boy is innocent, I know it. I just don't know why he isn't returning home, unless...."

"Unless?"

"He could be hurt, unable to return," Duke Mahio said.

"Well, the search and rescue operation is still on. If he's out there, they'll find him," Big Brah said.

"The other option is...." Duke Mahio hesitated.

"The other option is?" Big Brah prompted.

"I don't want to say this, but I have to, it's for my boy. He doesn't have any wiles or guiles. Any father would be proud of him. But it puts him at a disadvantage in this situation.

"We're talking Jim Bordeta's daughter here. I've known the father for a very long time, since college. He's a cold fish, full of wiles and guiles. The mountain apple doesn't fall too far from its tree.

"The daughter's got to be like the father. I fear for Kaipo. What if Jim Bordeta is using his daughter to ensnare Kaipo, make him look like a killer and a kidnapper, just to get back at me?"

Big Brah took a deep breath. "Enmity," he murmured.

"Yes, deep enmity." Duke Mahio agreed.

"But, why?" Big Brah asked.

Duke Mahio said, "We were a love triangle in college. Jim and I, we both fell in love with the same girl, Luana. But Luana loved me, chose me and we married. We had Kaipo, we were a happy family. But Jim never recovered from it.

"Sure, Jim married, his parents arranged it. His wife, Jean is his distant cousin. They did have two daughters. But an arrangement can't be as satisfying to a couple as love. Still, I'd hoped he'd move on.

"A few years ago, my wife Luana, she was everything to me, she loved the ocean, and she died in a boat accident. I was fool enough to invite Jim to her funeral. Let bygones be bygones, I thought.

"Didn't happen. Jim attended the funeral. You know what he told me afterward? That I didn't deserve Luana, since I couldn't even keep her safe, alive!

"That's the kind of man Jim is, unforgiving, cold. He insulted me, even during a tragedy. He knows I love Kaipo, he's all I got left of Luana. I believe, Jim's behind all this, otherwise it doesn't make any sense."

"Is there a specific reason you suspect Jim Bordeta?" Big Brah asked.

"Yes. I can give you not one, but two reasons. One, I already told you. The jewelry theft. Makes no sense for Kaipo to steal what's already his.

"I love Kaipo. I want him to have everything I do. He knows that, so why should he steal? Two, look at the woman Kaipo's supposed to have murdered. Helen Hokui.

"Helen's someone close to me, my property manager, an employee. Makes the whole situation stink. Makes it look really bad for me. I don't know how long I can take it anymore. Again, Kaipo has no real reason to kill Helen. It's got to be all part of Jim's mischief!" Duke Mahio said.

Big Brah reassured our client. "I understand what you're saying. Mahalo for bringing this matter to my attention. It's my job to find the real killer. I'll find out what really happened. I'm on it. As soon as I have something substantial, I'll report back to you," he said.

Duke Mahio made as if to get up and then decided against it. Still in the visitor's chair, he leaned forward. He adjusted the business-like glasses on his nose.

He adopted a confidential air. "Don't take this otherwise, Big Brah, but I hear, you know, the island gossip, you and Jim Bordeta have gotten in touch with each other…."

Big Brah smiled at the implication. He explained. "Inevitable, brah, no investigation in this matter can be complete without finding out Nohea Bordeta's role in it. I'll have to involve the Bordeta family."

"But I don't trust Jim!" Duke Mahio said.

Big Brah soothed Duke Mahio. "You have my word. My investigation will focus on finding out the truth, who the killer really is. You mustn't think Jim Bordeta can influence me to do otherwise. I know you don't trust Jim, but please, you must trust me," he said.

Duke Mahio took a deep breath and then let it out slowly. He looked at Kali and then me. He returned his gaze to Big Brah. "I trust you. Just keep in mind I don't trust Jim, okay?"

"Okay," Big Brah said.

Duke Mahio left, his mistrust for Jim Bordeta confirmed. Big Brah, Kali and I returned to the kitchen and the aroma of the mutton stew slow cooking in the crock pot. During an investigation, we ate, when we could.

I enjoyed the irregular hours. For dinner that evening, we started with a salad. Cucumber, avocado, radish, seaweed, basil, cilantro, red onion, sweet green chilies tossed in sesame oil with a twist of lemon.

Yum. Big Brah loved salads and vegetable dishes. He ate the salad with an appetite. The mutton stew, yummy, easily my favorite. The side, an appetizing blend of white and brown rice.

For dessert, cubes of ripe mangoes dipped in chocolate, Kali's current favorite. Kali was a big fan of wholesome desserts. The sweet richness of the ripe mango and the chocolate together melting in my mouth, beyond yummy. Not having slept much the night before, that night, I slept harder than an island hog did after a day's foraging.

Big Brah and Kali hadn't slept at all the previous night. They slept longer. I was first up, in the kitchen.

The tall kitchen windows let in plenty light and air. I made French toast and coffee for all of us and extras. Poli`ahu and Wiliwili had on their big eyes full of love. Purr love! I served Poli`ahu and Wiliwili treats in their bowls. There was the sound of a car. The car sped up the driveway. Someone was in a hurry.

The car screeched to a halt outside the house. Poli`ahu stopped eating, fixed her gaze on me and meowed. Had I heard the car? Wiliwili simply raised his head and looked at me.

I put the container with the treats back in its place in the kitty supplies bin. "All right, go on. I'm getting the door," I said.

Both of them went back to eating. I headed toward the front door. The doorbell rang twice, before I got the door open.

The new arrival had pink hair cropped at the

shoulders, a flowery sarong-dress and the mole on her chin. I never forget a face, anyway. "Lily! What can I do for you?" I said.

Lily didn't look happy. "Umi, I want to see Big Brah," she said.

I gestured for her to come in. "What's it about?" I asked, casually.

She followed me across the foyer to the office door. "It's about Noah. You remember, my boyfriend?" she said.

"Yes." I seated her in the visitor's chair.

"Well, he's got me worried. He's been acting really strange," she said.

"What kind of strange?" I pulled the blackout curtains and opened the windows to let in the spring morning light and air.

With a worried frown, she said, "He won't tell me. Just says it's about Kaipo."

Kaipo. Suddenly Lily had all my attention. "I know Big Brah and Kali won't want to miss this. You sit right here. Let me go get them," I said.

# Chapter 10 Who you calling riffraff?

Big Brah and Kali had descended to the kitchen in their t-shirts, shorts and rubber slippers. Kali made a conspiratorial face and lowered her voice. "We heard the sounds, who's the visitor?"

"Lily," I mouthed.

Kali had big eyes. Her big eyes widened. "It's got to be about Noah!" she whispered, prophetic as ever.

Big Brah stood calm and tall next to her. Kali turned and looked adoringly up at Big Brah. "Koa, are you ready?" she whispered.

Kali had cut her hair short. Her short hair had turned out curly. Big Brah and I? Let's just say so far as hair was concerned we were military men.

Kali ran a hand through her curls. "I'm ready, let's take our French toast and coffee to the office," she said.

Big Brah smiled fondly at Kali. "Let's go," he said.

Big Brah, Kali and I entered the office through

the inside door. Lily was still in the visitor's chair. We had our breakfast plates and coffee mugs. Big Brah and Kali sat down in their chairs behind the tidy desk.

I placed the breakfast plate and steaming coffee mug meant for Lily on the part of the tidy desk nearest her. I put my grinds on my desk. I took my place.

I parted the clutter on my desk to get a better view. "Lily, you can go on now," I said.

Lily squirmed. She looked at Big Brah and Kali. "I'm so sorry, hope I'm not disturbing you," she said.

Kali smiled, reassuringly. She indicated the breakfast plate with French toast and syrup on it and the steaming mug. "Please eat, drink and tell us your story, there's nothing we'd like more," she said.

"Are-are you sure? What I have to say may not be very important," Lily said.

"You're important to us, Lily, don't worry," Kali said, softly.

Lily stopped squirming. A sad expression played on her face. She fixed her gaze on the tidy surface of the desk. She spoke in a low, hard-to-hear voice. "I think I told you about Noah, the first time we met, inside Mahio Mansion."

Kali and I both looked at Big Brah, instinctively.

Big Brah remembered everything. "You met him Tuesday night at the Tavern. You praised

Kaipo. You told Noah how good Kaipo would be in love: Kaipo wouldn't hold back. Noah got jealous," he said.

Lily perked up. If Big Brah remembered, he must think it important. "Yes, yes, that's exactly right," she said.

"Since then, what happened?" Big Brah prompted her, gently.

Lily said, "Noah won't tell me, he only says it's about Kaipo."

"Jealousy," Big Brah murmured.

Lily looked up, a startled expression coming over her face. "You think so? I never meant to make him jealous," she said.

This was new love. As love ripened and grew sweeter, the jealousies faded away. No worries.

Big Brah shrugged and smiled. "I wouldn't worry about it."

Kali said, "Give it time."

The sad expression returned on Lily's face. "But last night, Noah, he calls me, he tells me, he's done something bad. I must forgive him," she said.

"Did Noah tell you what he did?" Kali asked.

Lily was on the verge of crying. "Yes, he told me he has done something bad to Kaipo. I made him jealous of Kaipo. I'm responsible."

I kept a box of tissues on my desk for such occasions. I delivered the box to Lily. Just in time. Big tears rolled down Lily's cheeks. She grabbed a bunch of tissues from the box and wiped the tears that wouldn't stop flowing. Helpfully, I moved the trash bin closer to her.

She spoke, in-between sobs. "I asked Noah what he had done. He wouldn't say, only he wanted to go away to suffer for his sins."

Suffer for his sins!

Lily said, "What sins? I cried out. But Noah wouldn't say, so frustrating. Kali, Big Brah, I know Kaipo is missing. What if Noah did something bad to him?"

Could Noah really do something bad to Kaipo?

Lily said, "I couldn't sleep last night, thinking what to do. If I told Uncle Duke, it's only going to make him worry worse. How do I even tell him?

"Uncle Duke has been an angel to my mother and me. How can one of us cause harm to the person Uncle loves most in the world: Kaipo? Then, I remembered you. First thing, this morning, I'm here. Please, please, you must help!" Lily said.

A long silence followed, interrupted only by the sounds of Lily blowing her nose. Big Brah and Kali looked at each other, letting Lily recover from telling her tale.

At last, Big Brah said, softly, "Lily, on Tuesday night, when you told Noah about Kaipo, why, what did you really have in mind?"

Lily started to cry again but softly this time. "I love Noah, he means the world to me. I want to spend the rest of my life with him. I wanted him to hurry up, ask me to marry him. So I told him, in love, Kaipo wouldn't hold back.

"I never meant to make him jealous, I was only showing him a good example. I never imagined he'd even think of harming Kaipo in any way," she said.

Big Brah heaved a sigh. "I understand the situation," he said.

Lily gazed at him, looking confused. "What? Aren't you going to do anything about it?" she said, a plea in her voice.

Lily was suffering. Noah was suffering. My heart was mush. Always softhearted, Big Brah would surely do something. Pure Big Brah love.

Big Brah smiled. "Lily, I'll act immediately, only if you finish eating breakfast with us," he said.

Over breakfast and talk story, Big Brah asked, "What is the name of Noah's boat?"

"Noah's Ark," Lily said.

I shivered. Noah's Ark had indeed chased after Kaipo and his gals the night of the murder. The man Music Man had seen was Noah.

"Where does Noah live?" Big Brah said.

"Noah lives alone, in the small house on the coast surrounded by fruit trees, near Mahio Mansion. I was there last evening. The place was locked, the boat gone," Lily said.

Big Brah reassured Lily we would find Noah. Lily left, happier. Big Brah, Kali and I visited Noah's small home.

The home was surrounded by fruit trees. Next to the green banana patch, a fancy fishing boat was hitched to a new truck. In big, bold letters, "Noah's Ark" was painted on the side of the boat. As we got out of the big, black truck, a man emerged from the home.

His hair was short, like mine. But he had a week-long beard. He had a bold stance and intense eyes. At the sight of us, he strode forward confidently. He halted near us. His intense eyes appraised us.

Then, he addressed Big Brah. "You look familiar. Are you looking for someone?" he said.

"Yes, Noah," Big Brah said.

"That would be me," he said.

Big Brah indicated the boat and the truck. "And the boat?" he said.

Noah smiled. "Also, Noah, after me. I was out fishing last night, just got back," he said.

"And Friday night?" Big Brah said.

Noah's smile faded. "How's that any of your business?" he said.

Big Brah smiled, disarmingly. "I forgot to mention. Your girl, Lily, she didn't know you were out fishing last night. She was worried. She called on us this morning," he said.

"Oh, Lily! She sent you! Why didn't you say so?" The smile was back on his face. "I recognize you, now. You're Big Brah!"

Big Brah nodded, approvingly. "This is Kali, and Umi," he said, gesturing our way.

"Of course, I know you all," he said.

Kali smiled. I bowed my head.

Noah looked at each of us in turn, his gaze even. "Tell Lily, I'm sorry, I worried her. I'll call her. Did she tell you any of what I've been saying to her?"

"About Kaipo? Yes, she told us," Big Brah said.

Noah laughed. "I didn't mean any of it. I got nothing against Kaipo," he said.

"But you told Lily, and this is what worried her the most, you'd done something bad to Kaipo," Big Brah said.

Noah stopped laughing. "Yes, I told her that, I regret it. Obviously, I made it up. Just drama. Lily and I, we're working through a serious issue. Hope you'll let us have our privacy," he said.

Big Brah nodded. "Of course, privacy first," he said.

Noah smiled. "I'm sure you understand. Besides, I couldn't have harmed Kaipo at all. Friday night, I was home alone, watching TV 'til after midnight, when I slept. I never even stepped out of the house, believe me," he said.

But Music Man had seen the boat "Noah's Ark" at the harbor.

Big Brah said, "And your boat?"

Noah's smile widened. "My boat? It was here the entire time," he said.

Now, Noah was lying. Big Brah didn't flinch, but Kali and I exchanged a secret glance. Why was Noah lying? Was it to hide a crime, or was it something else?

Time would tell. We exchanged pleasantries a while longer, then we left. Back inside the big, black truck, it was mid-morning, as we rode down the scenic coastal highway. Big Brah drove. Kali was in the passenger seat, while I had the backseat.

Big Brah glanced at Kali. "Any idea why Noah is lying?" he asked.

Kali thought for a moment. "In their love story, Lily and Noah are working out an important issue. Lily wants Noah to hurry, and Noah, I think, is confused. Noah doesn't know Lily's heart, fully, not yet, but give him time, and he will. Then he'll stop lying, and the truth will come out." She predicted.

Big Brah listened to Kali's prediction carefully, as he always did. He believed Kali, no questions, always. He nodded, his eyes on the road. "You're right," he said.

Adoring as ever, Kali looked his way. "You know, the turnoff is just ahead, why don't we swing by my office? The autopsy report may provide some answers," she said.

Big Brah, Kali and I left the big truck parked in the lot outside the two-story, gray county building. This time, we headed to the right of the building, where Kali's office was located.

We walked down a ground floor corridor, past the door of Kali's locked office to the open door of the temporary office of her substitute, Dr. Lohai.

Kali entered the office, Big Brah and I behind her. The office was a big, windowless room.

The room had overhead lighting and bare, undecorated walls. A desk and a few chairs were the only furniture. There were unopened boxes of medical equipment. Temporary office, for sure. Dr. Lohai was a big man and no part of his body had escaped the accumulation of fat.

Dr. Lohai's round head was bald, his face and belly rotund. He had a big mouth and lots of small teeth. He was completely at ease, as he sat behind the desk doing paperwork. He looked up.

His big mouth cracked into a happy, comfortable smile, displaying his many small teeth. For someone who had spent forty years of his career more with the dead than the living, Dr. Lohai had a cheerful disposition. He laughed. Every part of his big body moved.

It was fascinating to watch. He gestured for us to sit down. "Well, well, well. Soon as I heard the Waialeale Detective Agency was investigating the Hokui murder case, I had a feeling you'd visit," he said.

Big Brah and I sat down.

Kali smiled, taking a chair. "Tell us about it then," she said.

Dr. Lohai's big mouth straight-lined. "Dirty business. I'm confident the cause of death was head trauma," he said.

"Can you speculate on how the head trauma came about?" Kali said.

Dr. Lohai said, "A natural object, likely a rock. Now, here's the tricky part. Someone could have hit the victim with a rock. But it could also be, she was pushed off the boat, hit her head on the rocks and died instantly."

What an awful way to die. Big Brah always said the dead had a way of letting their last wish be known. The victim, she would want her murderer found.

Dr. Lohai said, "Either way, it suggests the involvement of the boat's occupants."

Kali asked, "How about the time of death?"

"The body was found in water, so it's harder to get an estimate. I'd say between midnight and 4 a.m. Now, I hear there was a phone call, no two phone calls, right before 1:30 a.m. from the victim's phone. That means she died sometime after 1:30 a.m. but before 4 a.m.," Dr. Lohai said.

Kali looked at Big Brah and me to see if we had any questions. We were detectives not medical examiners. We didn't have any questions.

Kali got up. She smiled at Dr. Lohai. "Mahalo," she said.

Dr. Lohai was also up on his feet. He came around his desk and hugged each of us in turn, solemnly. "Hope you find the murderer. I'll help in any way I can," he said.

Big Brah, Kali and I walked silently back to the truck. The sun was overhead and warm. I couldn't get over how awfully the victim had been murdered. I shivered.

Big Brah stopped suddenly. "The police have been searching for Kaipo and Nohea. Maybe they found something. Since we're here, why don't we go find out from Loni?" he said.

We found Loni in his corner office. The office door was open. Behind his expansive desk with the framed photographs of his wife and daughters, Loni lounged in the executive chair. He stared dreamily out of the open window at the quaint rooftops, rolling plains and mountains, while he tugged at the ends of his mustache.

Big Brah stood in the doorway and knocked on the open door lightly with his knuckles. Loni started. Alert now, he looked toward the door, where the three of us stood. He was pleased to see us.

Loni smiled. "Come in, come in!"

Big Brah, Kali and I entered.

"Sit, sit." Loni gestured at the empty chairs across the desk from him.

We sat down.

"What can I do for you?" Loni asked, hospitably.

"Last we left you, you were on your way to the chief to get approval for the search," Big Brah said.

"Yes, I remember. The chief agreed. The search has been very successful so far," Loni said, with a little laugh.

"Does that mean the police have Kaipo?" Big

Brah asked.

"Not quite," Loni said, "but we've made progress. For example, we've examined the passenger list of every flight departing the island since Friday night and interrogated the boarding agents.

"Kaipo, Nohea with him, they were not on any of those flights. All the boats belonging to either family have been inventoried, none are missing.

"The west side boat, airplane and chopper rentals didn't rent a boat, plane or chopper to anyone answering either of their descriptions, so they didn't leave the island on any other private craft. All this means, they're hiding somewhere on the island, confirmed!" Loni shouted gleefully.

Big Brah nodded, approvingly. "I agree, that's progress," he said.

Loni smiled, pleased. "Earlier this morning, I was in a meeting with the search and rescue mission crew. I don't know if you heard it on the news, but the search and rescue has been called off. Standard procedure. It had been seventy-two hours.

"But the search and rescue crew mission chief, he's a friend of mine. He doesn't give up, procedure or not, if he thinks there's a chance of rescuing someone.

"But he assured the chief, and me, the crew has done everything possible to find Kaipo and Nohea. But there's absolutely no sign of them out on the ocean. Kaipo and Nohea aren't hiding there or waiting to be rescued." Loni rubbed his hands together. "My idea to search the island is going to succeed! To begin with, Chief has approved two days of the search."

"But a day has gone by," Big Brah said.

Loni smiled again. "Only a day. Chief's given us two days. We have an entire day left. It's a small island. We're going to find Kaipo and Nohea and please the chief!"

Big Brah got up. "Good luck with the search. Mahalo for seeing us," he said.

Kali and I followed Big Brah out of Loni's office. What had happened to Kaipo and Nohea? The answer was like the elusive big wave you had to paddle around to find while surfing. We headed home in the big, black truck. No trouble, until we were nearly home. The truck drove past the agency's reader board and turned the corner.

I was ready for the sight of our two-story paradise. As usual, our home was there. But in front of the garage, there were two vehicles. Unusual. A conservative gray sedan with shining chrome and tinted windows, and a yellow sports car, like new, very stylish. Most unusual. The truck pulled over to the side of the driveway and stopped. Big Brah and Kali exchanged glances. They looked back at me silently.

I said, "Let's go see who they are."

Big Brah and Kali looked at each other again and nodded. We got out of the truck. I followed them, as they walked up the driveway toward the parked vehicles. The door of the yellow sports car cracked open.

The crack widened slowly. Our client, Duke Mahio emerged. Thinning hair, business-like glasses, he was dressed casually in shirt, cargo shorts and sandals. His wonderful tattoos showed. He still needed a shave.

He looked annoyed. "I'm sure glad to see you, Big Brah," he said.

The door of the conservative gray sedan now swung open. Jim Bordeta emerged. His hair was brushed back. Dark sunglasses hid his mismatched eyes.

His mouth was a straight line. "I'd like to have a word with you, Big Brah," he said, stiffly.

Big Brah looked from Mahio to Bordeta. The rivals didn't look at each other.

Big Brah addressed both of them. "This has to be about the murder. Why don't we go inside? Sit in the office and talk story?" He proposed.

Mahio said, "Look, I'm your client. You should see me first, then the riffraff."

Bordeta glared at Mahio. "Who you calling riffraff? I'd like to hear what lies you have to say. I want to be there," he said.

Big Brah raised his hands, trying to appease both the bickering men. "I'll see you both, in my office," he said.

Both men turned to glare at Big Brah. Making calming gestures, Big Brah moved slowly away from the men toward the front door. "Come on in," he said.

Without a word, both men followed Big Brah inside. Kali and I exchanged glances. Whew.

Inside the office, the lights were on. The blackout curtains remained drawn to keep the midday heat out. Big Brah had also prudently turned on the cooling.

We would need the cooling. Duke Mahio was firmly seated in the visitor's chair. Big Brah had already pulled up another chair from the conference table to seat Jim Bordeta next to Mahio.

Bordeta sat gruffly, holding the sunglasses he had been wearing outside. Big Brah, Kali and I took our places.

Big Brah faced both men and smiled at them encouragingly. "All right, we're doing good, brahs. Tell me, how long since the two of you last talked?" he asked.

Mahio made a face at Bordeta. "I told you what he told me at Luana's funeral five years ago. After that, what's there to talk?"

Bordeta didn't bother glancing at Mahio. "I stand by every word I said. In fact, let me say it better this time. Luana's death wasn't just an accident, you killed her!" he said.

"I killed her? Why would I kill her? I loved her, she loved me. She chose me. You just can't get over it!" Mahio said.

Bordeta said, "All I'm saying is, Luana died,

because of your negligence."

"My negligence? More like her sweet love for the ocean! She loved to go diving. All I did was let her go. My bad, I know. I regret it, everyday!" Mahio said.

Bordeta stared straight ahead at Big Brah. "That same negligence, like a sea monster, now rears its ugly head again. Kaipo, your son. Look what he's done to my daughter."

Mahio talked to Bordeta's profile. "He's done nothing to your daughter. Kaipo is as sweet and innocent as Luana used to be. I know it, they share the same love for the ocean."

Bordeta's voice was loaded with sarcasm. "Is that why Kaipo was teaching Nohea to surf?" he asked.

"To be honest, I believe he was," Mahio said.

"You sure it wasn't to charm Nohea into going out with him?" Bordeta said.

Mahio shrugged. "I don't know about that. Kaipo couldn't be attracted to your daughter, impossible. I know for sure, Kaipo is innocent!"

With a sideways glance at Mahio, Bordeta asked, "If he's so innocent, why are you here? Why haven't you informed the police?"

Mahio looked uncomfortably at Big Brah. He had told Big Brah why he couldn't go to the police. The surveillance video. He didn't say anything.

# Chapter 11 Soul marriage

Bordeta sensed victory. He turned to glare at Mahio. "There you go, this is all your ploy, isn't it? To get back at me, just because I said those words at Luana's funeral?" he said.

"You're a cold fish, Jim."

"Yes, Duke. You're the lovable dolphin Luana wanted."

"I was a fool to think you'd change. Shouldn't have told you anything." Mahio heaved a sigh.

Mahio looked at Big Brah. "This morning, when I drove down to meet you," he snuck a thumb toward Bordeta, "he was already parked outside your garage. I thought maybe the tragedy moved him, I told him what I'd come to tell you. I shouldn't have."

"What is it you wanted to tell me?" Big Brah asked.

"It's about Lily. From what I understand, her boyfriend, Noah, he was gone fishing last night. You visited him this morning, found him. He called her, right after you left.

"Noah was mad at Lily. Why had she involved you, in what's clearly their personal matter? Lily, she's crying, depressed, couldn't even talk to me.

"Lily's mother, Aunty Maria, she's my housekeeper, she told me all this. So I told her, I'll go tell Big Brah, there's no need to pull either Lily or Noah into this.

"Much as I'd have liked Kaipo and Lily to get together, I know Noah, he spends a lot of time with Lily. He's a good boy," Mahio said.

I wondered whether he would still think Noah was a good boy if he knew what Lily had told us. That Noah had done something bad to Kaipo. Big Brah didn't say anything.

"I don't want you to bother Noah and Lily," Mahio said.

Big Brah took a deep breath. He was about to say something.

Jim Bordeta broke out into a sarcastic laugh. "Ask Mahio why he doesn't want them bothered. I'll tell you why? The housekeeper's daughter and boyfriend. Lily and Noah sound like accomplices. Kaipo's and his. Look at the victim. Helen Hokui. The property manager. Father and son wanted to get rid of her. They did, they got rid of Helen," he said.

Mahio was up on his feet, fuming. "Big Brah, I'm done taking any more nonsense. My son's missing, is all I know. I've told you what I came to tell you. Now, I'm leaving."

Mahio strode to the door and let himself out. Soon, we heard his car start and drive away. Bordeta sat with us in silence.

At last, Bordeta said, "I'm sorry. I didn't mean to get between you and your client. But this is important. I'm doing this for Nohea."

Big Brah said, "I understand. But what is it that brought you over today?"

"After talking to you, I couldn't sleep last night. I talked it over with Jean, my wife, over breakfast this morning. And, it felt right to see you again, repeat my appeal to investigate your own client first, so I came over," Bordeta said.

Big Brah nodded. "I understand," he said.

Bordeta got up. "I'm going to the PD to see Rice. I've asked Loni be there. I'll be telling them to focus their investigations on Mahio," he said.

Jim Bordeta left. A cold fish, indeed. I heard his car start and then leave.

Big Brah chuckled. "He'll be back. I imagine Rice didn't tell Jim Bordeta about the fight Kaipo had with Helen Hokui, since it didn't involve Nohea. Now, Bordeta's also going to see Loni.

"Loni knows about the fight, of course. Randy Hokui told Loni the fight was about robbing the Mahio family safe. If Bordeta learns about the fight, and what it was about, he's sure to return!" he said.

Not knowing when Jim Bordeta would return, Big Brah, Kali and I went to the kitchen. Big Brah and Kali made lunch. Spicy ahi poke, steamed rice and butter stir-fried vegetables. I sat at the kitchen table with Poli`ahu and Wiliwili, doing college work. As the goddess would have it, Jim Bordeta returned right after we finished lunch.

Grim-faced, Jim Bordeta sat in the visitor's chair and faced Big Brah and Kali. From behind my cluttered desk, I had a good view of the three of them.

Bordeta hadn't bothered to take off his sunglasses, his mouth as straight line as ever. "I had a good meeting with Rice and Loni at the PD. I'm happy to say they're focusing their investigation on Kaipo Mahio. In fact, they provided me with more proof of Kaipo's shenanigans.

"You saw how Mahio was defending his son, so I had to make sure you knew what I learned. Apparently Kaipo had a brawl with Helen Hokui, in front of everyone, at the Tavern. Just the night before he murdered her, did you know that?" he said.

Kali and I exchanged glances. Big Brah had been right. Bordeta had heard about the fight and he was back.

Big Brah was patient as ever. "Yes, I know about the fight, Thursday night, at the Tavern. What about it?" he said.

"Then, you also know what the fight was about? No, don't tell me, I'll tell you. Kaipo wanted to rob the family safe! Helen, poor woman, didn't want to. What kind of a boy has Duke raised? Wants to rob his family safe. Brawls with property manager, when she tries to stop him, kills her.

"I don't mind letting Duke Mahio know. I'm telling you this, so you can convey my message to him. You saw, he and I can never get along. Kaipo Mahio isn't suitable for a girl like my Nohea.

"Nohea's sweet, innocent. I'm sure she doesn't want to have anything to do with a criminal like Kaipo. I agree with the police. Kaipo is holding my sweet Nohea captive!" Bordeta said.

Big Brah bowed his head. "The police are searching for Kaipo. The deadline's tomorrow. Loni is confident Kaipo will be apprehended. Your daughter will be safe," he said.

Jim Bordeta took off his sunglasses. Holding the sunglasses between thumb and forefinger, he waved the sunglasses in the air to emphasize. "I'm pretty sure, your client, Duke Mahio, he's behind all this. Kaipo is just a boy, he can't be doing this by himself. I'm sure Duke's the mastermind.

"It's Duke's son, his property manager, his housekeeper's daughter and her boyfriend. We need Kaipo. Soon as the police get him, I want the truth out of him. I'll expose Duke for what he is, once and for all!" he said.

Big Brah heaved a sigh. "We all want the same thing. Kaipo found, the truth known," he said.

Jim Bordeta left, obviously to brood about Duke Mahio, until the police found Kaipo. Big Brah, Kali and I looked at each other.

I spread my hands. "Jim Bordeta hates Duke

Mahio, obvious. But when he says Kaipo Mahio isn't suitable for a girl like Nohea? I mean, it's true Kaipo had a fight with Helen Hokui, but I fear, Jim Bordeta would disapprove of Kaipo, no matter what. He can't just disapprove of Kaipo. That's over-the-top lacking in aloha."

"You're right, Umi." Kali looked my way.

Kali's parents lived on the mainland. Her parents disapproved of her choice of Big Brah. Or else they'd be married years ago.

Kali was still sorting out issues. "Jim Bordeta has no right to disapprove of his daughter's choice. It's Nohea's choice, everyone in this world has the right, the freedom to choose the person he or she loves. His disapproval, it bothers me," she said.

Big Brah took Kali's soft and capable hand in his comfortingly. From time to time, they had to walk over hot lava because of Kali's disapproving family. During the spring vacation, Kali had a rule.

She didn't check mail, e-mail or text messages from her bad family. That helped. But Big Brah was Kali's great comfort. They were soulmates. Kali held Big Brah's hand with both of hers. She looked at Big Brah adoringly. Theirs was a soul marriage. Then a silence fell over us. What were we going to do?

Big Brah was on it. "If Loni finds Kaipo, with all the evidence Loni has, I don't doubt Loni will charge Kaipo with murder," he said.

I agreed. "Jim Bordeta will see to it, Loni does charge Kaipo!" I said.

Kali reasoned. "If I were Kaipo, I'd know I haven't murdered Helen Hokui, but someone did. Until the police find the killer, I'd continue to hide," she said.

Big Brah nodded, approvingly. "If we want Kaipo to come out of hiding, we have to find the real killer," he said.

Purposefully, Big Brah got up. He picked up the agency phone and the keys of the big, black truck from the table. "Come on, we're going to Duke Mahio's. I want another look at the surveillance video. I have an idea."

Big Brah's ideas were usually of the unexpected kind. I looked forward to the surprise. It didn't take us long that otherwise lovely spring afternoon to get to Mahio Mansion in the big, black truck.

Inside the mansion's old-style living room, with its high ceiling, bamboo and rattan furniture, Big Brah, Kali and I sat down with Duke Mahio. Without Jim Bordeta, Duke Mahio was not fuming. He was calmer. The big windows filled the spacious room with mid-afternoon light and air.

Big Brah indicated the state-of-the-art big screen in the room. "The surveillance video you showed us, is there any way it could have been tampered, messed around with?" he said.

"No way, I handled it myself. No one else has

seen it," Duke Mahio said.

Big Brah took in a deep breath, gazing at the big screen. "I want to see the surveillance video, again, slow. This time, give me the remote," he said.

Duke Mahio had the surveillance video running for us in minutes. In slow motion. Heels, thin legs, skirt, shirt, Helen Hokui's face, smiling. The top of her head. Black hair.

The way her body moved. Yes, she was talking. The man. Sandals. Khaki pants. Bead bracelet, shiny gold plate. Big Brah hit the pause button on the remote. The video stopped. Yes, "Kaipo" was stylized on the gold plate.

Big Brah said, "This bracelet, the police discovered it next to the body. Was it something Kaipo wore all the time?"

Duke Mahio was apologetic. "I don't know that for sure. You see, after his mother passed away, Kaipo and I, I told you, we moved apart. These kind of knickknacks, his mother would have known about him. I didn't, sorry. He does wear a bracelet often. Luana used to buy him bracelets, she loved to dress him up. Kaipo enjoyed it too. But this bracelet, I don't know how long he had it, sorry," he said.

Big Brah hit the start button. The video started again. Shirt. Neck. Face.

Big Brah paused the video. "Are you sure that is your son, Kaipo?" he said.

Like Helen Hokui, Kaipo was smiling.

Whatever fight they had the night before was forgotten. I stared at the face.

Wide forehead, thick, black eyebrows, high cheekbones and angular face, all a lot like Duke Mahio's. Abundant black curly hair, thick eyebrows and a mustache made him look younger.

Duke Mahio stared at the face on the screen. "I-I think so. Kaipo looks like me, only younger, and the mustache...yes, that's him all right. Helen talked to me over the phone, shortly after the videos were recorded. She told me, she'd seen Kaipo at the safe," he said.

Big Brah let the rest of the video of Kaipo with Helen Hokui play. Clearly identifiable. She with straight, black hair. He with curly hair.

They did seem to be getting along just fine. Big Brah forwarded the video 23 minutes, as Duke Mahio had done, the first time we watched it. In slow motion, sandals, khaki pants, bead bracelet, shiny gold plate.

Big Brah paused the video to check the gold plate. Yes, "Kaipo." The video played again. Shirt. Neck. Face.

Big Brah paused the video, again. "Are you sure that is your son, Kaipo?" he said.

For a moment, all of us stared at the face. *Duke Mahio, younger, with more hair*, I thought. But why was Big Brah asking the question again? It had to be something to do with his idea.

Duke Mahio took a good look at the face. "I'm

sure," he said.

Again, Big Brah let the rest of the video play. "I'm going to need copies of both videos, so I have images of Kaipo, the stylized bracelet and Helen Hokui," he said.

With digital copies of the surveillance videos downloaded to the agency phone, Big Brah, Kali and I exited Mahio Mansion. We had taken another look at the surveillance videos. We even had the videos with us. Now, what was Big Brah's idea?

# Chapter 12 Greek tragedy

My excitement mounted, as Big Brah drove us in the big, black truck to the island's picturesque downtown. Quaint rooftops. Quirky businesses. Just a few streets.

Big Brah parked the truck in front of a boutique. The signboard on top of the door displayed "Cosplay, Silicone Bodysuits." The boutique was a popular, new business on our island.

"Cosplay, Silicone Bodysuits" provided costumes, for every party. Lots of theme costumes. Kids loved to play make believe in these costumes. Costume play or Cosplay for us grownups. Cosplay was the new fun on the island.

I laughed out loud. "What're we doing here?" I said.

Big Brah explained his idea. "The video wasn't tampered with. That means, if Duke Mahio is right, and Kaipo didn't rob the safe, then the person in the video is someone else. An imposter. An imposter who wore a costume, a very lifelike costume, a silicone bodysuit. Cosplay," he said.

I was out of the truck fast. Big Brah and Kali followed me to the door below the signboard. Two information wanted posters were stuck on the wall next to the door.

The slanted rays of the late afternoon sun fell on the posters titled Information Wanted. Below the title was a familiar face. Thick eyebrows and mustache. Kaipo's face. The poster had his full name, Kaipo Mahio. He was wanted as a person of interest. The phone number of the police hotline to call with any information was printed in bold.

I pointed to the Information Wanted poster. "Kali, Big Brah, look!" I said.

While they looked, I took the opportunity to see the next poster. Nohea Bordeta. She looked a lot like her younger sister, Iekika, and her mom. The same thick, wavy black hair, big eyes and shapely chin.

Kaipo and Nohea had their innocent faces up on a wall for all to see. Suddenly the urgency of finding out what had happened to them rose as fast as stream water in a flash flood.

Briskly, I opened the door to the business. "Come on," I said.

Big Brah and Kali followed me. I entered a rectangular room with hushed lighting, low ceiling and shiny floor. There a doorway at the back to what looked like a bigger room. The walls had several lifelike bodysuits of men and women. A bit creepy how lifelike they were.

Behind the sales counter to my left, a man my age with a blue goatee communed with a phone.

He greeted me with a friendly smile. "First time here?" he said.

"Yes." I smiled back.

"No matter," he said, making me feel at ease, "I'm from another island, so am new to the entire place."

I widened my smile, welcoming him. Big Brah and Kali were behind me.

The man with the blue goatee smiled at us as a group. "My name is Agamemnon, let me show you around," he said.

Agamemnon came around the counter. He was small, chubby and moved surprisingly fast. "Our showroom is this way," he said.

Agamemnon disappeared through the doorway into the bigger room. I followed him into the showroom. It was a huge room with bright ceiling lights.

On the walls and in all manners of glass cases, exhibits were everywhere. A smile on his chubby face and hands behind his back, Agamemnon stood by.

Big Brah, Kali and I strolled around the room, each of us caught up in wonder at the strangeness of the exhibits in Cosplay's showroom.

A display of wigs adorned a wall. Another wall showcased torsos. Athletic, ripped, big belly, pregnant and corset bodysuits, to name a few. Masks, chests and hips. Inside glass cases, assortments of eyebrows, ears, noses, lips, chins, cheeks, necks, beards and mustaches. There was a special section dedicated to themes. Always popular. All so real, amazing.

Role playing paradise. In awe. I wandered back to Agamemnon with Big Brah and Kali.

Agamemnon cleared his throat. "Is there anything particular you're interested in?" he said.

From behind me, Big Brah spoke up. "Yes, what if I wanted to dress up as someone else?" he said.

Agamemnon ran a hand over his goatee. "You have two options. One, you can buy anything you like in this room. All merchandize come with wear instructions. I can help you with that."

Agamemnon peered past me at Big Brah I guess to estimate Big Brah's size. "Otherwise, you can go for our specialty, a customized silicone bodysuit," he said.

Big Brah stepped forward. "All right, the customized bodysuit. What would I have to do?"

"Character or friend?"

"Friend," Big Brah said.

Agamemnon smiled. "I ask, for a good reason. If you told me character, well, even if you chose a particular look for your character, we know how the character looks like, so all I'd do is take your measurements, so the suit can be made to your size. I'm pretty good with characters.

"I'd make the suit myself. If it's a friend, you'll have to work with my uncle. He's the senior artist, and well, he'll take your measurements. You'll have to tell him how your friend looks like," he said.

Big Brah thought for a moment. "I'd like to see your uncle, then," he said.

Agamemnon made an apologetic face. "I'm sorry, my uncle, he works at home. We have an artist's shed in our backyard. He doesn't always come to the store, you'll have to make an appointment," he said.

"How early can I see him?" Big Brah said.

"Today's almost over. Uncle starts his morning late, so I'd say noon, tomorrow," Agamemnon said.

Noon, the next day. Big Brah, Kali and I looked at each other. On the island, for a costume appointment, next day would be lightning fast. But, noon tomorrow was Loni's deadline.

What if the police did find Kaipo? They could. It was a small island. Without us uncovering evidence of Kaipo's innocence, Loni would surely arrest Kaipo.

Big Brah stepped forward. "Agamemnon, brah, I need a big favor. I'm really sorry, but this can't wait until noon tomorrow. My name is Koa Waialeale, this is my colleague Kali and my assistant Umi. Together, we're investigating the boat murder, you must have heard about it?" he said.

Agamemnon's eyes widened. Slack-jawed, he stared at Big Brah.

Then, he snapped out of his surprise and nodded. "You were also in the news. They said you're investigating the murder on behalf of Duke Mahio," he said.

"That's correct. I'd sure appreciate your help," Big Brah said.

"Uncle's home, the address is 2332 Waihale. I'm sure he'll assist you in any way he can," he said, helpfully.

Big Brah thanked Agamemnon profusely. "Mahalo nui loa for all your help today."

Big Brah, Kali and I headed to the outer room. Agamemnon followed us.

"What's your uncle's name?" Big Brah asked.

"Hades."

Big Brah stopped for a moment. We all did. Big Brah said, "Hades, Greek mythology, as in the lord of the—"

"Yes, underworld," Agamemnon said, making a sad face, "I get that a lot."

Big Brah, Kali and I turned away to hide our smiles.

Agamemnon called out after us. "I'll call Uncle. Let him know, you're on your way," he said.

We smiled all the way back to the big, black truck. Inside, we burst out laughing. Big Brah started driving. The laughter died down.

I said, "Seriously, first Agamemnon, then

Hades. What is this, a Greek tragedy?"

Big Brah chuckled. "Remind me, *akamai*, who was Agamemnon?" he said.

"In the Iliad, the king who commanded the Greek army that battled to free Helen of Troy," I said.

Big Brah nodded, approvingly. Kali flashed me a smile. Akamai. Genius. I glowed all the way to our destination.

Waihale Lane was situated in one of the wettest spots on the island. It rained here all the time. It was only early evening, but the light had turned poor already. Its headlights on and windshield wipers active, the big truck drove down the rain slicked asphalt road. There was plenty wilderness on both sides of the rural road. Lone mailboxes and long driveways revealed the location of homes shrouded by tall grass and wild trees.

We crossed a patch of wild trees. A gravel driveway came up on our right. By the driveway, there was a black, metal mailbox with the number 2332 on it.

Rain lashed the mailbox. The truck turned into the gravel driveway. At the end of the gravel driveway, there was a neat, single-story home.

The truck stopped in front of the home. The rain was coming down hard. We waited for the rain to ease up. No one came out. Several minutes later, the rain died down to a drizzle. We got out of the truck.

The home was surrounded by leafy ti trees planted at regular intervals. Agamemnon had mentioned the artist's shed at the back his uncle worked in. Big Brah, Kali and I strolled around the home, following the ti trees. The shed had a concrete floor and a tin roof.

The shed had no walls. Rainwater dripped down from the edges of the tin roof. Under the roof, there was a desk cluttered with hand tools and an incomplete bodysuit. Work in progress.

The floor was cluttered with boxes, opened and unopened, and silicone body parts. But, no artist. We returned to the front of the home.

Big Brah rang the doorbell. The chime sounded inside the home, but no one opened the front door. We looked at each other. Agamemnon had told us his uncle was home. So, where was Hades?

Kali shook her head. "Something's fishy," she said.

I said, "What're we gonna do?"

"Stakeout," Big Brah said.

# Chapter 13 Sea turtle, dolphin and octopus

Stakeout with Big Brah and Kali was always thrilling. Big Brah drove the truck off the gravel driveway into a gap in the trees. Wild bushes on both sides of the truck provided perfect cover.

The driveway and the front of the house were visible. But no one approaching the house would notice us tucked in the bushes. Big Brah, Kali and I waited, patiently. I got time to observe the bushes that grew wild all over the island. This was a wet spot. The leaves on the bushes were green and plentiful. Small yellow-and-red flowers bloomed in colorful clusters. Tiny, green berries flourished in clumps. The ripened berries were black and ultra sweet. Water dripped down the branch of a tree onto the hood of the truck.

Drip, drip, drip. The evening grew darker. Lights approached down the driveway. There was the sound of tires crunching gravel. A car.

I tensed. A big sedan, the car stopped in front of the house. The driver killed the headlights and plunged the surroundings into darkness. I strained my eyes to see what was going on.

A figure got out of the sedan. Small, chubby and vaguely familiar. The car door slammed. An exterior light turned on. In the light, the figure unlocked the front door and entered the home. The lights turned on inside.

Swiftly, Big Brah, Kali and I made our way across the gravel path. Big Brah rang the doorbell. We waited. The familiar figure opened the front door. At close range, I could see his goatee. Agamemnon. Darn. I was hoping to see Hades.

On seeing us, Agamemnon started. "Wh-what are you doing here?" he said.

Big Brah was relaxed and friendly. "Your uncle wasn't home, so we decided to wait," he said.

Agamemnon stared slack-jawed at Big Brah for a long moment. "Yes, of course, of course, you waited. I thought you'd call, silly me," he said.

Big Brah said, "Your Uncle still isn't home, but we saw you, so here we are."

Agamemnon recovered. "I have to tidy up. Please give me a minute. Sorry to keep you waiting," he said, closing the front door.

Big Brah, Kali and I waited.

Soon, Agamemnon opened the front door, again. "Come in, come into the living room, I have news for you. It's about Uncle."

The living room was lit up by lamps placed in each of its four corners. There was a couch, loveseat, armchair and coffee table on a cozy rug.

The coffee table was littered with cosplay fliers and magazines.

There was a desk and a chair against a wall. There was a lamp on the desk. A sheet of white paper was stuck prominently under the desk lamp. Clearly nervous, Agamemnon sat on the couch, running a hand over his goatee again and again.

Agamemnon gestured for us to sit down. Big Brah and Kali together sank into the loveseat. I got the armchair.

Agamemnon stopped caressing his goatee. "You say Uncle wasn't home when you arrived. Tell me what happened," he said.

Big Brah said, "We checked the shed at the back. You'd told us he'd be working there. He wasn't. Then, we rang the doorbell. No one answered. So we waited."

Agamemnon said, "Waited, ah, yes. You should've called me. After you left the showroom, I called Uncle. He answered right away. I told him you were on your way to see him, I told him...." His voice died.

Agamemnon looked miserable. "I told him you were private investigators, I shouldn't have," he said.

Big Brah, Kali and I looked at each other. Whatever could Agamemnon mean?

"Mind explaining what you mean, brah," Big Brah said, casually.

The expression of misery stayed on

Agamemnon's face. "It's why we moved from the other island to here, Uncle has a history.

"Over there also, he got mixed up in an investigation. Uncle had done nothing wrong, he's an artist, he liked making the silicone bodysuits, but a customer had used a bodysuit while committing a crime.

"For days, cops, private eyes, reporters, everyone in town stomped all over poor uncle's work shed and home. I was in high school, I escaped with my friends. But for Uncle, no respite.

"He couldn't work, he couldn't do anything. A corrupt investigator pinned the blame for the crime on Uncle. Since then, he abhors investigators," he said.

A silence ensued. At last, Agamemnon said, "It's been so many years. In the heat of the moment this afternoon, I'd forgotten Uncle's history. I sent you home, called him, told him about you. Big mistake."

"Your uncle must have told you something. What did he say?" Big Brah asked.

"Not much. You don't know him. I do. He can keep things to himself, really well, if he wants to. He didn't let on anything at all to me.

"Uncle told me he'd be home, waiting for you, no worries. Or maybe it didn't sink in until after we finished talking? Either way, I had no warning, same as you," Agamemnon said.

"No warning, about what?" Big Brah said.

Agamemnon sighed. He got up surprisingly fast and made his way to the desk. He lifted the desk lamp and took the sheet of paper from under it. He set the desk lamp back and returned with the sheet of paper.

He handed the sheet of paper to Big Brah. "This," he said.

Big Brah took the sheet of paper. Agamemnon turned to look at Kali and me. "No warning," he said.

Both Kali and I peered at the sheet Big Brah was examining. The words had been hastily handwritten with a black marker. Big Brah read the note out loud. "Sorry, can't take another investigation. The shop's yours 'til it's over. Need a vacation. Am going camping. Don't tell anyone. Hades."

Big Brah handed the sheet back to Agamemnon. "I'm sorry," he said.

By the time we got back home, disappointed and hungry, it was night. Big Brah, Kali and I went to the kitchen. The familiar bright, overhead lights in the kitchen comforted. Moreover, Poli`ahu and Wiliwili were waiting for us.

Their eyes big with aloha, they did their purr-purr and mrrp-mrrp kitty hula. Petting Poli`ahu and Wiliwili, I forgot everything else. Drowned by pure kitty love, the disappointment from the investigation seeped out of me. I felt better already. Big Brah and Kali went upstairs to freshen up. From the refrigerator, I got the kitty food I had cooked earlier. Chicken in chicken liver gravy. I fed the cats.

Both Poli`ahu and Wiliwili came away from their bowls, licking their whiskers. Big Brah and Kali appeared. They got busy cooking.

First, crispy *tempuras* fried in clear butter, with a dip made of shoyu, ginger and brown sugar. Mouthwatering. We ate the appetizers, while dinner cooked.

Dinner was a ginger, wild basil and coconut milk chicken curry and butter-fried noodles. I savored it. Sleuthing makes me sleepy. That night, I slept. The following morning, I woke up early.

Big Brah and Kali were still in bed. I decided to make them breakfast in bed, a tradition in our house. After all, it was Kali's spring vacation. In so many of my summer vacations in grade school, Big Brah and Kali would bring the breakfast plates up to my room, and we would sit around and eat breakfast together. Some of the best story times. I entered the kitchen and turned on the lights.

Poli`ahu and Wiliwili slumbered on in their chairs at the round table, unbothered. "Wake up, sleepyheads," I said.

Poli`ahu raised her head, meowed and fell back asleep. Wiliwili opened an eye, gazed at me for a long moment, shut the eye and went back to sleep. Typical. I got busy in the kitchen.

Big Brah's homemade bacon, guava jam, toast and butter. Eggs. Omelet for Big Brah, sunny sides up for Kali and soft-boiled eggs for me. A pitcher of fresh orange juice and a carafe of coffee. Coffee mugs. Sugar and cream. The sounds of my activities finally woke Poli`ahu and Wiliwili up.

I balanced everything on the big tray and headed upstairs. Poli`ahu and Wiliwili followed. Big Brah was there at the top of the stairs, waiting for me.

He took the tray from me. "Kali's outside, in the lanai. Go, I'll bring the tray," he said, kindly.

Relieved of the burden of carrying the tray, I raced ahead to the upstairs lanai. The eastern horizon was a myriad shades of pink. The fresh morning breeze was cool. The ocean was serene. The serenity of the surroundings was enhanced by the excited calls of birds. The lanai had comfortable rattan chairs and a table.

Kali sat at the table, familiar grin on her face, her arms open and ready for me.

Morning hug. Warm and soft. "I was planning breakfast in bed, but this is better!" I said.

"Sweet Umi, you're just like your Big Brah, always doing good deeds." She looked up at Big Brah, as he arrived with the breakfast tray. She grinned, happily. "I'm so lucky to have both of you," she said.

"Ahem." Big Brah looked back at Poli`ahu and Wiliwili who were following him.

Kali laughed, contented. "All four of you!" she said.

The breakfast wasn't nearly as yummy as the ones Big Brah and Kali could conjure up, but it fulfilled its purpose. I was gathering up all the used plates and mugs back on the tray, when the agency phone rang. Big Brah had it on the table.

He picked up the phone and glanced at the screen. "It's Loni," he said, and answered the phone.

I heard Loni's muffled voice from the other end.

"Yes, it's Big Brah." Big Brah listened, then said, "Sure, we'll be there, mahalo."

He disconnected the call and then looked at us. "Loni is holding a special meeting, at his office, we're invited. Rice won't be there, he has other duties to attend to, but Loni's invited both Mahio and Bordeta."

"Sure to be fireworks, then," I said.

"The police still haven't found Kaipo and Nohea. I have a feeling this meeting's meant to explain why not," Big Brah said.

Loni sure had some explaining to do. At 10 sharp, Big Brah, Kali and I trooped into Loni's spacious corner office. The sun was up, the morning still cool. The big window brought in light and cool air.

Loni looked grim. He sat straight in the executive chair behind the desk with the framed photographs of his wife and daughters. Across from his desk, he had five chairs. Only two of the chairs were occupied, but the individuals sat as far away from each other as possible. The rightmost chair was occupied.

I recognized the back of the head from the thinning hair. Our client, Duke Mahio. And in the chair farthest to the left, his hair gelled carefully in place, Jim Bordeta. Loni greeted us with a nod and gestured for us to sit down.

Duke Mahio got up to greet us. He was still stooped and needed a shave. Jim Bordeta kept sitting, stiffly. He didn't greet us. Finally, we all sat down.

Loni tugged at the ends of his thick, black mustache, thinking. He faced us. "I've called all of you here today, because I have something very important to say," he said.

Typical Loni. None of us said anything.

Loni said, "As you know, the police has been searching for Kaipo. We believe he has Nohea captive. The search will end at noon today. Now, there's still a couple hours left, but here at the PD, we're proactive.

"We won't wait for the deadline. We're acting ahead of time. That's us! So far, none of the search team members, they haven't reported any breaks. They still may, in the next couple hours, but let's just assume for the sake of this meeting, they won't." Loni gazed at each one of us in turn and then at a point above and beyond us.

Slowly, Loni brought his gaze back to our

level. "What does this police failure mean? No, it doesn't mean the police failed, it means we learned something new from it. What did we learn?"

Jim Bordeta swiveled in his chair. He glared beyond Big Brah, Kali and me at Duke Mahio. It was clear why he thought the search had failed. Mahio was behind it all.

Loni also swiveled, more imperiously, to fix Duke Mahio with a wicked stare. "Mr. Mahio, sir, with due respect, you're a senior member of our community. I respect that. At the chief's behest, I have acted with great respect. But I have to say, the only reason the search failed was, to put it bluntly, you must be hiding Kaipo!"

Jim Bordeta smacked the arm of his chair, happy. "Dammit, you're good," he said, to Loni.

Loni showed white teeth under his black mustache. Kali and I stared slack-jawed at Loni. Duke Mahio squirmed in his chair and kept looking at us uncomfortably. He didn't know what to say.

Big Brah rescued Mahio. "That's preposterous! Loni, brah, Duke Mahio here has hired me to find Kaipo. He wouldn't hire me, if he was hiding Kaipo, would he now?" he said.

Jim Bordeta face-palmed. On the other hand, Mahio nodded. He agreed with Big Brah and looked assertively at Loni.

Loni was unimpressed. "Big Brah, I don't know why you're involved in this. I know you wouldn't be involved with anything dishonest, at least knowingly. But the PD?

"The PD must act, always, in public interest. In this case, there's simply no other reason for the search to fail. Mr. Mahio must be sheltering his son," he said.

"That's not true," Big Brah said.

"What's not true?" Loni asked, incredulous.

"Mr. Mahio isn't sheltering his son," Big Brah said.

Loni made a show of reconciling. "Okay, all right, if you say so, Big Brah. But you've been looking for Kaipo. Have you found him?"

"Unfortunately, no, not yet, but I may," Big Brah said.

"When?"

"Soon."

"How soon?"

"I can't give you a timeline." Big Brah conceded.

Loni thumped the top of his desk, triumphant. "No timeline. Why? Because you work for Mr. Mahio. But I work for the people, the public. I can't not act."

Duke Mahio recovered his voice, but he sounded shaky. "What is it you want to do?" he said.

Loni shifted his gaze from Big Brah to Mahio. "There is one other reason the search has failed," he said.

Jim Bordeta wanted Loni to focus just on

Duke Mahio. He slouched in his chair. "No!" he said, loudly and face-palmed, again.

Duke Mahio looked exhausted. "What is this reason?" he asked.

Loni tugged at the ends of his mustache, thinking. "Normally, when we search for persons of interest, in a case, the response we get isn't as much as if we search for the criminal. Let's say, someone, not you, someone else is hiding Kaipo."

Jim Bordeta's hopes of nailing Duke Mahio were dimming.

Loni said, "As long as this person thinks Kaipo is just a person of interest, he or she doesn't bother much. But as soon as this person learns Kaipo is a wanted criminal, he or she now faces the added pressure of harboring a criminal. This person may succumb, call the information hotline."

"So what are you saying?" Mahio said.

"What I'm saying is, because of your standing with the chief, we were deliberately soft. We searched for Kaipo as a person of interest. Now, I don't know whether you know the whereabouts of your son.

"But, you've hired Big Brah here to find him, and even Big Brah can't find Kaipo. So, we'll continue to search for Kaipo again, but this time, we'll advertise we're looking for a thief, a kidnapper, a killer, a criminal," Loni said.

Duke Mahio was aghast. Wordlessly, he rocked in his chair. Hopeful again, Jim Bordeta sat up.

Loni said, "Rightfully, the public has to be warned, as soon as possible, such a dangerous character is at large."

Duke Mahio sat silenced.

Once again, Big Brah rescued him. "Criminal? How can you call Kaipo a criminal? There's no proof he's a thief, kidnapper or killer," he said.

Loni slammed the top of his desk and got up, fuming. "I have proof." He planted his palms on the table and glared down at Big Brah. "I found his bracelet next to the dead body, didn't I? What more proof do you want?"

"Motive. Kaipo has no real reason to murder Helen Hokui," Big Brah said.

"Of course, he has motive."

"How?" Big Brah said.

Loni said, "Let me remind you, Big Brah, Kaipo fought with Helen Hokui on Thursday night. He threatened to kill her."

"People say things. They don't always do those things," Big Brah said.

"Kaipo wanted to rob the Mahio safe. He wanted Helen to join him. She said no. He threatened to kill her," Loni said.

"Like I said, a threat doesn't always translate into action," Big Brah said.

"No, it doesn't, but it can evoke a response," Loni said.

Big Brah looked taken aback. "What response?" he said.

Loni gazed smugly down at Big Brah. "I know for sure Helen Hokui agreed to rob the safe with Kaipo," he said.

Duke Mahio frowned. He shot a worried glance at Big Brah. He was still thinking of the surveillance video.

Big Brah took a deep breath. "How can you be so sure?" he said.

Dramatically, Loni slid a drawer open on his side of the desk and produced a zip lock bag from it. Inside the plastic bag was an amazing necklace. Platinum embedded with sparkling diamonds in the shapes of a sea turtle, dolphin and octopus.

"The goddess help us!" Duke Mahio exclaimed. "That necklace belongs to Luana, it was her favorite. I'd recognize the turtle, the dolphin, the octopus any day."

Loni looked pleased. "The victim wore a scarf. Underneath, I found the necklace. She was wearing it. At first, I didn't think it was significant. But as soon as I learned the fight was over robbing the safe, I deduced this necklace was going to be important evidence.

"This means Helen did end up robbing the safe with Kaipo. Otherwise, how would she have possession of this necklace? But Kaipo, he killed her, so he could have it all. But, you know how it is? Kaipo got everything else, but this one necklace eluded him, because she hid it from him."

Loni sat down. "And therefore, Kaipo had an excellent motive for killing Helen Hokui," he said.

Big Brah picked up the bag and showed the necklace to Duke Mahio. "You sure this is from the safe?" he said.

"Yes, yes, I'm sure," Duke Mahio said.

Big Brah sat silenced. Loni kept smiling and nodding, clearly enjoying the silence.

At last, Loni grew solemn. "I must act, Mr. Mahio, to protect the general public, of course, from a criminal like Kaipo," he said.

And a criminal like you, Mr. Mahio, for harboring Kaipo, Loni didn't say.

Loni raised index and middle fingers splayed apart in the air. "Two more days, the police will search for Kaipo, but as a wanted criminal," he glanced at Jim Bordeta, "and Nohea with him. If we find him, great. If not, I will have to take further action. What that will be, I don't know. Chief and I, we'll be meeting to decide. I suggest, all of you be back, in this room, at ten sharp on Friday morning," he said.

Big Brah, Kali, Duke Mahio and I left Jim Bordeta with Loni, so Loni and Jim Bordeta could brood about Duke Mahio. Outside, the bright afternoon sunshine bathed the parking lot. We made our way back to our rides. We got to Duke Mahio's yellow sports car first.

Duke Mahio adjusted his business-like glasses and looked at Big Brah. "I can't believe this. Kaipo and Helen. My son, my employee. He convinces her to rob the safe with him, then Kaipo heartlessly kills Helen for all the jewelry. Why? The jewelry belonged to him, he didn't have to do this," he said.

Big Brah nodded. "There's something wrong," he said.

Duke Mahio said, "But the evidence is there. The necklace Helen Hokui was wearing, when she died, I'm sure it was stolen from the safe. She couldn't be wearing the necklace, unless she had robbed the safe with Kaipo. I didn't even talk about the surveillance video during the meeting, but you and I know it exists, and Kaipo and Helen are in it."

Big Brah said, "I have my doubts both about Loni's interpretation of the jewelry found on Helen Hokui and about the surveillance video."

Duke Mahio sighed and shook his head. His shoulders slumped. "But Kaipo's bracelet was found next to the body. They're going to look for Kaipo as a wanted criminal. Somehow, I feel as if I've let down his mother, my Luana. It's all right for Jim Bordeta to be so belligerent, he has a partner, a wife, while I have to do this alone. What do you think will happen?" he said.

Big Brah placed a supportive hand on Duke Mahio's shoulder. "I can imagine how you're feeling. Unfortunately, hearing he's being accused of murder will only make Kaipo hide more fiercely. But rest assured, we're working very hard, we'll prove Kaipo innocent," he said.

Somewhat reassured, Duke Mahio got into the yellow sports car. He waved. "I'm counting on you," he said.

Big Brah, Kali and I watched the yellow sports car leave. *To prove Kaipo innocent will be a big task*, I thought.

# Chapter 14 Definite imposter

Big Brah, Kali and I got back in the big, black truck. Big Brah started the truck. He had a surprise next step. "Cosplay's showroom is nearby. I want to find Hades. He has gone camping. Agamemnon may know if his uncle had any favorite camping ground," he said.

There was another surprise at the Cosplay storefront. The front door had a "Closed" sign on it. Yesterday, the uncle, and today, Agamemnon. Both gone. Creepy.

What was going on? Guilt, no doubt. Without a word, Big Brah turned the truck back. We headed toward the coastal highway.

"Where we going?" I asked.

"2332 Waihale," Big Brah said, "I have an idea."

Goody, another Big Brah idea. All the way to the rain-soaked neighborhood, Big Brah didn't explain his idea. In a situation such as this one, creepy and mysterious, both Kali and I knew better than to ask. He did ask I run a search on my phone for the owner of Cosplay.

I did. "Hades Akapalua, sole proprietor," I read

out.

Some relief. At least Agamemnon hadn't lied about that, otherwise it would have been too creepy.

"No mention of Agamemnon, he must be an employee," I said.

The afternoon sky darkened. Dripping rain. The truck sped down the wet asphalt. At the black, metal mailbox with the house number on it, the truck turned into the gravel driveway. We had no idea if Agamemnon would even be home or gone like his uncle.

The neat home surrounded by ti trees came into sight. Outside the home, there was a vehicle protected by a car cover. Anywhere else on the island a car with a cover on it meant the owner had gone on a vacation.

But here, where it rained so much, without a carport or a garage, a cover could be a necessity. From the shape and size of the cover, the vehicle was likely a sedan, but I couldn't be sure. The truck came to a stop behind the covered vehicle.

Following some kind of instinct, Big Brah, Kali and I got out of the truck in the dripping rain and trekked to the back, as we had done before. With rain dripping down from the edges of its tin roof, the shed was pretty much like we had last seen it. But, a surprise.

The lights were on above the big, cluttered desk. A man dressed in a regular shirt, shorts and sandals was at work. He was in the chair. His head was bowed. His hands worked on a silicone bodysuit. At the sound of us, he raised his head our way. The blue goatee. Agamemnon.

I felt a surge of relief. Nothing creepy. Agamemnon was here.

Agamemnon raised his hand in a friendly wave. "The investigators! Good to see you again," he called out.

Big Brah, Kali and I got under the tin roof of the shed and out of the rain. Closer and under the bright light overhead, short and chubby, Agamemnon looked much the same as he had last night.

Agamemnon set aside the silicone bodysuit on top of all the clutter on the big desk. I glanced curiously at the suit he was working on. The face looked unfamiliar. Definitely not a character. That moment, I thought nothing of it.

With surprising rapidity, Agamemnon came toward us, a welcoming smile on his innocent face. He rubbed his hands together. "What can I do for you today?" he said.

Big Brah was at his friendly best. "We went to the showroom, found it closed, so here we are. Thought you said you work at the showroom, and your uncle works here."

"Yes, but with Uncle gone, I have to do everything. Uncle was supposed to finish an order today, so I'm doing it for him. I couldn't be in both places, so I closed the showroom. I'll be back there tomorrow," Agamemnon said.

"But you told us, your uncle was the senior artist. He did friends, while you worked on characters," Big Brah said.

Agamemnon shrugged. "What can I do? It's an emergency. It's true, I'm working on a friend now. I have to deliver the suit to the customer," he said.

Big Brah chuckled. Agamemnon looked on, amazed. Big Brah stepped up to the desk, picked up the unfinished bodysuit and examined it.

He peered at Agamemnon over the top of the bodysuit. "Or, is it that you're also wearing one of these suits?" he said.

Agamemnon stared slack-jawed at Big Brah. He took a step back. No words came out of him.

Big Brah dropped the unfinished bodysuit on the desk. "You're not in your twenties, as you look. Agamemnon is. You, are the uncle, so you're older, in your forties. Your bodysuit bulks you up. You are slimmer. You forget and you move too fast," he said.

Agamemnon grasped his cheeks with both hands and an expression of total horror came over his face. He took another step back, wordlessly.

Big Brah moved casually closer to him. "Your real name is Hades Akapalua. Agamemnon is, as you would say, a friend, a character of your own invention," he said.

Agamemnon didn't say a word. He continued to look horrified.

"Am I right, brah?" Big Brah chuckled.

Slowly, the look of horror on Agamemnon's face faded. "I'm sorry," he said.

Agamemnon's shoulders drooped. He looked ashamed. "I knew your reputation, I should never have tried to fool you. Don't know if you'll believe anything I now say."

I got Big Brah's idea. Trying to fool Big Brah was not a good idea.

"Just tell us the truth, brah, and you'll do just fine," Big Brah said, forgivingly.

To tell us the truth, Agamemnon, or Hades Akapalua took us into the house through the back entrance. Kitchen, storage room, bedroom, bathroom and we were in the living room.

Hades Akapalua opened the window. It had grown darker outside. More rain. He turned on the lamps in all four corners of the living room and gestured for us to sit down. "Please give me a minute to change." He disappeared into the house.

We sat down, same as before. Big Brah and Kali in the loveseat, me in the armchair. Soon, Hades Akapalua returned and sat down on the couch. No blue goatee. No beard. And a balding head. Having shed his bulk, he was slimmer and somehow taller.

But he kept his voice the same. "I've always wanted to be an actor," he said.

There was a silence. Big Brah, Kali and I watched him, waiting.

Hades Akapalua bowed his head, shook his head several times and then looked up at us again. "When I was younger, I jumped at every acting opportunity I got, I worked bit roles.

"But I wasn't going anywhere. Then, I got into these silicone bodysuits. Fired my imagination. I could be anyone I wanted, at any time.

"Soon I started making the bodysuits. At first, I made them for my own enjoyment. Then the desire in every artist, to share, hit me. I came to this island, started Cosplay.

"It felt good to see others get a thrill out of what I already found exciting, Cosplay. Life was good. Then, on the first day of this month, April Fool's day, a customer arrived at the showroom.

"From the very beginning, I knew this person was trouble. He or she was in a silicone bodysuit," he said.

"You couldn't tell whether it was a man or a woman?" Big Brah asked.

"No, but the bodysuit was that of a man."

"Interesting, how did he look like?" Big Brah said.

"Short hair with a bald patch, bushy eyebrows, clean shaven," Hades Akapalua said.

"Hold on." Instinctively I pulled out the mini sketchpad I always carried around from the pocket of my cargo shorts. Big Brah, Kali and Hades Akapalua looked on. I sketched the man Hades Akapalua had just described.

I got answers for a few more questions: shape

of face, round, nose, regular, eyes, small, chin, double, clothes he wore, shirt, jeans, sneakers, and all the while, I kept sketching furiously. His experience with bodysuits apparent, Hades Akapalua was understandably very precise with the details. When I was done, I held up the sketch for them to see.

Hades Akapalua looked impressed. "Yes, I'd say that's him. But, remember, it was first April, so I thought initially, the bodysuit was a prank on me," he said.

I was engrossed by his story. "Wait a minute, we couldn't tell your bodysuit, so how did you know this person was in a silicone bodysuit?" I asked.

"Good question. The answer's simple. His bodysuit wasn't half as good as mine. It was the work of an amateur, himself. He could fool others, but with my experience, I could see through it easily. He knew he wasn't as good at it, so he'd come to me.

"Now, I deal with cosplay enthusiasts all the time. I know them. Smart. Big imagination. Not this person.

"I got different vibes. Dumb. No imagination. Just focused on a selfish motive. I know his type."

There was a silence. I knew the type he was talking about. Selfishness made everything stink.

Hades Akapalua sighed. "I told you about the trouble I got into on my home island. I wasn't making it up. I got mixed up with the wrong crowd of shameless, selfish people, I know them only too well.

"I tried to get rid of the customer, but he insisted. He wanted a customized bodysuit, a friend. I told him, he'd have to get out of the bodysuit he was in so I could get measurements, and he laughed at my concern.

"Told me to assume the bodysuit he wore didn't change his dimensions. I told him I'd need a photograph of his friend. He laughed at that too, told me his friend was imaginary, but he'd tell me how he looked.

"I didn't believe him, but there wasn't much I could do to refuse service. He got his wish a couple days later, I delivered the bodysuit he wanted to him.

"Long story short, the bodysuit I made for him, the face, the torso, unfortunately, has a strong resemblance to someone in the news recently." Hades Akapalua stopped, shaking his head.

"Kaipo Mahio," Big Brah said.

Hades Akapalua stopped shaking his head. "That's right," he said.

"Did he give a name, this customer?" Big Brah said.

"No name, paid cash, I told him he could come back if there was a problem with fitting. Never returned. I figured he knew enough to make changes himself."

"Is there any way for you to recognize this customer?" Big Brah said.

Hades Akapalua shook his head. "I believe the sole purpose of the bodysuit he wore was to make sure I didn't recognize him, if we were to meet again. He succeeded."

"His voice?" Big Brah said.

"Possibly, but I suspect he was altering his voice, again to hide, each time he talked with me," Hades Akapalua said.

Darn. I got the feeling our time here was being wasted.

But Big Brah smiled. "Why did you make up Agamemnon?" he said.

"When I saw the photographs of Kaipo Mahio associated with the murder, I knew I was in trouble of some sorts. I knew someone would come asking questions, suspecting. I was tired of having my life disrupted.

"I told you about the corrupt private investigator who pinned the blame for the crime on me. It was a minor offense, and I got off easy, but I hated all private investigators. I was wary of them. Agamemnon was so perfect.

"I combined my love for acting with my love for making these suits, and kept my life from being disrupted. I was disguised as my nephew, but I still hadn't decided on a name. Then I saw you, and it just came to me, Agamemnon. By the way, call me Hades," he said.

"Okay, Hades. Is there a way for you to

recognize the bodysuit you made of Kaipo Mahio, if someone else was wearing it?" Big Brah said.

"As a matter of fact, yes. Look, Big Brah, I wouldn't tell anyone else, but you've been kind, understanding and completely nonjudgmental, so I'll tell you. I don't always do this, but I told you I got bad vibes from this person, so I added a mole at the top of the right ear, so I could identify the suit, always. People rarely notice such a detail, but I know," he said.

Big Brah took out the agency phone. Kali and I craned over his shoulders. Big Brah played the first video of Kaipo with Helen Hokui. An image of the top of Kaipo's head.

Big Brah paused the video and made the picture larger. The right ear. The top of the ear. A tiny black blemish. My heart missed a beat.

I blinked to make sure I wasn't imagining it. But, the black mark stayed. Sure enough, there was a mole!

Big Brah showed Hades the picture. "Is this the mole you added?" he asked.

Hades took a long look at the picture and nodded. "Yes, my work," he said.

Swiftly, Big Brah started the second video. Kaipo alone, this time. Another image of the top of Kaipo's head. The top of the right ear. The mole.

Big Brah showed Hades the new picture. "Are you sure?" he said.

"See the curve of the ear, I remember exactly

where I added the mole, where it is in both the pictures. So yes, I'm sure," Hades said.

Big Brah, Kali and I exchanged looks. Wow. A huge break. Our time with Hades hadn't been wasted after all. Big Brah showed him the picture of the bead bracelet with the stylized gold plate.

Hades shook his head. "I rarely sell bracelets, unless it's part of the costume. But I can tell you where it's from. Jewelry Quartet. Just a few shops away from Cosplay's showroom. They're into selling jewelry."

I tucked the mini sketchpad away. Big Brah got up. Kali and I followed. I had no doubt our next destination was going to be downtown. Jewelry Quartet.

Big Brah gazed down at Hades. "Mahalo for all your help, brah. I'll make sure no one bothers you about this. And next time, will you promise not to assume all of us are corrupt?" he said.

"I promise," Hades said, contritely, "but before you leave, will you truthfully answer my question?"

"Sure," Big Brah said.

Hades got up from the couch to stand with us. "The question is important because I pride myself both in acting and making costumes. What clued you in to Agamemnon?" Hades asked.

Big Brah laughed. "The name." He ruffled my hair fondly. "Akamai here remembered Agamemnon commanded the Greek army that fought the Trojan War to free Helen of Troy. Perhaps, the name came to you, because you too had an association with a different Helen, the victim, Helen Hokui. In any case, I figured the name was made up. And if the name was made up, the rest of you was made up too," he said.

For the first time that afternoon, Hades looked happy. "So it wasn't the acting or the bodysuit that gave it away," he said.

Big Brah shook his head, always eager to make a good person feel better. "No. The acting was masterful."

"The costume was a masterpiece," Kali said.

Hades broke into a grin. "If there's anything else I can do, just let me know."

Big Brah, Kali and I headed out of the rain zone in the big, black truck. I let out a loud cheehoo!

Big Brah couldn't stop chuckling. Kali just gazed and gazed at him in open admiration. I was happy. The case was a hard coconut cracked open. What was inside?

The thief in the surveillance video was not Kaipo but an imposter. My mind raced. Who could it be? The person had to be friends with Helen Hokui. They had been in the video together.

I remembered visiting her home. Her brother, Randy Hokui had told us he was his sister's friend and confidante. Surely, he could have been the imposter. But then, I remembered something important. The person in the video hadn't limped.

Randy Hokui couldn't walk without a limp or a walking stick. So yes, I had no idea who the person was, but I hoped Big Brah and Kali would figure it out. Soon, Big Brah drove the truck down a sunny stretch of downtown, our destination Jewelry Quartet.

The slanted rays of the late afternoon sun fell on the store front. Big Brah parked the big, black truck outside. We got out, the day warm around us. Big Brah and Kali held hands. The Jewelry Quartet was a mom-and-pop shop.

The quartet referred to the couple's four children, two boys and two girls. The shop had a glass front and a display with its name painted on the glass in red. The glass door had an "Open" sign on it. I followed Big Brah and Kali into the shop.

The shop was a big rectangular room with a regular ceiling. My feet sank into the softness of the carpet. The temperature was several degrees cooler here. The air had the pleasant smell of an air freshener. The fragrance of plumeria.

The glass wall had thick curtains. Daylight streamed in through a couple of windows at the back. Under the windows, the matriarch, Weimana and the four children sat on cushions around a long table with short legs. After school the entire family was in the shop. At the sight of us, they waved but kept crafting jewelry.

We were regulars here. The lights were on in the many glass cabinets, illuminating exquisite displays. Necklaces, lockets, leis, bracelets, rings, earrings, ankle bracelets, bangles, they were all there. The patriarch, Manama had a contented look on his fierce face. A nice, round paunch testified to the contentment.

Manama approached us with a smile. "Big Brah, Kali, Umi, good to see you again," he said.

"We're here on business today," Big Brah explained, "we're investigating the boat murder."

Manama's broad brow furrowed. "Is it about the bead bracelet?" he said.

"Yes."

Manama took a step back and folded his arms. "But I've already told the police everything," he said.

"Mind telling us what you told them, brah," Big Brah said.

Manama rubbed his chin with a knuckle, thoughtfully. "Let me see, where to begin. Oh, yeah, Lieutenant Loni was here the other day. He showed me the bracelet, confided it had been found next to the dead body.

"I recognized the bracelet, immediately. I had sold it, only last week. I told Loni that, and he was interested. Loni asked me about the buyer. Now, I usually don't talk about my customers with nobody, but this was a police case. A murder, so I decided to tell Loni everything.

"I told Loni, a man with a head of curly hair

and a mustache had come into the shop looking for a bracelet. The man looked affluent, familiar. I recognized him.

"He was Duke Mahio's son. I am active in the local chamber of commerce. I see Duke Mahio often. The family resemblance was obvious, but I couldn't remember his name.

"I showed him a lot of bracelets. He didn't like any of them. Finally, he picked up a bead bracelet with a gold plate. 'Can I have it stylized, my name on it' he asked. I was happy to, so I asked for his name. Kaipo.

"I got it done for him, told him the stylizing was free, but the bracelet cost $200. Then, Kaipo did the rudest thing, an act that had no aloha. He took the bracelet from me and ran out of the shop.

"I shouted after him. But he didn't stop. He'd parked his car somewhere close to make a fast getaway. I was so shocked. This has never happened on the island. It took me a while to get to the front door. By then, Kaipo was gone," Manama said.

"Did you tell anyone else about it?" Big Brah asked.

Manama shook his head. "No. I didn't want to, I was too shocked. How could Duke Mahio's son, clearly rich, father owns a mall, how could such a man steal, for a mere two hundred dollars? I wasn't going to bother anyone, but the matter was still in my head. Then I heard in the news what he did with the boat, the woman dead. Finally, Loni comes and tells me all. Why am I not surprised?" he said.

Big Brah took out his phone, played the video and zoomed in on the bracelet for Manama to see. "Do you recognize it?" Big Brah said.

Manama peered at the picture, carefully. "That stylization, I did it myself. Note the whirl I put at the top of the K, you can't miss it. Yup, that's the bracelet I sold Kaipo," he said.

Manama had sold the bracelet to Kaipo or to the imposter in a silicone bodysuit made by Hades? There was only one way to find out.

Big Brah said, "While he was trying out the bracelets, you must have had a chance to look at Kaipo closely. Did you observe a mole at the top of his right ear?"

Manama grinned. "Funny you should say that. He tried out a clip-on ear stud. He had difficulty putting it on, so I helped him. It was his right ear too. Sure, there was a mole on top of the ear," he said.

Big break. Big Brah, Kali and I looked at each other animatedly. We would talk about the mole later. Big Brah thanked Manama. Big Brah took out his wallet and extracted a couple of c-notes.

He handed the c-notes to Manama. "I'm sorry about Kaipo's misbehavior. This payment is late, that's all," he said.

Manama took the c-notes. "If you say so, Big Brah. You know Weimana, me and the children, we have a lot of respect, a lot of aloha for you all, as a family," he said.

Family to family respect. Pure aloha. Big Brah, Kali and I waved goodbye to Weimana and the children on our way out of there.

Back inside the big, black truck, Big Brah said, "Kaipo or imposter?"

"Imposter," Kali said.

"Definite imposter," I said.

Big Brah nodded, approvingly. "The imposter procured the suit from Hades. Then he used the suit as a disguise to steal the bracelet from Manama," he said.

Evil imposter.

I had to ask the question. "Who can the imposter be?"

Big Brah started the truck. "Whoever it is has to be friends with Helen Hokui."

Kali agreed. "She was with the imposter in the video."

Big Brah said, "It's time we visited her office, see if anyone there knows anything about her secret friend," he said.

The truck backed and then rolled forward, our destination Helen Hokui's office. I frowned all the way to Mahio Plaza.

The mall front had a big neon sign with "Mahio Plaza" in red. The property manager's office was at the back. We left the truck in the big parking lot. The sky was red from the setting sun. The lights had started to come on.

On Wednesday evening, midweek, the mall was mostly empty and quiet. The exception was the food court.

As we made our way past the food court, the aroma of food, curry, barbecue and grilled fish filled my nostrils. People chattered and laughed, sitting around the tables in the courtyard. The lights were on in the property manager's office.

Big Brah grabbed the handle of the big, glass door with the words "Property Manager" on it. He looked at Kali and me. "Ready?" he said.

# Chapter 15 A wanderer, a free spirit

Kali nodded.

I said, "Yes."

Big Brah swung the door open. We entered a carpeted double office. The ceiling had lights over each office. A partition hid the other side. On the wall above the partition, a clock displayed the time. The clock was presumably visible from both offices. A desk faced the partition.

A big framed photograph of a couple standing together adorned the top of the desk. The man was lanky and supported himself with a walking stick. With his untrimmed beard, Randy Hokui was instantly recognizable. Standing next to him, the tall woman with black hair had to be his sister, Helen Hokui, and this was her desk. In the framed photograph, Randy and Helen Hokui had the red neon sign of Mahio Plaza behind them. They had made it good here. Grinning at the camera, they looked happy. A head peeked from behind the partition.

A woman with salt and pepper hair and

rectangular glasses said, "Can I help you?"

Big Brah introduced us and told her we were investigating the murder of Helen Hokui.

She came around the partition, revealing a slim, fit figure inside a frilly office dress and platform heels. "Helen, poor girl, can't believe she died the way she did. She was my coworker, we shared this office. My name is Sherry Nemy, I am the other property manager. Helen and I, we shared duties. I have been here, like forever. Helen was new, I was getting her up to speed, she depended on me for a lot of things," she said.

"That means you have a lot to tell us," Kali said.

"I was finishing up, getting ready to leave," Sherry said.

Kali looked at Big Brah and me, and we nodded promptly, guessing what she had in mind.

Kali looked back at Sherry. "Then you must be hungry," she said.

Sherry smiled, wanly. "I live alone, I usually pick up dinner from the food court," she said.

Kali said, "We're also hungry. Would you mind if we all went to the food court, ate and talked story?"

Sherry smiled. "Not at all," she said.

At the food court, we lined up to order. It wasn't a big line. Soon we had our dinner plates and drink containers on disposable trays.

Kali insisted on paying for all of us. Sherry

protested.

Kali said, "After all, we're investigating. We wouldn't want you to be hungry talking to us."

Sherry gave in. We carried our food trays to the open-air part of the lively courtyard. This part of the courtyard had fewer people dining. It was quieter and easier to have a conversation. The sky had lost its redness and turned gray.

Bright lights fringed the courtyard, illuminating everything. The ocean breeze had started, making the surroundings pleasant. We set our trays down on an empty table and sat down.

Big Brah had a steaming bowl of saimin, a noodle soup that was a local favorite and a sandwich to go with it. I had chicken *katsu*, breaded chicken, another local favorite, and fried noodles. Kali had *ono* fish and fried rice. Sherry Nemy had a bento box with shrimp tempura and salmon musubis.

Big Brah and I volunteered to go get the drinks. We had a surprise consensus. Green tea, for everyone. Then we settled down to talk story. I was ready to learn more about Helen Hokui. See if we could figure out who was impersonating Kaipo with her. I ate the chicken katsu and fried noodles with gusto. The food tasted surprisingly good. Big Brah sat across from me.

Big Brah spooned saimin into his mouth, gulped it down and glanced diagonally across at Sherry Nemy. "Tell us about Helen. What kind of coworker was she?" he said.

Sitting to my left, Sherry Nemy finished chewing on a shrimp tempura. "Helen was a sincere worker. I liked her. I know Duke also liked her. I don't think we ever thought something so bizarre would ever happen," she said.

Big Brah, Kali and I ate our food, listening to her intently.

Sherry Nemy sipped green tea. "She was new to the island, didn't have many friends, her work was her social life. Her brother, Randy, he came to pick her up after work sometimes. He has a bad leg, needs a walking stick. He complained walking on the mall concrete hurt his leg, but it didn't stop him from coming. He was the only family she had. They were fond of each other. But Helen had needs. You know, after work, she saw another man," she said.

Kali set her fork down. "So it wasn't only her brother who was picking Helen up in the evenings," she said.

Sherry Nemy picked up a musubi and rolled its wrapper down. "That's right! There was this man who she was seeing, for a while. I remember him. He was balding, and he had bushy eyebrows," she said.

Big Brah, Kali and I looked at each other. Sounded like the man who had bought the Kaipo bodysuit from Hades. Big Brah nodded briefly at me. I whipped out my sketch pad. I showed the sketch to Sherry Nemy.

Sherry Nemy giggled. "Why, yes, that's him, you know him already?" she said.

I shook my head. "No, not really. I just sketched him from someone's description," I said.

"That's a good sketch, very lifelike. You have serious talent, Umi," she said, with an approving nod.

I sensed an art lover in Sherry Nemy. I would have asked her about it, but the investigation was more important. I did not know I would be learning about her love for art and artist soon. "Mahalo," I said.

"What was his name, this man?" Big Brah asked.

"Bran. I never got a last name," she said.

"Bran," Kali repeated.

Sherry Nemy took a bite of the musubi. She chewed and swallowed. "Yes. Bran. He used to come almost every evening. He was always punctual, he showed up at closing time. They didn't talk much inside the office. I can hear everything from the other side. Just hellos, and how have you been, but I could tell they were intimate," she said.

"Intimate? How could you tell?" Kali asked.

"Funny, isn't it? Coming from me, I've never been married, never really been intimate with any man or woman. But, I grew up in a big household with brothers, sisters, uncles, aunts, grandparents, I had plenty opportunity to observe couples being intimate in the middle of a whole bunch of people. It's just in the way you say things, or the things you don't say. I can't explain, I just know." She laughed.

Kali laughed too. "Okay, I believe you," she said.

Big Brah and I smiled and ate in silence.

Sherry Nemy said, "Helen and me, we used to come to this food court for lunch. So, one day, I asked her about Bran. Who is this man who comes picks you up every evening? At first, she was coy. I joked with her. I told her what I just told you, I told her I knew she was intimate with him. It made her even more hesitant, and I enjoyed it. I won't lie. When you're a confirmed single like me, these are the things that please you." Sherry Nemy ate another bite of her musubi.

"So what did Helen say to you?" Kali prompted.

"She told me, Bran works at a bank, and yes, she liked him. I asked her if she was seeing him on the weekends also, and guess what she told me?"

Sherry was getting to the juicy part.

Sherry said, "Yes, she was! Now, if a couple see each other over the weekend, they'd be intimate, don't you think? So, I teased her some more about it. Of course, I didn't tease her too much, this is a workplace, she could be offended. But she was sporting and didn't take any offense. In fact, the very next day, after she had told me about Bran, she asked if I'd like to go to the food court for lunch, and I agreed. We became friends." She took the last bite of the musubi and dropped the wrapper on the disposable tray.

"Did you ever get to talk to Bran?" Kali asked.

Sherry Nemy adjusted the rectangular glasses on her nose. "Yes, I did. There was this one time, Helen was in a meeting elsewhere. The meeting was unexpectedly running late, so she wasn't in the office. It had been a tiring day. I looked up at the wall clock, it was closing time. I took off my glasses, I was rubbing my temples, when I heard the door open.

"I got up to take a look. Without my glasses, I couldn't see like normal, but I'm not entirely blind. Bran was standing awkwardly, staring at the framed photograph Helen had of herself and her brother on her desk.

"I told him Helen was late due to a meeting, she'd be back soon, and he looked grateful. Did he need a drink, or anything? He shook his head, told me he'd take a walk around the mall.

"I figured he worked at a bank, probably sat all day, he needed the exercise. He came back after Helen returned, and she was extra apologetic, whispered she'd make it up to him," she said.

"Did you ever see them together outside the office?" Kali said.

"Funny you should ask, but I did see them together, many times. I told you, I buy dinner and take it home from here. Well, Helen and Bran often sat here in the courtyard and ate dinner," Sherry said.

"How were they together, you must have observed," Kali said.

Sherry giggled. "Oh, I observed Helen and Bran all right. It's what I live for. I'd wave to them, if they saw me, and they waved back. But most of the time, they'd be sitting at a table, across from each other and...."

"And?" Kali prompted, helpfully.

"And they'd be eating and they couldn't stop looking at each other, you know? So romantic. I told her about it. Don't you guys talk, or do you just worship each other, I teased her. By then, she had lost her initial hesitation. She told me, Bran was the most attentive man she'd ever met," Sherry said.

"Did she talk about the future? Of what they would do together?" Kali said.

"Once or twice. At work, you can't talk too freely about relationships. If anything, Helen knew the rules of the workplace. So she never talked about the future in that way. But what I got from her, she wanted to be with Bran. Bran wanted to be with her. They'd work out a future together," Sherry said.

"Did she mention where he lived?" Kali said.

Sherry frowned, thinking. "I can't remember her mentioning it." Then, she giggled. "But I asked her," she said.

"You asked her where he lived, what did she say?" Kali said.

Sherry said, "He lived in the same neighborhood she lived in with her brother. That's how they met, at the park. Both of them sat under the same tree, alone, until they started talking. Helen hadn't been around long. I got the feeling neither had Bran. Perhaps, since they were both new, trying for friends, they bonded. Strange are the ways of love, don't you think?"

Kali smiled. "Strange for sure, but do you think she was really in love with him?" she said.

"I believe Helen was in love with Bran." Sherry looked up at the stars that had started to appear in the night sky. "I hope Helen's up there, somewhere, making peace with what happened to her, here on the island."

Amen. The stars were all out in the night sky, by the time Big Brah, Kali and I said mahalo and goodbye to Sherry Nemy and returned to the big, black truck. While the police searched for Kaipo, we now had a different search. Bran.

Two clues. Bran worked at a bank. He lived in the same crowded neighborhood we had visited to meet Randy Hokui. I had an intuition about what we were going to do next.

Big Brah confirmed my intuition. "It's late, but we're fed, so we can work, right?" he said.

"Yes!" Kali said.

"Cheehoo." I called out from the backseat.

Big Brah nodded, approvingly. "This mystery

has become too interesting now to let go," he said.

Kali and I waited. I breathed shallow, waiting for what I knew he was going to say.

Big Brah drummed the steering wheel. "If anyone else knows anything about Bran, that person is going to be Randy Hokui. After all, he's told us he was his sister's friend and confidante. Helen Hokui impressed Sherry, a coworker. Surely, Helen Hokui must have confided in her brother about her love. So, how about we pay him a visit?"

"Makes sense," Kali said, right away.

"Cheehoo," I said.

Big Brah started the truck. "This will also give us an opportunity to scope out the neighborhood where Bran lives," he said.

Kali said, "Our chief suspect is Bran."

"I agree," I said.

Big Brah drove the truck out of the Mahio Plaza parking lot. "I know it's late to pay someone a visit, but these are special circumstances. Even Randy Hokui will want his sister's killer found. He's probably in the living room armchair, drinking beer from a tall can and watching the small TV on the corner table. Hopefully he won't mind," he said.

Kali gave Big Brah's profile her admiring look. "Especially after what you did for him this morning," she said.

"Wait, what?" I was puzzled.

Kali turned to me and smiled. "Is why I was saying this morning at breakfast, you brothers are so alike. Both of you are busy doing good deeds."

"Good deeds?" I said.

Kali rested a palm on Big Brah's arm affectionately. "While you fed the family, Li'l Brah, your big brah was on the phone, you'll see."

I sat up, alert. I was ready for this. As Big Brah had predicted, Randy Hokui was in the living room armchair. He was drinking beer from a tall can. He watched the TV on the corner table. The small TV played an old movie.

On seeing us, Randy Hokui used a remote to silence the movie. He sat with his lanky frame planted in the armchair, his walking stick propped up against the chair. We had rung the bell. Without getting up, he had told us to come in. The room around him had gone through a tremendous transformation.

The room wasn't messy or smelly. The furniture was still sparse and worn. But it smelled good in here. The room was clean of beer cans, pizza boxes, spilled beer and half-eaten pizza slices.

The floor looked good as new. There was a new rug under the coffee table. The table was clean and polished. A box of fragrant fresh-baked pizza decorated the table. The couch and loveseat looked invitingly clean. As it was in most homes in this neighborhood, the window had its blinds closed for privacy. Big Brah and Kali had no problems seating themselves in the loveseat, while I sank into the couch.

Even Randy Hokui looked better, refreshed. "Big Brah, I think I told everyone I talked to how I was missing Helen's housekeeping. The problem isn't just my leg, I can handle the limp, but I also have a problem bending. Everyone listened, but no one did anything about it, except you," he said.

Big Brah smiled and looked my way. "I called Cousin Koma," he said, explaining.

Cousin Koma ran an island-wide home cleaning business, his slogan "No mess too big to clean." I looked around the clean room. "I see his paw prints all over the place," I said.

Kali smiled. "You see," she said.

Randy Hokui watched us. "No really, Big Brah, I must say, most kind. Koma has been helping me out the entire day, personally, because, he told me, it was you who called. Koma left just an hour ago, even got me pizza and beer before leaving. I don't even know how I can pay you for this," he said.

Big Brah smiled, pleasantly. "You don't have to pay me. This is your moment of grief. I understand your sister was a good employee," he said.

Randy Hokui nodded. "So she was, so she was. I just can't believe it, Helen's gone. I can handle she's gone, she used to be out of the house often, but that she won't return? Ever?" He put a hand over the left side of his chest where his heart was and his eyes filled up with tears. "That hurts."

For a while, we sat in commiserating silence. At last, Randy Hokui stirred. He blinked back his tears. "I'm sorry, I'm getting carried away, the grief. But you're in the middle of an investigation, how's it coming along?" he said.

Big Brah folded his hands on his lap. "We're here to ask for your help in the investigation," he said.

Randy Hokui took a deep breath. "Anything," he said.

Big Brah unfolded his hands and gestured with them as he talked. "Your sister, she was seeing a man, Bran. Did she talk to you about him?" he said.

Randy Hokui nodded. "Yes, often. Why?"

"We met her coworker, Sherry Nemy," Big Brah said.

"She told you about Bran?" Randy Hokui frowned.

"Yes."

"How people like to gossip," Randy Hokui said, irritably.

Big Brah reassured him. "Oh, Sherry Nemy didn't really want to talk about it, we got it out of her," he said.

"What makes you investigate poor Helen's private life?" Randy Hokui asked.

"She was the victim of a murder. Very often a

victim's private life provides us with clues to the murderer," Big Brah explained, patiently.

"You should be going after Kaipo, not Helen," Randy Hokui said.

Big Brah spread his hands. "I'm committed to finding out who killed your sister. You can help by telling us whatever you know about Bran," he said.

Randy Hokui took a deep breath and let it out slowly. "Okay, Big Brah. I don't know why you don't believe me when I say Kaipo killed my sister, I'm sure of it. But ever since my sister and I moved to this island, I have got to know your reputation to search for the truth. I'm cooperating with you, because I wish my sister's killer be caught. In that goal, we are united," he said.

Big Brah nodded, approvingly. "I can agree with that," he said.

Randy Hokui sat up in the armchair, felt for the walking stick and found it leaning against the chair. He propped the walking stick vertically up between his feet. Clutching the walking stick, he gazed at the three of us one by one.

His gaze settled on Big Brah. "What is it you want to know about Bran?" he said.

"Everything. Let's start from the beginning," Big Brah said.

A sour look came on Randy Hokui's skin-over-bones face. "It's all the fault of this damn leg. It hurts, if I walk. I couldn't go out with Helen, when she wanted to go for a walk. So she had to go out alone. Helen got into the habit of walking to the park, sitting under a tree she liked before walking home."

Big Brah said, "How did your sister meet Bran?"

Randy Hokui said, "Bran started to join her, under the tree. Helen didn't notice him for a while, but then she became aware of him. A few days later, she told me the same man shows up every day, at the park, under the tree. We figured he lived in the neighborhood."

Big Brah said, "When did you see Bran the first time?"

Randy Hokui said, "I told Helen, if Bran bothers you, I can come along, tell him off. But she told me, no, it was okay. Bran was quiet, she rather liked him, she could handle him. Several days went by. She continued going to the park every day. One day, she returned from her evening walk, excited.

"The man had summoned up the courage to greet her. I asked her, what did you do? She laughed. Why, brah, I greeted him back, she told me. His name's Bran. We're going to be friends, you don't mind?

"I laughed too. I didn't mind. If anything, my sister was austere. I always prodded her to go out more often. I was glad she was at last meeting other people." Randy Hokui balanced the walking stick on his chair.

He leaned back in the armchair. "It was a Saturday, and it was raining hard. When evening came, Helen was disappointed, she wanted the rain to go away. But the rain kept coming. She decided to go to the park anyways.

"I didn't stop her. I knew why she wanted to go to the park. Bran. Talking to him, she had started coming back late. That evening, I waited, sitting right here, in this armchair. She was gone for a long while.

"I sat here and listened to the rain. Just when I was getting worried, the doorbell rang. Helen never rang the bell, she walked right in, so I thought what the heck, but I called out 'Come in.' Helen stood in the doorway, dripping wet, but with a smile on her face.

"Before I could say anything, she stepped inside, revealing a man standing behind her. He was a regular looking guy, I noticed his thick eyebrows right away. Like Helen, he was also soaked. He grinned from ear to ear. She introduced him. Bran.

"Bran had also decided to brave the rain to see Helen. I shooed them inside, told them to change, get warm. They went into her bedroom, didn't come out. I went to bed. I got up Sunday morning. The two of them were in the kitchen talking and laughing, sipping orange juice. Bran didn't leave until Monday morning, when they both went to work."

By this time, Randy Hokui had progressed to

leaning back in the armchair. He gazed up at the ceiling, and he talked as if to himself. "From that day on, Bran started picking Helen up from work. Sometimes, they'd go over to his place, sometimes they'd be here. I guess my presence slowed them down, they started going more and more to his place. They were in love. I asked her if she wanted to marry him. She told me, yes. She wanted to marry Bran, but she wanted to wait for him to ask her. Helen was sweet, she didn't want to rush him," he said.

Big Brah said, "Is there a way we can meet Bran?"

Randy Hokui continued to gaze at the ceiling, as if he hadn't heard Big Brah's question. Big Brah waited, patiently. Kali and I looked at each other. This was the big moment. If we could meet Bran, we had him.

At last, Randy Hokui straightened in the armchair and brought his gaze back to our level. "As you can imagine, with this bad leg, I don't get around much. Honestly, I don't know where Bran lives.

"I never asked Helen either. Obviously, they met at the park, so he must live close by. But ever since Helen's murder has been on TV, Bran hasn't once shown his face. How can he? He's probably as devastated as I am," he said, with a sniff.

Big Brah looked at me and signaled. I handed him my mini sketchbook opened up at the right page.

Big Brah got up and showed Randy Hokui the sketch. "Is this Bran?" he said.

Randy Hokui squinted at the sketch. "I think —yes, that's him!" he said.

Big Brah returned to the loveseat and sat down next to Kali.

Randy Hokui studied Big Brah. "Are you looking for Bran, because you think he murdered my sister?" he said.

"Yes," Big Brah said.

"Impossible."

"Impossible?"

Randy Hokui said, "Yes, impossible. Bran wasn't the violent kind. He was a wanderer, a free spirit. If I'd thought he had anything to do with my sister's murder, I'd have called the police at once. But, it wasn't the case. Bran was broken by Helen's death, no way could he have killed her. He loved her. I'm telling you, you're chasing after the wrong man. Sorry. Go after Kaipo, he's the real killer."

# Chapter 16 Anticipation
## is everything

Big Brah got up, and Kali rose with him. I got on my feet. Big Brah thanked Randy Hokui politely, and we left, disappointed.

His face grim, Big Brah drove the big, black truck out of the crowded neighborhood. I gazed out of the window. The streets. The neon of the local mart and the gas station. A few people crossed the road at the traffic lights. The darkness of the park.

Kali sounded puzzled. "Randy Hokui still thinks Kaipo is guilty," she said.

Both Big Brah and I glanced her way to see what she was getting at.

Sometimes when she was with us, Kali did her thinking aloud. As was the case this time. "Oh, Bran knows we have the surveillance video. But he doesn't know we have Hades' testimony to prove the thief impersonated Kaipo," she said.

Big Brah nodded, approvingly, as he drove. "Yes, even if Randy Hokui thinks Bran is innocent, Bran is still our chief suspect."

"Bran and Helen stole the jewelry," I said.

Kali said, "They planned the robbery in advance. First, they established Bran with a bodysuit, so no one knew how Bran really looked like."

I said, "At work they fooled Sherry Nemy. At home Randy Hokui and at Cosplay, they fooled Hades Akapalua. What happened to Bran and Helen Hokui to end this way?"

Big Brah said, "They used the bodysuit not just to hide Bran's true identity, but also to frame Kaipo for the Mahio safe heist."

Cunning greed.

Big Brah said, "After their heist of the Mahio safe, Helen and Bran had a fallout. Jealousy took over. Likely Bran wanted all the jewelry for himself. It's a lot of money."

Kali and I chorused, "Bran killed Helen."

Big Brah said, "Yup, we're still looking for Bran."

I was inspired. "Our new problem is finding the suspect. His name's Bran, he lives in this neighborhood. Bran works in a bank, but we don't know how he really looks like, since he's always been in disguise. So there's no way a normal person can find him, but then we're not normal," I said.

Big Brah immediately proved we were not normal, by saying, "Let's go home. I have an idea."

We returned home. I was tired but inspired.

Big Brah wasn't done yet. He led Kali and me into the office. With the lights on and the windows open for fresh air, we sat down in our places. What was Big Brah going to do?

He surprised both Kali and me by calling Cousin Koma and requesting him to come over. We shouldn't have been surprised though. It was true Cousin Koma ran an island-wide home cleaning business successfully. But it was a small island. There were only that many homes to clean that many times.

Whenever Big Brah needed him, Cousin Koma eagerly moonlighted as a detective. He often worked with us on investigations, carrying out tasks Big Brah assigned him. Never failed, Cousin Koma always delivered. His cleaning business provided the perfect cover for covert work. Such as finding Bran without alarming the perp.

In fifteen minutes, we heard Cousin Koma drive up to the house no doubt in one of his white cleaning vans. In a couple more minutes, Cousin Koma was in the visitor's chair. Along with his home cleaning business' slogan, no mess too big to clean, Cousin Koma had a few other identifying features.

For example, the mane of orange hair and the flowing white beard he took great pains to maintain. It made him look, well, unique. Otherwise, he was a small man of slight build with a deep, resonant voice.

Always laidback, he settled back in the visitor's chair, his eyes half-closed. "You called, Big Brah?" he said.

"Yes, brah. Mahalo for the job you did today with Randy Hokui."

Cousin Koma said, "Randy Hokui needed help with the cleaning. He limps, he can't bend, he has bad legs. He doesn't move much."

Big Brah said, "I hope you'll continue with him. We just came back from seeing Randy. Randy, he was plenty pleased with your work, so mahalo, again."

Cousin Koma stroked his flowing beard. He did this, whenever he was pleased. "Mahalo, Big Brah, it's always a pleasure running errands for you," he said.

"Koma, I need you to do one more thing." Big Brah signaled to me.

I brought him my mini sketch book showing the page I had sketched Bran.

Big Brah showed the sketch to Cousin Koma. "His name's Bran. He lives in the same neighborhood as Randy Hokui. He works at a bank. Can you find him?" he said.

Cousin Koma took the sketch book from Big Brah and gazed at the sketch through his half-closed eyes for a long moment.

Then, he set the sketchbook down on the tidy desktop. "Who's he?" he said.

Big Brah explained the situation to him. Cousin Koma's eyes opened all the way to normal.

He took another good look at the sketch. "So, this is the murderer," he said, almost to himself.

I had sketched the murderer. I shivered.

Cousin Koma said, "I'm gonna need a picture on my phone, is that cool?"

I nodded silently. Wordlessly, Cousin Koma used his phone camera to get some clear images of my sketch of Bran. Big Brah waited patiently.

At last, Cousin Koma gazed up at Big Brah. "How long do I have?" he said.

Big Brah shrugged, still silent.

"I suppose that means as soon as possible," Cousin Koma said.

"Yes," Big Brah said.

"I'll find him. I'll let you know soon as I have something," Cousin Koma said.

After Cousin Koma left that night, the mystery bothering me, I tossed and turned in bed for a long time. I slept in. I got up late to the strong aroma of butter-fried salmon floating up from the kitchen. I stretched and got out of bed. I had a feeling today was going to be a busy day. I found Big Brah and Kali in the kitchen.

Poli`ahu and Wiliwili slumbered in their chairs at the kitchen table. On the table, there were three big bowls of steaming rice topped with fried salmon, two soft-boiled eggs and sautéed mushrooms.

Her hair all curls, Kali greeted me with a grin. "Perfect timing, Umi. We just finished making breakfast," she said.

In a loose tank-top, shorts and floppy slippers, Big Brah tousled my hair affectionately. "C'mon, let's eat," he said.

We sat down in front of the steaming bowls. For a while, we ate in silence. Big Brah and Kali had butter-fried the salmon to perfection. The fish tasted delicious with the soupy rice. I savored the eggs and mushrooms.

To honor the yummy breakfast, Big Brah smacked his lips satisfied. "Umi, Kali and I have been talking story," he said.

"Talking story. What's the tea?" I said.

Kali said, "Kaipo didn't steal the jewelry. The fake Kaipo, disguised as Bran stole the jewelry. We have evidence."

"Agreed."

Kali said, "Like you said last night, Umi, finding Bran is gonna be a big problem."

I said, "I tossed and turned last night thinking about it. We have our best person on the job. Cousin Koma. I could think of nothing better. Now, what do we do?"

Big Brah said, "Today, we focus on the connection between the murder and Kaipo. We'll verify whether the Kaipo involved in the murder was the fake Kaipo, that is Bran, or the real Kaipo Mahio, our client's son."

I approved. Big Brah was big on details. "Good plan," I said.

To verify who the Kaipo involved in the

murder truly was, Big Brah, Kali and I rode the big, black truck first to Bordeta House. Our goal was to find out from Iekika how well she knew Kaipo and how much of him she had seen on Friday evening, when Kaipo had picked Nohea up. We found Iekika taking a walk in the garden in front of the house.

It was a beautiful spring morning the air cool and bracing. In front of us, the windows of Bordeta House glinted in the early morning sunlight. The garden was filled with the fragrance of early spring gardenias, plumeria and jasmine. Black haired, big eyed and shapely chinned, Iekika was happy to see us.

She spoke brightly. "I heard your truck coming up the hill. Do you have any news of Nohea?"

"No," Kali said.

Iekika's face fell. She was dressed in a light jacket, shorts and sneakers. "Mom and Dad are inside, should I call them?"

"Actually, we wanted to talk with you, if that's okay," Kali said.

"Me? Of course it's okay. Mom and Dad won't mind either," Iekika said.

"Good, then. We wanted to ask you about Friday evening," Kali said.

"I'm sorry, I should've told Mom and Dad about it earlier, but I was so embarrassed, I didn't know how to. You saw how my dad gets mad, even if he hears the name," and here she lowered her voice, "Mahio."

Kali smiled, encouragingly. "I saw that," she said.

"So what was I to do? But, when you were there, I summoned up all the courage I had and blurted the truth. Mahalo for helping me!" she said.

Kali smiled, again. "You did good, the truth will help us find your sister," she said.

Iekika sniffed. "Will it, Kali? I really miss Nohea. She isn't just my big sister, she is also my friend. I'll tell you whatever you want to know."

"Tell us then, when did Nohea start seeing Kaipo?" Kali said.

Iekika's eyes widened. She giggled. "We're going to discuss love, wow. I can do it, I'm all grown up now. But when Nohea first told me about this boy Kaipo in her class, I was a tween.

"Nohea was still a high school senior. Kaipo and Nohea were in an advanced science class together. She told me, she liked him. I wasn't interested in boys back then, so I didn't pay much attention.

"Nohea went to college, I grew up. But Mom and Dad, they're always busy. Without them, Nohea and I got to spend a lot of time together. So, she kept telling me bits and pieces of her thoughts about Kaipo, how they both loved the marine biology classes. How he loved to surf and how she dreamed of surfing with him someday. But she didn't tell me who Kaipo really was, until they were both juniors in college.

"It happened right here in the garden. Nohea and I, we used to come out here for a walk, often. She was talking about Kaipo, and I was interested, listening. We were giggling and laughing, having fun. I asked her, why she didn't bring him home. Poor Nohea. Her beautiful face clouded up like the sky on a stormy day. She was close to tears. I asked her, what happened?

"Has Kaipo been mean to you? She shook her head and smiled through her tears at me. Sweet, innocent Iekika, she said to me. It isn't that at all. The problem?

"Kaipo is Duke Mahio's son. Even my younger self knew how bad this was. I gaped at her in wonder. What're you going to do? I asked her. Nohea was always kind. I am younger than her, and she never likes to scare me. She laughed, trying to make light of it. She told me laughing, she'd have to run away with Kaipo."

Iekika's young face became solemn and her voice turned small. "I think that's what she's done, run away with him."

Kali nodded. "Hope wherever they are right now, they're safe," she said.

Iekika shook her head. "Dad doesn't think so. He thinks Kaipo wants to negotiate his own safety so he's holding Nohea hostage. I keep telling him, Kaipo wouldn't need to hold Nohea hostage, she'd go with him willingly," she said.

"When did this talk of running away

happen?" Kali said.

"Last fall. Nohea started junior year in college. I started my sophomore year in high school," Iekika said.

"After that, did Nohea talk about going away with Kaipo again?" Kali asked.

Iekika shook her head. "No, never. I told you, she was always concerned for me. Protective big sister, she didn't want to alarm me.

"But every now and then, she'd tell Mom, Dad and me that she was going on a field trip. Later, she'd tell me, I went surfing with Kaipo. Honestly, the surfing alarmed me quite a bit. Nohea wasn't so good in the water."

Iekika's features softened. She strolled down memory lane dreamily. "Nohea assured me, she was safe with Kaipo. I feel safe with him, no matter what I do with him. But in the water, he's just the best. I'm in love with him."

Nice.

Iekika said, "If I was still in middle school, I'd probably not understand love. But in high school, I do. I giggled and told her, you rock sis, and she turned shy. I complained to her.

"I asked her why she didn't tell me before she went out surfing, why only after? She looked at me for a long time, so long that I figured it out. She was afraid I'd blurt out her plan to Dad, and he'd catch them together. Terrible.

"I told her, I'd never tell Dad, or anyone. She made me promise. Then finally, last week, she confided in me," she said.

"Confided in you, what did she say?" Kali said.

"Nohea was excited, I've never seen her so excited. She told me, she was going out with Kaipo again, Friday night. This was going to be special. I asked her if they'd go surfing in the moonlight. She told me yes, dreamily. I figured there was more to it.

"I'm grown up now. I know about all these things, so I asked her, if he was going to ask her to marry him. She patted my head, caressed my hair, but it still didn't prepare me enough for the surprise.

"Kaipo had already asked her to marry him. She had told him, yes. Now that they were both twenty-one, they figured they had the right to get married anytime. Blew my mind.

"I asked her what they were going to do. I expected her to say, they were flying to Vegas to get married, or something. But, she said they were renting a boat and going out on the ocean. I asked her if they were taking a priest along, and she said, no, not required.

"I was relieved, at least she wasn't planning on doing anything crazy, just having some Friday night fun. After all, like all the other couples, she couldn't go to the Tavern with Kaipo. Because of Dad! So, they were renting a boat for privacy," Iekika said.

"Did you ever get to meet Kaipo?" Kali said.

"I asked to meet Kaipo. Nohea was careful.

She told me, if things didn't work out between her and Dad over Kaipo, she didn't want me to suffer. So, it was better that I never risked being seen with them," Iekika said.

"But Friday night, Kaipo came over here to pick Nohea up, did he do that often?" Kali said.

"No, first time."

"You must have seen him then," Kali said.

Iekika giggled, again. "Yes, Heki opened the front door. I was upstairs, helping Nohea get ready. I could see the lanai from the window. I got a glimpse of Kaipo: curly hair, mustache, so dreamy!" she said.

"You never got a closer look at Kaipo?" Kali asked.

Iekika shook her head. "No, only Heki got a close look at him. Kaipo didn't come inside, and Nohea, of course, she left with him," she said.

"Why were your parents under the impression Nohea left with Heki?" I said.

"Because I told them that."

"Why?" I said.

"Because they'd believe it."

"Why would they believe it?" Kali said.

"Because Nohea and I, we'd both decided to tell them Heki had a crush on Nohea. You see, Nohea is like a true big sister. She wanted Heki and me to spend time together, get to know each other. But Mom and Dad, they're old school. Nohea and I, we didn't know how they'd react, so we made up that story, so Heki could be in the house. Mom and Dad didn't take the crush story seriously, and we were all good. Heki didn't have a crush on Nohea."

Kali smiled, a knowing look on her face.

With a shy expression, Iekika said, "Heki has a crush on me."

That explained Heki.

Kali said, "Of course, Heki didn't leave with Nohea. He stayed with you. You didn't want to tell your parents he stayed with you, so you told them he left with Nohea, right?"

"Right. You know my parents. Heki and I, we realize we're young couple, we've lots to learn. We're watching Nohea and Kaipo, to see how they do, before we go tell Mom and Dad."

"Taking it slow is the wise thing to do," Kali said.

Looking very mature, Iekika smiled. "Mahalo, Kali," she said.

"One last thing, Iekika, before I let you go."

"Anything, Kali."

"Is there a way we can ask Heki about Kaipo?"

Iekika giggled. "You must see Heki. He saw a lot of Kaipo. Heki told me everything, you must hear it from him, he's funny!" She gushed.

"How do we meet him?" Kali asked.

"It's spring break. Heki's working at the mall. Da Pet Shop!" Iekika said.

Time to see the young lover. The Bordeta Shopping Center was on the west side of the island. It took Big Brah, Kali and me about an hour to get there in the big, black truck. The shopping center could have been a replica of Mahio Plaza, but for the neon sign saying, "Bordeta Shopping Center."

The west side was the drier side of the island. The sky here was a flawless blue. It was a Thursday morning. Lunchtime was still an hour away. The mall was quiet as we entered.

A quick look at the mall directory. "Da Pet Shop" was to our right, located at the corner of the mall. No problem finding it. We entered through a glass door.

Overhead lights shone down on aisle after aisle of shelves stacked with food and supplies for all the beloved island pets. Shy cats, friendly dogs, cute hamsters, colorful birds and abundant fish. The familiar pet store odor was all around us.

From behind a sales counter, a woman with white hair welcomed us with a smile. She wore a colorful sarong-dress, making her look young.

I strolled over to the counter, Big Brah and Kali behind me. "Where can I find Heki?" I asked.

The woman behind the counter gave me a warm smile. "Your friend?" she said.

On the island you had family. Everyone else was your friend. I nodded.

She pointed beyond the aisles. "He's at the back. We just got a truck, he's helping unload it," she said.

Outside, a group of four teenaged boys were

gathered behind the open backdoor of a supply truck. "Heki," I shouted.

A big, strong boy separated from the group and jogged toward me. He had a team t-shirt colored green and white.

Green and white were the island school colors. I knew the school colors well. So did Big Brah and Kali who were behind me. The boy halted in front of me. He had short hair, only a wispy mustache and a faint beard.

He still had a ways to get to manhood. His young face cracked into a grin. "My name is Heki, you must be Umi. Brah, big fan, you're still legend in school," he said.

Even back in school, I used to be solving mysteries with Big Brah and Kali. Gratifying, when the next generation recognizes you. "Mahalo, brah," I said, modestly.

He looked past me at Big Brah and Kali and then back at me again. He lowered his voice. "These your big brother and his girl Kali, brah?" he said.

I nodded, briefly.

His eyes widened. "Legends!" he said.

"Are you going to help me or what?" I said.

He turned his attention on me. "About that, my girl, Iekika, she called me, told me to level with you. I told her, I will. She told me, you want to ask me about Kaipo," he said.

"Did you know him from before?" I asked.

Heki shook his head. "No, I didn't. But I got a

good look at him on Friday evening," he said.

"What did you see?" I asked.

Heki made a face. "Nothing unusual. He was excited about something, Kaipo couldn't stop smiling. When a man smiles that much, I know it's about a girl. And it was. I knew Nohea was going to go out with him. Kaipo was happy, he had a right to be happy," he said.

"Did you observe anything about his face, his body that strike you as unusual, like he may have on a costume or something?" I said.

Heki's face brightened. "A costume? Like the ones in Cosplay? Brah, I love those costumes. I'm going to wear a costume to junior prom. I'm asking Iekika to come with me," he said.

Junior prom was still a ways away for him. Dreams. Typical for his age. *Anticipation is everything,* I thought.

"So was Kaipo wearing a costume?" I asked.

Heki grew solemn. His smooth forehead wrinkled, as he tried to remember. At last, he said, "Could be, he was wearing a costume. He did behave kind of funny, but like I told you, I thought he was excited about snagging da gal!"

"What do you mean funny?" I said.

"Kaipo had a bouquet of roses. Soon as he saw me, he dropped the flowers." Heki giggled like a girl.

"That could be, he was nervous," I said.

Heki stopped giggling. "Could be, but it was funny," he said.

"Funny," I agreed. "Anything else?"

"Yes, when Nohea came down, Kaipo gave me a hug and thanked me. I was like, brah, hug your girl first. But, Nohea also stood by and let him. It's as if both of them knew they weren't going to see me in a while, or when they next saw me something big like this would've happened," Heki said.

Heki hadn't seen them in a while, and something big had happened. "Now, Heki, I want you to think carefully, try to remember what you saw. Did you see a mole at the top of Kaipo's right ear?" I said.

Heki's forehead wrinkled, again. He didn't say anything for a long while. "A mole, a mole, a mole. You know, I never notice moles, things like that. Did Kaipo have a mole, which ear now?" he said.

"Right ear," I said.

"Uh, I can't remember. He may've had a mole, or maybe he didn't," Heki said, thinking hard.

I waited.

"I can't remember, sorry." Heki looked downcast at failing to answer my question.

I tried to do what Big Brah and Kali always did to good people. Made them feel better. "Don't worry, Heki," I said.

Heki was still worried.

"A small mole is hard to notice. You did good!" I said.

Heki smiled and looked me in the eye. "I did

all right, you say?" he said.

Feeling very big, I smiled encouragingly. "You did great, Heki."

I was still feeling very big by the time we exited "Da Pet Shop" and made our way back through the mall. It was closer to lunchtime. The mall was crowding up. Beckoned by the many enticing smells from the Food Court, the crowd thronged. We followed the crowd. We would be asking cousin Keni, Alba and Music Man the same kind of questions we had been asking Iekika and Heki. Green tea and coconut water were the favorite local drinks.

While the food court at Mahio Plaza specialized in green tea, the food court here at the Bordeta Shopping Center was known for its chilled coconut water. To eat on the way to our next destination, the eastside harbor, we got bento boxes of sushi and golden-brown wontons. We got plenty of coconut water.

Work made us hungry. By the time Big Brah parked the big, black truck outside rent-a-boat's white shack at the harbor, all three of us had finished every last morsel of the musubis and wontons. We had drunk the last drop of the chilled coconut water.

Due to all the bad publicity, the harbor was deserted. As we ascended the steps to Keni's office, Keni swung the door open for us. Short and pony-tailed, Keni wore the red rent-a-boat t-shirt and navy-blue shorts. But he wasn't smiling.

# Chapter 17 Bliss for an artist

Keni looked weary. He had us sit down in the visitor chairs and then seated himself in his chair behind the sales desk. The spring afternoon flooded in through both the windows. Posters, prices and pictures of boats decorated the walls.

Keni swiveled in his chair from side to side. "Is good to see you, but I'll be happy to see the end of all this. Any news of Kaipo?" he said.

Big Brah shook his head. "No, but I had to ask you a few questions, will that be okay?" he said.

Keni nodded. "Of course," he said.

"Have a lot of people been bothering you with questions?" Big Brah said.

"Yes, but for you, Big Brah, I'm always ready to answer more," Keni said.

"Okay, then. You told me you saw Nohea Bordeta with Kaipo a couple of months ago. Right?"

"Right."

"You never saw her again."

"Nope."

"But you continued to see Kaipo regularly?"

"Yes, like once every ten days."

"This month, did you see him prior to Friday night?"

"Yes."

"Yes?"

"Yes, he was in here on Wednesday, sat where you're sitting, Big Brah. He wanted to know about my specialty boats and how he could rent one."

"Didn't that strike you as odd, considering he's rented from you so many times before?"

"Hmm. I don't know where you're going with this, Big Brah, but now that you mention it, maybe a little odd, especially since, as you say, he knew how to rent the boat, and my entire inventory of boats, they're all on my website. Kaipo could have just looked them up."

Good, Kaipo hadn't looked up information about the boat, denying Loni anymore evidence. Kaipo had protected his girl.

Big Brah grinned. "But, well, it's the island. It's simpler to drop by, share aloha, be close."

Thinking, Keni reached behind his head and absent-mindedly adjusted his ponytail.

Big Brah said, "Tell me, Keni, did you see anything different about Kaipo on Wednesday?"

Keni frowned. "Kaipo's face looked funny. I figured something was going on with him and Nohea, so he was excited. Young love, you know."

A dreamy look came over Keni's still young face. Eni was his wife. "Eni and I, we used to be that way."

"Did he look any different, like his hair, or mustache, or anything at all?" Big Brah asked.

"Aue, Big Brah, I didn't even think to look. If I had, maybe I'd have noticed something, but you know how excited I get when I talk about boats. I forgot everything, while I extolled the virtues of each of my specialty boats."

Big Brah chuckled. "Yes, Keni, I know what your boats mean to you. Tell me, what else happened on Wednesday?"

Keni said, "Well, I didn't see how Kaipo got to the harbor. I wasn't looking for it, so I don't know. Kaipo walked into the office, around ten in the morning.

"Kaipo told me, he wasn't going to rent a boat today, but he was looking for a specialty boat Friday night. I got talking about the boats. When I described the 'Honeymooner,' he was sure he wanted it.

"I had a few good boats left. I wanted to tell him about them, but he was sure. Okay, if that's what you want, I told him. I'll reserve the boat for you. Kaipo jumped up, happy. He shouted, I'll be back, from outside the door, before letting the door close."

"Kaipo did come back, Friday night, to claim his reservation, what happened then?" Big Brah said.

Keni gestured toward the window that overlooked the parking lot and the harbor road beyond. "Friday night, yeah, I'd been waiting for him. I saw a truck drive by with two people inside, I figured it was them. Sure enough, minutes later, Kaipo walked in, my guess had been right. He was fidgety, nervous and there was something wrong with his eyes," Keni said.

"Interesting, what was the matter with his eyes?" Big Brah said.

"Maybe it was the excitement, but his eyes were red, either from rubbing or crying. Love can be so emotional. Eni and I, we're still like that." Lehi was their daughter. "One of the first words Lehi learned to say was...emo!" he said, proudly.

"Children learn everything from their parents," Big Brah said.

"Yes, so true, Big Brah, so true. But, Kaipo, on Friday night, I didn't notice anything else. He'd been here before, he knew the rules. He was out of here in no time at all," Keni said.

Big Brah got up to go, knowing Keni wouldn't mind. Keni didn't get up.

Keni swiveled himself from side to side and gazed up at Big Brah. "There's one other thing, Big Brah," he said.

"What is it, Keni?" Big Brah said.

Keni lowered his voice. "My brah next door, you know, Alba. Since you saw him, he's been moody, alone, won't even talk to me. I wonder what's going on with him. Please, will you see him, make sure all's well with him," he said.

Typical of Keni to be concerned about his

neighbor. Kali and I also got up.

Keni sprang up and scurried around the sales desk to hug each of us in turn with a smile. "I hope Kaipo and Nohea are safe. Big Brah, Kali, Umi, I know you'll be able to get them back, safely," he said.

Big Brah nodded. "We'll see Alba next," he said.

Ross T. Alba's office was the same as we had last seen it in the night, but it was afternoon. The lights on the low ceiling weren't turned on. The daylight from the single window illuminated the room.

Outside the window, Alba's albatross, the white seaplane, bobbed on the water. Alba looked different. With his ears fanned out, his small eyes too close together and his big nose, he still resembled one of the cute island bats that lived in the trees. Same as last time, he had on regular jeans, a t-shirt and a green "Fly like a Bird" baseball cap.

But somehow, when Alba got up from his armless, swivel chair behind the clean desk to greet us, his movements had a gravity they had lacked before. His voice was quiet and his nasal tone subdued. "I was thinking about you. I'm glad you came. Please sit down," he said.

What was going on? The chair Big Brah had unfolded and sat on was still there, as he had left it. Big Brah got back on the chair, hugging its back. Kali and I sat down in the other chairs. Alba seated himself and gazed at Big Brah.

Big Brah smiled, encouragingly. "What made you think about us?" he said.

"This whole situation, I've had time to think about it deeply," Alba said.

"And?"

"And I'm sorry, I didn't tell you the entire truth the first time we met here," Alba said.

"You didn't?"

"No, sorry, I didn't. But, in my defense, I didn't realize the truth until this morning," Alba said.

"This morning, how did that happen?" Big Brah said.

"I've done nothing but think these last few days. Last night I slept little, thought a lot more. Finally at daybreak, I saw the light. How I had deluded myself. What my true destiny is," he said.

Delusions. True destiny. Those were big realizations. Alba must have done some heavy thinking.

"Tell us about it," Big Brah said.

Relaxing, Alba wheeled his chair back. He crossed his legs. "First, my delusion. It's about my crush. I told you, I used to have a crush on Nohea Bordeta in college. Well, these last few days, she's gone. I couldn't stop thinking about her, about my life. Then, it hit me. I was so affected by her disappearance, because I still had a crush on her." Assessing our reactions, Alba paused to look at Big Brah, Kali and me.

Alba was talking about his heart. Big Brah nodded. Kali smiled. Both were sympathetic. I wanted more. I listened intently.

Reassured, Alba wheeled his chair back a few more inches. "I still had a crush on Nohea. I'd never realized it, until she was gone. But slowly, the realization sank in. Is why I hated Kaipo so bad. I started thinking about all the things I'd told you, you know, about Kaipo. How he was a bad lab partner."

Alba uncrossed his legs and relaxed some more. "I mean, if I was over Nohea, would it still bother me that Kaipo was a bad lab partner way back in college? Or, he was renting boats next door? No! Truth was, I hated Kaipo even today, because I wasn't over Nohea. I told you, Kaipo was a bad lab partner. Wrong!" Alba said.

Big Brah raised an eyebrow. "Wrong?"

"Yes, wrong. I realized the truth, since the last time we talked. So please forgive me, if this contradicts what I told you. Kaipo wasn't careless at all.

"He was actually carefree and a free spirit. He used to do a bulk of the work, but he didn't care to take the credit for it, never talked himself up.

"In fact, Kaipo was the opposite. He didn't say anything about all the work he'd already done, only talked about what was left. Made me think, I was doing all the work. But I realize now, I wasn't, I wasn't doing all the work. Kaipo was just being kind to me," Alba said.

Big Brah let his eyebrow fall back into place. "Kind, interesting," he said.

"Yes, kind. If Kaipo was being kind to me, just a lab partner who he hardly knew, guess how he'd behave with the girl he liked? I concluded, it's this kindness that attracted Nohea to him. I told you, Nohea loved Kaipo, but Kaipo was too selfish to truly love her back."

Alba closed his eyes and shook his head. "I regret saying that." He opened his eyes. "It isn't true, Kaipo is capable of loving Nohea. In fact, I'm one of the few people who has observed Kaipo and Nohea more than others. I should know. What I've always witnessed was genuine love. I had to go back to spy on them, again and again. To get more of pure love," he said.

Having finished his confession, Alba fell into a relaxed silence. Big Brah, Kali and I exchanged glances. To me, Alba's realization and subsequent confession had been a long time coming.

Big Brah stirred. "Mahalo for telling us, brah, that took courage. All of us appreciate the truth. You're saying you've seen Kaipo and Nohea a lot together, mind if I ask you a few questions about them?" he said.

"Sure."

"You knew Kaipo in college, but did you see him, when he rented the boats?" Big Brah said.

"I got into a conversation with Keni. He told me about Kaipo renting a boat. This was very early on, about the time Kaipo first started. I told Keni how I hated Kaipo and warned him Kaipo was a potential bad customer. The truth is, Kaipo wasn't better or worse than anyone else, and accidents will happen. Of course, Keni didn't listen to me. I'm now glad he didn't listen to me. But I'd asked him to tell me, whenever Kaipo rented a boat.

"Anyways, Keni humored me. Often, he'd call me, and tell me, hey, your buddy Kaipo, just rented a boat. Of course, Keni meant it as neighborly gossip, he never guessed my true reaction to it. I'd go out and follow Kaipo's boat in my albatross." Alba regarded the white seaplane through the open window, an expression of pride on his face.

Big Brah nodded. "Did you ever get close to Kaipo?" he said.

Alba thought for a moment. "Last week, Wednesday, Keni called me to say Kaipo had just left his office, but Kaipo wasn't renting a boat today. Call it curiosity, or my old hatred of Kaipo, I went out the door, just to glare at him.

"Kaipo had descended the steps from Keni's office. He was just standing there, looking spaced out. I hadn't really observed him this close, since our college days. So, yes, I got close to him," he said.

"So, you were outside your door, and Kaipo was at the bottom of the steps from Keni's office?" Big Brah said.

"Yes."

Big Brah leaned forward. "Did you observe anything different about Kaipo?" he said.

"Anything different? Well, since I knew him, he'd grown his hair wilder. He had a bigger head of curls than I remembered. Also his mustache, more defined, thicker and he'd put on a few pounds," Alba said.

"A few pounds, interesting, whereabouts? Did you notice?" Big Brah said.

Alba frowned, trying to remember. "Hmm. I'd say around the face, also his shoulders, his torso in general," he said.

"Then what happened?" Big Brah said.

"He went away toward the harbor without noticing me. I figured he'd parked at the harbor, and I got back inside," Alba said.

Big Brah nodded, approvingly. "For my next question, I'm afraid you may have been too far away from Kaipo to see, but did you observe a mole on Kaipo's right ear?" he said.

For a moment, Alba looked startled. Then he smiled. "I don't remember him ever having a mole. Even if I was closer to him, I doubt I'd see such a thing," he said.

"What about Friday night, did you see him then?" Big Brah said.

"As a matter of fact, yes, I did see him again. Keni called, as usual. He'd told me on Wednesday, Kaipo was going to be here on Friday. Around seven, I was prepared. I didn't wait for Keni's call.

"I was outside, pretending to tinker with my

albatross, when Kaipo got the boat out of the boathouse. Usually, by the time I get out, he'd already have the boat out and on its way to the harbor dock. But Friday night, I got a pretty good look at him again," Alba said.

"Was it the same Kaipo you observed on Wednesday?" Big Brah said.

Alba frowned. "I think so," he said.

"Anything different?" Big Brah said.

"Kaipo looked happy, he had a smile on his face. But the boat went away fast, and it was evening, so the light wasn't the best," Alba said.

"Would you say he was excited about something?" Big Brah said.

Alba nodded vigorously. "Definitely, more excited than happy, I'd say that," he said.

"Did you observe anything strange about his eyes?" Big Brah said.

"Strange? What kind of strange?" Alba said.

"Reddened due to crying, rubbing or getting something in them," Big Brah said.

Alba chewed on his lower lip, again trying to remember. "He had his eyes squinted, is all I could see," he said, at last.

Big Brah took a deep breath and let it out slowly. He glanced at Kali and me. He was done with his questions. "Mahalo for answering my questions," he said.

"By answering your questions, I hope I'm helping you find Kaipo and Nohea. Please bring them back safe. Hope this makes up for all the bad things I told you earlier," Alba said.

Big Brah nodded. "I'm glad you took time to think things over. Meditating helps solve problems," he said.

"Yes, yes, you're so right about that, Big Brah. Meditation helped me get over my delusion, it helped me find my true destiny, you know, my true calling, all with such clarity!" Alba's small eyes started to shine. He was getting excited.

Big Brah looked out of the single window at the white seaplane, the albatross, gleaming in the bright, afternoon sunshine. "You told us about your delusion, do you want to share your true calling?" he said.

Alba looked proud. "You're looking at it, my albatross. My true calling came to me early this morning. I love flying. I dropped out of college, so I could fly. Truly, really, my crush on Nohea, it was just that, a crush. What I really want to do in life...is fly."

Big Brah chuckled, looking at Kali and me. "We own an amphibian aircraft, we call it our ocean bird. We know the joys of flying," he said.

At the mention of our ocean bird my heart soared. Flying was so fun. The ocean bird lived in a hangar. The hangar was separated from the boathouse by a wild stretch of bushes and coconut trees, Big Brah didn't say.

"No kidding, I didn't know you were aviation enthusiasts!" Alba exclaimed.

Big Brah said, "Enthusiasts yes, but we love

sleuthing more. What about your crush on Nohea?"

Alba smiled, looking strong. "I'm totally over the crush. If I find someone who shares my passion for flying, then sure. Otherwise, romantic love isn't for me," he said.

After seeing Alba, his words, romantic love isn't for me continued to ring in my ears. On our island of natural beauty and aloha, love and romance were hula dancing everywhere. How long could Alba resist romantic love? Big Brah, Kali and I strolled down the harbor road to see Music Man. As we got closer, the strum of his melodious ukulele greeted us.

With dreads, dark skin and long fingers, Music Man sat in his backpack chair under the shade of the wide fronds of the coconut tree by the dock. At the sight of us, he stopped playing. He rested the ukulele on the side of his backpack chair and beckoned us.

Big Brah, Kali and I joined Music Man in the shade. Away from the warm afternoon sun, it was cooler. This wasn't his home. Music Man didn't have chairs here. We sat down on the sandy ground in front of him.

Music Man looked worried. "I been thinking, what I tell you about Kaipo, remember?" he said.

Big Brah nodded. "You told us how he left with two women, one of whom was the murder victim, Helen Hokui," he said.

"Yes, the second woman was Nohea Bordeta.

So, I been thinking, not much else I do, after the music, that's all I do, think," Music Man said.

"Tell us, brah, what did you think?" Big Brah said, conversationally.

"You know how I say, Kaipo left with two women. Fake love? I fear I was wrong."

"Wrong, in what way?" Big Brah said.

"It may not have happened the way I tell you."

"No?" Big Brah said.

"No."

"Then, tell us how it happened," Big Brah said, interested.

"Well, Kaipo and Nohea, they arrive first. A truck, I see before. Kaipo drives it, I think, it must be his truck. Kaipo takes a moment to get out, not usual. He park, he jump out, but on Friday night, he slow to get out.

"I hear the sound of a car. The red sedan. She parks, where I told you the car was. There are coconut trees between the truck and the red sedan. She parks behind truck, so Kaipo, or Nohea, they don't see her, I don't think.

"Then, Kaipo go to get boat, same as usual. Nohea waits in the truck for him to bring boat to the dock. Kaipo get boat, he secures the boat same as usual. He come over to me. I see Nohea go fast into boat. I play the reggae number Kaipo always ask for. He goes into the boat, and if they leave now, everything like normal. You with me so far, brah?" Music Man gazed down at Big Brah, an intense expression on his face.

Big Brah nodded. "Yes, you had told us all this," he said.

Music Man looked away over our heads at the lapping harbor water behind us. "You know why I tell you all this, why I spend so much time thinking about it?" he said.

"No, why?" Big Brah said.

"I tell you this, because I believe in love, brah. There was a time, I was in love. I was young, no patience, very confident. I grow up in the big city, I play my music in the big clubs. People talk recording contract for me. I'm gonna make it big, they say.

"I busy. I play, I sing my heart out for people, under them big city lights. I love what I do. I make people laugh, cry, be happy. What can be better bliss for an artist?

"Then, one day, I work late. I'm a on a break, getting a drink at the bar, when this woman get on stage. I look away, there are many who sing covers of my songs. Then, I look again.

"She had the face of an angel. Long, black hair down to her hips. A smile so playful. I think, I'm in love. Her eyes on me, she sings a cover of one my songs.

"Afterward, I go ask her out. She gave me that playful smile. I hold my breath. Finally, she say, yes. From that day on, she, me, we a couple. I want her, she want me, we together, always, always," Music Man said.

Big Brah rested his hands on the sandy

ground behind him, leaned back and continued to listen attentively.

Music Man continued. "Then, one day, we home, late night, it's almost morning, early. She tell me, baby, while we still together, let's get out of here.

"I no believe her. Why? I ask her. She tell me, she got recording contract of her own. I'm a surprised. She deserve contract, why she want to leave? Like me, she from the big city, so she got nowhere to go. I ask her. She say, she love me, want to be my woman, not recording artist.

"But music is my life, hers too, I say. No, our love is her life, she argues. I told you, I was young, no patience, very confident. I call her every name I know.

"I rage at her. Tell her off. I can't give up music, not for love, not for anything, I told her. Poor thing, she cried. She cried, didn't get up, the whole day. Evening arrives.

"Finally, she get up, give me the saddest look, then we both go to work. From that day, we never talk about it, we just work. Everyone know we lovers, no one says nothing.

"Then, she gets a bigger contract, but me, I'm still stuck with my old one. Then, another big contract for her. Me? Still stuck with same old job.

"She made it big, so big, she a star. Big city too small for her. She bigger star in many, many big cities, all over the world. But sad, she, me, we never see each other anymore. She tell me, she will, but then, she don't.

"I understand. I find a new home, here on the island. I play my music, far away from her, I don't want to bother her. But, my love for her, it still burn inside. I no want anyone to say I was with two women, or my love was fake.

"I'm sorry, I told you that about Kaipo. What if, his love was pure, and I made a mistake? Saying bad things, spreading rumors about pure love is wrong.

"Helping pure love is the right thing to do, it is the island way. I shouldn't have said something so bad about pure love, unless I'm sure. Now, I'm not sure, so I regret telling you Kaipo's love was fake," Music Man said.

Big Brah took in a deep breath and let it out slowly.

Kali said, "So, are you saying Kaipo's love was pure?"

Music Man said, "What else can it be? Day after day, I see them right here. He bring boat, comes over to me, she run into boat. I sing them the love song he want, they leave.

"When they leave, they look happy, eyes for each other. When they return, after time together, they be even more happy. Every time I see them, it make me feel good. That's pure love, when you make even a stranger watching you happy," Music Man said.

Big Brah, Kali and I nodded.

"So you watched them. Did you see anything different about Kaipo on Friday night?" Big Brah said.

Music Man said, "I told you about the other woman."

"Yes, we'll talk about her in a minute, but what about Kaipo himself. Did he look different, behave any different than he usually does?" Big Brah said.

"On Friday night? Kaipo...well, he was excited, not usual, but more. He nervous, not like before, there be something going on with him for sure," Music Man said.

"What about his face, anything different?"

Music Man looked away behind us at the harbor water, thinking. Then, he shook his head. "Can't remember," he said.

"How about his eyes, were they red?"

Music Man's gaze swung back to Big Brah. "Yes! Left eye, I remember, red," he said.

"Could it be, he rubbed his eye, or cried, or," Big Brah turned to look at Kali and me significantly, "Kaipo got some makeup in his eye?"

Music Man shrugged. "Could be. Whatever it was, it didn't bother him, so I forgot about it," he said.

"Did you ever notice a mole at the top of Kaipo's right ear?" Big Brah said.

"A mole? No, never, but I no look so close at his ear, can't really say," Music Man said.

"Okay, so tell us, Kaipo and Nohea are in the boat. You're singing them the love song Kaipo's asked you to sing. At this point, the usual is, they go away. But, on Friday night something different happened, what?" Big Brah said.

"Yes, yes, is what I've been wanting to tell you. Kaipo and Nohea, they come out of boat together, they not do this ever before," Music Man said.

"Are they happy, or are they worried, or what?"

"Happy, always happy, when they together. It's as if they forget the rest of the world, they so focus on each other," Music Man said.

Big Brah nodded, approvingly. "Then what happened?" he said.

"They go to his truck, parked over there." Music Man pointed.

All of us looked the way he pointed. Just the coconut trees and beneath the trees sandy soil. None of us said anything. We were all trying to imagine what had happened here Friday night.

Music Man grew more intense. "I think they were in the mood to celebrate. They get champagne bottles from truck. They simply forgot about the drinks, remembered just in time, ran back to get them," he said.

"That's likely, they were having fun, forgot the drinks," Big Brah said.

"Yes, yes. I told you last time, I thought they create distraction, so I not notice the other woman get into boat, but here's how I could be wrong. First, the other woman, she followed them here. I assume they're together. On the island, people follow people they know places. It's common. Less common, people follow people they don't know, so I not think about it, 'til later. What I'm saying is, the other woman, she may not be with Kaipo," Music Man said.

# Chapter 18 Fool Music Man is playing music

"Not with Kaipo, interesting," Big Brah said.

Music Man spoke more forcefully, warming up to the idea. "Just think, what if, the other woman, the victim lady, she not with Kaipo. Maybe, she follow him here, then when she see he not looking, Nohea's not looking, she runs into boat," he said.

"Stowaway," Big Brah whispered, his eyes faraway.

"Yes, yes, that's what I'm talking about. I see it clearly, now. I think she look their way, when she run into boat. At the time, I took it, she was trying to tell them all is going by plan. Fool Music Man is playing music, he not see me," Music Man said.

There was a silence. The harbor water lapped. The shadows of the trees had grown longer, as the late afternoon sun dipped westward. At last, Music Man's melodious voice broke the silence.

Music Man said, "I was a fool. I should have warned Kaipo, you got a stowaway in your boat.

That way this whole trouble never happen. But, I didn't. I regret it now." His eyes filled up with tears.

Big Brah got up. He went behind Music Man and rested a hand on each of Music Man's shoulders. "Don't worry too much about it. I'd have made the same mistake as you, any human being would," he said.

Music Man blinked back his tears. He shook his head and smiled at the same time. "You think so? If anything, I'm just human," he said.

Big Brah let go Music Man's shoulders, patted them again to reassure and then returned to his place on the ground next to Kali. "You never told us the name of your girl," he said.

Music Man was embarrassed. He threw back his head and laughed. "I better sing you a number. What would you like?" he said.

"The name," Big Brah said, chuckling.

"Sing us a song about her," Kali said.

"You persistent," Music Man said to Big Brah, and to Kali, "all my songs are about her, but here's a number I named after her. You'll like it, it is called, 'Laika Lahaina.'"

The strum of the ukulele and Music Man's mellifluous voice filled our ears. The beauty of the spring afternoon deepened around us. The cool, refreshing breeze from the ocean, the music of the birds and the rhythmic rustling of the wide coconut fronds above us provided the perfect backdrop. The lap of the water kept up a steady beat. Music of pure aloha.

Music Man sang song after song dedicated to his love, Laika Lahaina. It was easy to forget everything else for a while. When he was done, Big Brah, Kali and I hugged him.

He hugged us back fondly. "Mahalo for listening," he said.

"Mahalo for the songs," Kali said.

"Mahalo for taking the time to think, to care, to take the time to tell us everything," Big Brah said.

"Everything Kali and Big Brah said, and you're awesome," I said.

Back inside the big, black truck, I let out a cheehoo. "So, Helen Hokui wasn't on the boat by invitation. She was following Kaipo and Nohea, saw the opportunity and got in stealthily. That much is proven. But, what do you think, will Loni accept Music Man's word for it?" I said.

In the driver's seat, Big Brah chuckled. "I have an idea. There's more evidence inside the 'Honeymooner' that Helen Hokui was a stowaway. We'll need Loni to show us the boat, again. I say, we go to the PD, and I'll show you what I mean," he said.

I thumped the backseat, approving. The cheehoo, the thumping. Kali smiled at my antics, fondly.

Big Brah extracted the agency phone he carried from the pocket of his cargo shorts. "But first, I have to do one other thing," he said.

Kali and I exchanged smiles. What did Big Brah have to do?

Big Brah held the phone. "What else did we learn from Music Man?" he said.

"Helping pure love is the right thing to do," I said, eagerly.

"Right on," Big Brah said.

Kali grinned. "Music Man's love is pure! Do something, Koa," she said.

Big Brah nodded, approvingly. "I'm going to call someone I know, an agent, a music industry insider. See if he can deliver a message to Laika Lahaina. It will be our way to help Music Man's pure love!" Big Brah said.

A few minutes into the call, I heard Big Brah say, "Tell her, her love is here on the island, we call him Music Man!" he said.

In a few more minutes, while Kali looked on dotingly and I admired from the backseat, Big Brah finished the call. The call over, the outcome unknown, Big Brah started to drive.

The truck drove up the harbor road, gathering speed. By the time Big Brah, Kali and I followed Loni into the police yard behind the gray county building, it was evening.

The yard was quiet. Its vehicles and boats were motionless and suspended in time. Loni had been reluctant to agree showing us the boat, but he couldn't just say no to Big Brah. Especially when Big Brah reminded Loni, Big Brah would be happy to share the new evidence from the boat.

Loni turned back to look at us doubtfully, as we trailed behind him. "What is this new evidence, Big Brah?" he said.

Big Brah walked faster and caught up with Loni. "I want to start with the galley," he said.

"The galley? What's in the galley?" Loni said.

Big Brah chuckled. "You'll see," he said.

It was a little hard to see inside the "Honeymooner's" cabin. The boat wasn't powered on. The evening light streaming in through the portholes cast long shadows inside the cabin's confined space. The boy scout he was, Big Brah was prepared. He had brought the small but powerful flashlight he kept inside the big, black truck. We walked past the living room, the walls decorated with prints of romantic paintings by island artists. We got to the galley.

Fully equipped. Storage drawers. Refrigerator. While Loni looked on impatiently, and Kali and I watched from the doorway, Big Brah went to the refrigerator and opened it. He shone the flashlight inside.

Two bottles. Champagne. Unopened. The rest of the refrigerator? Empty.

Big Brah closed the refrigerator and turned to Loni. "I have an eyewitness who says he saw Kaipo and Nohea get out of the docked boat at the harbor. They strolled back to their truck parked under the coconut trees to fetch these bottles. I just wanted to make sure he had seen that right. Yes, the eyewitness did see Kaipo and Nohea with the champagne bottles," he said.

Loni shrugged. "I already knew Kaipo and Nohea were on the boat. What else, Big Brah?"

Using his flashlight, Big Brah led us into the bedroom. The big bed, the silk sheets and the luxury pillows still were like things from a princess fairy tale. He stopped by the door of the walk-in closet. Right behind Big Brah, Loni also stopped.

Big Brah turned back to Loni. "This is the walk-in closet, where you think Nohea and Kaipo locked the victim up. Wrong. I'll prove to you the victim willingly hid inside the closet, without Kaipo or Nohea being aware of her. The evidence is right inside the closet," he said.

Kali and I were behind them. We exchanged looks. How was Big Brah going to prove the victim was a stowaway?

Loni folded his arms. He heaved a sigh, his thick, black mustache drooping. "How're you going to do that, Big Brah?" he said.

Big Brah carefully turned the knob and pulled the door open. He held the flashlight with his other hand and shone it inside. The closet was still empty. On the left wall, the shelf was visible. There was the wooden rod below the shelf with the clothes hangers. I examined the floor. The fallen hanger was there next to the white circles painted on the teak floor. Big Brah signaled to me.

I stepped past Loni, so I could hold the door. Big Brah carefully took one long stride into the closet, bent down and gingerly picked up the hanger on the floor. From inside the closet, he handed it to Loni.

Big Brah pointed to a set of scratches where the wood had flaked and discolored. "Take a good look at these scratch marks. You know how they got here?" he said.

Loni held the hanger up to the level of his eyes and examined the marks. Then, he lowered the hanger. "I'll hold on to this piece of evidence, Big Brah, if you like," he said, his voice dripping with sarcasm, "but no, I don't know how these scratch marks got on this particular clothes hanger."

Big Brah chuckled. "Let me demonstrate," he said.

Big Brah retrieved one of the hangers from its resting place on the rod and brought it back to Loni. He held it up in front of Loni, so Loni could see. "Check this specimen for scratches, see if it has any scratch marks?" he said.

Loni's eyes scanned the hanger, first one side and then the other. "No scratch marks," he said, crisply.

Big Brah took the hanger. He placed the hanger on the teak floor, so it would come in the way of the door closing and then nodded at me. Intuitively, I let the door go.

The door swung, slowed and then crunched the wooden hanger. But the door stayed open a crack. Big Brah pushed the door open from the inside easily.

He picked up the hanger. He showed the damage to Loni, Kali and me. Scratch marks had appeared on the hanger's wooden surface identical to the scratch marks on the other hanger. Big Brah, Kali and I exchanged triumphant looks. We knew what this meant.

Loni was unfazed. He feigned ignorance. "What do the scratch marks on this specimen indicate, Big Brah?" he said.

"It shows the door wasn't ever locked from outside. The victim wedged the hanger in your hand to stop the door from closing. So Kaipo couldn't have locked her inside. She was in there to hide," Big Brah said.

"What about the kick mark on the inside?" Loni said.

"She kicked the door all right, but it wasn't because she was locked inside. More likely, she was kicking it open," Big Brah said.

Loni held the hanger between thumb and curled-up index finger and tapped the hanger against the open palm of his other hand. He squinted at Big Brah for a long moment.

Then Loni turned and quickly made his way past Kali and me. "Good job, Big Brah, good job!" he said.

Big Brah looked at Loni's receding back and then at Kali and me. He lifted his shoulders and let them fall. Had Loni accepted Big Brah's explanation?

Big Brah, Kali and I trooped up to the cockpit

of the luxury cruiser. The evening had darkened. Transparent plastic sheets still protected the cockpit's teak floor, stainless steel appliances, grill, cooler, seats, pilot's chair, digital throttle, cup holders, joystick and wheel.

Loni was there, looking pleased. "Did you say you also had a new witness, Big Brah?" he said.

Big Brah looked at Kali and me and then at Loni. "Yes, Music Man," he said.

For a moment, Loni widened his eyes to show his incredulity. "Music Man! You mean the bum in the dreadlocks? Ha! He, a witness?" Loni burst out laughing.

Then, with a glance at me, he contained himself. "I mean, yes I know the gentleman who calls himself Music Man, and well, he is a rather unreliable witness, don't you think?" he said.

His gaze went from Big Brah to Kali then me. We just stared back at him.

"Tough crowd," Loni muttered. Then, he returned his gaze to Big Brah and spoke in what I suppose he considered a reasonable way. "Well then, Big Brah, mahalo for showing me this new, er, evidence. You seem to be fascinated by how the victim got on the boat.

"Good research, good job. Now, we know for sure how the victim got on the boat. After their fight at the Tavern, no doubt she was following him around, to keep an eye on him.

"Good employee that she was, she was trying to stop him. She even robbed the safe with him, only so she could stop him. Too bad, somehow, Kaipo discovered her presence, decided to do away with the nuisance permanently. Kaipo killed her."

With that final conclusion, Loni stepped smartly onto the rear platform and down the boarding ladder over the engines. Big Brah, Kali and I followed.

On the ground, Loni tapped Big Brah's broad chest with one end of the wooden hanger playfully. "Be there for the meeting tomorrow, bring your client," he said.

Big Brah asked Loni, "Loni, brah, you don't think all this makes any difference to the case?"

"The evidence is okay."

"Just okay, Brah?" Big Brah said.

Loni said, "But you need a more reliable witness."

"A more reliable witness?"

Loni said, "As it stands, no, this new evidence and new witness make no difference at all to the case."

Loni was frustratingly stubborn. Back in the big, black truck, Big Brah was in the driver's seat.

Kali said, "If Loni thinks Music Man is a bum and an unreliable witness, then we need another witness."

"Noah," Big Brah said.

I said, "Noah works for the county, same as Loni. Loni can't think of Noah as a bum."

Big Brah said, "Problem is, we have to get

Noah to tell us the truth."

Kali frowned. "We need to find out, what's the bad thing Noah did to Kaipo."

"Loni's being stupid," I said.

Big Brah said, "I say, we go see Noah."

By the time we reached Noah's place, the small home surrounded by fruit trees, it was totally dark. No lights inside or outside the home. The truck's headlights completed the disappointing story.

The fancy fishing boat, "Noah's Ark," and the new truck we had seen it hitched to were both gone. Noah wasn't home. He had gone fishing, again. We were disappointed. We started for home. There was a surprise on the driveway outside our garage.

The big, black truck's headlights revealed Duke Mahio's yellow sports car. In no time, we had him inside the house. The lights turned on, as we entered the office.

I pulled the blackout curtains and opened the windows to let in the fresh air. Duke Mahio sat down in the visitor's chair. Big Brah and Kali sat down in their chairs behind the tidy desk. I sank into my chair behind the cluttered desk. What, now?

Duke Mahio adjusted the business-like glasses on his nose. "I just wanted to tell you about Lily," he said.

Big Brah sat up. "What about her?" he said.

"Noah must still be mad about her coming to

see you. He was gone fishing, all of last night. She called him several times, he didn't answer. Her mother told me today, Lily is beyond sad. She can't stop crying," Mahio said.

Big Brah nodded, sympathetic. "Yes, I can imagine. We were at Noah's place a short while ago. Unfortunately, he's gone fishing again tonight," he said.

Mahio said, "You see, they used to go out fishing, but together. Now, she can't figure out the matter with him. He doesn't want her with him, he wants to go alone."

"I'll be seeing him first thing tomorrow morning. He'll be back then," Big Brah said.

Mahio sighed. "Yes, I want you to help Lily. She's like a daughter to me. The other thing that's bothering me is, Loni's meeting tomorrow. What will he do, if the police still haven't found Kaipo?"

Big Brah said, "That I can't tell. We were with Loni a short while ago, he expects us to be present. He told us, he'd be talking to the chief about it, so it will be up to them to decide. We'll all be there at ten sharp, find out together. What I can tell you is, we are beginning to uncover flaws in Loni's story of what happened."

Duke Mahio looked pleased. He leaned forward. "Flaws? Good, I'm sure glad to hear that. What are they?" he asked, eagerly.

Big Brah never discussed the details of an ongoing investigation with anyone other than Kali and me. He made an apologetic face. "I'm sorry, brah, but I don't discuss an ongoing investigation, it disturbs my focus," he said.

Duke Mahio looked taken aback. "Disturbs your focus, why, that kind of makes sense. When I'm thinking about something, I don't discuss it with others, until I'm done with my own thinking, so okay, I understand. But how about the surveillance video, should I show it to the police?"

Big Brah took a deep breath and let it out slowly. "You'll have to make that decision yourself. But I can safely share this with you. I have evidence to prove the man in the surveillance video wasn't your son, but an imposter," he said.

Duke Mahio gaped at Big Brah. "An imposter, who?" he said.

"I don't know, but I'm going to find out," Big Brah said, his face grim.

"This imposter, could he also be the murderer?" Duke Mahio said.

"Likely."

Kali said, "In the surveillance video, you identified the imposter as Kaipo by the bead bracelet. The gold plate had his name stylized on it. The bracelet was found with the body."

Big Brah said, "So, yes. The thief in the video is likely the murderer."

Duke Mahio was impressed. "I can see you've been working hard."

Kali said, "We'll be working harder to find the

murderer."

Duke Mahio gushed. "I knew the reputation of the Waialeale Detective Agency, now I'm experiencing it myself."

Big Brah said, "We won't rest until we find the murderer."

"I feel better already, mahalo," Duke Mahio said.

Duke Mahio left, feeling better. Big Brah, Kali and I headed for the kitchen. We were famished. It was time to raid and reheat the frozen goodies in the refrigerator.

Soon we were at the round table with hot plates stacked with one of Big Brah's savory delights. Layers of pasta, kalua pork, grilled eggplant and sautéed taro leaves with lots of cheese and sauce, all homemade. Delicious. The island-style lasagna was a special family recipe.

I savored it. We were almost done eating when the agency phone that Big Brah had set down on the table jingled. The caller was the music industry insider Big Brah had called earlier. Big Brah's message had been delivered. Within minutes the star had canceled all her engagements through her web presence. Laika Lahaina didn't mention why.

The insider told Big Brah Laika Lahaina was flying to the island in her private jet. The caller wanted directions. How to find Music Man?

Big Brah told the caller how. Big Brah chuckled, happy. He set the phone back down on the table. He looked at Kali and me, inviting comments.

"She's dropped everything. She's flying to the island to see him. Promising!" Kali said.

Big Brah nodded, approvingly.

Kali said, "Yes, they'll be together, again."

Confidently, I said, "I can predict what's gonna happen next! Laika Lahaina will have Music Man tour with her, make him as big a star as she is."

Big Brah loved mysteries. He loved being mysterious. He chuckled. "Not so fast, Umi. Let them meet first, spend time and catch up."

"We'll see what happens," Kali said

"Wow. It's gonna be great," I said.

Big Brah, Kali and I looked at each other. "Whatever happens, Music Man totally deserves the happiness!" We chorused.

Meanwhile, we had to see Noah in the morning. Big Brah and Kali were already up and about, by the time I got to the kitchen the following morning. The air was filled with the familiar aroma of a breakfast pizza baking in the oven.

All three of us had changed out of our home clothes into work shirts, shorts and sandals. Poli`ahu and Wiliwili were close, spreading and sharing aloha. Kali poured kitty treats into their bowls. One look at us, and you could tell, a family, right here.

Pure aloha.

Kali greeted me with a cheery smile. "Ready for the big day, Umi?" she said.

I nodded, enthusiastically.

Big Brah got the pizza out of the oven, sliced it and got it over to the round table. "Just in time, Umi," he said, with a chuckle.

Another Big Brah and Kali special, the breakfast pizza was beyond good. Homemade thick crust. Topped with local cheese, crushed garlic, early spring basil, onions and roasted chicken. Fresh scrambled eggs on the side. Yum.

All washed down with a nutrient-rich chocolate milkshake. Big Brah's recipe. After breakfast, Big Brah, Kali and I set out in the big, black truck. Our destination once again was Noah's home by the coast not far from Mahio Mansion. I was lost in anticipation of the big day ahead. First, Noah. Then, Loni's meeting. What was going to happen? The windows were down.

The morning air was cool. The sun had risen. The red blaze was still low on the eastern horizon. In the early morning sunlight, the ocean glimmered and glittered, as we got to the small home surrounded by fruit trees.

"Noah's Ark," the fancy fishing boat and the new truck the boat had been hitched to were both there in front of the home. I was ready for more Noah action. The sound of our truck must have warned Noah.

As soon as we got out of the big, black truck, Noah emerged from the home, as before. His hair was short like mine. He had a bold stance and intense eyes. With confident strides, he drew close to us and halted.

Noah looked exasperated. "You, again?" he said.

Big Brah kept his face expressionless. "Yes us, again," he said.

"I already told you, I know nothing about Kaipo or the murder."

Gently, Big Brah said, "It's okay, I know what you did to Kaipo."

Noah stared slack-jawed at Big Brah. Then, he recovered, smartly. "You only know what Lily told you, that I did something bad to Kaipo. Well, I didn't, okay?" he said.

Big Brah sighed, softly. He bowed his head and gazed at the ground. "Noah, it's no use lying to us, I know what happened," he said.

Noah fixed an intense stare on Big Brah. No help at all, Big Brah continued to look at the grassy ground casually. Noah turned his intense eyes first on Kali then on me. Last time, Noah had lied to us. Kali and I knew to keep our faces carefully expressionless. He got no help from us either.

At last, Noah spoke, slowly. "Why don't you come inside, tell me what happened," he said.

Big Brah nodded approvingly. The three of us followed Noah into the living room. White carpet. Leather-upholstered furniture. Everything in mint condition.

A single person's delight. This condition could change very fast with a baby in the house. With an impatient hand gesture, Noah invited us to sit down. Quickly, he sat down in the armchair. He watched us, hands hugging the arms of the armchair.

Big Brah and Kali sat down in the loveseat. I got the whole couch to myself. The clean coffee table had a phone on it. Noah's, no doubt.

When we were all seated, Kali and I looked at Big Brah. This was new, even to us. What did Big Brah know about what Noah had done?

# Chapter 19 I love akule

Noah fixed his intense eyes on Big Brah. "Now tell me, what happened with Kaipo and me?" he said.

Big Brah met Noah's eyes, candidly. "Last week, on Tuesday night, what Lily told you about Kaipo made you jealous," he said.

Noah shook his head. "Nonsense, I don't do jealousy. Who do you think I am?" he said.

Big Brah soothed Noah. "Wrong use of words, forgive me. Jealousy is a petty feeling. I agree you don't do jealousy. That's very good. What I really meant was, by telling you about Kaipo, Lily really hurt your feelings," he said.

Noah had that look of exasperation on his face, again. "Listen, Big Brah, my feelings can't be hurt so easily by something Lily says," he said.

Big Brah made a placatory gesture with both hands. "Of course, of course, your feelings can't be hurt so easily. That's a good thing, shows you're strong!" he said.

Noah just stared at Big Brah intensely, waiting for Big Brah to continue.

Big Brah continued. "Again, wrong choice of

words, Lily didn't hurt your feelings, but she confused you," he said.

Noah frowned. "You could say that," he said.

"You, then set out to find out a few things about Kaipo," Big Brah said.

"What if I did? I didn't do anything wrong." Noah had lost his edge.

"No, nothing wrong in finding things out, but you followed Kaipo," Big Brah said.

"Nothing wrong in following someone, is there?" Noah looked defensive.

"But, there was something wrong about you following Kaipo. What was wrong was your motive," Big Brah said.

Noah's intense stare faded.

"You know what your motive was!" Big Brah said.

Noah blinked. "You're right. I followed Kaipo, not just out of curiosity. I wanted to dig up something bad about him," he said.

Big Brah nodded. "So you could tell Lily, Kaipo wasn't as perfect as she thought, right?" he said.

"Right." Noah agreed.

"Such evidence would prove to Lily, once and for all, for her, you were the man! Right?" Big Brah said.

"Right." His confession out in the open, Noah was calmer.

"Mind telling us what you did?" Big Brah said.

Noah was smarter than he looked. A hint of a smile passed through his features. "Thought you said you knew what happened. Why're you asking me?" he said.

Big Brah chuckled, softly. "I'll tell you what happened. You followed Kaipo around on Wednesday and Thursday. You found nothing wrong with him.

"By Friday evening, you'd have been close to giving up. Then, you followed Kaipo to Bordeta House, saw him pick Nohea up.

"At first, you couldn't believe your good luck. Everyone knows about the feud between Duke Mahio and Jim Bordeta, you did too.

"You figured Kaipo was having a secret affair with Nohea. This was something you could tell Lily to prove Kaipo wasn't so perfect after all. Excited, you followed Kaipo and Nohea to the harbor.

"You watched them leave in the 'Honeymooner.' You had followed Kaipo to the harbor on Wednesday. When Kaipo went into rent-a-boat, you figured he'd rent a boat sometime soon. You were prepared for it. You had your boat ready. You couldn't resist following Kaipo and Nohea," he said.

Noah blinked a few times. "Then, you'll also know where I followed them to," he said.

Big Brah nodded. "Yes, you followed them to Forbidden Beach," he said.

Noah now looked dazed. "How do you know all this? I haven't told anybody, not even Lily," he said.

How had Big Brah known all this? He had figured it out, of course.

"You need to tell Lily, everything," Kali said.

Noah said, "How can I? Now, she'll laugh at me."

"No, she won't," I said.

Noah said, "She won't, why?"

"Because she loves you," Big Brah said.

Noah said, "But she loves Kaipo more."

"No, she doesn't," we chorused.

Noah was not easily convinced. "Lily and Kaipo, they're childhood friends. They've known each other so much longer."

Big Brah said, "Sure, they're childhood friends. A childhood friendship is a wonderful thing. But Lily, she is also your friend. She loves you, Noah. She just wanted you to hurry up."

"Propose to her." Kali encouraged.

"Get on with it." I urged.

Big Brah said, "Lily tried to tell you by using Kaipo as an example."

"Really, is this true?" Noah looked from Big Brah to Kali and then to me.

Noah needed help. This time, both Kali and I nodded.

Big Brah said, "Yes, it's true. Lily didn't mean to confuse you, far from it."

"Lily was trying to help you," Kali said.

"Lily doesn't love Kaipo," I said.

Big Brah smiled. "Lily loves Noah," he said.

His anguish apparent, Noah leaned forward

in the armchair. He clutched his head with both hands. "The last few nights, I have been running away from Lily. I feel bad. Lily has called me so many times." He stared at the phone on the coffee table.

"Call her, then," Big Brah said, softly.

Big Brah, Kali and I watched him. Slowly Noah let go his head, took a deep breath and exhaled. Something was going on inside him. A decision, likely.

His eyes intense again, Noah turned to Big Brah, "You've cleared my confusion. I was about to propose to Lily. I was nervous, hesitant. She must have sensed my hesitation. Lily tried to help me. I completely misunderstood. But I'm going to make it up to her, right away."

A good decision. It was always gratifying to help pure love. Big Brah, Kali and I smiled.

To my surprise, Big Brah said, "Noah, you're bold and confident. It's not like you to be nervous or hesitant. Lily thought it was her words about Kaipo, but I figure you had another problem."

Noah sighed, nodding. "My job with the county has ended. I am unemployed."

Unemployed. Loni would have Noah on the same "bums" list as Music Man instantly. *There goes Noah's usefulness as a witness,* I thought. I didn't know how wrong I was.

Big Brah sympathized. "Let us know if we can help," he said.

Noah continued. "I owe you plenty for

helping me already. Ask me anything, I'll answer all your questions, best I can," he said, decisively.

Big Brah nodded, approvingly. "The something bad you did to Kaipo, you gonna tell us about that, brah?" Big Brah said.

Noah smiled. "You miss nothing, do you, Big Brah? You're right, if I had only followed Kaipo, it wouldn't have troubled me as much. But after he rented the 'Honeymooner' and brought the boat over to the dock," Noah sighed, looking at his phone on the coffee table, "like every phone, my phone has a camera. I filmed Kaipo, the boat, the entire departure, so I could show it to Lily. I had no idea this would turn out to be a murder!" he said.

A really big wave of excitement raced toward me. Noah had a recording of the entire departure. Talk about evidence for Loni. I was set to ride the big wave.

"Mind if we take a look at this video?" Big Brah said.

Noah got up. He picked up his phone from the coffee table, messed around with it and then invited us to watch the screen as he played the video. Big Brah, Kali and I also got up and gathered around him to watch. The audio quality was clear.

Noisy calls of the shorebirds. The image shuddered, shook and then was steady. I recognized the place. The eastside harbor. In the fading light of the evening, the dock was visible past the coconut trees. A splash of red and white. The "Honeymooner." A man jumped out of the boat onto the dock.

The man bent to secure the boat. Then, he walked over to the coconut tree where Music Man sat. Music Man's backpack chair, his dreads, all visible. The camera zoomed in for a close up of the man. Curly hair, mustache, the resemblance to Kaipo, uncanny. But did he have a mole at the top of his right ear? We were about to find out.

As Kaipo talked to Music Man, there was a movement off screen and the camera jerked. The camera caught the cause of the movement. A woman, running.

The woman looked a lot like Iekika, only older. Long, wavy black hair, big eyes and shapely chin. Nohea Bordeta certainly.

Nohea disappeared into the boat. The camera focused back on Kaipo and Music Man. Kaipo finished with Music Man and returned to the boat.

Then, Kaipo and Nohea both came out of the boat. They strolled leisurely toward a parked truck, theirs, no doubt. Again, the camera caught another movement, jerked and moved away. A thin woman with black hair came into focus, presumably Helen Hokui.

Helen Hokui got out of the red sedan where we had found the sedan parked. She ran forward. She looked furtively in the direction of Kaipo and Nohea, just as Music Man had told us she had.

The strum of Music Man's ukulele and his melodious voice could be heard in the background, as Helen Hokui sprinted the last few steps to the boat and disappeared inside. Stowaway, definite stowaway.

The camera now turned in the direction Kaipo and Nohea had taken. Both of them, laughing, chatting, unawares, holding something. A close up, and yes, they held champagne bottles. The camera followed them all the way into the boat. The video ended abruptly.

"Sorry, I'm not much of a camera person, but I was desperate," Noah said.

"You did good," Big Brah said, "can you pull up a close-up image of Kaipo?"

Noah messed with his phone again. "What're we looking for?" he said.

"A mole at the top of his right ear," Big Brah said.

For a moment, Noah looked startled. But he did as Big Brah had requested. He didn't just bring up one close-up of Kaipo. He brought up several images of Kaipo, very close. In image after image, I could see no mole. Darn.

Big Brah, Kali and I exchanged glances. This had to be the real Kaipo. Darn, again. The big wave of excitement was down to a ripple.

But Big Brah never gave up easy. "You followed the 'Honeymooner' to the Forbidden Beach. Then, what happened?" he asked.

Noah moved away from us and bent down to put the phone back on the coffee table. "The full moon was out, it was like daylight. I could see everything," he said.

"You waited?" Big Brah said.

Noah straightened, turned back toward us and spread his hands. "Only for a short while. The moon was so bright, I was afraid they'd be able to see my boat from the beach. So, I didn't stay long. I turned back, got home, watched TV late, slept, like I told you," Noah said.

"In the short while you waited, what did you see the 'Honeymooner' do?" Big Brah said.

Noah thought for a moment and shrugged. "The 'Honeymooner' just went into the boathouse," he said.

Boathouse. Why the boathouse?

"The boathouse, interesting." Big Brah looked significantly at Kali and me. "Noah, how sure are you of this?"

"Very sure," Noah said.

The boathouse was a place of interest for sure. But we had to attend Loni's meeting. Back inside the big, black truck, the clock on the dashboard display showed close to ten. We'd have to hurry to get to Loni's office on time. But Big Brah showed no desire to move fast or treat the meeting as an emergency. Whistling a happy tune, he took his time starting the truck.

Once he had the big truck started, he let the truck idle. He continued to whistle the same happy tune, gazing out of the windshield. Kali looked at his profile, smiled and turned to look at me. I raised my shoulders and made a face. Wish I knew what Big Brah was thinking. Big Brah started driving at a leisurely pace.

Still smiling, Kali asked him on behalf of both of us. "What are you thinking?"

Big Brah stopped whistling. "I was thinking about what Loni may have in store for us," he said.

"Hope Loni's found Kaipo," I said.

Big Brah chuckled, unworried. "Otherwise, we're in trouble," he said.

I don't know how Big Brah stayed calm at the most happening of times and still managed to get the job done. At ten sharp by the clock on the wall above the window, we were inside Loni's office. We were seated in front of Loni. Light and air spilled in through the window. The open window had a view of the rooftops, the rolling plains and the mountains. Loni sat hunched up behind his desk with the framed photograph of his pretty wife and young daughters.

Loni looked tense. His thick, black mustache drooped. With thinning hair, business-like glasses and a salt-and-pepper beard, Duke Mahio sat uncomfortably in the rightmost chair. Big Brah sat next to our client.

Big Brah had stopped whistling the happy tune, but he retained the unworried air about him. Next to Big Brah, Kali had an attentive frown on her face. She was paying attention to what was going on. Big Brah had warned us of trouble. Kali gave my arm a reassuring squeeze to tell me: you know your Big Brah and Kali have any trouble covered. Don't worry.

I wasn't worrying, but Jim Bordeta sitting stiffly on my left surely was. His hair was gelled in place. His mouth was a permanent straight line. With his mismatched brown eyes, he glared at Duke Mahio every now and then. Both dads had similar attire: shirts, jeans and sneakers. Nothing had changed between them.

Loni looked grimly at all of us. "Since we last met, two more days have gone by. We have searched for Kaipo as a wanted criminal with vice, homicide and the entire PD involved. Sadly we still haven't found Kaipo, and Nohea with him," he said.

Jim Bordeta glared past me, Kali and Big Brah at Duke Mahio. "This can only mean one thing!" he said.

Loni raised a restraining hand. "I'm coming to that, all in proper order," he said.

Jim Bordeta subsided.

Loni looked up at the wall clock and then back at us. "We've still got until noon for the deadline to expire, but as always, here at the PD, we're proactive. We get things done before time. So, the chief and I, we have already discussed the situation. I recommended this action to the chief. The chief accepted my recommendation.

He has given me the authority to take this action." To make sure we understood how important this made him, he looked at each of us in turn.

Even Loni's fan, Jim Bordeta muttered, "Oh, get on with it," irritably.

Loni continued, importantly. "I told you this in our last meeting. If we can't find them, it can only mean one thing." He turned to stare at Duke Mahio in the eye. "Sir, you're hiding Kaipo and Nohea!"

Jim Bordeta slapped the armrest of his chair. "Yes!" he said.

Duke Mahio sank down in his chair, shaking his head. He had a nervous frown. Big Brah glanced at Duke Mahio, looking puzzled. Duke Mahio had left our home last night, feeling better about the investigation. He should be standing up to Loni confidently. Why was he slouching?

Loni nodded, a satisfied expression on his face. "Your body language says it all," he said.

"Guilty!" Jim Bordeta said.

Loni said, "Yes, guilty. Mr. Mahio, your housekeeper must have informed you I interrogated her this morning about your movements on the night of the murder."

Oh, that was Loni's source of confidence. This morning, Loni had interviewed Lily's mom, Aunty Maria. But, why?

Big Brah gazed inquiringly at Loni. "What did you learn?" he said.

Loni raised an appeasing hand. "I'm coming to that, Big Brah, I'm coming to that. Everything in proper order," he said.

Big Brah waited.

Loni heaved a sigh. "This morning, I visited Mahio Mansion. I interrogated Duke Mahio there. He told me he was home all of Friday night. Minutes later, I interrogated the housekeeper, Aunty Maria. She told me, Duke Mahio, he was out on the ocean all of Friday night," he said.

What?

"Guilty!" Jim Bordeta said.

"Yes, guilty." Loni agreed.

At last, Duke Mahio found his voice. Indignation written all over him, he turned and spoke to Big Brah. "Kaipo's mother, Luana and I, it was our tradition to go fishing Friday nights. Since she passed away, I still go out fishing, to remember her. When Lieutenant Loni here asked me what I did Friday night, I was outraged by his tone. He was implying I had something to do with the murder and Kaipo's disappearance, so I didn't tell him I was out that night. What difference did it make, where I was? It's Kaipo who is missing. What reason can I possibly have to murder my property manager Helen?" he said.

Big Brah nodded. "I understand," he said, placidly.

Loni had been listening on to every word Duke Mahio uttered. "What kind of fish did you catch?" he said, sarcastic.

Duke Mahio talked to Loni now. "I got lots of *akule*," he said.

Loni leaned back in his chair, theatrically threw his head back and laughed out loud. "Akule? The small fish?" he said.

Duke Mahio turned sideways to look at Big Brah and Kali for support. "Nothing wrong with akule. Kaipo's mother used to love akule, she had so many recipes for the fish," Duke Mahio said.

"I love akule," Big Brah said.

Kali nodded. "Koa and I, we have several recipes," she said.

Duke Mahio hadn't looked at me for support, but I was always compelled to stand up for all things small. "Akule can grow big," I said.

Pityingly, Loni looked at Duke Mahio, Big Brah, Kali and me. "Yes, I can see all of you are in this together," he said.

I supposed Loni meant we were all together in our love for akule, the small fish, and he would be right. But I was wrong.

"You know what fish I catch?" Loni said.

Before Duke Mahio, Big Brah, Kali or I could say anything, Jim Bordeta said, "You're a big fish kinda man."

Loni nodded, proudly. "Yes, ahi. I fish ahi," he said.

Everyone in the room nodded, acknowledging the island's favorite big fish ahi.

Loni continued. "Whatever your favorite fish, Mr. Mahio, on Friday night, you had the opportunity to murder Helen Hokui, pick up Kaipo and Nohea and take them to a secret hiding place known only to you and them," he said.

Duke Mahio sat up in his chair, looking more confident. "Helen Hokui was found on the rocks. Those rocks are so dangerous, it would be an impossible task to get my boat in and out safely," he said.

Loni leaned back in his chair, a smug look on his face. "Impossible?" he said.

Unnerved, Duke Mahio turned to Big Brah and Kali for help. Both Big Brah and Kali looked apologetic. They didn't say anything. Confused, Duke Mahio turned his gaze back on Loni.

Loni now had a smug grin plastered on his face. "Big Brah and Kali, you were famous in high school, the two of you got a boat in and out through those rocks at will, did you not?" he said.

I looked at Big Brah and Kali. Action heroes. This was something they hadn't told me. Probably because they didn't want me to try it. At least not alone, since they had done the dangerous task as a couple, keeping each other safe.

Sitting there, all quiet and serious, you would never imagine they had such an adventurous streak in them. I was proud, so proud of my Big Brah and Kali.

Big Brah nodded. "Yes, but that was a long time ago," he said, in his modest way.

Kali shrugged, sweetly. "We were young, we were in love, we could do anything. But we didn't recommend anyone else try to get the boat in and out of the dangerous rocks," she said.

Loni agreed, wholeheartedly. "Naturally, you were responsible, kept each other safe. But you did prove beyond doubt, it can be done." He turned to stare full on at Duke Mahio. "That means Mr. Mahio, you don't have an excuse. Your housekeeper, she's been with you a long time. She's been there, since the time of your parents. She's seen you since you were very young. She told me you have always been exceptionally good with boats.

"Apparently, you and your late wife, Luana, shared an interest in boats. In fact you did go boating around the island a lot. The two of you had boasted to Aunty Maria about being able to go in and out through those very rocks, am I right?" he said.

Duke Mahio looked nervous. "I already told you Luana and I used to go fishing Friday nights. Sure, we could get the boat in through those rocks, but I meant, I couldn't do it alone," he said.

"You'd only have to bring the boat in alone. On the way out, you'd have Kaipo to assist you. You could have taken your boat in and out of there, no problem," Loni said.

"No problem," Jim Bordeta said.

Duke Mahio opened his mouth to speak and then closed it without saying anything. He looked shaken.

Loni moved to rest his elbows on the desk and leaned forward. "The PD has been burning all its resources searching for Kaipo. Chief says, this can't go on indefinitely. At noon today, we'll stop searching for Kaipo actively," he said.

Duke Mahio recovered his voice. A defiant look came over him. "I don't need you to find Kaipo. I have Big Brah," he said.

Loni grinned, smugly. "Yes, you do have Big Brah. I suggest you use him. So, here's what I'll do for you." Loni raised his index finger slowly and then waved it in the air. "I'm giving you one day. Today is a Friday, so tomorrow, Saturday, at noon, I want you to bring Kaipo, and Nohea with him, to my office, right here. Otherwise—"

"Otherwise, what?" Duke Mahio said, still defiant.

"Otherwise, Mr. Mahio, I'm going to have to arrest you," Loni said.

Duke Mahio was up on his feet, his chair rolling away from under him. "I won't stand for this, I don't know where Kaipo is, I—"

Big Brah tugged at Duke Mahio's shirt sleeve. Duke Mahio turned his gaze downward at Big Brah, confused. Gently, Big Brah signaled for Duke Mahio to sit down. Duke Mahio gazed at Big Brah for a long moment.

I got up and rolled Duke Mahio's chair back for him. Duke Mahio sat down. I got back in my chair. Kali had her big eyes on Big Brah. What was Big Brah going to say?

# Chapter 20 Always too dramatic for police work

Big Brah got up. He got behind his chair, rolled it back a few paces and placed his hands on its back. Duke Mahio, Jim Bordeta, Kali and I had to swivel in our chairs to see him. Kali smiled at Big Brah encouragingly. She squeezed my arm to say enjoy the Big Brah show. Jim Bordeta and Loni exchanged nervous glances. Duke Mahio gazed at Big Brah, silently.

Big Brah spoke, softly, to Duke Mahio. "Brah, you have hired me to find Kaipo. But, if I find him, what will you do with him?" he said.

Duke Mahio looked taken aback by the question. He turned his head to look peevishly at his rival dad, Jim Bordeta, and then said to Big Brah, "I will scold him. He shouldn't have troubled Nohea like this. I'll make sure he never sees Nohea, ever again."

Noting the irony of the situation, Big Brah smiled at Kali and me. Then, he spoke to Jim Bordeta.

"You, brah? If I brought Nohea back to you,

what would you do?" Big Brah said.

Jim Bordeta fumed, his mouth a straight line. "How does it matter what I'll do? Kaipo has kidnapped my daughter. I want you to release her, immediately. Once you do, well," he paused to glance at Duke Mahio, reconciling and then continued, "yes well, rest I'll do as you would. I'll scold her. Tell her never to see Kaipo, ever again," he said.

This time, Big Brah, Kali and I, all three of us exchanged smiles. Big Brah had taken on this case to fight for love. Loni and the dads were not getting the irony of the situation.

"I don't know where Kaipo is, no one does," Big Brah said.

"You know," Jim Bordeta said. "If you know, Duke knows it too, you work for Duke!"

Big Brah smiled to pacify Jim Bordeta. "Let me explain. I believe Kaipo is hiding. Nohea is hiding with him out of her own freewill. And the real reason they are hiding now, the real reason they have been hiding all along?

"Is this feud between their dads! A dad's job is to keep the children safe, not drive them out of their homes, especially when they need your help, your guidance the most. For the first time in their lives, your children have fallen in love! If the two of you can stop fighting, both your children can return home safely," he said.

From behind us, I heard Loni make a sound of disbelief. "By the deadline, tomorrow noon, Big

Brah?" he said.

"No, not by the deadline, not by any other condition. They are smart kids. They have found a hiding place no one can figure out. More important, they are good kids. They want their fathers to be happy with their choices, especially this one, their mate for life. Unless Kaipo and Nohea see their fathers are genuinely happy to see them again, they won't ever return," Big Brah said.

There was a tense silence. The gentle breeze of the spring morning blowing in through the window could have been the fabled island monster breathing fire into the room prior to a full-blown attack. It was that tense.

Loni sighed, loudly. "More drama, Big Brah! You were always too dramatic for police work, back in high school, and now," he said.

"I'm never in anything for the drama, Loni, you should know that by now. I find the truth, and I just stated the truth," Big Brah said.

All of us swiveled in our chairs, so we could watch both Big Brah and Loni.

Loni looked frustrated. "All this talk is going to get us nowhere," he said.

"We talk, so we can all get to the right place, not a place where we keep on hating each other. But a place where we can all share love, aloha. A place we can all be proud of," Big Brah said, softly.

Loni clutched his head with both hands. "Noon tomorrow, I am arresting the father here.

I don't care he's your client, or not!" he said.

"Arrest him then, but you still won't get Kaipo," Big Brah said.

Duke Mahio started. He gaped up at Big Brah, aghast.

Loni let go his head, placed both hands on the top of the desk and glared at Big Brah. "If you're not careful, Big Brah, you may risk getting arrested yourself, as an accessory!" he said.

Big Brah grinned. "Go ahead, arrest me. You still won't get Kaipo," he said.

Duke Mahio spoke, his voice almost choking with feelings. "What're you saying, Big Brah? You'll let Kaipo languish, let me be arrested, let yourself be arrested, and you still won't find Kaipo?" he said.

All of a sudden, still fuming, Jim Bordeta was on Duke Mahio's side. "Duke, you have Big Brah on contract to find Kaipo, don't you?"

"I-I didn't think it necessary to have a formal contract," Duke Mahio said.

Big Brah was big on legalities. "You don't need a formal contract, my word is sufficient reason to initiate any legal action against me," he said.

Big Brah was making it easier for the men to be threatening.

Jim Bordeta completed his threat. "You can have his private investigator's license revoked for breach of contract."

All three of them, Jim Bordeta, Loni and Duke Mahio, silently watched Big Brah for his reaction to their threats. Kali and I exchanged glances.

I have to confess we, Big Brah's diehard fans, even we were worried. Arrest? Private investigator's license revoked? These weren't things you associated with Big Brah.

Awards, merit citations, yes. Arrest, license revocation, never. Big Brah threw his head back and laughed out loud.

Jim Bordeta looked even more annoyed. He looked at Loni. "Arrest him, now!" he said.

Duke Mahio looked mortified. "Thought you were more reliable than the police. I never should have hired you!" he said.

Loni had worked with Big Brah many more times. But he was clueless. "I want Kaipo, by noon tomorrow," he said, adamant.

"What will you do, if you do get Kaipo, by noon tomorrow?" Big Brah said, softly.

"Arrest him, of course, for the murder, for sure." Loni looked at both the fathers, taking them into his confidence. "The kidnapping charges, we'll see how we feel about that," he said.

Big Brah said, "In other words, you'll separate Kaipo from Nohea, even if the dads didn't. I can't allow that unless—"

"Unless, what?" Loni exploded, in exasperation.

"Unless, Kaipo is guilty of the murder. Then, he may deserve to be separated from his love. Unfortunately, as of this moment, I have not concluded my investigation. It's going to take me some more time to determine what happened on the boat and who the real murderer is.

"If I determine, Kaipo is the murderer, I will bring him back, to serve justice. If he isn't the murderer, then, yes you can arrest me, have my license revoked, but I won't bring Kaipo to you," Big Brah said.

The three men stared at Big Brah. They didn't know what to make of Big Brah's offer. Duke Mahio was our client, the man who had gotten us involved in all this.

He reconciled a little. "So, you're saying, you will find the real murderer after all?" he said.

Big Brah nodded, reassuring. "Yes, brah, I'm not going to let you down. I will find the real murderer, and I'm confident it isn't Kaipo. Therefore Kaipo will have one less reason to continue hiding. Who knows? Kaipo and Nohea, together, they'll figure out maybe they should return? But, I'm going to make sure they get to decide what they want to do," he said.

The experience of all the years Loni had spent working with Big Brah on the big cases now kicked in. Suddenly, Loni was all smiles.

Loni said, "I see the problem. I think Kaipo is the killer, and you, Big Brah, you think someone else committed the murder. All right, all right. I can live with that. It's part of police work to learn to live with different opinions. You must make sure who the real killer is, I agree."

Duke Mahio nodded, vigorously. "It's the right thing to do to find the real killer," he said.

Jim Bordeta looked doubtful. He shrugged. "I guess, I've waited this long. I can wait another day," he said.

"Then, I see no problem," Loni said, quite grandly. "Take your time, Big Brah. You have until noon tomorrow."

Big Brah got up and nodded briefly. Kali and I got up. Big Brah turned and headed for the door. Kali and I followed him out of there.

Back inside the confines of the big, black truck warmed by the sun, I shivered. "Were they really going to arrest you, revoke your license?" I said.

In the driver's seat, Big Brah was grim. "Umi, we took on this investigation to protect love by delivering justice. I was making sure we did. Threats don't bother me. I know we're doing the right thing," he said.

I heaved a sigh of relief from the backseat. "Mahalo for making it so easy," I said.

Big Brah turned to Kali, an inquiring look on his face. "What's on your mind?" he asked, softly.

Kali gazed at Big Brah in open admiration. "You did good, Koa. You did good," she said.

I was proud of my Big Brah. "To protect love by delivering justice. Let's go!" I said.

Big Brah chuckled, pleased. "Loni's talk about bringing boats in and out of the dangerous rocks made me think. I want to know what happened there. Let's go to the crime scene," he said.

Back to the crime scene. The dangerous rocks. A symbol now of the adventurous streak of the action heroes: Kali and Big Brah! I was eager to see the rocks. How had Big Brah and Kali got in and out of there? The truck rolled forward.

We followed the coastal highway, until we were above the calamitous rocks. The truck slowed as we got close to the sandy road spiraling away from the highway. The truck crunched the sand all the way to where the ground leveled.

Big Brah parked the truck. We got out, as before. It was near noon and our shadows small. There was the startling blue ocean. Beautiful. Below us, the shocking rocks. Big waves pounded the rocks. White spray spouted skyward.

Big Brah pointed to the farthest rock outcrop. "This is counterintuitive, I know, but see those rocks? If you want to bring a boat in, you head straight at those rocks," he said.

"Wow," I said. "Scary."

Kali smiled reassuringly at me.

Big Brah said, "Scary, yes. You've gotta have faith. Right before you hit the rocks, there's a strong rip current that's going to lift your boat and throw you over there." He pointed.

I looked toward the direction he was pointing. There were a couple more rock outcrops. These rocks were bigger with the ocean spray rising even higher.

These rocks looked even more dangerous.

"Sheesh, how does that help?" I said.

Kali smiled reassuringly, again.

Big Brah chuckled. "If you're patient and don't panic, you just hold on. The current delivers you right into the channel between those rocks," he said.

The channel ended in a sanctuary. A pristine beach nestled against towering steep cliffs. The ocean was the only way to get to the beach. On the island, we lovingly called this sandy haven Sacred Beach.

Wondrously, I said, "The channel is calm, protected from both sides. This allows you to bring the boat in all the way. Safe to Sacred Beach."

"Very good, Umi. You're getting it already," Kali said.

I swelled up with pride.

Big Brah held Kali's hand. "That's what we did."

I was in awe. Looking at them I believed love delivered you to a haven even through dire rocks.

Big Brah said, "But I doubt Duke Mahio would have done it that way."

"Because he was alone?" I said.

Big Brah shook his head. "Doesn't matter Duke Mahio was alone. If he really wanted to get to the 'Honeymooner,' it would have been easier for him to drive here." He pointed at the rocky path descending down. "And trek down to the rocks where the 'Honeymooner' was found," he said.

I said, "Do you think Duke Mahio drove down here, helped Kaipo as Loni suspects?"

Big Brah shook his head, firmly. "I think Duke Mahio loves Kaipo way too much to put his son in danger. Duke Mahio didn't go down to the 'Honeymooner,' but someone else may have," he said.

"Who?" I cried out.

"Bran!" Big Brah said.

As soon as Big Brah mentioned Bran, I thought of Cousin Koma searching for Bran. Cousin Koma had told us, he would let Big Brah know, as soon as he had something. We hadn't heard from him, since then. But Big Brah had something more pressing at hand.

"Let's follow the killer's footsteps," Big Brah said.

Despite the sun high above us, I shivered. We started down the rocky path. I imagined Bran, as he climbed down this very path on his way to murder Helen Hokui.

Bran had to be anxious and stressed. It would have been a full moon night, and he had probably brought a flashlight that he didn't have to use. Also, the night would have been cooler than the midday. It took us several minutes to get down to the rocks.

No doubt it had been the same for Bran. The ocean spray was now close, cool and welcome under the warm sun. I imagined Bran chatting with an unsuspecting Helen Hokui here. In the innocent moonlight, taking her closer and closer to the water, so he could discard her in the ocean. The cruel blow to the head.

We stopped near the water's edge, the ocean spray in our faces. Big Brah stood there communing. After a while, he turned back.

Big Brah shouted above the din of the crashing waves. "Let's go," he said.

We started up the rocky path. I imagined Bran. He had to have been in a hurry to leave the scene. Big Brah though climbed unhurriedly. Kali was even-paced. The steep climb back up took us several minutes longer. Provided he had legs as strong as ours, Bran could have made it back in the same time. Big Brah, Kali and I made it back to where we had left the big, black truck. We climbed into the truck.

Big Brah started the truck. "If Bran killed Helen Hokui, then what happened to Kaipo and Nohea?" he said.

The truck lurched back, made a smooth turn and started up the sandy road.

I said, "Helen was a stowaway."

Kali said, "She was hiding from Kaipo and Nohea. After Helen was sure the couple was gone, she'd come out of hiding."

Big Brah said, "So, Kaipo and Nohea escaped before Bran got here. Or at least, I hope they escaped."

Big Brah fell silent, thinking. The truck

was back on the coastal highway. At last Big Brah spoke. "We're on to something. Kaipo and Nohea escaped before Bran got to Helen Hokui. Otherwise, Bran would be holding Kaipo and Nohea captive. That didn't happen. If it had, the police would have found Kaipo and Nohea, and with them Bran," he said.

"That makes sense," I said.

"What makes even more sense, we eat lunch somewhere. I'm hungry," Kali said.

Big Brah nodded, approvingly. "I was also thinking of lunch. The night prior to the murder Kaipo met Helen Hokui at the Tavern. I'm curious to know what happened between them. Let's go to the Tavern," he said.

Big Brah wanted to go back to the scene of the fight. He would commune and figure things out. Cool. As we drove to the tavern, Kali slipped into a trance.

In her trance states, Kali thought up a storm. Then she came up with something brilliant. As Big Brah parked the truck in the Tavern's parking lot, he shot me a glance. What was going on with Kali?

Big Brah and I were both curious to know. It was lunchtime. The restaurant was crowded. Bright, petite and with an important smile, Mohua sat us down at our usual table.

Mohua inquired if we had any more questions for her. Kali shook her head briefly. Mohua looked relieved. She took our orders and disappeared. Big Brah gazed out at the green mountains, thinking.

Kali was still in her trance. As often happened, I was the normal member of the family. Mohua appeared with our drink: a clear pitcher of iced green tea. The rich, aromatic brew was a welcome sight. She also had our appetizers.

Crisp, golden-brown spring rolls with a spicy, tangy red sauce. The spring rolls and the dip were gone almost as soon as she left them. I sipped the green tea and let the cool drink soothe my throat. Big Brah and Kali also sipped drinks, both still silent.

There was some serious thinking going on at the table. What were they going to come up with?

I shivered, just in anticipation. Big Brah had been so relaxed about it, I had paid little attention to Loni's deadline. But it hit me. We had less than a day to find Bran.

I was clueless. I had no idea how to go about it. Well, Big Brah and Kali had better do some deep thinking. We needed it. Soon Mohua returned with our food. As she put the lunch plates down on the table, she looked at Kali and Big Brah.

Kali and Big Brah were both still silent. Mohua shot me a sympathetic look to say: so you normal. I smiled back, proud. Mohua left. We started on our lunches, mute.

We had all ordered another island favorite:

local teriyaki burgers with macaroni salad on the side. The burgers smelled good and came with a big, green leaf of lettuce, sliced tomatoes, onions and cheese, all fresh.

I ate heartily, my anticipation growing. Mohua took our empty lunch plates away, with a pleased smile. We had forgotten to order any dessert.

But Mohua didn't forget her friend, Kali, appreciated wholesome desserts. Mohua left us a big plate of malasadas: small, browned balls of fried dough, sweetened. Delicious.

Complimentary, of course. Despite her trance, Kali looked at Big Brah significantly. Mohua had just practiced aloha. She should be thanked for the giving.

With his mind on the investigation, Big Brah still managed to acknowledge Kali's look. To make up, Big Brah would pay extra gratuity. A generous amount considerably more than the price of the malasadas. Cheehoo for aloha. But Big Brah and Kali, they needn't have worried.

A few years ago, when Mohua's father had gotten mixed up in a crime, Big Brah had rescued the father. The father was a good man, innocent. Big Brah had never thought to charge him a cent. Ever since, the entire family treated us as their own. At last, Kali slipped out of her trance.

She smiled brightly at first Big Brah and then me, her big eyes shining. Big Brah and I looked at each other. We had waited this long. This was going to be good. Big Brah also abandoned whatever he was thinking and paid attention to Kali.

Kali tucked a strand of her thick, black hair behind her ear, purposefully. "I have figured out a few things about the case," she said.

I was glad people was talking again! Kali and Big Brah were masters of the understatement. "A few things? I bet you've figured out how it all happened," I said.

Big Brah chuckled, happy. He was always pleased when Kali shone. "Interesting, I've puzzled over what happened here, it fits," he said.

They were sitting across from me. I gazed at them now. They really did make a sweet couple. Made me proud.

I spread my hands. "All this figuring out, all this puzzling, you better enlighten me, fast," I said.

Both of them laughed. With typical generosity, Big Brah said, "Kali, you go first!"

With equal magnanimity, Kali said, "I only got a small piece of the puzzle, you probably have the whole thing. You go first. I'll fill you in with mine, as you go along!"

Big Brah nodded, approvingly. "Fair enough! Let's begin, here at the Tavern. It's Thursday night, Kaipo and Helen Hokui are at that table." Big Brah snuck a thumb toward the lush palm hiding the table beyond us. "Why did they fight?"

I had brainstormed on cases with Big Brah

and Kali on so many occasions, I had gotten good at it. "According to Loni, they fought over robbing the safe," I said.

Big Brah said, "Loni's assigned motive is weak. From the surveillance video, we already know Fake Kaipo also known as Bran robbed the safe. When she was murdered Helen Hokui was wearing the platinum necklace with the sea turtle, dolphin and octopus. I suspect Bran didn't see the necklace. Loni found the necklace under her scarf. Duke Mahio confirmed the necklace was from the safe. Helen Hokui had to be in on the theft with Bran.

"Clearly, with the Kaipo suit and the Kaipo bracelet, Bran and Helen wanted to frame Kaipo for the theft. The real Kaipo didn't know about the theft, why? Because it was in Bran and Helen's interest to hide their intention from the person they were framing. That would be Kaipo," Big Brah said.

I had a sudden idea. "Is it worth asking Mohua about the mole, to see if it was the real Kaipo, or Bran who fought with Helen Hokui?" I said.

Big Brah thought for a moment. "Suppose, while they were here, the real Kaipo walked in. Or, a longtime friend stopped by their table to see them. It would be too awkward, they would be found out. Too risky. No, I'm sure this was the real Kaipo. The real Kaipo had a real fight with Helen, but why?" he said.

Kali spoke up, her voice bubbling with

excitement. "Maybe if I told you what I have figured out, it will provide the answer," she said.

Both Big Brah and I fixed our gazes on her. What was she going to say?

Kali grinned. "You know what Cousin Keni told us. He told Kaipo about the 'Honeymooner.' Kaipo wanted the boat, and wouldn't hear of any other," she said.

I nodded, animated.

"Yes, I remember," Big Brah said, encouraging.

Kali said, "Then, Iekika. She told us, she had even asked Nohea, if they were taking a priest along, in order to get married. Nohea had replied, no, not required. Iekika thought Nohea wasn't getting married, just looking for some Friday night fun. But, what if, for Friday night fun, Kaipo and Nohea got married?"

# Chapter 21 Not lost but found

Married? Meaning Kaipo and Nohea were not lost but found!

Kali gestured animatedly with her hands. "Think about it. The champagne bottles, we found them not in the cockpit cooler but in the galley refrigerator next to the bedroom. Why? Because they got married. Afterward they expected to start their honeymoon onboard. After all, they didn't have a home they could go to and share their joy, a home where they'd be loved as a couple...." Kali's voice trailed away, as she shared the pain from the lack of aloha Kaipo and Nohea must have felt.

But their love had surmounted the problem and found them a way.

Kali shrugged. "Deprived of a loving home, they chose one of Cousin Keni's lovingly customized boats for their honeymoon. Not bad."

Big Brah nodded, slowly. "I think they did all right. If they intended to get married, it would be something they'd want kept secret until afterward. So even if their families objected, they'd be married already," he said.

Kali said, "And, if Helen Hokui learned about Kaipo's plan to marry Nohea on Friday night, and she told him she knew. Or worse, she blackmailed him: I'll tell your father, or hers. Then sure, Kaipo lost it. He was here alone, without Nohea, and not surprising, he threatened to kill Helen, if she told anyone about the wedding."

Big Brah said, "That explains why Helen followed Kaipo to the harbor. When she sensed opportunity, Helen hid inside the boat's cabin. So she could continue spying on Kaipo and Nohea. Find out exactly what was going on between them." Big Brah picked up the small, black folder Mohua had left us, read the bill and tucked greenbacks into the folder from his wallet.

The plate of malasadas was now empty. Mohua arrived. She held a tray in her right hand. I couldn't see what was on the tray. Big Brah had already paid. Deftly Mohua picked up the bill folder with her left hand. She smiled at the empty malasada plate. From the tray, she served another plate full of the sweet delights. On the Tavern. Mohua winked at Kali.

Now Kali couldn't have Big Brah compensate Mohua for the fresh plate of malasadas. He had already paid. Kali smiled benignly back at Mohua. Friend.

Mohua left. Kali looked inquiringly at Big Brah. Big Brah nodded, briefly. Anticipating what

Mohua would do, he had remembered to pay for extra plates of malasadas. Pure aloha.

Big Brah helped himself to a malasada. "Come on, let's finish the malasadas, fast. I have a plan," he said.

While we speed-ate the malasadas, Big Brah revealed his plan of action. "Finding out what happened to Kaipo and Nohea is an important piece of the puzzle to find out how Bran murdered Helen Hokui."

Kali and I agreed.

Big Brah said, "Noah confirmed to us, the 'Honeymooner' traveled from the harbor dock to the Forbidden Beach."

I caught on. "The 'Honeymooner' went into Makoa Alika's boathouse," I said.

Kali said, "The boathouse is where we should head to next."

"In the ocean bird," Big Brah said.

A swoosh of excitement lifted me. The ocean bird was our twin-engine amphibian aircraft. We flew the bird for business and pleasure. The amphibian's dual land and water capability made the aircraft useful on the island. The ocean bird resided in the hangar at the water's edge inside our property. That afternoon, after returning from the Tavern and freshening up, Big Brah, Kali and I left the house through the kitchen door, on our way to the hangar.

We got to the boathouse down the meandering garden path. "Makoa Alika, when we saw him, I thought he wasn't leveling with us," I said.

Big Brah nodded. "I felt the same way," he said.

We walked on in silence. The garden path continued around the boathouse. There was wilderness on both sides. Wild bushes and coconut trees.

"Why're we taking the ocean bird, why not the big boat?" I said.

Big Brah walked with his head bowed, eyes on the ground in front of him. "Makoa Alika's already told us to use the beach. If he sees the big boat, or us, he may not come out, at all. Today, the challenge is to attract his attention, but in a way that shouldn't make him mad, but provoke his curiosity. So he comes out to see us. We get the truth out of him. The ocean bird's gonna help us. Just watch," he said, mysteriously.

The mystery deepened. We belted up inside the ocean bird. Big Brah was at ease in the pilot's seat. Kali was excited in the copilot's seat. I was giddy in the cabin seat closest to the cockpit. Getting over her excitement, her voice steady, Kali chatted with the aunties at the island air traffic control. Soon we were all set.

The hangar doors opened. The ocean bird moved slowly out. The afternoon sun was bright. In front of us, the ocean stretched blue.

Big Brah sped the ocean bird up. "Here we go," he said.

The ocean bird surged forward purposefully. The familiar sinking feeling in my stomach, and we were airborne. Cheehoo! The ocean bird gained height.

Below us, the island. We were flying over the eastside harbor. Fly like a bird. Rent-a-boat. The coconut trees. The boat ramp. A multitude of cars were parked under the coconut trees. The dock. A crowd was gathered around Music Man.

I saw TV cameras. Laika Lahaina must have arrived to see Music Man. Excitement there. But we were on a mission. Big Brah flew the ocean bird northward, following the coastline.

The dangerous rocks, cliffs and Sacred Beach passed below. We had been down there only hours ago. The big waves and the spray of the water was visible. We turned the northeast curve of the island.

To our right appeared revered waters. Since ancient times, islanders worshipped these waters where *mano,* the beloved shark, thrived. The water was blue and looked pure and innocent. To our left was the beautiful shoreline.

Every now and then, the waves found a way inside secret bays, coves, inlets, deltas and beaches, all the way to where the reserve started. The Forbidden Beach came into view. From the air, the beach looked even more gorgeous.

The blue water. The golden sand beach. The grassy hill. The wilderness. The island was already paradise. The forbidden land of the whale reserve was a paradise within paradise.

The ocean bird banked toward the pristine beach. Makoa Alika would be staring up at us right about now.

"Let's get seen from below," Big Brah said.

The ocean bird flew over the golden sands of the Forbidden Beach. Below the treetops on the left, the boathouse peeped out. The bird flew over the grassy hill on which Makoa Alika had stood.

Beyond the grassy hill, there were the ruins of the ancient heiau: rock platform and pillars. Kahunas all, Makoa Alika's ancestors had been the priests who worshipped at the heiau.

Next to the heiau, there was a home with its own water and solar power supply. The home had a neat shingle roof. Near the sturdy home, there was a large catchment tank supplying the water. Nearby, the shining panels of a solar farm smiled up at us. The heiau and the home were surrounded by miles of wilderness.

Rolling plains. Ridges. Valleys. Pristine nature. Big Brah turned the ocean bird around. Once again, we flew over the heiau. Someone had emerged from the home, no doubt a member of the Alika family. A young woman. She was excitedly waving up at us.

Big Brah said, "That should do it. They have seen us from below. I'm going to land the ocean bird now."

We flew over the grassy hill and the beach. The ocean bird banked and lost height rapidly.

Big Brah brought the ocean bird in for a water landing. The ocean bird kissed the water. Smooth. The ocean bird lost speed and slowed down.

"I'm gonna get us to the boathouse," Big Brah said.

*Will Makoa Alika be waiting for us?* I thought.

The ocean bird surged forward on the water like a boat. Like ours, Makoa Alika's boathouse was situated at the end of an inlet. The ocean bird moved slowly up the inlet and stopped outside a massive closed door.

The door looked pretty solid. No way were we getting in there without help from the boathouse owner. A movement on the shore to the right caught my eye. Big Brah and Kali saw him too. Makoa Alika.

In helmet, cape and malo, he carried the sharp spear he had thrown at Big Brah. Big Brah had succeeded in getting Makoa Alika's attention but had provoked more than the kahuna's curiosity. I could feel the wrath of his piercing eyes.

Big Brah waved cheerily and turned the nose of the ocean bird shoreward. In minutes, Big Brah, Kali and I joined Makoa Alika on the shore. The sun was warm on our backs and the sand soft under our feet. Makoa Alika was as I remembered him from last time.

He had permanent frown lines between his eyebrows. Long beard. Whale-tooth necklace.

Bands and triangles tattooed in black ink on his bare chest. Makoa Alika wasn't pleased to see us.

He clutched the menacing spear. "I told you, you could enjoy the beach. Why're you snooping here?" he said.

Big Brah made a placatory gesture and smiled to rob his words of any offence. "Sorry, brah. I wanted to talk with you. So I had to fly over your land, attract your attention," he said, honestly.

Big Brah's honesty melted Makoa Alika, somewhat. "My daughter, Moli, she loves airplanes, she saw you."

His daughter Moli loved airplanes. If that melted Makoa Alika's heart, we would take it. I remembered Moli's excited waving.

The older man relaxed his grip on his spear. He glanced at Kali and me. "Moli loves to be in the air. I blame it on her mother naming her after a seabird."

A seabird? Then I remembered. *Moli* was Hawaiian for albatross. First Alba and now Moli. Our island albatrosses sure loved to fly.

Makoa Alika fixed his piercing stare on Big Brah. "What is it you wanted to talk about?" he asked, in a quieter voice.

Big Brah took a deep breath and let it out slowly. "Kaipo and Nohea, I want to talk about them," he said.

Makoa Alika snorted. "What of them? I already told you, they didn't surf here on Friday night," he said.

"I remember. Just as you told us, I don't doubt Kaipo and Nohea didn't surf. But you didn't tell us they were here and their boat went into your boathouse," Big Brah said.

"Into the boathouse? Nonsense. They'd need me to open the door for them," Makoa Alika said.

Big Brah lifted his shoulders about an inch and let them drop. "Then, you must have opened the door for them," he said.

"Why would I do such a thing?" Makoa Alika said.

To make himself as nonthreatening as possible, Big Brah sat down on the sand. He squinted up at the kahuna. "Kaipo and Nohea wanted to get married. You're a priest. You let them in," he said.

There was a silence. The crash of the waves rolling onto the beach was louder. The chorus of the shorebirds amplified.

At last, Makoa Alika said, "It's true, I'm a priest. I conduct weddings in the way of our ancestors. But Kaipo and Nohea, they'd have been required to make a prior appointment," he said.

Big Brah nodded. "I believe they did get a prior appointment, from you. You were expecting them. They arrived as expected. You let them in," he said.

"You know everything," Makoa Alika said, bothered. He clutched the spear, again. "Why don't you tell me what happened next?"

Big Brah rose, drawing himself to his full height. "Sorry, brah, that's all I do know. After that what happened, I don't know. Is why I'm here, I hope you'll tell me," he said.

Silence, again. This time the crash of the waves and the calls of the shorebirds was muted. *Here's where we find out what happened to Kaipo and Nohea,* I thought. My ears were tuned only to Makoa Alika.

Makoa Alika's grip on the spear relaxed. He laughed his high-pitched laugh. "Tell you what happened? Why should I tell you anything about Nohea or Kaipo? I watch the news on TV. You're working for Duke Mahio. While the police search for his son as a wanted murderer, the father stands around and watches. Or, should I try to help Jim Bordeta? The man knows his daughter loves Kaipo. But he's trying hard to have Kaipo arrested. What lousy parents."

Makoa Alika's high-pitched laugh earlier hadn't been caused by amusement.

Makoa Alika accused Big Brah. "You're helping the lousy parents!" he said.

"No, brah. I'm as bothered at the parents as you are. But I'm trying to protect Nohea and Kaipo. I'm trying to protect their love," Big Brah said.

"How?"

"By finding the real murderer," Big Brah said.

Makoa Alika moved his spear from hand to hand and gripped the weapon with both hands.

"Then, why're you here? I don't see any murderer around here. No, I think you're trying to find the kids, so you can drag them back to their parents and the police," he said.

Big Brah sighed. "You married them, didn't you?" he said.

Makoa Alika glowered at us. He didn't say anything.

Big Brah looked at Kali, me and then back at Makoa Alika. "Kaipo and Nohea, they left their boat in your boathouse. You left the boathouse door open, so they could leave. Yes, you married them, at the sacred heiau, next to your home. Is why you're protecting them, now. It's your sacred responsibility. The heiau has always been a refuge. As priest your duty is to protect those who seek your shelter."

Wow. Makoa Alika was carrying out his sacred duty. No joke.

Big Brah said, "After the wedding ceremony, when Nohea and Kaipo got back to the boathouse, the boat was gone, right?" he said.

The boat was gone? Kali and I looked at Big Brah for more.

"How could that happen? A boat can't just disappear on its own," Makoa Alika said.

For the first time, Big Brah smiled. "Must have puzzled Kaipo and Nohea, and you," Big Brah said.

"Answer my question, how could the boat disappear?" Makoa Alika said.

"The answer is simple. Helen Hokui was hiding in a closet in the cabin. After Kaipo and Nohea left, sensing them gone, Helen came out of her hiding place. The boat was hers now. She left with it," Big Brah said.

Makoa Alika looked disgusted. "And crashed the boat on the rocks?" he said.

Big Brah nodded, slowly. "A dangerous maneuver. Helen was trying to bring the boat in through the rocks. She lacked the experience and the expertise. She crashed the boat. But she survived," he said.

Makoa Alika frowned. "How did she die then?" he said.

"A man by the name of Bran, not his real name either. Bran met Helen Hokui on the rocks, killed her," Big Brah said.

"Just like that? Why would this Bran kill Helen Hokui?" Makoa Alika said.

"Bran and Helen Hokui had stolen jewelry from the Mahio safe. Bran wanted it all. He killed her," Big Brah said.

"This Bran, why is it he isn't in the news, and no one knows about him?" Makoa Alika asked.

Big Brah said, "Because I haven't told anyone."

"Why?"

Big Brah said, "I wanted to make sure the sequence of events was just as I told you. It's important I know Helen Hokui was alone when she crashed the boat."

I said, "Unaware of the stowaway, Kaipo and

Nohea left Helen alone in the boat. Helen stole the boat."

Kali said, "That can only be if Kaipo and Nohea got out of the boat here."

Makoa Alika thought for a moment. "I'll be honest with you," he said.

Saying nothing, Big Brah, Kali and I watched the kahuna for honesty.

Makoa Alika sighed. "I did marry Nohea and Kaipo," he said.

Big Brah, Kali and I looked at each other and smiled triumphantly. Kaipo and Nohea had to be safe. But where?

Makoa Alika must have observed our triumphant smiles. "I did open the boathouse door for the 'Honeymooner.' My wife, Kala helps me with the weddings. She was getting the couple ready. Kaipo was happy.

"Kaipo told my wife, after the wedding all his troubles will be over. No hiding Nohea. He told my wife Helen Hokui had been following him around and found out about his plans with Nohea. Helen Hokui was blackmailing Kaipo. The night before at the Tavern, he had gotten into a fight with her."

Sounded pretty honest so far.

Makoa Alika said, "After the wedding, Kaipo and Nohea returned to the 'Honeymooner.' They left the way they had arrived. What must have happened is Helen Hokui either emerged from her hiding place or they found her."

That could have happened.

Makoa Alika said, "Somehow, Helen Hokui managed to overwhelm Kaipo and Nohea. Maybe she took them by surprise, maybe she had a gun."

A gun! Violent.

Makoa Alika said, "She took the boat into the shark-infested waters nearby."

Shark-infested waters! Dangerous. Instantly I got a bad feeling.

Makoa Alika said, "Helen pushed Nohea and Kaipo into the ocean. She raced away in the boat, leaving them to die."

Left them to die! Shocking. Dumbfounded, Big Brah, Kali and I looked at each other. Big Brah frowned. He almost never frowned.

"Are you saying, Kaipo and Nohea are dead?" Big Brah said.

Makoa Alika shrugged. "Unless they were exceptional swimmers, I don't know."

Kaipo was a good swimmer. But Makoa Alika didn't think it would have made a difference.

Sagely, Makoa Alika said, "What difference would it make if they were good swimmers? Their parents didn't want them. Not together as a married couple. The police wanted to lock Kaipo up for a murder he didn't commit."

Wow.

Makoa Alika calmly concluded. "So, better them dead than alive."

What?

Makoa Alika helpfully pointed out. "This

gives you what you need to catch this Bran: Helen Hokui crashed the boat, she was alone," he said.

Understanding, Big Brah shut his eyes and nodded. He stopped frowning. He opened his eyes.

He sighed. "Kaipo and Nohea gone forever, this will be terrible news for their ohanas," he said.

My heartbeat accelerated.

Makoa Alika was unrelenting. "Evil is anyone who stands in the way of true love. Evil is anyone who separates true lovers. This is the way of our ancestors. The right way." He dug his spear deep into the sand.

"You don't think the parents deserve a second chance?" Big Brah said.

Makoa Alika shook his head with surety. "No," he said.

That no rang in my ears. The immense cliff of disappointment had sprung up so suddenly. Big Brah, Kali and I were quiet all the way back to the hangar. We secured the ocean bird and trudged back to the house, disappointed and dejected. We went to the kitchen. No one was in the mood for food.

Poli`ahu and Wiliwili sensed our mood. Consoling us in whatever human grief we were immersed in, they lovingly brushed their soft fur against us and caressed us with their tails. Big Brah, Kali and I flopped down in our chairs at the round table. Poli`ahu and Wiliwili joined us.

They sat in their chairs with solemn faces.

At last, Big Brah got up. "Let's go to the heiau. It'll make us feel better," he said.

I kissed Poli`ahu and Wiliwili. Without another word, Kali and I followed Big Brah out of the kitchen. It would get cooler at the heiau. In the foyer, Big Brah picked up a light jacket for Kali from the hat-rack. We stepped outside.

The high clouds in the sky had turned blood red, as the sun set in the west. The birds conveyed their endless excitement at the end of another day. An evening breeze had started, cooling.

Kali put on the light jacket. She slipped her hands into its pockets to be extra snug. She smiled a mahalo at Big Brah. Outside the heiau's small lava rock boundary, we stopped.

The sky was azure streaked with red and the sand golden. The cool breeze from the ocean was on our backs. But the smells of the ocean swirled all around us. Behind us, the waves rolled in endlessly.

The waves would always come rolling in. I looked inside the heiau at the whimsical shapes and figures made of myriad rocks. I could always count on these rocks for their silent aloha. I thought of Kaipo and Nohea. Had their lives, their love, really ended, as Makoa Alika had so cruelly suggested? I teared up.

I remembered praying to the goddess, right here, under the bright moonlight. "Goddess, let nothing bad have happened to Kaipo and Nohea," I had said.

Afterward Big Brah and Kali had explained we were taking on the case to protect love. I remembered my doubts. How did we know, Kaipo and Nohea, their love was true not fake?

Time will tell, Big Brah had wisely answered. Meanwhile, we were detectives and we had to search for the truth. So, we had searched for the truth. What had we found? The Kaipo in the surveillance video was Bran.

The Kaipo who got the bracelet made and took off without paying: Bran, again. The scene at the Tavern. The real Kaipo, but he was protecting his love.

*Goddess, how could you let this happen?* I thought now, blinking back my tears. A mynah couple flying in harmony descended on the rocks inside the heiau. The small brown birds had cute yellow beaks. I watched them hop from rock to rock on their small, yellow feet, moodily. Big Brah and Kali folded their hands, closed their eyes and prayed. A realization hit me. Kaipo and Nohea were in love, and pure love always found a way to live on. If their love was pure, Kaipo and Nohea would also find a way to live on. I clung to the hope.

The happy mynah couple hopped closer. I smiled at them. I felt better. I closed my eyes.

I prayed to the goddess, fervently. "Let nothing bad have happened to Kaipo and Nohea,"

I said, over and over.

I opened my eyes. As usual, Big Brah and Kali were patiently waiting for me to finish. A loving, reassuring group hug and we were all feeling better. We strolled back up the garden path to the front of the house, the evening darkening. The gentle breeze swirled around us. We were in the goddess' loving arms. The goddess was always involved in our lives. What was her divine wish?

I didn't know it then, but we were going to have one memorable evening.

# Chapter 22 *In some other realm*

First up, Loni. His unmarked, green sedan was parked in front of the garage. He saw us coming up the garden path, and he jumped out of his car.

His arms outstretched, he came stumbling across the grass to us. He gave each of us a warm hug. "Kali! Umi! Big Brah! I'm so glad to see you," he said.

Big Brah was the last to disengage from Loni's hug. "What brings you here?" he asked, conversationally.

Loni's hands moved, but he resisted the temptation to swat at one of the flying bugs that swarmed in the evening. "Can we go inside? I wanted a word with you," he said.

So polite. The change in Loni was mysterious but a polite Loni was pleasant. Big Brah, Kali and I exchanged smiles. We escorted Loni to the office. The lights turned on. Loni headed to the visitor's chair. Big Brah and Kali sat behind the tidy desk.

To let in the cool breeze, I pulled the blackout curtains back and opened the window. The first stars winked in the sky. Loni sat down in the visitor's chair and waited for me to sit down. Unheard of. Loni never gave me so much respect. I took my place behind the cluttered desk.

Finally Loni turned his gaze on Big Brah. Below Loni's thick, black mustache, his lips parted. A display of white teeth. Loni kept up the smile for a while.

Big Brah regarded Loni, patiently waiting for him to speak. Kali and I exchanged glances. It was clear Loni had come to make amends for the performance in his office.

Loni must have talked it over with the chief or with his wife, Beatrice. Beatrice made excellent musubis and cupcakes. Loni had her framed photograph on his office desk.

Loni started to shake his head, and his head kept shaking as he spoke. "I'm so sorry, Big Brah. After you left, I had a meeting with the chief, and Chief? He outright told me to apologize to you. He has full confidence you've not been harboring Kaipo or Duke Mahio in any way," he said.

"What about you, brah, you have the same confidence in me?" Big Brah said.

Loni stopped shaking his head. "Confidence? Yes, I have the fullest confidence in you, Big Brah."

Loni looked at Kali and me, contritely. "I have confidence in all of you, the entire Waialeale Detective Agency."

Big Brah chuckled softly. "Mahalo," he said.

But Loni wasn't done yet. He stayed rooted

in his chair. "That's not all, Big Brah. I went home early, and I was brooding about the office. Beatrice asked me to tell her the whole thing," he said.

Big Brah folded his hands behind his head and leaned back in his chair to listen. Kali and I suppressed smiles. Had Beatrice also scolded Loni? If yes, then good. Loni deserved to be scolded.

Loni examined the clean top of the desk, frowning. There wasn't anything on the desk to examine, so he had to be embarrassed. "I-I don't know how to say it, Big Brah, it's awkward, but I have to do this. You see, when I told Beatrice everything, minus of course those things that involve official police work, she, um, well, it surprised me, but she scolded me!"

Kali and I secretly air-fived each other. Good! Even Big Brah had to make an effort not to smile.

Loni appeared to have found a tiny blemish on the desk. Show, of course. There was no blemish on that desk. I had wiped it clean myself.

Loni used a finger to wipe the imagined blemish. "Surprising...but, it made me realize how wrong I was to say all those silly things about love, and how love shouldn't figure in an official investigation. I understand love. Beatrice, she reminded me, of our love, we have been married years, our lovely daughters...."

Big Brah nodded, approvingly. Even Kali and I joined Big Brah in our approval of Loni's ohana.

Loni shook his head. "But I shouldn't have said those things. Of course, I'm going to give Kaipo a second chance. If Kaipo loves Nohea, and Nohea loves him, and their love is true...."

Big Brah slipped his hands out from behind his head and sat up. "Are you willing to accept then, that there is a killer out there, and the killer isn't Kaipo?" he said.

Loni's face contorted as if someone was slowly peeling off his thumbnail such was his pain. But he had to go home and no doubt Beatrice would ask him how it went, so he was determined not to blow it.

Somehow, Loni controlled his pain. "Yes, I'm willing to consider someone other than Kaipo as the killer," he said.

Big Brah, Kali and I exchanged looks. Was Loni's acceptance of Kaipo too late?

Loni got up. "I forgot something."

Loni strode stiffly out of the room. We heard him outside slamming his car door. He was back in minutes with a tote bag. He didn't sit down.

Loni stood by the visitor's chair. "There is one other thing. The chief will attend the meeting tomorrow noon. It's a Saturday, the weekend. Chief wants the meeting somewhere informal. Any suggestions?" he said.

Big Brah glanced at Kali and me to see if we were going to say anything before he spoke. "Why, yes. I suggest we gather in this room. We'll even provide snacks, soft drinks," he said.

Loni smiled. "Very generous of you, Big Brah," he said.

"You or the chief won't mind if I invite a few more people, all related to the case, do you?" Big Brah said.

Loni made a face and shrugged. "The chief and I, we have confidence in you, Big Brah," he said.

Big Brah also got up. The meeting was over.

Loni handed the tote bag to Big Brah. "Beatrice made these musubis and cupcakes for you. Hope you'll like them," he said.

Kali and I exchanged looks. For once, Loni was trending pure aloha territory. All right. Kali and I were willing to forgive Loni. After the service Beatrice had done to make Loni see light about Kaipo, if she had served us lava rocks, Big Brah, Kali and I would have devoured the rocks gladly. The musubis and cupcakes were nothing like lava rocks.

After Loni left, we sat in the office and ate the musubis. Beatrice had packed a mix: ahi tuna, *unagi* and salmon. There were plenty cupcakes, a choice of chocolate, vanilla and mac nuts. Delicious.

I got coconut water for all of us from the office refrigerator. Satisfying dinner. We were done with the food and drinks. I heard the sound of Duke Mahio's sports car approach the house and behind it an unknown vehicle.

Big Brah and Kali looked my way. They knew I

would be able to tell who it was. "Who is it, Umi?" Kali asked.

"Duke Mahio, but it isn't only him," I said.

Big Brah opened the front door and brought the visitors into the office. It wasn't only Duke Mahio. With him, he had Noah, Lily, Lily's mom, Aunty Maria and Sherry Nemy from the unknown vehicle. With big rectangular glasses, salt and pepper hair, Sherry Nemy had on a short dress and platforms. Strangely she had a relaxed air about her.

Pink haired, in a flowery summer dress, Lily looked radiant, but her eyes were red from crying recently. Bold and confident, Noah was solemn. His intense eyes were on Lily.

Aunty Maria, Loni's star witness from the morning looked a lot like Lily. As I pulled up chairs from the conference table to seat all five of them across from Big Brah's still tidy desk, I observed Aunty Maria closely.

Aunty Maria's hair was also cropped at the shoulders like Lily's, but hers was colored black, not pink. Dressed in a flowery, summer dress a lot like Lily's, she had an air of aloha and patience about her that I connected with instantly. Aunty Maria sat down first.

Sherry Nemy sat on Aunty Maria's left. Next to Sherry Nemy, Lily and Noah sat down. They held hands. Making sure all of his family was seated, Duke Mahio finally sat down on Aunty Maria's right. The women in the middle. The protective men on both sides. That night, they looked like a quaint ohana. When all of our guests were seated, Big Brah, Kali and I took our places.

"What brings you here?" Big Brah asked, pleasantly.

Lily held up Noah's hand in hers above the desk, so Big Brah and Kali could see. She said, radiant, "Noah proposed to me. We're getting married, but when," gloom slowly shrouded her face, "depends on Kaipo and Nohea returning safely."

His eyes on Lily, Noah nodded solemnly. "Big Brah, Kali, Umi, for bringing us together, a big mahalo," he said.

Kali said, "Your love brought you together."

I said, "We merely helped."

Big Brah said, "It's island custom to help true love."

Both Noah and Lily melted and looked immensely pleased.

Duke Mahio said, "Lily and Noah are already part of my ohana. Now they are part of the Plaza ohana as well. They're going to be my new property managers."

*A neat solution to Noah's unemployment problem,* I thought. Noah and Lily would be together, working. But if Noah and Lily were going to be property managers, what was going to happen to Sherry Nemy?

Duke Mahio said, "Sherry's been in our ohana,

with me and Luana, for a very long time."

Sherry Nemy spoke up. "I always loved acting, costumes, makeup, role playing. But I was young, shy. Luana mothered me. Duke, here has helped me build my confidence."

Duke Mahio said, "Helen was to help us. With her gone in this way, murdered. I told Sherry, see how life is short. It's never too late to pursue your dreams."

Sherry Nemy said, "I have always wanted to be an artist. You know, make those costumes, play with makeup and jewelry."

I knew it. I had sensed the artist in her, the first time, when I had showed her my sketch of the murderer.

Smiling, Aunty Maria rubbed Lily's back, affectionately. "I'm so happy for all of you," she said.

Sherry Nemy got up. "I stopped by to say, no matter what, I'll still be available for this investigation. This is important."

Kali thanked her, solemn-faced. "Mahalo, Sherry," she said.

Sherry Nemy smiled, wanly. "I have to work late. I'm still the property manager."

After Sherry Nemy left, her vehicle no longer unknown to my ears, Duke Mahio turned his head to look proudly at Aunty Maria, Lily and Noah. "I told you, Lily's like a daughter to me," he said.

"Mahalo, all of you, for sharing your

happiness with us," Kali said.

Big Brah nodded, approvingly.

Duke Mahio turned his gaze back on Big Brah and Kali. "Normally, we'd be having a celebration. I'm here to apologize for my behavior at the PD. Sorry, I don't know what came over me, it must be the stress. I'm so glad I came to you for help regarding Kaipo, please don't take any offence at what I said," he said.

"No offence taken, brah, I understand the stress," Big Brah said, generous, as usual.

There was a comfortable silence. Grateful, Duke Mahio turned his head slowly to look at Aunty Maria. "Will you say it?" he said.

Aunty Maria nodded. She looked at Kali and then at Big Brah. "Ever since Kaipo's mother, Luana died, she was my best friend, I have looked after Kaipo, like my own son.

"I have been his mother, I am his mother and I'm going to be his mother. Kaipo has all the right in the world to choose the girl he loves.

"Kaipo chose Nohea Bordeta, and I don't care if Duke here still fights with her father Jim Bordeta. I will not let Kaipo and Nohea suffer for it.

"I'm here to tell you, Kaipo and Nohea, their love for each other will be fully accepted. Both will be welcomed back to a loving home, and that loving home is mine," she said.

I was misty-eyed.

Kali clapped her hands, applauding. "Yes!" she

said.

Big Brah nodded approvingly, again.

Duke Mahio rubbed his forehead, wearily. "I'm so sorry, Big Brah. I should have put in more time with Kaipo, while he was still around.

"I told you, after Luana's untimely demise, Kaipo and I, we'd drifted apart. So true. But it never should have happened. Kaipo is the symbol of the love Luana and I will always have for each other.

"I should have protected Kaipo, held him closer. Instead, somehow I pushed him away. Friday night, Kaipo should have been on the boat with me, fishing akule, not alone with Nohea," he said.

*Here it comes,* I thought. The diatribe about how the evil Nohea had taken his innocent son away from him. But, no.

Duke Mahio said, "Nohea should have been with Kaipo, making me proud. Making Luana, watching over us from the stars, also so proud. Our son, the symbol of our love, has found his love, no more happy moment for us parents, no?"

Big Brah looked at Kali and me and then at Duke Mahio. He nodded. "You really feel happy for Kaipo?" he said.

Duke Mahio said, "Yes, I feel happy for Kaipo. I feel so relieved, I see light. I was so wrong to doubt Kaipo. Of course, he's made the right choice. From what I hear, Nohea's a good girl. So what if she's Jim's daughter. Jim's not too bad himself."

I nearly fell out of my chair. Kali's eyes widened in surprise. Only Big Brah had a serene expression on his handsome face. He had endured the threat of license revocation in Loni's office. There the two warring dads had united against Big Brah. Big Brah had sacrificed to bring about the precious unity.

Duke Mahio said, "This afternoon, at the PD, after you left, Jim and I got talking in the parking lot. We went to the Tavern, and we just kept talking. All these years. So much catching up to do. You know, Jim's not a bad sort. Luana, she loved Jim like a brother. Much like Lily here loves my Kaipo, like a brother."

Hearing this, Lily and Noah cuddled each other. Aunty Maria smiled.

Duke Mahio continued. "Jim confessed to me, his was a crush. As soon as he met Jean, he forgot about Luana. Soon Jean was his entire world.

"Unfortunately, Jim and I, we continued to fight. After Luana passed away, the fight grew worse. It was my bad, I fought with Jim.

"I should have seen him as the brother Luana saw him as. I do see him as a brother now. Jim's daughter, therefore, is more than welcome in my house.

"Nohea will have all my love and blessings, same as Kaipo. And for teaching me this lesson, the hard way, by scolding me, when I needed to be scolded, I will always be grateful to you, Aunty

Maria. You are Luana's best friend indeed, and mine too!"

Gosh. I was ready to cry. If only Nohea and Kaipo were safe.

Noah, Lily, Aunty Maria and Duke Mahio left soon after. Big Brah, Kali and I sat in the office, silent for a while. I heard the distant sound of another vehicle. The vehicle got closer. Jim Bordeta's large gray sedan.

"It's the Bordeta ohana," I said.

Big Brah ushered the family into the office. Mom, Dad, Iekika and they had another person with them. Big and strong, Heki. *Was the Heki out of the bag?* I thought.

Heki grinned at me. He greeted me with a hand gesture islanders did to show aloha for each other. The *shaka*. I also did a shaka for him. But Heki was otherwise solemn due to the occasion. Iekika's big eyes were full of laughter and pain.

Laughter, because of her own happiness having Heki around. Pain, because she didn't get to share her happiness with her big sister Nohea. The four of them sat in order. Jim Bordeta, his wife Jean, Iekika and Heki.

Iekika and Heki, the kids, they didn't hold hands, as Lily and Noah had done. With our guests seated, Big Brah, Kali and I took our places.

Big Brah welcomed our guests with an easy smile. "What brings you here?" he said.

Kali also smiled at the young couple benignly.

Iekika spoke excitedly, gesturing with her hands. "Mahalo, Kali, for being my role model. Like you told me, I have decided to take it slow. But, I told Mom and Dad the truth about Heki. Heki comes to see me, we're friends. I also told them everything about Nohea and Kaipo, their love, and this time, Mom and Dad, they listened. So, here we are, Heki and I, we're together. Mom, Dad, you don't mind, do you?"

Jim Bordeta shook his head silently, his face full of anguish.

Jean Bordeta said, "Silly, you should have told me this right away. So what if your dad and I were busy? You know, I've always had time for you and Nohea!"

"Yes, true." Iekika conceded.

Both Iekika and Heki looked very relieved. Friendship first, then maybe love later? Silently, I wished them well.

His hair gelled in place, Jim Bordeta fixed his mismatched eyes on Big Brah. "I've been a terrible, terrible dad to Nohea," he said.

Next to him, Jean Bordeta laid a soothing hand on her husband's arm. Her thick hair, big eyes and shapely chin were like Iekika's. "Don't be too hard on yourself. Jim, these things happen in some ohanas," she said.

"Yes, but why did it have to happen in ours?" Jim Bordeta said.

Jean Bordeta said, "There is a way forward. For every problem in an ohana, the solution is always the same: love, aloha."

I would have thumped my desk in joyful agreement. But it was still a serious meeting. I refrained.

Jean Bordeta continued. "It's true you've asked for Kaipo's arrest, Duke's arrest, knowing Nohea loves Kaipo, and that was wrong. But now, after all these years, you've summoned the courage to meet with Duke, and strike peace with him. You did it, for Nohea, and Kaipo," she said.

Big Brah nodded, approvingly. "It took a lot of strength for you to strike peace with Duke. You did good!" he said.

Jim Bordeta looked relieved for a long moment. The look of anguish returned on his face. "I wish I could have Nohea back, Kaipo back. You were so right in Loni's office, Big Brah.

"It was us, the dads, who made it tough on our kids. It's why they had to be secretive. Now, I don't know. I only hope they're safe.

"It was my job, as a parent, to keep them safe. Instead I was focused on hating Duke. I see that, now.

"I regret it. If I had a second chance, I'd do all this very differently. Duke feels the same way. He told me so, at the Tavern, earlier. Kaipo and Nohea, I hope they'll forgive us," he said.

Jean Bordeta took a heavy breath. "If we do get a second chance, no matter how busy Jim and I get with our work, our lives, I'm going to make sure both Nohea and Kaipo know. They and their love for each other will be fully accepted. For the love they have for each other, they'll be stars in our eyes, always," she said.

There was a long silence. Big Brah, Kali and I looked at each other. It was rather sad, really. Here, Jim Bordeta was repenting, as Duke Mahio had done earlier. Aunty Maria and Jean Bordeta each guaranteed the young couple a happy home. But for Kaipo and Nohea, was it too late? I shivered.

We were done with our guests. Big Brah studied the top of his desk. A grain of white rice from the musubis we had eaten earlier had fallen on the top. A few scouts of the tiny black ants we had on the island had already gathered around the grain of rice.

Anyone else would have reached for the spray bottle of a surface cleaner. Not Big Brah.

Big Brah was an avid entomologist. He peered at the ants, studying them. Gently he tapped the surface of the desk near the ants with a finger. Kali and I watched. To our amazement, the ants picked up the grain of rice. They fell into a formation. Carrying their feast, they disappeared down the desk.

Big Brah looked pleased. Things were going our way tonight. Even the ants had obeyed Big Brah. Then the agency phone on top of the tidy desk jingled.

Big Brah glanced at the screen. "It's Koma," he said, and answered the phone.

Big Brah's face grew animated as he listened to Koma. At last Big Brah said, tersely, "Just hang out with him. We'll be right there!" He finished the call.

Big Brah faced Kali and me. "Koma says he's pretty sure Bran isn't living in the neighborhood. Koma was at Randy Hokui's to see if Randy needed help. The two of them got talking about Bran. Koma says Randy has something of great importance to say about Bran!" he said.

Kali and I were on our feet faster than Big Brah. In no time, we were inside Randy Hokui's clean and fresh smelling living room. Orange-maned and white-bearded, Cousin Koma was there. He wore a cleaning apron over his regular clothes. He looked concerned.

Randy Hokui was draped on the armchair, his bony face pinched. The walking stick was propped up against the chair. Big Brah and Kali sat down on the loveseat, and I had the couch. Cousin Koma just stood. He had opened the door for us.

Randy Hokui sighed. "I understand, Big Brah, you had Koma here looking for Bran in the neighborhood. You're really wasting your time, his time, everyone's time. I already told you, Bran has nothing to do with the murder of my sister. Kaipo killed Helen, I'm convinced," he said.

"But you had something important to tell us about Bran," Big Brah said.

Randy Hokui sighed, deeper. "Bran? Bran's

gone," he said.

I gasped, silently. Kali looked puzzled.

"Gone? What do you mean?" Big Brah said.

"I mean gone," Randy Hokui said.

"Why?" Big Brah said.

Randy Hokui looked weary. "On Wednesday, shortly after you left, I went back to watching TV. I wanted to keep my mind occupied. That way, it hurt less, inside.

"I was almost done watching, it was late, when I heard the doorbell. It was Bran. I didn't know what to say to him. I guess, our grief, it was the common bond now.

"I realized Bran was in far worse shape, than I was. Bran was in shock. He was always quiet, but now, he was something more than quiet. He'd never mentioned any family.

"I didn't know how to console him, so I asked him about his family. Then, he told me something startling. His name wasn't even Bran, he'd made that up to meet Helen, and he didn't have a family.

"Whatever family Bran ever had, he'd left them far behind. I asked him about his job at the bank. He told me something even more startling. He didn't have a job, not at the bank, or anywhere else. I asked him, then what do you do?"

Randy Hokui's voice grew quieter. "Bran was a wanderer, he wandered from place to place in search of spirituality. Never before had he lived in any one place for so long. His love for Helen had made him want to stay here forever.

"He'd never ever forget Helen, he'd carry her in his heart everywhere he went, and he was going away, from the island, forever. I asked him where he was going. Everywhere.

"All around the globe, to every spiritual place on the planet. Why're you doing this? I asked him. For Helen, if I lost her in this realm, surely I'll find her in another. I could see he was too far gone.

"I wished him luck. I let him go. Helen would have wanted to set him free. In some other realm, who knows, maybe Helen and Bran will be together," Randy Hokui said.

If Bran was wandering to a spiritual place, around the globe or in another realm, he was surely gone.

# Chapter 23 Sharp, evil-looking spear

The optimist, Big Brah was not giving up so soon.

"Did Bran say where he was going first?" Big Brah said.

Randy Hokui shook his head. "Not that I remember."

"A religious group, or place?" Big Brah said.

"No."

"What about his belongings?" Big Brah said.

"He didn't have much, whatever he had, donated to charity. I don't know which one."

"He told you Bran wasn't his real name. Did he tell you what it was?" Big Brah said.

"No, what he was telling me was so shocking, I forgot to ask!"

Big Brah fell silent, stumped. Kali frowned. Cousin Koma looked even more concerned, close to distraught. Tomorrow noon, Big Brah was supposed to announce the murderer. Bran.

But now, the night before, we had new problems finding Bran. His name wasn't really

Bran. We didn't know his real name. For convenience, we continued to call the murderer Bran.

Bran didn't live in the neighborhood anymore. He was a wanderer.

We didn't know where Bran lived. He didn't work in a bank. He didn't even work. We didn't know how he really looked like. He had always been in disguise.

Darn. Bran was now an impenetrable mystery. Leaving Randy Hokui still draped on the armchair, Big Brah, Kali and I exited the place, silent.

Distraught, Cousin Koma followed us out. The streetlights cast long shadows in the small yard. Cousin Koma stood at the gate and waved goodbye sadly. Big Brah, Kali and I slowly boarded the big, black truck. Suddenly Big Brah stopped, struck by a thought.

"I forgot to tell Koma what to do next," Big Brah said.

Big Brah ambled back to the gate. Big Brah told Cousin Koma something. I couldn't hear what. Cousin Koma perked up. He nodded vigorously. Big Brah's talks had an energizing effect.

Soon Big Brah was back inside the truck, and we were on our way home. All silent. That night, I tossed and turned, thinking about the mysterious Bran. Where could he have gone?

How were we to find Bran? The deadline to

find the killer was almost here. Big Brah would find a way. But how? Puzzling over the answer took my mind off the heartache of Kaipo and Nohea being missing. I dozed off. The sound of Cousin Koma's cleaning van outside the house woke me up.

The bedside clock told me I had slept for less than an hour. Still, it was late. Big Brah's footsteps flopped down the stairs and then the front door opened and closed. Muffled voices, from the foyer. Soon the front door opened and closed again. I heard the sound of the van start up and drive away gathering speed.

I told myself I had to be dreaming and drifted back to sleep. I woke up to the welcome smells of breakfast floating up from the kitchen. I was there in no time. The tall windows let in the light and air of another beautiful spring morning on the island.

The birds chirped, outside. Poli`ahu and Wiliwili were up and about, their tails high and their ears pointy. They were onto us. They knew something big was going down today. I poured kitty treats into their bowls. But, surprise.

Big Brah wasn't there.

Kali greeted me with her usual smile. "Get any sleep? Cousin Koma was here so late, woke us up," she said.

I sat down in my chair at the round table. "I heard him right, then," I said.

"Yes, and Koa told me to tell you, Koma left

two boxes in the foyer. You are to carry them into the office and set them by the conference table. Your big brah wants to conduct the meeting at the conference table," she said.

"I heard their voices in the foyer, I'd told myself it was a dream," I said.

Kali left making breakfast to come over to me and tousle my hair fondly. "You told yourself it was a dream? So cute!"

I grinned at her. Kali went back to making breakfast. Meanwhile Poli`ahu and Wiliwili finished the treats. They climbed onto their chairs at the table alongside me.

"Where's Big Brah?" I asked, as Kali returned with two steaming breakfast plates.

Kali set the plates down on the table. Macaroni, cheese and meatballs.

Kali sat down. "Big Brah, he's taken the ocean bird and gone visiting Makoa Alika," she said.

Makoa Alika. I knew the kahuna was involved in this. Had Big Brah figured out where to find Bran? Did Makoa Alika follow Helen Hokui in his boat because she broke a kapu? Did he see something he didn't tell us? The big clue to finding Bran. The big kahuna sure was hiding something.

I picked up my fork, thoughtfully. "Did Big Brah say why?" I started to eat.

Kali shook her head. "Only, he may be late, so he wanted us to get things organized for the big meeting," she said.

I swallowed a mouthful of the macaroni, cheese and meatballs. "Very yum," I said.

Kali smiled happy and ate. After breakfast, she got back to making the snacks and drinks for the guests. Big Brah had left the agency phone to invite everyone who had been involved in the case. I sat at the round table and used the phone. I had to tell each invitee the same exact thing.

Big Brah was going to announce the killer in the Helen Hokui murder case. So, please be here at noon.

*How's Big Brah gonna announce the killer?* I thought, every time I finished with an invitee. My curiosity was an albatross, soaring high. But I couldn't find Alba.

No one else was left uninvited. Not even Music Man. I didn't have a number for him. Keni volunteered to convey the message to Music Man.

Keni said, "Tell Big Brah, Laika Lahaina's at the harbor with Music Man. Tourists and locals are flocking here, business has picked up like crazy. You know the best part, Umi.

"Duke Mahio and Jim Bordeta stopped by together to pay for my boat's repair. They're friends now. I must have looked incredulous, what magic has Big Brah worked, this time? They told me, going forward both their mall delis will serve the special coconut water and green tea, as a symbol of their new friendship. Aloha is strong on the island. I'm renting more boats than ever, Alba's been flying all morning."

I said, "Explains why I can't find Alba."

Keni had a smile in his voice. "Big Brah is going to announce who the murderer is? Sure, I'll drop by for the meeting, Umi. Big Brah has turned this thing around for all of us at the eastside harbor, it's the least I can do," he said.

Afterward, while Kali finished with the snacks and drinks, I went to open up the office. The boxes Kali had told me about were in the foyer.

Two regular cardboard storage boxes sealed with duct tape. The boxes weren't heavy. I carried them into the office, no problem.

Big Brah had told Kali he was going to conduct the meeting at the conference table. I set the sealed cardboard boxes down, one on top of the other, by the chair at the end of the table where Big Brah would sit.

Then my thoughts racing, I went about pulling the curtains back, opening the windows and tidying up. What was in the boxes?

Maybe Bran's meager belongings. Cousin Koma was more than capable of finding the charity Bran may have donated to. Perhaps the belongings had a clue to where Bran was. But more importantly, why had Big Brah gone after Makoa Alika this late in the day? It could only mean one thing.

Big Brah agreed with Randy Hokui. Bran wasn't and couldn't be the killer. If so, Big Brah had to suspect Makoa Alika. Why else would Big

Brah go?

I shivered. I was going to find out, pretty soon. I set up the conference table with all the existing chairs.

I got additional folding chairs from the store room, unfolded them and put them in a neat circle. The folding chairs formed a second row to the existing chairs. I was done. The office clock was on the wall next to the conference table. I glanced at the clock.

Just past eleven. Was time moving faster? Soon the guests would start arriving. Still no sign of Big Brah. I refrained from hitting the panic button. I went to check on Kali.

The kitchen was full of aromas from Kali's dishes. Kali had the food in platters. Assorted musubis. Sushi. Bite-sized sugar cookies dipped in chocolate. Arare or rice crackers, an island favorite. Cucumber sandwiches. Egg salad sandwiches. She had the drinks in pitchers.

Iced tea. Coconut water. Lemonade. I helped her carry everything to the office. We stacked the platters of food and pitchers of drinks on Big Brah's tidy desk. My desk was too cluttered.

Besides Big Brah wouldn't mind. I had already stacked plates, forks, glasses and paper napkins on the conference table for the guests to help themselves. Prep work, done. Kali and I looked up at the clock on the wall above the conference table.

Forty minutes past the hour. I could almost

hear the distant sound of a car approaching. The first guests were about to arrive. Still no sign of Big Brah.

It was most unlike Big Brah to be late. But this had been a case where he had been through a couple of other unlikely things: threatened to be arrested and have his license revoked.

Kali was unconcerned. She never lost her confidence in Big Brah. "Umi, time to freshen up," she said.

Ten minutes to twelve, we were back in the office, refreshed. This time, I didn't imagine the sound of a car approaching. It was real. I opened the front door.

Surprise. His hair was crimped five times on the top, a style he had adopted, when he had decided to join the force thirty years ago. He was small and dapper, our police chief. I tried to greet him, but he would have none of it.

He hugged me instead. "Umi, where's Big Brah? I owe him an apology for Loni's atrocious behavior," he said.

I grinned. "Big Brah will be pleased to hear you say that, but he isn't home, yet," I said.

Chief's forehead furrowed. "Isn't home? Don't tell me he's still immersed in the investigation," he said.

"Yes, he is," I said.

The chief hadn't become chief for nothing. He was a leader. "Let me help you, Umi. You bring the guests in, I'll chat with them. You know, talk story to keep them occupied, until Koa returns." He headed for the office door.

I said, "Kali's in there."

"Loni and Rice will be here soon." The chief didn't slow down.

"Mahalo, Chief," I called after him.

The chief disappeared into the office, and the other guests poured in. I had no time at all to think, as I greeted them and exchanged aloha with them, as island custom demanded. The surprise?

Music Man showed up with Laika Lahaina. I greeted the happy couple. Laika Lahaina was a head taller than Music Man even with his dreads. Her skin was exquisitely darker. She had her arm wrapped around him.

She giggled. "Now that I've found him, I'm not letting him go," she said, her voice magically musical.

Music Man spoke in his melodious voice. "I say mahalo to Big Brah for all this," he said.

Music Man and Laika Lahaina made an awesome couple. Their music together was bound to be super happy. Then I sipped from the bitter-sweet drink of hellos and goodbyes. *Many on the island will miss Music Man,* I thought. But I was happy for him. "So, what're you going to do, the two of you?" I couldn't help asking.

Her big bosom heaving, Laika Lahaina laughed. Music Man squeezed her arm. "No worries. I've left it all up to my girl here," he said.

I had already guessed. "You'll go on a worldwide tour first and then settle in the big city," I said.

Laika Lahaina laughed. "I am going to live here with him," she said.

"What about your music?" I asked, a trifle alarmed.

"We'll sing on the island. You'll find us both under the coconut tree by the dock at the harbor," she said, still laughing, her joy apparent.

Big Brah had known. Music Man and Laika Lahaina weren't going to go away. Instead, love had found a way, a path that was different from the ones usually taken. I took a sip of the sweet drink called pure aloha. Nice.

As I joined all the guests in the office, I heard the most welcome sound. The sound of the ocean bird returning to its roost. I sighed, relieved. Big Brah had made it on time.

It was exactly noon by the clock on the wall. Big Brah ambled into the crowded office through the inside door. His handsome face was serious. There was a surprise. He had brought Makoa Alika with him.

Until then, the gathered crowd had been enjoying the refreshments noisily, even if it was a solemn occasion. The crowd now silenced.

Makoa Alika didn't look happy or pleased. He wore the traditional garb, helmet, cape and kapa malo, but he had a surly expression on his fiercely bearded face.

What silenced the crowd even more was the sharp, evil-looking spear he held menacingly. The office smelled of food. Big Brah indicated the food platters and drink pitchers on his desk to Makoa Alika. Would he have some?

On the island, it was rude to decline a hospitable offer of food and drinks. Makoa Alika declined Big Brah's offer. The silence in the room deepened. Undeterred by his companion, Big Brah hugged Kali and me and went to his place at the conference table.

Small and dapper, the chief was already seated to Big Brah's right. His thick mustache prominent, Loni sat next to the chief, importantly. Behind the chief and Loni sat the huge Rice from Vice comfortably. With no hair on his head and face, Rice had his conspicuous eyebrows close together. He was concerned. To Big Brah's left, Duke Mahio and Jim Bordeta sat with each other.

His thinning hair and business-like glasses in place, Duke Mahio had an expectant air about him. Next to Duke Mahio, Jim Bordeta had his hair gelled in place and regarded Makoa Alika suspiciously with his mismatched eyes.

Makoa Alika strolled down slowly to the other end of the conference table. He sat down on the back-most folding chair.

Makoa Alika looked around at the gathering, scoping them out. The silence grew tense. Makoa Alika's gaze stopped at Jim Bordeta and Duke

Mahio.

Makoa Alika glared at the dads. Kali and I stationed ourselves halfway down the table on either side. We were ready to bring our guests any more refreshments they wanted, and we were going to make sure there was no trouble.

Big Brah started the proceedings. "Mahalo, all of you, for coming at such short notice. It shows you care," he said.

There was a murmur around the table, more mahalos mostly, as everyone replied at the same time.

Big Brah allowed the murmur to subside. "No, really, if you're here, it means you've somehow helped me find the murderer," he said.

Another murmur rose, this time louder. They had all come to find out who the murderer was. The moment was close.

Big Brah spoke and the murmur died down. "To reveal the murderer, we have to understand the sequence of events leading up to the murder. First, Helen Hokui wasn't entirely innocent herself.

"She and her boyfriend, this man we will call Bran, they schemed to rob the Mahio jewelry. Everyone on the island knows the jewelry is worth a fortune.

"I suspect Bran has previous criminal records on other islands. Helen Hokui arrived on our island about a year and a half ago. She took up a job as Duke Mahio's property manager. At first, her brother, Randy Hokui," and here Big Brah paused to smile at Randy Hokui who sat quietly next to Loni, "mahalo, for coming, Randy, you visited her office in the evenings, but soon she met Bran, and Bran started picking her up after work."

Randy Hokui adjusted his lanky frame on the chair and nodded. "That's true," he said, heavily.

Sherry Nemy sat next to Randy Hokui. She had on her rectangular glasses and wore a frilly office dress. She also nodded.

"You, Randy," Big Brah smiled at Sherry Nemy, "and you Sherry, both of you thought Bran and Helen were in love. I'm afraid that wasn't so. Bran and Helen, their love was fake.

"What they were really doing was scheming to rob the Mahio safe known for its valuable jewelry. So they wouldn't get caught, they were also scheming to frame Duke Mahio's young, innocent son, Kaipo.

"Kaipo was immersed in love and oblivious to the threat. We all knew about the old enmity between Duke Mahio and Jim Bordeta. Soon Bran and Helen learned about it.

"Doubtless, Helen or Bran followed Kaipo around, in order to learn about his movements, so they could frame him. They discovered Kaipo secretly rented boats at the harbor, took a girl out on the ocean, for privacy.

"It must have been easy for them to figure out the reason for the secrecy. The girl was

Jim Bordeta's daughter, Nohea. Helen and Bran decided to use the information to fulfill their purpose of stealing the jewelry and framing Kaipo for the theft. So, Bran went to Cosplay."

Slight and balding, Hades Akapalua had been slouching in a chair next to Sherry Nemy. He sat up and paid attention.

Big Brah smiled at Hades Akapalua. "Bran wanted you to make a bodysuit resembling Kaipo Mahio. To allay your suspicion, he had come to your shop on April Fool's Day to create the illusion that it was all a prank.

"You made him a fine bodysuit, without knowing its true purpose. Unknown to Bran, you had marked the bodysuit with a mole on top of the right ear. Bran used the bodysuit to dress up as Kaipo Mahio and visit the 'Jewelry Quartet.'"

Manama was seated next to Hades Akapalua. His fierce face broke into an embarrassed smile at the mention of his shop.

Big Brah smiled at Manama. "You noticed the mole on top of this Kaipo's right ear. In other words, it was Bran in the bodysuit.

"Bran bought a bracelet with 'Kaipo' stylized on it. Bran then did something the real Kaipo would never do. Bran ran out of the shop carrying the bracelet, without paying for it. Bran did this drama so you'd remember him as Kaipo vividly.

"You did remember Bran as Kaipo vividly. Then, it was time to blackmail Kaipo about

Nohea. Thursday night, Helen met with the real Kaipo at the Tavern."

Mohua was there in one of the back row folding chairs, listening on bright-eyed.

Big Brah smiled at Mohua. "Helen told Kaipo she knew about Nohea. Kaipo must have been on edge. He was secretly planning on marrying Nohea the very next day. It was also the perfect time to strike for Helen and Bran. Hence, the fight.

"Helen and Kaipo had many witnesses of the fight, and Kaipo wasn't going to tell anyone the real reason for the fight either. Friday morning, dressed as Kaipo Mahio, Bran, Helen with him, robbed the Mahio safe.

"To frame Kaipo further, Bran wore the bracelet with 'Kaipo' stylized on it, the bracelet he had stolen from Manama's shop. Afterward, Helen grew greedy.

"Without telling Bran, Helen wore a platinum necklace, studded with diamonds in the shapes of a sea turtle, dolphin and octopus, very beautiful, but it wasn't hers to wear."

Loni was sitting next to the chief and throughout Big Brah's discourse he had been nodding importantly. At the mention of the necklace he had recovered from the body, Loni looked even more important.

Big Brah looked at Loni, solemnly. "You recovered the necklace from the body. You also found the bracelet. The bracelet was left there by

Bran in order to frame Kaipo. But we'll come to that, soon.

"Let's continue with our sequence of events. So, Helen, wearing the necklace hidden under a scarf continued to follow Kaipo around. Both Bran and she knew it was only a matter of time the theft, the surveillance video, everything would be discovered, and then they would need all the information they could get on Kaipo.

"To get the dirt firsthand on Kaipo and Nohea, Helen followed Kaipo to the harbor, saw opportunity and hid herself inside the 'Honeymooner.'

"Helen didn't know what she'd let herself in for. Kaipo and Nohea were going to get married at Makoa Alika's ancestral family heiau that very night."

Makoa Alika had sat surly-faced all this while. He didn't flinch. If anything, he looked just as surly.

Big Brah gestured with his hands. "You married Kaipo and Nohea," he said, softly.

There were gasps around the table and everyone looked at Makoa Alika.

"What if I did marry Kaipo and Nohea?" Makoa Alika said, bothered.

"Kaipo and Nohea left the 'Honeymooner' in your boathouse and went up to the heiau to get married. In the while, Helen Hokui got out of the walk-in closet, her hiding place in the luxury boat. She panicked and called her brother," Big

Brah said.

Randy Hokui shook his head. "No, Helen told me she was with Kaipo. Kaipo was right there. He had convinced her everything was all right," he said.

Big Brah took a long breath and exhaled slowly. "You lied about the call," he said.

Randy Hokui's bony face showed confusion. "I-I lied?" he said.

"Yes."

Randy Hokui grew agitated. "What could I lie about? There's a record of the call, on both our phones," he said.

Big Brah said, "Yes, you knew there would be a record of the call. Precisely why you made up this lie. Your sister did call you. Helen was in trouble. The 'Honeymooner' was inside the Alika boathouse. Helen was alone in the luxury boat. She did not know what to do. She was calling for your help."

There was a stunned silence. Randy Hokui tried to speak, but no words came out of his mouth.

# Chapter 24 Insane allegations

Big Brah spoke in a solemn voice. "When you, Randy, you heard the situation on the phone, you saw opportunity. You could get rid of Helen and keep all the money from the jewelry for yourself. Greed.

"You told Helen to bring the boat in through the dangerous rocks. You'd be there, pick her up and bring her home, safe. You thought the rocks would get her."

All eyes were on Big Brah. "Helen survived the rocks, but she didn't survive you.

"You were there, waiting for her. You boarded the crashed boat. You hid the deadly rock you were carrying. You used the rock to kill her. You threw her body into shallow water. You had already used the bracelet to frame Kaipo for the jewelry theft. You wanted to frame Kaipo for the murder.

"So, you dropped the bracelet right next to Helen's body. To give yourself an alibi, you used her phone to call your phone a couple times. Then you left her phone on the boat for the police to find. Everyone would think Helen was calling you, while you claimed you were sleeping at home."

"You can't prove any of these insane allegations," Randy Hokui said.

Big Brah nodded. "I'll come to the evidence in a minute, but you lied to us about a couple other significant things. Helen did tell you the code to the safe, so you could rob the safe as Fake Kaipo," he said.

Randy Hokui shook his head vehemently. "All garbage talk. I'm not listening to this. None of you should," he said.

There was an awkward silence. Orange-haired and white-bearded, Cousin Koma had been observing everything from a back row chair.

Big Brah turned to Cousin Koma. "Last night, when we left Randy Hokui's home, I told you to search the home for these items. Mahalo for bringing them to me," he said.

I had stacked the two boxes from Cousin Koma next to Big Brah's chair. Big Brah swiveled his chair toward the taped cardboard boxes. I was prepared. I threw him a box cutter.

# Chapter 25 Flash
## of arms and legs

Big Brah caught the box cutter. He extended its blade and cut the tape. "Helen was your wife. You were posing as brother and sister."

"More garbage talk," Randy Hokui said.

Big Brah reached into the opened box, took out a document and held it up. "Here's your marriage certificate."

Marriage certificate. Such deception.

Big Brah said, "She was your wife but the love you had for each other was fake! You were bonded by greed."

Big Brah set the certificate down. He got up and slowly extracted a bodysuit from the box and held it up so everyone could see. The lookalike had short hair with a bald patch, bushy eyebrows and a smooth chin. "Bran," he said.

Big Brah set the Bran bodysuit carefully down on the table and picked up another bodysuit. Curly hair, mustache. I could see the mole on top of the right ear so high was my focus.

It was the Fake Kaipo bodysuit. There were

gasps all around. Big Brah laid the bodysuit out on top of the conference table. "The Fake Kaipo, the work of an extremely skilled and dedicated cosplay artist, my friend Hades Akapalua," he said.

Sitting next to Hades Akapalua, Sherry Nemy turned to gaze admiringly at the artist through her big, rectangular glasses. They had the same interests and made a sweet couple. "You've serious talent, Hades," she said.

Dramatically, Hades rose. He put a hand on his heart and bowed low. Matching Hades' drama, Sherry Nemy offered him her hand. He kissed Sherry Nemy's proffered hand. I applauded, mentally. Born on the island, this friendship was blessed to be sweet and lifelong.

Big Brah indicated the boxes to Duke Mahio. "The rest is all the jewelry from the safe. Brah, will you please come over and check everything is okay," he said.

Duke Mahio jumped up. He couldn't wait to do as Big Brah had asked him to do.

Big Brah sat down. He looked at Randy Hokui. "Are you ready to confess you were Bran?"

Smugly, Loni put a heavy hand on Randy Hokui's shoulder, as if Loni had known all along. Big Brah nodded approvingly, at Loni. Kali glanced my way. I nodded. We were ready for any trouble.

Randy Hokui stared bitterly at Big Brah. "This is ridiculous, I couldn't have been on the rocks.

My legs. They're weak. I need a walking stick!" he said.

"Another lie. You don't have a limp. Your legs are just fine," Big Brah said.

Suddenly, Randy Hokui jerked out of the reach of Loni's hand. Randy Hokui sprinted up, making for the door, his limp, his bad leg, all forgotten.

I watched the action in slow motion. Kali was on Randy Hokui's side of the table. Randy Hokui careened past Kali, his eyes on the door. He shouldn't have dared.

Like Big Brah and me, Kali deeply disliked liars, thieves, murderers and fakers of love. Like me, she also learned the martial arts with Big Brah. Kali froze, focusing.

Randy Hokui sprinted harder. He was going to make it to the door and escape. Kali moved.

There was a flash of arms and legs. Randy Hokui hit the hardwood floor with a loud thwack. Kali froze, watching him. Suddenly athletic, Randy Hokui got up with surprising agility. Kali stood between him and the door.

Randy Hokui was taller than Kali. He must have fancied his odds against the diminutive Kali. "Love is for you suckers. I'm leaving." He yelled out.

Randy Hokui sprinted for the door again. Kali moved faster with more purpose. There was another flash of arms and legs. Randy Hokui hit the hardwood floor with a louder thwack and a loud groan.

Randy Hokui was also a coward. He lay on his back, howling. "Don't hurt me, please, I'll confess everything. Yes, yes, I stole the jewelry, I murdered Helen, but please, please, don't hurt me," he said.

Kali remained firm and focused ready to stop the criminal from escaping. Big Brah and I ran to Kali's side. Loni also jumped up and joined us. The rest stood up ready to help. Disdain, disgust and disapproval at the heinous criminal was palpable in the room. Loni got down on his haunches and handcuffed Randy Hokui.

Importantly, Loni marched the murderer out of the door. The chief and Rice looked on proudly. Fake love had perished and Kali had struck the final blow.

Big Brah hugged Kali. "My hero," he whispered to her.

Kali didn't reply. In his arms, she just snuggled. I was proud, watching them. They were my heroes.

Big Brah gestured for the others, still excited, to quieten and settle down again. Everyone did. Kali stood next to Big Brah and put her hand on his shoulder affectionately.

# Chapter 26 Ohanas
## deserve a second chance

Big Brah said, "I have one other thing, I have to take care of. I took on this case to protect love, that of Kaipo and Nohea's. They are a young island couple, and the love between them is natural and true. Such pure love should prosper, not be doomed."

Big Brah looked at Makoa Alika. "The police searched for Kaipo and Nohea everywhere else on the island. No one thought of searching the whale reserve where you maintain strict kapu. I knew Kaipo and Nohea had to be hiding there.

"Makoa, we have you to thank for playing the role of a parent to Kaipo and Nohea. You blessed their wedding, you took care of them, you protected them. You did your duty as the priest of the ancient heiau.

"You did all this selflessly, without a thought for your own profit in any way, just as you saved Pilialoha. On our island, brah, you are a true hero," he said.

Makoa Alika was unmoved. But I could see the

cracks forming.

Big Brah said, "Makoa, you had to make sure I caught the murderer first, before you'd let Kaipo and Nohea out of your care. So you made up the tale about Kaipo and Nohea being lost in shark-infested waters. Fortunately for me, this is what gave you away."

Makoa Alika was taken aback. His frown returned. "Gave me away. How?" he said.

Big Brah smiled. "I figured, you wouldn't let the couple you just married perish. No way. If such was the case, you'd rescue the newlyweds even from shark-infested waters. You're a hero."

Makoa Alika grinned. "It takes a hero to recognize another," he said, gladly.

Big Brah spoke in his softest voice. "Makoa, are you convinced Kaipo and Nohea can return to the world, now?"

Makoa Alika turned his gaze on Duke Mahio and Jim Bordeta. The dads were sitting side-by-side, their feud forgiven and forgotten. They were responsible businessmen and dads.

Makoa Alika sighed. "I have been observing the two of you, I can see you're friends now, genuinely. Yesterday, Big Brah had asked me, if you deserve a second chance, and I had told him, no, you don't.

"But today, he asked me, if the children, Nohea and Kaipo deserved a second chance, and I couldn't say no. Our children, they deserve second chances.

"Besides, Nohea and Kaipo are the sweetest children any parent can ever wish for. Now that the killer has been identified, and after seeing you all, I'm convinced both ohanas deserve a second chance!"

Spoken like a true dad. There were cheers around the table. Several thumps. Kaipo and Nohea had been in the care of the Alika family. But where were Kaipo and Nohea?

Big Brah said, "I flew Kaipo and Nohea over in the ocean bird, along with the Alika family. Alba helped."

Alba helped. Is why I hadn't been able to reach him. Big Brah had hired him.

Big Brah said, "Kaipo and Nohea have been patiently waiting outside the door, waiting for me to tell them to enter."

I glanced at the faces of those waiting for the newly-married couple. Not just the dads. Aunty Maria. Jean Bordeta. Lily. Noah. Iekika. Heki. Sherry Nemy. Hades Akapalua. Cousin Keni. The chief. Rice. Manama. Mohua. Music Man. Laika Lahaina. Cousin Koma. All of them connected by Kaipo and Nohea's love for each other. Anxious. They all wanted Kaipo and Nohea back.

Big Brah raised his voice. "All right, you can all come in, now!" he called out.

The inside door to the office opened, slowly. With curly-hair and mustache, Kaipo entered holding hands with a shyly smiling Nohea. Nohea had big eyes, thick hair and shapely chin, just like her mom and little sister. A pleased Kala Alika was right behind them.

Kala Alika had a frizzy mane of salt-and-pepper hair and looked very attractive in a sleeveless dress. The tattoos on her arms showed. She had a pleased smile on her face. She walked in, the Alika children behind her. My gaze travelled to the back of the enthusiastic group.

To my amazement, a couple holding hands were the last to enter. With his small eyes, big nose and fanned ears, Alba walked in with the biggest, silliest grin on his batlike face. The slim, attractive island girl gazing wondrously at Alba looked familiar. I had seen her from the air. She had to be Moli, our island girl albatross. The birds had found each other! Big Brah had played Cupid. Everybody was happily soaked in aloha.

Everybody hugged each other and especially the newlyweds. Kaipo and Nohea had endured an ordeal. But their love had been true, and true love always found a way to live on. Ecstatic, Big Brah, Kali and I joined the jubilant madness. Time for a *luau*. Time to party. Time for some *hoihoi*.

To celebrate pure love, in two days, all agreed to Big Brah's grand luau at our heiau on the beach. Everyone was to bring all their family and friends. Loni was absent, with the murderer. I made a note to invite Loni. No celebration of this investigation could be complete without Loni, Beatrice and their sweet daughters. Besides Loni would no doubt secretly brood if he missed Big

Brah's luau!

For any of Big Brah's luaus, all our numerous cousins on the island always attended. Hard to reach, our cousins lived in many crazy cozy nooks. Cousin Keni was busy renting boats. Cousin Koma immediately took on the task of informing all of our cousins. Two days later, Big Brah, Kali, Wiliwili, Poli`ahu and I were at our heiau on the beach.

Tiki torches flared, illuminating the surroundings. The grand luau was ready with lots of food. Made with seasonal island ingredients, the food was naturally delectable. Kali was excited to get everyone started with appetizers. Mohua assisted. For his island ohana, Big Brah loved to cook. He had conjured up a wholesome feast of surprises and old favorites.

For sure, everyone stacked their luau platters with goodies including Big Brah's new akule curry and his always popular cabbage fried rice. Kali's healthy, scrumptious desserts sweetened moods and palettes. I helped. Served generously, aloha was the most delicious ingredient. Family, food and fun. The two feuding dads were feuding no more.

Duke Mahio and Jim Bordeta were now an ohana with aloha, a force to reckon with that night. The dads were enthusiastically ready to make amends for all their misdeeds. Hades Akapalua, Sherry Nemy and Manama were going to get new shops for costumes and jewelry at both island malls. Police charities received generous gifts. For being the heroic priest who cared for Kaipo and Nohea, Makoa Alika received big checks.

For being, well, just the best island hero ever, Big Brah got the biggest checks, from both dads. The Alika family blessed the occasion by singing a sacred mele. The chief enthusiastically performed karaoke.

The chief's performance was the best. Immensely honored, Music Man and Laika Lahaina sang together. Their endearing songs of enduring true love filled our hearts. My all-time favorite lovebirds, Big Brah and Kali electrified the celebration with their mesmerizing hula dance. On our island of natural beauty and aloha, pure love was in full blossom. Total bliss.

# Umi's island speak

Adobo: fish or meat dish cooked with vinegar and garlic
Ahi: tuna
Ahuula: cape made of feathers
Akamai: intelligent, supersmart
Akule: fish found in the waters around the island
Aloalo: hibiscus
Aloha: love
Anole: garden lizard
Arare: crispy rice cracker
Aue: an exclamation of exasperation, alas
Aunty: address to show love and respect

Big Brah: older brother
Big Sister: older sister
Braddah: brother
Brah: brother

Cheehoo: joyous whoop
Chicken katsu: breaded chicken
Chicken skin: goose bumps

Fire dance: a performer dances with fire batons
Fly, fly: a game played with whomever you can lift up, swing around and make "fly, fly!"

Goddess: island goddess, goddess Pele
Grinds: food

Haka: fierce face
Haupia pie: sweet, coconut-y pies
Heiau: temple
Hoihoi: joyful fun
Hoku: full moon
Honu: sea turtle
Hula: island dance

Kahuna: traditional spiritual leader
Kakau: traditional method of tattoos inked by hand-tapping
Kapa malo: traditional garment
Kapu: sacred law
Karaoke: karaoke
Keiki: child(ren)
Kupuna: ancestors

Lanai: porch
Laulau: meat, salted fish and taro leaves cooked in a ti-leaf wrapper
Lei: garland
Lilikoi: passion fruit
Li'l brah: younger brother
Loco moco: rice topped with burgers, sunny side

up eggs and gravy
Luau: party

Mahalo: thank you
Mahalo nui loa: thank you very much
Mahiole: traditional helmet
Mainland: continent
Malasada: sweet, fried dough treat
Mana: life energy
Mano: beloved shark
Mele: song-poems
Mochi: sweet rice flour treat
Moli: albatross
Musubi: layers of meat and rice in a seaweed wrapper
Muumuu: comfy dress
Mynahs: beautiful brown birds

Nani: beautiful

Ohana: family
Ohia: first tree to appear on new land created by lava
Ono: fish found in the waters around the island

Pau: done
Papa: patriarch
Pohaku: lava rock
Poli`ahu: goddess of snow
Pono: righteously good
Pua lehua: the lehua flower

Pua`a: feral pig

Sarong: wraparound dress
Shaka: a hand gesture islanders use to show love
for each other
Spicy ahi poke: fresh tuna with mustard
Stuffs: things

Talk story: exchange stories
Tempuras: fritters
Ti: island plant with big leaves
Ti-leaf: leaf of the ti plant
Tutu: grandparent
Tutu kane: grandfather

Ukulele: stringed instrument
Uncle: address to show love and respect
Unagi: freshwater eel

Wiliwili: flowering, island tree

# Umi's island poetry

## Pure aloha

Sweet little black hen sings her clucking song.
Proudly she guides her family around the yard.
Kind, protective rooster is the attentive guard.
Patiently, both nurture their chicks to make
them strong.

They pause by shade and puddle as they skip
along.
He tells them stories learned from his father
bard.
Sweet little black hen sings her mother's
clucking song.
Proudly she guides her ohana around the yard.

Rooster and hen teach their chicks right from
wrong.
To cherish, love each other and party hard,
as they had learned in that beautiful yard.
All happy, rooster, hen and chicks dance along.

Sweet little black hen sings her clucking song.

# Acknowledgement

I have many people to thank and reasons to be thankful for:

Rita and Mele, my awesome publishing team.
My island ohana, full of aloha.
My favorite fiction writers, you are a part of me.
My kind readers, this is all for you.
My dear reviewers, your encouragement is the best.
The goodness I see in human hearts keeps me grateful and hopeful.

Mahalo.

--Ishwar

# About The Author

## Ishwar Chandra Sen

Ishwar Chandra Sen is a poet, storyteller and novelist. A lifelong learner of human nature, he sees the goodness in human hearts. Ishwar and his fictional heroes are inspired by the same goodness. Ishwar lives with his family in Hawaii.

# Books By This Author

## Family For Sure

Welcome to the fictional island of natural beauty and aloha! Solve a murder mystery with the Waialeale detectives. Bighearted Big Brah is loved by all. Big Brah's able assistant and li'l brah, Umi is all heart. All Big Brah needs is his beloved girlfriend, Kali. Full of suspense and twists, this novel will entertain and also surprisingly soothe you!

On this island, love and family, aloha and ohana are cherished and practiced, yet someone has been found murdered. Big Brah has to solve the case. Umi and Kali are by his side to work for justice.

Family for sure is an entertaining cozy mystery with a message of love and family.

A special Sen Fiction mahalo for our first reviewers on Goodreads and Amazon. You are our heroes.

Revealing rave reviews:

After reading this book I couldn't wait to read more. Murder mysteries aren't my usual read but the story was fun! The characters as well as the twist and turns were easy to follow and remember. What I loved the most through it all though was the feeling of family and being immersed in Hawaiian culture. Big Brah and Umi are such a great team and I grew close to these characters. The evidence and story was perfectly written in a way you couldn't guess who the murderer was and you couldn't wait to find out.

Great Read!!
I had the pleasure of living in Hawaii from 1991 until 1996 and most of that time I lived in the beautiful town of Waimanalo. Reading this book brought me back to the sounds of Hawaii and the true beauty of the people. A great cozy read that took me home again.

Read this for sure
Hawaii 5.0 in novel form! This book was wonderful from start to finish. It begins on a fictional island when a wealthy woman hires Big Brah and his little brother Umi to solve her husband's murder. Everyone on the island knows and loves Big Brah. They respect him. They trust him. They cooperate with him. His investigations help the island police force.

In true island fashion, such a serene and laid back feel. And that goes for Big Brah's murder investigation. He has own style. He operates on his own time table. The attention to his customs and traditions stays steady throughout. And it was all just so comfortable. I want to live there!

The investigation introduces you to all kinds of characters, plot twists, motives, and scenarios. I never quite caught on as to who I really thought was the suspect. I definitely did not have it figured out.

No gore. No spice. This was 100% a cozy mystery of a whodunit. I am excited to join Big Brah and Umi in later books, as the author says they will absolutely be back. Just an all around good feeling novel. I did think Umi seemed a lot younger than he was supposed to be. So, I just changed his age in my version and kept reading. Lol

# Sen Fiction

Kind reader,

BIG BRAH, KALI and UMI will return!

Visit our website at https://www.senfiction.com for the latest news about the detective trio.


Sen Fiction, Hawaii is a publisher of fiction eBooks and print books.
Contact us at https://www.senfiction.com/contact-us.